ALSO BY ANN ARENSBERG

Sister Wolf

Group Sex

INCUBUS

INCUBUS

a novel by

Ann Arensberg

ALFRED A. KNOPF

NEW YORK

1999

THIS IS A BORZOI BOOK
PUBLISHED BY ALFRED A. KNOPF, INC.

Published in the United States by Alfred A. Knopf, Inc., New York, and simultaneously in Canada by Random House of Canada Limited, Toronto. Distributed by Random House, Inc., New York.

www.randomhouse.com

Library of Congress Cataloging-in-Publication Data
Arensberg, Ann, [date]
Incubus : a novel / by Ann Arensberg. — 1st ed.
p. cm.
ISBN 0-394-55696-8
I. Title.
PS3551.R398153 1999
813'.54—dc21 98-41732
CIP

Manufactured in the United States of America
First Edition

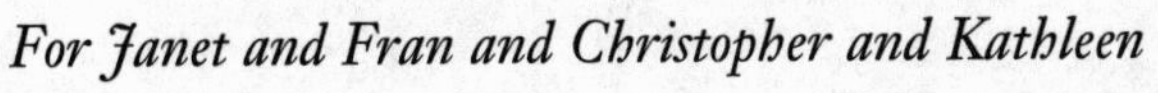

For Janet and Fran and Christopher and Kathleen

Christ before us, Christ behind us,
Christ within us,
Christ beneath us, Christ above us,
Christ to the left of us, Christ to the right of us,
Christ when we lie down, Christ when we sit down,
Christ when we arise,
Christ all around us.

EIGHTH-CENTURY IRISH PRAYER,
"St. Patrick's Breastplate"

"I think we're property."

CHARLES FORT, *The Book of the Damned*

INCUBUS

Preface

My name is Cora Whitman and I spent three months in the underworld, the summer of 1974, a season when the rains failed. Or perhaps the underworld erupted in those parched months, covering the land of the living with killing ash, blending the upper and lower regions into one. Perhaps, more correctly, the underworld came to me.

Every night we pass over the boundaries of the underworld. Are the dreams we bring back from our journeys only dreams, or memories of experience? Sometimes a dream image dogs us as we hurry through the waking world: a man with no face; a house underwater. Like photographic negatives printed on untreated paper, these pictures will blur and fade as the day progresses. We may see them again, but not at our own discretion. You cannot enter the underworld at will. Its regions have never been charted by living mapmakers. There is no consulate that handles applications for passports.

From our side, the frontiers of the underworld are all but impassable. Are the borders as hard to infiltrate from the other side? Are the flesh eaters, castaways, and scarecrows we meet in dreams content to stay where they belong or do they want to travel? If they start to wander, how do we shut them out? When they get past our sentries, how do we send them back? The day world does not have diplomatic relations with the night world, let alone a recognized treaty of extradition.

If only we could stay awake around the clock, or discover a way of renewing our cells without sleeping. When we are asleep, our dreams overpower us like spring tides. We are carried through the rivers of the underworld, spinning and sinking, ripped by the beaks of snapping turtles, tangled in bottom weeds. Awake and upright, standing in the light of day, we believe that our dreams are the work of our imaginations. We like to think we "made them up," as we make up stories for children, tales of giants, elves, and mermaids, and other "imaginary" creatures. We take comfort from this notion. If the monsters we see in dreams were invented by our brains, then they live in a place inside our heads, and cannot harm us.

There is clandestine traffic from the underworld in every era, but particularly at the end of a millennium. Near the turn of any century, human beings behave like herd animals, driven headlong by panic toward the edge of an overhanging rock face. We see the breach between one century and another as a vertical drop, an abyss, when in fact it is no greater than the time between one year and the next, a single second in duration, the span of a handclap. The inhabitants of the underworld smell our panic, just as lions smell fear in inexperienced trainers. Attracted by the scent, which grows sharper as the century dwindles, they cross over in larger numbers, to claim us and use us for their purposes. Nineteen seventy-four was the beginning of the end of this century, the last year of the known universe, the last time familiar things could be taken for granted: the purity of the seas and waters; seasonal weather; the idea of Africa; the permanence of Art; the ethic of honest work for honest wages.

As of the census of 1970, the inhabitants of our village, Dry Falls, numbered 1,500. Between April and September of 1974, migrants from the night world swelled that population. Other migrations occurred in the state of Maine, in Oxbow, Whiting, Burnt Island, and suburban Bangor, and one major influx in the town of Haley Pond, which spread across the line to Garretson, New Hampshire. As reports came in from areas around the country, it was clear that Tennessee and Idaho were hit as hard as Maine was. While the nation as a whole was under siege that summer, none of the incidents fitted our local profile. We have documents, with photographs to support them, from Maryland, Missouri, and South Dakota, describing the appearance of human faces on cellar floors, a phenomenon never recorded in northern New

England. Red rains fell chiefly in the Finger Lakes region of New York, when, in at least two cases, the substance was identified as blood. Several witnesses at a boys' camp on the Allegheny River saw three moons in the sky on the night of July 22. (If the sighting had taken place downriver in Pittsburgh, it would have been explained as an optical illusion created by smog layers.)

Showers of blood, faces on floors, objects in the sky, the Dry Falls entity: they are one and the same. Angels appeared to people in religious times. Twentieth-century man has visions of spaceships. These appearances have physical reality. They cannot be dismissed as illusions, phantoms, or figments. Objects from the sky, by whatever name you call them, leave material evidence of their flights and landings: patterns on radar screens; scorch marks on the grass; fragments of an unknown, heat-resistant metal. In Brownsville, Texas, the Virgin Mary left her image imprinted on a tree trunk. The Dry Falls entity was experienced by its victims as a bodily affliction, the "incubus syndrome": respiratory difficulties; paralysis of the limbs; autonomic arousal. These psychic extravaganzas are produced by stage managers from the underworld, from dimensions invisible to humans with our limited mind-set, worlds above us and below us, before and behind us, surrounding and pervading us.

Who are they and what do they want with us? Do they mean to challenge our fixed ideas and expand our consciousness? Or are they trying to keep us in superstitious fear, to block the progress of our psychic evolution, lest we learn too much about them and gain the power to nullify them? Whatever they are, they have business with human beings. There is no way to know if their motives are benign or malevolent. At the moment we are their property and their creatures. They would go to any lengths to keep us from turning the tables.

My husband, Henry Lieber, and I have set up a private foundation, the Center for the Study of Anomalous Phenomena. In an effort to understand occurrences like the Dry Falls entity, and the larger reality we believe they represent, we will go on collecting case after outlandish case. We will examine every piece of data, no matter how unreasonable. We will cross-reference the facts and see what patterns emerge. As we feed in more facts, these patterns will be replaced by stranger ones. Perhaps in the future there will be no more "anomalies." The exception will be the rule; the abnormal the norm. All the facts will fit because the system has grown so capacious. Our minds will become so flexible that nothing will daunt us: comets in the daytime, dialogue with the dead, snowflakes the size of wagon wheels.

It is a lifetime's work and we are over halfway through our lives. I am forty-two and my husband will be fifty-six. We have no formal training so the work will go more slowly. On the positive side, we are not saddled with preconceptions. Henry has a doctorate in theology from St. John's Seminary. He was the rector of the local Episcopal church, St. Anthony the Hermit. Until recently my own chief interests were cooking and gardening. I wrote a recipe column that appeared in many Maine newspapers. There are two of us at the foundation, along with Adele Manning, who used to be Henry's secretary at St. Anthony's. We have recently been joined on a part-time basis by Jeremy Mulbach. A doctoral candidate in parapsychology from Portland University, Jeremy is an expert in statistics, computers, and spectral photography.

We need help from the public if we have any chance of succeeding. We need cases to study. We need firsthand reports and descriptions. We guarantee confidentiality. No names will be used without the consent of the subjects. We understand your feelings of shame and your desire for secrecy. When you told your story the first time, no one believed you. Contact with the unexplained sets the victim apart. The community withdraws its support, for fear of contagion.

By publishing the following account of our own experiences, we hope to make clear that we, like yourselves, are victims. Every aspect of our lives was altered by our encounters. Nothing is the same, either for us or for our fellow villagers. We no longer trust what we see, hear, taste, smell, or touch. When it thunders at night, we cannot sleep until rain begins falling. When we walk across the lawn, we test the ground for firmness. We have lost our sense of security, however false it may have been to begin with.

I have written up our case history as carefully as I could reconstruct it, using diaries, police records, pathology reports, and exhaustive interviews, corroborated by tape recordings. For the rest, I have relied on memory; but I believe that memory has served me. The events are recent in date and graphic in content. If anything, time only sharpens my recollections.

Correspondence should be addressed to the Center for the Study of Anomalous Phenomena, c/o Dr. Henry W. Lieber, Box 608, Dry Falls, Maine 04071.

PART I

Christ Before Us

Chapter One

When I sat down to make a record of the Dry Falls happenings, I made many false starts in my attempt to find some logical sequence. I am a pastor's wife and I can quote from the Book of Revelation, in which my task, or any writer's task, is spelled out plainly: "Write the things which thou hast seen, and the things which are, and the things which shall be hereafter." St. John was the chosen instrument of God. He transcribed his visions in the order in which God sent them. When it came to ordering events, I had no guidance. Many things were happening around us all at once; some I learned about too late for inclusion in this chronicle. I must choose a beginning blindly and with trepidation, as soldiers draw lots to "volunteer" for a suicide mission. I will mix up past and present as it suits my purposes. The future is still uncertain, so I can only guess at it. I was determined to publish my account, have it printed and distributed through the bookshops in my county. By so doing I will be following the mandate to St. John: "Seal not the sayings of the prophecy of this book; for the time is at hand."

I was not qualified to be the narrator of these incidents, although my stake in making them public was very high. I was an amateur whose experience was limited to one topic. I wrote about food—growing and cooking it—500 words a week, two typewritten pages. My readers in the state of Maine were undemanding. If a measurement was incorrect, they blamed the printers. My readers, after all, were familiar with my subject. They were cooks like me. I thought of them as my colleagues. Many of them sent me their families' favorite recipes. I reprinted the best in a yearly column called "Readers' Choices." I have met my readers at newspaper-sponsored contests. I have spoken at women's clubs from Kennebunk to Machias. Often they were more knowledgeable than I was, and more ambitious. They took courses in cake decoration. They were casual about *croquembouches*. If they had no need of advice, why did they read me? They cooked three meals a day. They ran out of fresh ideas. They looked to me to make their kitchen chores more interesting. Since I wrote for a newspaper, my words had the ring of authority.

Suppose I were to lecture to these groups of nice women on my present subject? I can picture a setting like so many where I have spoken, a community center, recently the scene of a flower show, trestle tables placed against the walls bearing withering exhibits, entries in various categories, on various themes, such as "Fruits of the Vine," "Table for Two," "Bringing a Meadow Indoors," and "One Perfect Rose." When they were settled on folding chairs with their cups of coffee, I would walk to the front of the room and begin to speak. I would tell them about our town and its time of emergency, about women like themselves whose bodies were used in sleep. I can see them averting their eyes, darting glances at friends, burrowing in their handbags. Two or three who were seated at the back might make a tiptoed exit. Unless I reverted quickly to culinary matters, I would lose my audience along with my credibility. On any issue other than menus and food preparation, my respected regional byline counted for nothing.

For as long as I wrote it, my little column was a link to humanity. It addressed basic needs—survival, nutrition, celebration. It was concerned with the continuance of life from season to season: planting, harvesting, putting food by for the winter. The document I am presently compiling takes up nonhuman matters, events that make hunger and survival seem benign and attractive. I must catalogue human reactions to nonhuman circumstances: fear, depravity, shame, hysteria, self-deception. I am obliged to spare no one, not my loved ones, my acquaintances, my countrymen. I have tracked down participants who were desperate to forget their experience. I have asked the most intimate questions from an impersonal standpoint. Unjustly, since I was as much a sufferer as anyone, the work I am doing will set me apart from my fellows.

I am sitting at the desk where I tapped out my column each week, a plank set on two metal cabinets with plenty of drawer space. The desk is the same, but the room it is placed in is different. In the rectory it sat in one of our three guest rooms (although sometimes I carried my typewriter to the kitchen table). Here it occupies a crowded corner of our only bedroom. The rectory was a fine old house, crowned by a belvedere, with Carpenter's Gothic trim and long French windows, a house that captured and stored the available light. There were many ideal locations for perennial borders: along the proper front walk paved with brick in a herringbone pattern; running the length of the fence by the sidewalk; on either side of the steps by the screened-in back porch. I never dug up the lawn as long as I lived there. I believe that borders should relate to existing structures.

Our new home is a two-story apartment in a white clapboard building on Main Street recently vacated by a chiropractor. Before Dr. Klinger, the building housed a firm of tax accountants; before that, it was a branch of the Huguenot Society of America. We tore down partitions that divided each floor into office cubicles or examining rooms, leaving us with a large open space on the ground floor (living–dining room and efficiency kitchen) and a bedroom, bath, and storage room upstairs. The place is snug, to put a good construction on it, but adequate to our needs.

Over the front doorbell is a discreet brass plaque bearing the name of the Center; but Henry and his employees work underground in the finished basement. The basement has a separate entrance down a half-flight of steps. Except for two high windows, it is lit artificially by rows of overhead fluorescent tubing. There is a washroom, a compact refrigerator, and a two-burner hotplate. The Center's offices and laboratory are self-contained, although we sometimes conduct interviews upstairs in the living room. I should mention that we offer our services free of charge. Many of our clients have been driven out of their homes, lost their jobs, or incurred hospital expenses because of emotional trauma. In the interests of our work we are living in straitened circumstances. Henry inherited money from his father, who made his fortune smoking and canning seafood. Conrad Lieber died when Henry was twenty-three and away at war. Henry rarely touched his legacy when he was a minister. He draws on it now to support the operations of the Center. He still pays himself an Episcopal clergyman's wages, except that a beautiful house and grounds were once part of the benefice.

The landing outside our bedroom is stacked with cartons, the overflow from the storage room. The cartons are filled with boxes of slides and tapes, newspaper clippings, and notes scribbled down at the time on anything handy—napkins, deposit slips, the insides of paperback book covers. Each carton is labeled and dated according to incident: the Manning Case, the Burridge Case, the Violette Brook Campgrounds Case, etc. Our bedroom is small, with one logical place for the bed, so my desk must face a wall instead of a window. If my desk faced the window (thereby blocking the major passageway), what would I see through the glass to cheer or please me? Outside there is a concrete yard with a drain in the center and a chain-link fence between us and Baldwin's hardware store. If I stared out the window too long at this sordid view, the gardener in me would take over, or whatever is left of her. A hurricane fence makes an excellent support for a vine garden—tomatoes, cucumbers, sweet peas, and a splash of blue morning glories.

Until I finish this chronicle, I am cut off from the natural world. I am living, for the present, in a world of words and abstractions. I am thin, where I used to be sturdy. I have lost my color. I cook by rote, in a hurry, only at suppertime. For the other two meals we open cans, jars, and boxes. We live like students in an off-campus dorm with a communal kitchen. Henry is quite content with these slapdash arrangements. Before we married he subsisted on creamed herring, sardines, and crackers. Sometimes when my back aches from sitting in one position, I invent a new dish in my head, although rarely in practice, such as a cornbread cake made with buttermilk and filled with vegetables—string beans, onions, garlic, red and green peppers. When will I be free to lead a more balanced life? It is more than two years since I put on blue jeans and struggled through the briars on my way up Pumpkin Hill, tearing my sleeves, getting long, mean scratches on my arms, until I found the place where the sweetest wild blueberries were hiding.

Did my love for the things of this earth bring on the trouble in the first place? Did my heedless, pink-cheeked vitality attract their notice? Did the smells from my kitchen tempt them out of their element? I am dealing in guilt and blame, which serves no purpose. Every woman in Dry Falls was an unsuspecting magnet. Adele Manning took "baths" in the light of the waxing moon. The Roque sisters, Claude and Arlette, who were in their late teens, camped overnight in Parsons Ravine during their menstrual cycle. Ruth Hiram, our librarian, grows old roses exclusively for their fragrance. Jane Morse often nursed her first child on a bench in the common.

If physical life was a powerful attractant, it was not the special property of the female population. Dry Falls is a prosperous farming community, the exception in Maine, teeming with life, surrounded by fields of feed corn and tender alfalfa, by pastures where mammals with distended udders are grazing, where circles of cow dung swarm with carrion insects. In the summer the farm hands work bare-chested, raising a sweat, bringing earth and manure indoors on the soles of their boots. We have chicken farms in the area, hens raised for eggs. Michel Roque breeds sheep and goats, and makes tangy cheeses from their milk. Evan McNeil's Highland Kennels is famous in New England for its Border collies, uncanny, intelligent herding dogs with a cast in one eye. Around here the life cycle operates at a sped-up pace. Something is always breeding in our vicinity—sprouting, dropping, hatching, whelping, fermenting. The township of Dry Falls fairly reeks of generativity, more than enough to call forth the legions of the disembodied.

If bodiless entities are attracted by an abundance of life, there are those in our community who are drawn to the immaterial. Among our year-round inhabitants are a number who have retired or escaped from cities, and whose interests are far removed from agriculture. Some of these peaceable refugees started a discussion group, meeting at one another's houses as often as they could manage it. They kept the group and its purpose to themselves. If they had broadcast the fact that their topic was psychical research, who knows what kind of chowderheads and dabblers might have begged for admittance? No one in the group was a professional parapsychologist; but they were well informed on the subject, serious and skeptical. Walter Emmet had scholarly credentials in another field, eighteenth-century American furniture and decorative arts. Mary Grey Hodges was a registered nurse, formerly in practice in Bangor, who founded our Visiting Nurses Association. David Busch had been a staff photographer for *Decade* magazine, who went off on his own to specialize in nature and landscapes. Lorraine Conner Drago was a local real-estate agent, a mundane career for a person with clairvoyant abilities. At age fifty-one, my husband, Henry, was their youngest member.

When Henry joined up, I remember hoping that Bishop Hollins wouldn't get wind of it. Our Bishop was the crusading sort of clergyman, not much interested in the spiritual life, let alone in spirits. He thought the mission of the Church was people helping people, like the Community Chest, the March of Dimes, or the United Way. On one of his official parish visits he scolded Henry for holding too many meditation sessions, and ordered him to start a bimonthly meeting of Parents Without Partners. Henry's psychical research group did nothing to ease the pain of divorce or stop world hunger, but it seemed to me they had some concern with human betterment. When they met at the rectory in October of 1973—four sober elderly people and my youthful husband—Mary Grey read aloud a paper on healer-treated water. Mary Grey read too fast and dropped her voice at the end of every sentence, but the message and its implications were far-reaching. If one healer could purify a tank of contaminated water, a squadron of healers might be able to revive Lake Erie.

After the reading I provided light refreshments—coffee, cider, and date bars made with oatmeal. Walter wanted to conduct an experiment in extrasensory perception. "Not a very rigorous experiment," he said. "Just a little stricter than a parlor game." He brought in a folding screen from the dining room, and placed a side table behind it. Behind the screen he opened a satchel and placed an object from his private collection on top of the table. Walter himself did not know the identity of the object. He had asked someone else to select it and wrap it in several layers of heavy brown mailing paper. Walter gave us ten minutes by the clock to receive impressions and to write down any images that came to us, however fragmentary. I played along, so as not to disrupt the atmosphere, but my mind wandered out to the kitchen where the supper dishes were soaking in the sink and the macaroni and cheese was hardening in its casserole.

Ten minutes later, Walter called us to order. "Nothing," said David. "It couldn't have any relevance. I kept getting a name with a 'k' in it—Kennett? Or Mackenzie?" Lorraine read her notes out loud: "wavy glass," "the size of a julep cup," "bubbles," "black flecks," "tilting sideways." Mary Grey's paper was blank. "I kept dozing off," she apologized. "I pass," I told Walter, "I have about as much ESP as a tree stump." Walter turned to Henry, whose notepad was covered with writing. When Henry closed his eyes he had seen a circle of light, golden light, with a red glow at the apex of the circle. In a moment the circle developed a foot, or base. "Like a bowl," said Henry, "a yellow bowl, but I think it was metal."

Walter started unwrapping the object before Henry had finished, tearing at the paper, wrenching the bands of Scotch tape. He pulled out a little footed cup, four inches in diameter, hammered out of brass, burnished to a soft golden luster. "One of my prizes," said Walter, handing it to Henry. "This communion cup belonged to the first rector of King's Chapel in Boston. He took it with him to deathbeds, when he was called out to give the last rites." There was a round of applause for Henry. David clapped him on the shoulder. "A religious object," he said. "You had an unfair advantage, padre."

Henry's accomplishment called for a round of drinks. I took orders and poured out the liquor. Henry asked for a brandy. Lorraine seemed a little less animated than the others. She had once taken part in the ESP trials at Duke University, when the great J. B. Rhine had given her a high mark for accuracy. Walter salvaged her pride. "You got through," he said. "You scored a hit. You, too, David." He explained that the communion cup was displayed on a cabinet shelf next to a beaker, a hand-blown colonial drinking vessel dating from the 1760s.

The name of the person who had selected the brass cup and wrapped it was Janet McKay, who did occasional secretarial chores for Walter.

The Uncanny was with us, a seventh presence in the room. I caught the group's excitement, a collective shiver. Henry's direct hit now seemed less dramatic than Lorraine's and David's oblique ones. A priest, after all, is supposed to be in touch with the invisible. I could see that their faces looked younger; years had dropped away. With his small, sharp features, Walter looked like a boy turned white early. Henry's face was so flushed and unguarded I was almost embarrassed for him. My own face, reflected in the mirror over the fireplace, looked as pretty as I get, with my bumpy nose, pale green eyes, pale hair, pale lashes and eyebrows. I looked like a piece of straw, but a fresh piece of straw before the weather starts to spoil it. I blessed Walter (who is actually a judgmental, self-centered little stickler) for bringing some spark to our lives just as winter was upon us.

At the time I believed no harm could come from these games, since their immediate effects were restorative and beneficial. I listened as they talked about agendas for the next month of meetings. I thought I might join them, if more of the sessions were like this one. It seemed their appetite for thrills had been slaked, at least for the present. In Henry's opinion, they were putting the cart before the horse, delving into parapsychology without more grounding in physiology and psychiatry. David suggested they read a new book on the two halves of the brain. Mary Grey offered to report on dissociation and multiple personalities. I decided not to join them after all, if they were going to be so studious. At least my husband had found a hobby, an interest outside his work. For some time I had wondered if his work were more burdensome than satisfying.

Chapter Two

Henry Lieber received his calling in a Belgian forest on the sixth of January, 1945. With no trucks, a crippled radio, and dwindling ammunition, Captain Lieber and his troops were marooned at Roche-les-Vierges, a cluster of farmhouses whose inhabitants had long since evacuated. Waiting for contact with the 41st armored infantry, last heard from to the south of them on the far side of the Sononmont River, they were surprised by German rocket fire on the night of the fifth, driven out of the pastures, and up to the thickly wooded highland.

Out of sixty-five men, thirty-two reached the cover of the forest, where trees were still standing from the campaigns of Julius Caesar. Working desperately slowly in ground that was partially frozen, they dug into foxholes as the sun rose behind banks of snow clouds. When the Germans renewed their assault at eight the next morning, the foxholes had little to offer by way of protection. Artillery fire brought down branches and trees on their heads, splintering the wood into daggers as lethal as forged steel. Within minutes Henry Lieber was sharing his foxhole with a dead man.

The thunder of the shelling, the shattering and crashing of tree trunks filled Henry's head and his chest, exploding both around and inside him. If Death was the absence of sound, he was ready to die. With his eyes closed, he gave himself up and waited for silence. Almost at once the battle noise receded, as if it were coming from a distance, perhaps his own memory. Finally he heard nothing except the whistle of a bird, and a faint gentle rustling like a breeze through a stand of long grasses. Then a voice spoke out of the stillness, as close as the body lying next to him: "Why are you troubled? Why do thoughts arise in your heart? I am with you always, even to the end of the world."

When the Bulge was closed on January 23, the Allied casualties numbered 81,000. Henry Lieber was alive, unimpaired in mind or body, and a few days short of his twenty-third birthday. As soon as he was released from active duty, he obeyed his calling as he had understood it. When he disembarked at the port of New York, he rode uptown and enrolled in St. John's Seminary. Conrad Lieber had died just before the invasion of Normandy, so Henry had no earthly father to disappoint. Henry's place in the family business would go to his cousin, a wide-awake young man who wanted to branch out into frozen fish sticks.

The failure rate at the seminary was high, since a good many entrants imagined, quite mistakenly, that divinity school was a prolonged retreat, an opportunity for leisurely thought and meditation. Ex-Captain Lieber thrived in this competitive setting, and obtained his doctorate three years later. By the time he was assigned to a parish in his hometown of Portland, Maine, he was already being referred to as "bishop material."

Henry never became a bishop or even a dean. His first post was All Souls and Ascension, a "social" parish, the kind that gives the Episcopal Church its reputation for snobbery. All Souls catered mainly to Portland's upper classes. Its middle-aged and elderly members had known Henry's father and mother. When he served communion to this gray-haired congregation, he felt like a child passing plates of canapés at his parents' cocktail parties. Because of its location in the old part of town near the waterfront, All Souls had some working-class members from the boatyards and the fisheries, as well as a group of servants from the households of the rich, who had retreated to the heights of Portland in the 1920s. The carriage trade, with its domestic staff, turned out full strength at eleven o'clock on Sundays. The working poor who lived in the neighborhood came on foot or by trolley to eight o'clock communion. Only on weekdays at Morning and Evening Prayers did the two congregations worship side by side, although most of the worshippers at these daily services were elderly women wrapped up in their private devotions.

Henry Lieber quickly identified his mission: to unite his divided parish into a democracy. To every committee—the vestry, the altar guild, home visiting—he appointed members from the old town as well as from the heights. If Mr. Bickford, a widower residing on Hill Street, was confined to his bed after surgery for phlebitis, Mrs. Raposo from Wharf Street was sent to call on him and make sure the private nurses were earning their keep. When Sharon Malone gave birth to the fifth of her children, Harriet Gould and her daughter, Amy Washburn, drove down to run errands, cook lunch, and watch out for the little ones. To the Bible-reading classes held in the Lenten season came Portuguese, Irish, Blacks, and Anglo-Saxons. When the roof sprang a leak, the brickwork needed pointing, or the steeple began, unaccountably, to lean sideways, young men of all estates worked in shifts to complete the repairs—stevedores, fishing hands, and college boys on short leave from Bowdoin. When Raposos, Malones, and Browns, with their scrubbed and groomed offspring, began to appear at High Mass on Sunday mornings, Father Lieber gave thanks, keeping some of the credit to himself, well pleased with the success of his efforts.

By the power of his office and the force of his personality, Henry Lieber had imposed reforms on his parish community. The poor accepted him because he lived in their midst; the rich respected him because they could vouch for his pedigree. Henry's flock was an outward model of Christian conduct, of charitable duties performed automatically and cheerfully. Even the signs of social difference had been reduced. The gentry came to church in plain wool coats; the workingmen wore pressed jackets and sober neckties. Some men like to ride the crest of their accomplishments, but Henry looked over the horizon to further challenges. He had managed to change the behavior of his parishioners, without, he suspected, transforming their inner hearts. He could point to only one example of genuine friendship—between Amy Washburn, whose early marriage to an alcoholic had ended in divorce, and Patricia Santo, a seamstress from Dock Street who was childless for no known reason. Patricia went often to Amy's big house while her husband was at sea. She was teaching Amy how to knit and was patient with her clumsiness.

Henry Lieber left All Souls and Ascension in 1958. He was thirty-six years old and overdue for a transfer or a sabbatical. He was exhausted in mind and body and he felt like a failure. Instead of listening to his body's wisdom telling him to rest and restore himself, he volunteered to work at a settlement house in black Harlem, where he ran interference for destitute families with the welfare system and started a program for teaching older people how to read and write.

In those days a white man in Harlem was a lightning rod for anger. Henry's tall, athletic frame kept trouble at bay for a while; but he refused to wear his clerical collar, which might have protected him. He liked to go on long walks to work out the kinks in his limbs and in his spirit, along St. Nicholas Avenue, where all social life took place on the sidewalks, up to Washington Heights, where he could see the Hudson River and the cliffs beyond it. On the streets around Rhinelander House he was recognized and left alone; but he wandered away from his territory once too often.

On the corner of 160th Street, one of the highest points in Manhattan, while he was ambling instead of striding, lifting his face to the early spring sun, he felt a sharp blow on the back of his neck and another between his shoulder blades. Before he could turn around to confront his attackers, a rain of stones descended on him. He bent over double, covering his head, and tried to stumble out of range. As suddenly as it had begun, the assault stopped. When he straightened up and looked behind him, the street was empty. As he made his way back to the settlement house he was no longer in danger. The sight of blood seeping down his forehead kept bystanders well clear of him.

The doctors at St. Luke's Emergency Room diagnosed bruises, superficial cuts, and a collapsed lung, a condition associated with stress. They kept him in a hospital ward for two weeks. He refused to be transferred to a private room. The Bishop of New York labeled Henry's illness "battle fatigue" and sent him to recuperate at Grail House when his lung was functioning normally. The Grail was an Episcopal order of celibate laymen. They lived on the little finger of the Finger Lakes in a vast shingled camp willed to the Church by a paper baron. Martin Kinder had bequeathed his lakeside camp and 100 acres, along with an endowment that, in the postwar economy, barely paid the heating bill.

The Grail brothers spent their days maintaining the property, shoring up one section of the house at a time while the rest went on deteriorating. They had no time to take a break to observe the canonical hours, so they recited the holy office wherever they happened to be working—replacing planks on the docks, grouting the chimneys, cleaning the spark plugs on the tractor, spraying for carpenter ants. Guests on retreat were provided with large rooms and plentiful meals, and urged to take advantage of the reclining chairs on the porches and in the garden. The sight and sound of the brothers at their ceaseless labors were apt to rouse even the seediest guests from the cushioned lounge chairs. Henry slept for twenty-four hours upon arrival and awoke to the noise of hammers and electric drills. Thereafter he joined Brother Joe on outdoor detail, and chopped enough wood for the stove to see Grail House through the winter.

Mindless work, clean air, and a diet of grains and vegetables gave Henry back his vigor and his customary optimism. Like many of the guests, he went through a period of wanting to take vows and join the order, a phase that died a natural death as soon as his release date was agreed upon. He was summoned to diocesan headquarters in Augusta, Maine, by his Bishop, Malcolm ("Coach") Hollins. Hollins put up his fists and darted a feinting blow to Henry's midsection, testing his reflexes, making sure that his boy was in shape for the next engagement. Henry told the Coach he was out of contention for the present. He asked for a small-town parish in a rural district, where class warfare was at a minimum. Bishop Hollins assigned him to the church of

St. Anthony the Hermit, located in the town of Dry Falls in the Lake Sebago region.

Where was God all this time? While Henry toiled in His service, was He looking out for him? God had passed the ball to Henry, who caught it and ran with it, scoring point after point for His church without flinching from injury. God gave Moses a detailed map of the Promised Land, describing the boundaries as precisely as any surveyor. The Son of God told Saul to get up and go into Damascus. His Mother, Mary, told Bernadette to build her a chapel. God's instructions to Henry were in no way specific. Henry Lieber was not a prophet, an apostle, or a saint: all God had given him was questionable proof of His existence.

Henry had worked sixteen hours a day, neglected his nutrition, taken a total of a month's vacation during his tenure in Portland. He had hankered after several nice women, one of whom he had known since Mrs. Weld's dancing classes. He broke so many dates that these ladies lost patience. His former dancing-school partner married a surgeon, whose hours were slightly more reasonable than a preacher's. If Henry denied himself the comfort of marriage and the pleasures of outdoor sport, he did so entirely on his own authority. He was not under orders from God to wear a harness with blinders.

When Henry was being stoned by boys in Harlem, undergoing the clerical equivalent of a nervous breakdown, was it God who pulled him out of the soup, or the fact that he had inherited Conrad Lieber's iron constitution? How had God kept Henry on the hook for so many years? Had He revealed Himself again, given Henry a peep, peeled off a glove, dropped a gauze scarf, unzipped, flashed His countenance? While Henry and I were courting, telling each other the story of our lives, I asked him these questions. How many times had he heard the Voice in the foxhole? "It never happened again," he answered, "or perhaps it did and I was so tied up I missed it." Season after season Henry prayed to a drawn black curtain. The curtain never opened. No magic show was staged for his benefit; nor did he expect one. "Prayer is not a slug," he said. "God is not a slot machine." I honored my suitor's persistence and his courage. He was hungry for the supernatural, but he curbed his appetite. Gardeners like me had it easier than religious believers. Most seeds would sprout if they got enough sunlight and water. Nature made a better idol than the Christian god: she was just as theatrical and infinitely more generous.

Chapter Three

I lived with my mother, Emily, until I married Henry Lieber. There was a father, or the absence of a father, who died when I was seven and my sister, Hannah, whose name means "the favored one," was nine. When I think about my father, Francis Whitman, I summon up an image of closed doors: the door to his bedroom, the door to his workshop in the barn, the door to his hospital room. Francis Whitman was a master cabinetmaker and woodworker, an unforgiving perfectionist in matters of craft and aesthetics. He resembled the furniture he designed and built in his workshop: very clean, unadorned, and offering little comfort. Francis restored antique furniture for historic houses and museums all over New England. These commissions were his bread and butter, but not his avocation. His original work was sought after by modern architects, especially his series of unmatched side chairs in Ceylonese ebony and his free-standing cylindrical bookcases mounted on casters.

Emily and Francis moved to Dry Falls from Portland after her parents died, leaving them their house and its contents. My grandfather Beaulac was descended from Huguenot lumbermen, exiles from the persecutions of Cardinal Richelieu, who fled from France to Cape Breton Island in 1630. Ruined by a pine blight that swept the Atlantic Provinces, my mother's people fled again to Maine in the late 1870s and remained in Portland manufacturing asbestos shingles. Our house on Rough Lane was my grandparents' summer residence and later their place of retirement until they died within a month of each other. A simple clapboard farmhouse, it was full of incongruous appointments and ornamentation, collected by Great-grandfather Beaulac as his fortunes improved, reflecting the taste of a late-Victorian merchant. Francis Whitman, with his spartan rules for beauty, was required to live among these heavy, old-fangled objects, not one of them the genuine, antique article, each one copied, or mistranslated, from an earlier period.

Almost immediately Francis moved into a cell-like, high-windowed back room, used by my grandmother for airing household linen. The room is still as he left it, with its cot and candlestand, and pegs on the wall for hanging his pared-down wardrobe. As soon as I was old enough for school, he left the house and set up separate quarters in the heated cow barn. Later on, when my sister, Hannah, was in a friendly mood, we would walk through the house playing our favorite game, trying to guess which object had driven Francis out. Was it the alabaster lamp with crimson fringe on its shade? The andirons topped by smiling Cheshire cat faces? Francis maintained that the furniture drained him of inspiration. As long as he lived in the house he did ugly work. As soon as he moved out, his business became successful. My mother would smile her uncertain smile at his eccentricity. Her eyes were so cloudy and distorted by her thick-lensed spectacles that none of us could read her expression or measure her reaction, although everyone seated at the table or around the fireplace suspected that Francis's barbs were intended for the heiress to the furniture.

When my father started to grow the tumor that took him out, he kept us ignorant of his condition and its prognosis. He cooked for himself in the barn during the last year of his life, and left my mother's share of his earnings in unmarked envelopes in the mailbox. I remember seeing him wave to me from a window when I was outside building a snowman, and once he came to the kitchen porch, walking with a cane, to ask for another pillow and an extra blanket.

Late that April Emily took us to Raymond to buy new sneakers.

On the way back Ellis Smalley from down the lane hailed the car and stopped us. He had seen an ambulance coming from our house with its sirens screaming. We turned around and drove straight to North Windham, to the only local hospital. The head nurse told us the patient had requested no visitors. We went back every day for a week and camped in the waiting room. When he finally lapsed into a coma, the night nurse took pity on us. She said we could stay in his room as long as he remained unconscious. With his prominent beaked nose, thin lips, and smooth, domed forehead, he looked as he had always looked, self-contained and indifferent. Francis never woke up to acknowledge us or dismiss us. He died by himself while we were downstairs in the cafeteria.

Some widows begin to live when their husbands die. My mother laid down one cross and took up another. She buried Francis on the sixth of May, 1942, the day the Allies surrendered at Corregidor. She was forty years old, graying, sallow, and self-neglectful. It was lucky she had money from my grandparents, because Francis had none to leave her. The war was both far away in Europe and the Pacific and nearby on the coast of Maine at the navy shipyards. We lived forty miles from Portland, out of range if Axis planes bombed our fleet; but we had a war of our own close at hand, a homely version of the big one. Part of Francis lived on in the body of my angry sister, who had her father's curved beak and high forehead and the coarse black hair inherited from the Whitmans.

When my sister was in her mid-teens, I dreaded coming down to breakfast. My mother and sister would already be stationed in the kitchen, both of them vying to do tasks best done by one person. Their backs were turned when I finally entered the room. They would be standing shoulder to shoulder, minding the toaster. When the timer pinged and the toasted bread rose up, each one would capture a slice and start to butter it. Sometimes they grabbed for the same piece of toast. Hannah would strike my mother's arm to make her release it. Emily cried out but retained her grip on the toast. Hannah pulled harder, tearing the piece in half. They would start to argue, a long-standing, frequent argument, over which was the thriftiest method of buttering toast. Emily scraped the top of the stick with the blade of a knife. Hannah sliced a pat, let it begin to melt, and spread the liquid. At the end of the meal, they rose to clear the table. Without fail, they reached for the same dish simultaneously. Just as inevitably, a glass or a cup tipped over; and Hannah would blame Emily's awkwardness or Emily's eyesight.

No one bothered with me. Their business was with each other. I ate my meals to a background of bickering, left the table unnoticed, and thus avoided helping in the kitchen. As I made my escape, my mother and sister might be squabbling about the garbage for the compost, whether to leave the orange rinds whole or cut them in pieces. Hannah might have opened the icebox and be running an inspection, quizzing my mother about the age of the various leftovers, little mounds of this and that plopped in cereal or soup bowls, covered with waxed paper fastened tight with a rubber band.

They lived in a world of desperate struggles over everyday matters—the conservation of butter, the way to fold towels, the depth of water in the bathtub. Hannah stalked my mother like a bird dog, leaving her no privacy. Emily took refuge outside but still Hannah followed her, pointing out branches weighed down by snow and in danger of breaking or places where the deer had chewed the bark off the yew trees.

One mild day in April, Hannah took it into her head to prune the clematis, the Duchess of Edinburgh, whose double white flowers bloom all summer. The Duchess requires only the lightest shaping, or she will not flower; but Hannah had cut the vines to the ground before Emily caught her. I heard such a howling I thought one of them had been injured. From the window I saw them wrestling for possession of the pruning shears. Suddenly Emily broke free and threw herself against the trellis. Hannah tried to pull her away. Emily held on tighter. I had learned over time that my role in these family disturbances was the same as that of a chambermaid who opens the door on two lovers. Like the maid, I would retreat until it was safe to come back. As I withdrew from the window I saw them on their knees, embracing. Broken sections of the trellis were lying on the ground around them.

My mother grew quieter and spent all her time in her garden. In her forty-fifth year she took up the subject of genealogy. Her sense of herself was steadily frittering away, so she began to construct an independent identity, building on facts and stories she had heard from her family. There was a branch of the Huguenot Society of America in town on Main Street. Monday, Wednesday, and Friday, when the Society was open to the public, she pored over books in its well-stocked but badly lit library. Finally I ventured to ask her what she was researching. Her face lit up at once in response to my questions. When Emily smiled, years, if not cares, dropped away, making her look like a young person burdened with worries. Interest and encouragement caught her entirely off guard, releasing a grateful flow of talk, breathy, eager, and unpunctuated. She ticked off the Beaulacs who had died for the Protestant cause, fighting at the side of their leader, Prince Henry of Navarre. The list was so long that I wondered how any Beaulacs had been left to carry the name and the faith down the intervening centuries. One of these ancestors came to life for me by the manner of his death. In a barn at Vassy, a town outside Paris, a company of Huguenots had met to worship in secret. The king's men set fire to the barn, burning everyone in it, among them a boy of fifteen, Antoine Ariste Beaulac. My distant cousin was exactly my age when the Catholics murdered him. After that I stopped asking my mother about her research. There might be something unhealthy about being related to Huguenots.

When Hannah was seventeen she became engaged to a Huguenot descendant. She was failing three subjects and quit high school in December of her senior year. Bobby Court was a tongue-tied young man who sold sporting equipment and acted as a wilderness guide who took groups on white-water canoe trips. Hannah was at loose ends and Bobby qualified as an older man, since he was over twenty-one. No man of any age had ever paid so much attention to her, although Bobby's courtship was conducted in silence, for the most part, and consisted in following her around and mutely adoring her. Hannah's friends were envious of her engagement, and soon began to think she was romantic and daring for quitting school, instead of an academic washout. No one looked very far into the future, least of all Emily. The young couple planned to live over the sporting goods store, which was right in town, within walking distance.

The wedding date was set for mid-October, on Bobby's twenty-second birthday. Hannah had a good word for everyone, including my mother, although of course they locked horns over issues like a train for the wedding gown. The war had been over for five years, but fabrics were still costly. Hannah had never worn a dress except under protest. Now she turned into an expert on fashion, arguing the merits of satin, peau de soie, or faille; cream, blush-pink, or oyster; stand-up collars versus portrait necklines. It was a good thing she settled on Grandmother Beaulac's wedding dress, the least expensive solution, under the circumstances, since the invitations had been printed and paid for and could not be refunded.

The bridegroom did not survive to see his wedding day. In the Huguenot tradition, Bobby Court expired before his time. He died in the open, by the banks of the Kennebec River, under empty blue skies at a Court family Labor Day picnic. The cause of death was an air bubble in his bloodstream. I was present at his death. Bobby was sitting in an old canvas director's chair holding a full plate of food, bright orange carrot slaw, charred spareribs, purple blueberry relish, yellow cornbread, dark green olives, pale green celery sticks. When Bobby pitched backwards, I thought the canvas had ripped. The Courts hung onto their furniture, indoor and outdoor, until it constituted a hazard to human safety. Bobby went down. For a moment his full plate was airborne. Each item of food left the plate in an orderly file, like planes taking off from the deck of an aircraft carrier. My only view of Bobby was the treadless soles of his sneakers. Hannah began to laugh because

Bobby had a history of pratfalls. Katrina Court was annoyed by the breakage and the waste of food. "Get up, Bobby," she directed. "Thank goodness I didn't use the best china."

Living with my sister after Bobby Court's burial was like living with a pound dog, a creature who snarled and bit and came to no one. Hannah asked for Bobby's clothes to remember him by and the Courts could not refuse her, although they thought it would have been more suitable if she had wanted his watch or his silver baby cup. She dressed in his clothes, her only keepsakes, which bore stains from food spilled by Bobby, holes and tears inflicted by Bobby on expeditions, and retained, in the case of woolen garments particularly, a sharp, musty reminiscence of his wilderness exertions.

Hannah slept in the house and shut herself up in Francis's workshop in the daytime. It would be more accurate to say that she spent the night in the house, since we knew from her complaining that she usually lay awake until the sun rose. Like many bad sleepers, Hannah was proud of her affliction. It was a mark of sensitivity, like her white skin, her heavy, peaked eyebrows, and her broad, flat fingertips.

No artist of any merit gets a full night's rest, and Hannah decided, at age nineteen, to become an artist. Francis Whitman had been only a craftsman, however gifted. Hannah took up sculpture, although she worked in wood, like her father. She started making fan-shaped pieces inlaid with strips of painted wood, and went on to fashion objects from the natural world, snail shells, eggs, and skeletons of birds and rodents. As a child, Hannah had watched her father at his workbench, or tinkered in a corner with a pocket knife and scraps of lumber. Francis never spared the time to teach her, but he let her stay as long as she was quiet.

Without instruction or encouragement from her father, she had no confidence in herself and worked with difficulty. Her motivation came in fits and starts. When she could not work, she paced the studio, smoking cigarettes. Sometimes she let me come in when I brought her a sandwich for lunch or called her to supper. If I picked up one of her pieces and admired it, she grabbed it out of my hands and said it was too sentimental, or too illustrative, or like something in a museum shop. Her successes made her angrier than her failures, even more aggressive than her usual disposition, since she worked in large part to gain revenge on the parent who had ignored her.

With her mind full of conflict and partially blocked inspiration, my sister was a textbook candidate for insomnia. When she stretched out in bed on her back, preparing for sleep, her imagination broke loose and started to ride her. Instead of turning her wakefulness to profit, making sketches or paper models for future sculptures, she fastened her whole attention on the blanketing darkness, listening for sounds and watching for shapes and movement. Someone else might have chosen to turn on a lamp; but Hannah was inclined to act against her interests. Insisting she could not sleep in a lighted room, she not only lowered the blinds but also drew the curtains. She maintained that coffee "acted like a sleeping pill," and drank a strong brew before bedtime without adding milk. By loading the dice in favor of a wakeful night, she managed to accomplish another unconscious objective. If she woke up late, blurred and heavy from accumulated fatigue, she could hardly be expected to work productively in her studio.

Lack of sleep and prolonged confinement in darkness can lead to a state of sensory deprivation. In this condition, as I have recently learned from my reading, a subject is apt to hallucinate, to see things or hear things. Hallucinations are perceived by the subject as real, unlike delusions, where he or she may be aware they are only imaginary. One night my mother and I were awakened by an uproar—footsteps running in the hallways, voices shouting from one floor to another. While I lay huddled under the covers, too frightened to move, my bedroom door burst open, hitting the wall. The figure at the threshold snapped on the overhead light. In the yellow glare stood a startled young policeman.

The house was swarming with policemen, weapons at the ready, answering a call about a break-in at number one Rough Lane. Hannah was downstairs in her bathrobe directing operations, ordering them to look for broken windows in the pantry and the cellar. When nothing was found, she accused them of being too hasty and made them retrace their steps, not once, but several times. Emily smoothed matters over by serving them cocoa and pound cake while Hannah continued to search the house by herself, insisting she'd been wide awake when she'd heard glass shattering. When the policemen were gone, she turned her bitterness on my mother. "You took their side. You let them think I was crazy."

Hannah left us on an ordinary day in early July, while Emily was taking some pink daylilies over to Ruth Hiram in exchange for a rooted cutting from her Thérèse Bugnet rosebush. I was working at Silver's Coffee Shop in the mornings. It was Ernie Silver who taught me to cook, not my female relatives. He started me out frosting sweet rolls and chopping salad ingredients; soon afterwards he showed me how to stew a chicken for pies and how to bake a meatloaf according to his secret recipe, with oatmeal instead of bread crumbs and a blue cheese surprise in the center. Ernie often gave me leftovers to take home. I was hurrying back on my bicycle, carrying yesterday's corn-and-lima bean pudding in the basket, since both my mother and my sister forgot to eat lunch unless I put it in front of them. I reheated the casserole and dished up a plate for Hannah, who had moved into the barn, like her father before her.

The barn door was open, letting in flying insects. I closed it behind me and set her plate on the workbench. The sunlight outside was so bright that the barn seemed dark and shadowy. I thought I saw her at the back of the room, sitting on the steps to the sleeping loft. "Lunch!" I called out. "It's getting cold!" Then my eyes adjusted to the dimness. Emily was sitting there, holding an envelope and a piece of paper, staring straight ahead, giving no sign of having heard me. "Ma mère," I said, reverting to our childhood usage. "Mère, what is it?"

I made my way back to her, skirting cardboard boxes and piles of shavings. When I reached her, she let the paper slide to the floor. I read it on my knees in the light from a grimy window. The script was jagged and slanted, written in a hurry. Hannah was on her way to Rochester, over 400 miles from Dry Falls in the state of New York. Two weeks later she wrote again, giving no return address or telephone number. She was working in a furniture factory applying the finish to a high-priced line of Early American reproductions. She was making ends meet and saving a little besides. We must not try to find her because she didn't want to see us. It was two and a half years later before she broke the silence again. This time she sent a Christmas card with her name scrawled at the bottom and no message, postmarked Albany.

I got my mother to myself when I was almost eighteen. Once I had found her, I did my best to keep close to her. According to all the schedules of normal adolescent development, it was time to leave home and break the maternal tie. My pattern of development had been just the reverse of average. I learned to be self-sufficient throughout my childhood. To cut the tie now would go against my heart's inclination. Instead of accepting a partial scholarship to a woman's college in western Massachusetts, I enrolled at Portland University so that I was free to come home every weekend. When I finished college, where I dabbled in botany, business studies, and English, I found jobs that allowed me to make my home with Emily. My friendships with men and women were conducted during the week, Monday to Friday. I led a kind of harmless double life, as an individual and as a daughter.

I worked briefly as a guide for a travel agency in North Windham, escorting groups of pregnant Catholic women to the shrine of St. Anne de Beaupré, the Lourdes of Quebec. After that there were stints of employment at the Shaker Village on Sabbathday Pond; as an assistant editor for *Maine Heritage* magazine, where I graduated from the SWOP page to a feature called "Maine Kitchens"; and, last of all, as the parish secretary at St. Anthony's, working for the newly appointed minister, Henry Lieber.

When Hannah ran away the temper of our household changed immediately, as if the dark red wallpaper with the raised fleur-de-lis design had been stripped and replaced with a coat of glossy white paint. We removed the Spanish armchairs to the attic, but left everything else just as it had been. Emily's French blood made her as close-handed as any native Yankee. If their religion allowed it, the French would take their belongings to the grave, like the Egyptian pharaohs.

We cleaned Hannah's room and aired it, washed and ironed the curtains, and made up the bed with fresh sheets. If Emily was mourning I saw only one outward sign of it. She placed a vase on my sister's bureau, and kept it filled with cut flowers in the summer, dried statice and silver pennies in the winter, forced branches of apple or forsythia in the springtime. She put flowers in my bedroom, too, and scented bags of lavender in my bureau drawers. She gave me my grandmother's locket with a picture of herself inside it as a smiling child. I do not believe she had intended it for Hannah, or she would have presented it to her at the time of her engagement.

You could say I regained a happy childhood long after the event. My mother and I read aloud to each other in the evenings on the screened-in porch, until the midges, which New Englanders call no-see-'ems, hung so heavily from the overhead light shade that we could hardly decipher the words on the page. Making up for lost years, we read childish books that had a moral—*A Girl of the Limberlost*, *Anne of Green Gables*, *Emily of New Moon*, stories about young girls growing up in isolated places. She taught me to drive the car. She made a lotion from rosemary and lemon balm for my teenage blemishes. Her garden grew like a jungle, overstocked and, in places, undisciplined. Emily was indulgent to weeds and allowed them their fair share of house room. Side by side we dug up the lawn with its sterile crop of grass and planted every foot of it. From the beams in the barn we hung herbs and everlastings to dry. Junior Freckleton, who owned the general store, was willing to pay cash for them. In early spring Francis's workbench was covered with pie plates and egg cartons, where seeds sprouted and leafed until they were ready to be hardened off for transplanting.

My mother was a garden witch. She knew without listening to the weatherman when all danger of frost was over for the season. Nothing ever died on her except plants that had been gifts from someone else's garden. Mildew and slugs steered clear of her, although they visited Marion Smalley down the lane. I was much older and married before

I recognized bud-wilt, black spot, cabbage worms, and leaf-miners; or realized that cantaloupes will not set fruit after an unexpected cold spell in the spring. I thought Emily was successful because she worked steadily from breakfast until suppertime, shoveling compost, repairing cold frames, staking vines, hanging netting over the raspberries—although now I remember her standing at high noon at the center of the garden for so long at a stretch that a chickadee came to rest on her shoulder. At those times I never went near her, any more than I would have interrupted a conductor directing an orchestra. Only once, twenty-two years after Hannah left, did my mother's powers appear to fail her, in the summer of 1974, when drought browned the lawns and pastures. Even then Emily's garden was the last in our community to wither; and at the peak of the heat wave it brought forth a crop of corn, a potful of puckered, stunted ears, somewhat flavorless but perfectly edible.

PART II

Christ Behind Us

Chapter Four

The first alarm was sounded on March 21, 1974. We made very little of it. In the event of a nuclear attack, chances are the emergency warning will be mistaken for a fire siren. March 21 was the opening day of spring. There was a layer of snow on the ground, melting when the sun shone and hardening to a crust after dark when the temperature plunged downward.

The next morning I made the rounds in my fleece-lined boots, checking for signs of growth in protected areas—the south side of the rectory, the entrance to the church, and the graveyard that lay behind the church at the edge of an apple wood. Along my back porch in the herb bed the chive plants were greening and would soon be thick enough to cut. The lavender and rue looked dead; but they were always the last to revive. Tucked into corners by the lug door to the cellar, crocus and waterlily tulips were sprouting on schedule. I walked down the shoveled brick path flanked by beds of peonies, bending down at several points to brush aside the snow and a light blanket of chopped leaves and pine needles. I saw the red knobs pushing up and covered them over again. A thicket of tall, woody lilacs and overgrown forsythia screened the rectory from the church next door, thirty yards or so away. I crossed the lawn, leaving squelching wet footprints behind me, and ducked through a gap in the shrubbery, getting swatted by branches.

Our church is a gaudy little building made of blue-gray granite, neo-Gothic in style like most Episcopal churches. The door on the western side is painted red. Red it stays, although once every decade there is a movement to change it. The stained-glass windows tell a one-sided version of the legend of St. Anthony, concentrating in broad detail on his temptations: naked women approaching the holy man as he slept; the Devil assuming the shape of pigs and goats; a big black bird with a human face snatching bread from St. Anthony's hand. The triple window in the apse above the altar shows Jesus stepping out of his rock-bound tomb, an angel on his left and St. Anthony kneeling prayerfully on his right. Our patron saint is dressed only in his own uncut hair and beard. At the ends of his fingers grow long nails curving like sickles. No one knew why a church in the northernmost state of the union should be named after a saint who lived in the Egyptian desert. A summer resident from Portland gave the money to build the church in the 1890s, so that he could worship the year round in the denomination to which he was accustomed, instead of having to make do with the Congregational service, where people prayed sitting down and sipped grape juice instead of wine at Communion. Since Herman Widerick owned a fleet of cargo vessels, it would have been more fitting if his church had been dedicated to St. Brendan, the patron saint of sailors and seagoing voyagers.

I sloshed around back to the churchyard and through the gates of the wrought-iron fence, which creaked as I opened them, in need of oil and a new coat of rust-resistant black paint. The snow was already receding from the markers and the monuments, as if grave dirt were richer and hotter than other soil.

There was a burial ground here before there was a church, even before Dry Falls was incorporated in 1811. The oldest stone in the churchyard was nearly illegible except for part of a date, 176—, and a last name, Huckins. The first name ended in the letter *a* so most likely it was a woman's, although Asa was a name given to men in colonial times, and so was Hosea. There are no Huckinses in these parts now and no one can remember any. Whoever the dead person was, he or she had no local descendants. The oldest grave stands at the far end of the churchyard near a spreading apple tree. Later on a mass of blue scilla surrounds the foot of the tree and the headstone and it looks as if the unknown Huckins was buried underwater.

Someone had paid a tribute to the stranger in our cemetery. As I came closer I saw a hodgepodge of offerings scattered on the ground. A frostbitten red florist's rose, sprigs of dried lavender, sage leaves, and some greenery I couldn't identify. An unusual assortment, chosen by a person with kind intentions and little money to spend, who wanted to convey a meaning or a message. People always give flowers to the dead, roses in particular, because Pluto lured Persephone into the underworld by holding out a rose. If I remembered my herb books correctly, lavender put a damper on the sensual passions and sage was a cleanser, the spiritual equivalent of Ajax. Herbs and flowers had their place on a grave, but why would anyone leave a cracked white cup and a small square mirror, the kind that might have fallen out of a dime-store compact? The cup contained a dark red liquid. I did not taste it, but it smelled like sour jug burgundy. Litter angered me, and I began to change my mind about my pious donor, who was probably a half-wit or a teenager.

Mary Fran Rawls was coming out of the church, carrying a trash bag. Mary Fran was our cleaner, Ernie Silver's waitress, and a ticket seller at the movie house over in Raymond. She lived with her mother, who took care of her fatherless little boy and gave her a bad time about working on Protestant territory. Mary Fran had on a pale blue sweater, too light for the weather, buttoned tightly across her thin chest, the sleeves too short for her long arms. Nola Rawls had no grounds for concern. Mary Fran was God's chosen waif, and her faith was unshakable. She always wore some light blue article, if only a ribbon in her hair, because that shade was the Virgin Mary's color. When Mary Fran was in labor with Patrick, sick and weak from childbed poisoning, the Virgin crowned with stars appeared to her and promised her a safe delivery. She had a rampant high fever at the time, and the doctors and nurses saw nothing out of the ordinary, except that the patient's temperature went down as suddenly as it had risen; but it was a lovely story, and it kept Mary Fran buoyed up through the course of her fourteen-hour workday.

"Put the bag down, Mary Fran. I'll help you carry it."

"There's something funny," she said. "Come inside and I'll show you."

Mary Fran led the way down the aisle to the chancel, bobbing a curtsy when we reached the steps to the padded altar rail. I wondered if she genuflected when she swept the stone floors, maneuvering her broom so her back was never turned to the cross. Our altar table is a plain slab of granite on a granite block. During the Lenten season it was bare of any cloth. At either end of the altar stood two branching silver candelabras embossed with birds and cupids' faces, Herman Widerick's gift.

"Look for yourself," said Mary Fran. "They were all here yesterday."

Each candelabra had five branches. Six of the candles were missing, all five from the sockets on the left and one from the right. Our candles were made of pure beeswax unadulterated by paraffin. They were costly to us on a tight church budget, but no burglar would have lifted them in preference to the candelabras or the chalice.

"How about these?" said Mary Fran, reaching into the mended pocket of her brown trousers. She pulled out a handful of dyed feathers, yellow, fuchsia, and black, and a clump of fine white down used for stuffing pillows. "They were all in a mess on the floor underneath the altar."

"Under the altar?"

"Well, the yellow one was on the top step and the other ones . . . It was awful." She looked at me with stricken eyes. "They were sticking up out of the chalice, like, you know, an *arrangement*. It's something bad. It scares me." She took my hand in her own rough hands as if she thought I needed comforting more than she did. "Don't worry, Cora. I wouldn't let you down. I'll be here next Tuesday the way I always do."

. . .

Henry believed that a church should always be open. Night and day, the door was unlocked and one light in the apse was kept burning. A house of worship was not a business with fixed working hours. It was an emergency room for the soul with around-the-clock access.

During his sixteen years at St. Anthony's, he had encountered many night visitors. Some belonged to his flock, some to other denominations, and some to none. A few of them took to their heels when they caught sight of Henry—I am thinking of fourteen-year-old Tommy Webb, whose father was a drunkard, albeit a peaceable one. Others required Henry's ears or his blessing, like the little widow from a suburb of Boston, passing through on her way to her daughter's, who needed to tell someone she was happy for the first time since her wedding day. Henry thought about keeping a supply of blankets and pillows in the vestry, since there were occasions when St. A's was used as an impromptu hostel. One night Frank Morse bedded down on a pew when he and Jane had a husband-and-wife and Jane locked him out. A tramp and his bird dog took shelter to wait out a rainstorm, leaving before sunup to catch a boxcar at the whistle stop in Milliken. If your car broke down late at night, you lost your house keys and didn't want to smash a window, the local inn was full or you couldn't rouse the innkeeper, there was a saying in town: "You can always go to Henry's."

For all that, no one took advantage of Henry's open-door policy. Both locals and wayfarers found some way to repay the favor. The Boston widow left a hefty contribution in the poor box, enough to pay old Anson Nye's oil bill for the winter. Frank Morse took it on himself to repaint the parish meeting hall. Some tourists from Wisconsin, the Strombergs, sent Henry an Easter card every year, since Maundy Thursday was the night they were stranded in Dry Falls. For a couple of months two summers ago we found a basket of fresh eggs on the church porch every week. We've also had anonymous donations of garden flowers (I particularly remember some spires of giant white delphiniums, their stems carefully wrapped in damp newspaper), but no one had ever left anything so cranky as those feathers and nothing had ever been stolen, broken, or violated.

. . .

When Henry was drafting a sermon he was as close to bad-tempered as he ever got. It was one of his few vanities that he spent hours preparing and then gave the appearance of speaking offhand, as if the words and ideas had come to him on the spot. Preachers who read their sermons lost their audience, lost the chance to scan the congregation, meeting eyes in the back pews as well as the front, in case anyone was settling down for a spell of daydreaming. This week Henry's text was from Luke, chapter four, verses one through thirteen, in which Christ goes three rounds with the Devil and comes up the champion. Two slices of toast lay uneaten on a plate beside his typewriter. When I entered his study he was tapping a pencil against his coffee mug. He greeted me as if I had disturbed him several times that morning already, with a flash of annoyance in his eyes, a quick frown, and a stiffening of his shoulders. He had five more days in which to finish his sermon, so I stood my ground. I held out the evidence, which I was carrying in a shallow cardboard box: the frostbitten rose, the dried herbs, the mirror, the cup of wine, and the feathers.

Henry got up and came around to my side of the desk. I told him my story and Mary Fran's and offered to show him the empty sockets in the candelabras. He picked up the items one by one, handling them cautiously. He lifted the cup to his nose, dipped a finger in the liquid and tasted it. "What is it?" I asked. "A practical joke? Teenage mischief?" Henry walked to the window and stood there looking out with his back turned. There was nothing to see from that viewpoint but a row of gray birches. I began to wish I had spared him this added burden. His head was bowed, either in prayer or discouragement. His posture disturbed me. There was something he knew or surmised that was outside my comprehension. Many laypeople thought that a clergyman could see behind veils—even clergymen's wives, who ought to know better. "Tell me what it is, Henry, please." I don't know if he heard me. He was opening the window, although his office was already underheated. A stinging cold breeze blew some filing cards down on the carpet. I treated his gesture as symbolic, an act of defiance, fresh air bracing his spirits, clearing away webs of suspicion.

I disliked being cold indoors. It was the subject of a thermostat battle between me and Henry. When I raised the setting, Henry would sneak it back down. I used to leave him threatening notes tucked behind the dial: "This thermostat is wired to a silent alarm at the police barracks!" I was still wearing my parka but my hands and feet were numb. I wanted to change my socks and make some cocoa. In some ways I was the wrong kind of wife for a man of God. I had a very low threshold of tolerance for anything mysterious. Henry scanned the heavens; I kept my eyes on the ground. Perhaps I was not even a Christian, although I liked old churches and organ music reverberating in high-ceilinged spaces. Most Christians lived seventy-odd years in suspense: Would God embrace them at the last? Or cast them out of His temples into a lake of fire? I hoped to become good compost when I died. It was only the prospect of an afterlife that made Death fearsome.

The longer Henry stood at the window, the more un-Christian I felt. I resented being kept on tenterhooks, risking pneumonia. Whatever he was keeping to himself, no matter how shocking, could wait until my body temperature returned to normal. I picked up the cardboard box and started to go. I had my hand on the doorknob when I heard the window slamming shut. "Leave it here," said Henry. He took the box away from me. I expected his face to wear a look of sorrow, but the expression in his eyes was as jarring as the feathers on the altar, a mixture of excitement and voracious curiosity.

Chapter Five

A pastor's job is something like woman's work. Once it is done it is almost time to do it over again. Like bed making and cooking, services are performed every day. The words change according to the calendar, but the rituals must be repeated from year to year, until the Second Coming. The moment it is swept up, dust begins to gather again in the corners. As soon as absolution is bestowed on a penitent sinner, weakness and wickedness accumulate, even in sleep. Special services such as Christmas and Easter vary the routine, but they also require more exertion, like baking and decorating for the holidays. The pastor and the housewife are rooted in the things of this world. They have little time for abstract thought and contemplation. Their dependents cling to their coattails or their skirts, holding them down, preventing them from dreaming and soaring.

Except in the case of adults seeking confirmation, or of young people who think they might be destined for the ministry, Henry rarely handled matters involving faith and doctrine. His day was made up of countless practical tasks. He unfolded and stacked the chairs for parish meetings. He took the church garbage to the town dump. When the choir director was sick, he rehearsed the singers. He visited sickbeds and stayed to write letters for the patients. He showed busloads of grade schoolers how to make rubbings from headstones.

Henry was losing interest in parish life. His parishioners would be the last to know it. Henry did not yet know it himself, so he could not speculate on the causes of it. He imagined he needed more exercise and decided to climb Mount Katahdin. He oiled his bicycle, caulked and painted the wooden canoe, booked a riding lesson with John Crowley and then canceled the appointment.

Henry was a tall man with the frame of an athlete—a powerful chest, long muscular arms and legs. There was no fat on him and surprisingly little slack. He toed in when he walked, a habit you observe in ballplayers. He carried himself with a stoop, as if to deflect attention from the breadth of his shoulders. His body was younger than his face. His blue eyes had faded to grayish; and his fine, sandy hair was losing color. His fair skin freckled in the sun; but the freckles no longer receded over the winter. Now his freckles were age spots.

Henry developed a habit, not quite a tic, of clenching one fist or both fists, and extending his fingers, usually when he was required to sit and listen. In a meeting, on the telephone, more than likely in private sessions with troubled parishioners, his hands began to work, opening and closing, clenching and splaying, clenching and splaying. If I saw him trapped in a corner at some social occasion, I went up to him and held his hand to interrupt the rhythm. This seemingly bridal behavior gave rise to a rumor about our passionate sex life. Around this time he began to hurt himself in little ways. He scratched his cornea attaching Concord grapevines to the arbor, not on a branch or a twig, but somehow on one of those green paper-sheathed wire ties. He dislocated his shoulder on his way from the living room to the kitchen, walking so fast he collided with a door frame. A cabinet sprang open, bruising him on the cheekbone. Paper cut his fingers. The furniture waylaid him, barking his shins.

That was the essence of physical comedy, a big man cut down to size by inanimate objects. If the Unconscious was lodged in the body and the Conscious in the head, then Henry's psyche was at odds with itself, playing hob with his excellent reflexes. No doubt he should have followed a regular program of exercise, if only to regain his normal coordination. A man of his build ought to give his body its due. If Henry had found an outlet in physical activity, it would have cured the symptoms, but left the disease untouched. Henry thought about climbing mountains and shooting rapids, imagining that feats of strength could make up for a lack of spiritual challenges. Speaking as his wife, I had firsthand proof that his spirit was ailing. Sex involved both the body and the spirit; and for the last ten months we had had a sexless marriage.

Why was I alarmed by his preoccupation with that box of rubbishy feathers he kept under lock and key in his bottom desk drawer? Or by watching him light a bonfire in our driveway to which he fed the candles the thieves had left behind? He dropped them one by one into the flames, waiting until each of the six had melted down and was utterly consumed. Why was I startled to find him standing in front of the altar, reading from the service for the consecration of a church? *If anyone destroys God's temple, God will destroy him.* I should have been grateful. Henry needed a shot of novelty, and life had injected one. Walter Emmet's psychical research group, started in the fall, had petered out after only four meetings, to Henry's disappointment. Walter spent the winters in Florida and Mary Grey Hodges went back to Massachusetts to attend her dying sister-in-law. David Busch was off to Alaska on assignment for the *National Geographic*. In spite of its lively beginnings, Walter's group was focused on book learning, dry stuff compared to the mystery on our own church doorstep. Instead of worrying about my husband's unpriestly obsessions, I should have been hoping it would sustain him longer than Walter's study group.

Chapter Six

There was a boarding school on Sinkhole Road, five miles north of Dry Falls. It is still in business, although enrollment fell off drastically in 1975. Burridge Academy, known as "The Sink" to students and townspeople, was founded in the 1940s by Miss Nancy Burridge, whose father, one of the developers of the machine gun, sold his patent to the Belgian government and made a fortune in the First World War. A suffragette and a Master of Arts in medieval literature, Miss Burridge had her own ideas about the instruction of young women. The school brochure still includes her statement of purpose: "to foster those feminine values that are neglected by traditional systems for educating men." Miss Burridge believed that women were the preservers of culture and men the destroyers, a notion that has made little headway since the Age of Chivalry.

The Burridge curriculum was weighted toward the arts and self-expression: free movement; free verse; freehand watercolor and drawing; art history; spinning and weaving; hand-built pottery. She created a course in Mythology that was given to every senior class. Forty years later, we would call such a course a "workshop." As I understood it, each student picked a different goddess to be her term project. They built shrines in the woods behind the school—a circle or platform of stones, a mound of earth—and collected the emblems that were sacred to their goddesses, such as an image of an owl for Athena; a dove for

Aphrodite; a sheaf of wheat for Demeter, or a clay figurine of a sow, her favorite sacrifice. The girls made costumes and headdresses—a full suit of cardboard armor for Athena, a papier-mâché mask of a she-wolf for Hecate. They wrote speeches for their goddesses and delivered them at a full-dress ceremony at the end of term. I have a copy of part of one such soliloquy in my files, spoken in May of 1974 by Mercy Locke, the student who had chosen to play the role of Demeter:

> I am She who mourns the loss of a virgin daughter
> I wander the grasslands of Arcadia where I heard her cry of terror
> I left her for an instant
> I left her gathering poppies by the river
>
> My tears salt the ground
> My tears blight the land and its harvests
> While my child is a prisoner in Hades
> Dragged below by the black-browed Abductor
> I will make Hell on Earth
>
> Nothing grows where I walk
> I scatter Death with my footsteps . . .

Burridge Academy graduates, who were stuffed to the gills with goddesses, could hardly be blamed for concluding that the gods were subordinates, drones who played bit parts in the Olympian drama. Their education, however progressive, was out of balance. Generations of girls were exposed to needless danger because Nancy Burridge belittled the masculine principle. We saw Burridge girls in Dry Falls buying ice cream cones and magazines. They came into town on free afternoons and weekends, riding their bicycles or walking in pairs, linking arms, a homogeneous, honey-colored crew with shiny hair and white teeth. They used our library and helped out at the annual book sale. Some came to St. A's or the Fourth Congregational on Sundays. We knew them generically, not personally, since they all looked like cousins.

Once in a while a few of them took on a separate identity. Mercy

Locke had red hair and Helen Akers was tall and walked with a limp, the result of a bicycle accident. Mercy and Helen were the geese in the Burridge Academy swanherd. They failed to conform to the physical standard, Mercy because her beauty was full-breasted and womanly, and Helen for the reason that pain pinched and sharpened her features. Neither girl was rebellious in the classroom; and both expected to graduate with honors. The present headmistress, Myra Littlefield, Miss Burridge's grand-niece, had some good words to say for the two girls, and some reservations: "Excellent college material. They'll be a credit to the school down the line. Most of our students are just kids, open books, easy to read. These two look you in the eye and you still can't imagine what they're thinking."

Henry made the acquaintance of Mercy Locke and Helen Akers one night very early in April. He had come to check the boiler in the church basement, which was acting up and shutting itself off. As he left by the main door, he noticed two bicycles propped against the churchyard gates and went over to investigate. The moon was full, casting dramatic shadows, stark contrasts of black and white over the cemetery. A light frost sparkled on the ground, still frozen under the trees, where snow lay in patches. In that lighting Helen and Mercy looked like frightened children, crouching behind a leaning tombstone that only half hid them, covering their faces with their hands to keep the approaching figure from noticing them. The midnight hour rang out from St. Anthony's bell tower. By the stroke of twelve, the dark figure was looming over them. Miss Littlefield would have been pleased. At that moment they were easier to read than the youngest of her charges.

Sticky tears blotched their cheeks as the tall man pulled them to their feet. They seemed reassured to discover that Henry was human. Helen clung to his arm. "We thought you were something else." Mercy saw Henry's collar. "We're sorry. Do you have to report us?" "Show me what you brought," said Henry. Mercy hung her head and pointed to a newer tombstone, a slab of marble on four short pillars, a sort of mortuary coffee table. On its surface lay three brown eggs in a nest of pine needles, an alto recorder, and a strand of red hair tied with black ribbon. "You owe me an explanation," Henry said, "and you owe me twelve dollars for the beeswax candles."

I settled the girls in one of our guest rooms, gave them nightgowns and toothbrushes, hung their jeans out to dry on a chair by the radiator. Henry telephoned the school and told Miss Littlefield he had found them in the graveyard. "They were spending the night there on a dare. We'll bring them back to you in the morning." Miss Littlefield laughed. "I'll have to punish them, of course. What do you suggest?" "Tire them out," said Henry. "You must have a pile of logs that need splitting."

I put it to Henry that he hadn't been entirely truthful. An impartial observer might conclude that he had lied to Myra Littlefield. He could tell I was teasing, but he met my eyes defiantly, like a boy protecting his turf from an inquisitive adult. "What did you expect me to tell her? I won't know anything positive until I grill them after breakfast." Before I went to bed I mixed up the batter for a batch of pancakes, adding some chopped pecans and wildflower honey. The young ones might need something to sweeten the ordeal ahead of them.

Washed, dressed, and fed, the girls followed Henry into our living room. A fire was burning in the grate, as much for light as for comfort. It was seven-thirty in the morning on a gray day with rain in the forecast. Henry sat them side by side on the sofa and took the armchair opposite them. He had allowed them only six hours of sleep, so they were heavy-lidded and yawning. I brought in cups of coffee, although coffee was forbidden at Burridge Academy. I began to hover in the background, but Henry stared me out of the room.

I returned to the kitchen and finished washing the breakfast dishes. I suppose I could have stripped the guest beds and done a laundry, or tested a recipe for my cooking column, which was due by the weekend. I had no intention of staying in the kitchen, busy and obedient, waiting for a secondhand report at Henry's convenience. I opened the kitchen door and found that their voices reached me quite clearly. I overheard some of the proceedings from the dining room, where I sat at the table out of sight with a pencil and an oversize message pad, a present from a houseguest, which bore the word URGENT in red capitals at the bottom of each page. In a combination of handwriting and shorthand (which I had taken for a term in college), I transcribed all I heard satisfactorily, feeling certain that Henry would thank me for it.

Mercy (high-pitched, deliberate, with a slight patrician drawl): Everybody is supposed to choose a different goddess but we took the same one.

Helen (eager to cooperate, rushing her words): Mercy picked Artemis and I picked Selene. They're not actually the same. Later on in history they got mixed up with each other.

Henry (low-keyed, unthreatening): Why did you choose them?

Helen: They rule the moon.

Mercy: The moon rules women.

Helen: If we go out in the moonlight we can synchronize our moontime with the phases of the moon.

Henry: Your moontime. Your menstrual cycle?

Mercy and Helen: (dead air)

Henry: (maintaining a judgment-free silence, like any good therapist)

Mercy: It was wrong to put the feathers in the church. It was a joke. We got them from the costume room.

Helen: We needed candles for our shrines. We thought church candles would work better.

Mercy: We brought the mirror so we could see the goddess's reflection.

Henry: You don't want to gaze at the moon directly?

Mercy: No, that's not it. We want to see her face. Her face emerges in the mirror.

Helen: What really happens is we see her features on our own faces.

Henry: You know what the moon goddess looks like.

Helen (beating Mercy to the draw): Well, it takes a long time. It takes a while to develop the skill. At first you only see colors, or the mirror begins to mist over.

Henry: Why did you choose the cemetery?

Mercy: There is a witch in the cemetery. Mistress Huckins. I think that's funny, a witch in a churchyard.

Helen: Mercy means that the church burned witches. We get really upset by that.

Mercy (belligerently): Do you know what a witch is? A witch is a woman who knows something.

Helen: They healed people with herbs. That's why men hated them.

Henry (only a wife would suspect that his patience was fraying, as any man's does, faced with unsystematic thinking): If I remember my mythology, Hecate was the goddess of witchcraft.

Helen: Good for you! She rules the dark of the moon. Artemis is the Maiden, Demeter is the Mother, and Hecate is the wise old Grandmother.

Henry (changing the subject prematurely, in my opinion): What about the eggs and the wooden flute?

Mercy (contentiously): That's pretty obvious. Women are fertile when the moon is full. It's our time of power.

Helen: We drink a toast to our Mother with wine and we sing her a song. She loves to hear us sing.

Mercy: Helen plays the recorder because her parents won't buy her a silver flute.

Helen: Come on, Mercy. They're very expensive. Plus which, Burridge is expensive.

Henry (hanging on the ropes): How many times have you visited the cemetery?

Helen (taking a moment to answer): The first time we went it was wonderful. We felt really connected. I don't know what went wrong.

Mercy: I do. We forgot to bring protection.

Helen: You were supposed to get sage leaves from the cook.

Mercy: You said you'd bring the salt.

Henry: Slow down. This is new to me. Back up a little. Something happened this time. Can you talk about it?

Mercy (close to tears): I don't want to.

Helen: You heard it too. You grabbed my hand. You nearly broke my fingers.

Mercy: I'm not the one who was whimpering.

Helen: All right, but when something starts growling that close by . . .

At this interesting juncture I heard the telephone ringing, as it always did in times of crisis or high drama. Ruth Hiram kept me on the line for ten minutes, asking me to speak at one of the library's monthly book teas. To put an end to the conversation, I agreed to review a new book on whole-foods cooking, by an author who believed that eggs, milk, and cheese are poison. It was too late, in any case, to resume my post in the dining room. Henry was starting the station wagon, backing down the driveway. I could see from the kitchen windows that Helen was in the passenger seat and Mercy in the rear. Helen was wiping her eyes with the ends of her scarf. Mercy was slumped against the back rest, scowling. High-handed of Henry not to invite me along. My mother was an acquaintance of Myra Littlefield's, and my Beaulac grandparents were in attendance when the school cornerstone was laid. I might have helped, as a woman, an additional feminine presence, to soften the encounter between the girls and their headmistress. A brazenly self-serving argument on my part. I was no better than the gawkers who collect at the scene of a traffic accident.

It took all day to catch up with Henry, who had pastoral duties at the Poland Community for Mental Illness. Schizophrenics liked to talk to a counselor who wore a collar, since so often their poor heads were bursting with religious images. The brains of these patients lacked some kind of protective membrane, like clairvoyants who are flooded by impressions and unable to repel them. They were restful patients, Henry told me, when I asked him how he worked with them. "There's not much you can do," he said, "except for listening and keeping them company." Late that afternoon I lured Henry to the fireside with jasmine tea and ginger shortbread. He compared his schizophrenics to the girls he had delivered to Myra Littlefield.

"Sometimes they hit on a drug that works wonders for one of them, keeps him on an even keel for a period of years. They call it a 'cure' when the hallucinations stop. I've seen some of these cures. They come back to Poland as outpatients. They look lost—you know, bereft. They keep their heads cocked a little to one side, as if they were trying to hear something. In a couple of years, those two kids will have that same lost look."

"Do you want them to be frightened for the rest of their lives?" I asked.

"I want them to remember that something remarkable happened.

Keep faith with it, not erase it. To take a little pride in being the one it happened to."

"Henry," I reminded him, "I'm waiting to hear what did happen."

It startled Henry to be wrested away from his speculations. He was caught up in the meaning of events, which the facts concealed. The truth was like a nutmeat protected by a tough shell of fact; and his job was to smash the resistant outer covering. I tended to think that the facts were truth enough, and that they took unkindly to human prying and tampering. It was one of the differences between us, between most men and women. I can't say it caused trouble, but it was a source of exasperation, especially on Henry's part. When he told me a story, I made him repeat himself. I pinned him down. When he baptized an infant, I asked him to describe the christening dress. A christening ceremony was short and straightforward, unless the godmother dropped the baby, but the Burridge girls' scare in the churchyard was strange and complex, full of details that tantalized me. At least he had written them down, the disreputable facts. He left me to read them while he went to take the evening prayer service. His notes were abbreviated and roundabout, dashed off on the backs of Xerox copies of a budget he had submitted to the diocese.

4/4/74. St. Wilfred destroyed the early Celtic church, sold it out to Rome. Humanity divorced from nature from that point on. I'm employed by a crippled institution. Kendrick's *Druids* missing from my library. Had my hands on it in early December. Must have lent it to Walter. Is that what the girls saw? Some green man or nature spirit?

Preposterous story. I'd think they were conning me except they were too distraught. All the trappings of a dime-novel horror story: looming black shape with glaring eyes, "zoo smell," "growling." Shape changed size, "high as a tree" → "low as a bush." Opaque (a "black cloud"). (N.B. Ask M. Littlefield what Shakespeare plays the senior class is reading.) Dispute about eyes: Mercy red, Helen yellow. Sequence: (1) smell, (2) growling, (3) sighting of shape. How close? They agreed it came as near as forty feet (twice the length of the living room).

Shape identified as *human*, in spite of animal odor, noises, eye color: "An animal would have been less frightening." Did it threaten them? "It kept moving closer." What did they mean by human? *Formerly* human, the spirit of a dead person? A resident of the cemetery? Insisted shape not only human but masculine. Not a ghost, a man, "a real man." Unshakable conviction on this point. It was a man and he was "real."

Pronoun of reference changed from impersonal to personal: "He wanted to rape us." Raped by a dark cloud, cf. Correggio's painting of Jupiter appearing to Io. Burridge students steeped in art history and mythology, overemphasis on goddesses. Where do the gods go? Tamped down into the unconscious, waiting to be split off under stress. Neurotic dissociation. I wish I were dealing with anyone but adolescents. Maybe nothing going on here but sexual repression.

M. less embarrassed than H. by topic of rape. Spoke for both of them, H. nodding, gripping M.'s hand. Why did they think he intended to rape them? M: "*We could read his mind.*" H: "*We could see it happening, like in a movie.*"

Now comes the anomalous detail, the flash of gold in the streambed, the skewed, off-center item that could rescue the tale from convention and/or pathology. M: "*There were others.*" What they "saw": other women, hundreds (?) of women, dressed in white, "nightgowns" (grave clothes?), lying still, face upward, on the ground beneath the trees surrounding the churchyard. Had they been/were they being raped? Answer shocked me: "No. Not yet." They were earmarked for rape, inventoried, stockpiled. "He knows who they are."

H. sheet-white, pupils dilated. M. dropped her coffee cup. Remorse: I had pushed them too far. Had to help them close off the experience. What could they have done to gain release from the shape? They brought up the sage and the salt again. (Same little spat: H. blamed M. and vice versa. Normal energy returning.) What could they do to protect themselves in the future? One of their "manuals" said to strew garlic around their bedrooms, take it up and burn it in the morning. Both girls owned gold crosses. Would I bless them? I said yes, if they prepared for confirmation. At this point they started fretting about school, missing classes, facing Miss Littlefield. Drove them back. They seemed relieved to be rid of me.

N.B. Keep in touch w/Myra. Girls may need counseling.

I was a teenage girl myself once. I had that advantage over Henry. Polly Ellis and I made a wax doll of our sports teacher, Miss Crocker. We stuck pins in its knees. If she were incapacitated—just a little, not seriously—we reasoned we could get out of gym, which we hated because we were scared of the balance beam. One day Miss Crocker was rushed to the hospital with a burst appendix. We knew we had caused it, although knees and appendixes were unconnected anatomically. We were sick with guilt, sympathetic stomachaches and spiking fevers. We swore off magic for a year, until we fell in love with a pair of brothers. We slept with their pictures under our pillows and always said their names backwards—that is, "Yar" and "Nnelg."

Teenagers think the world begins and ends with themselves. In other words, teenagers are religious because their universe is personal. They organize life, which is disorderly, by the use of invocation and ritual, as in "Make him call in the next ten minutes and I will never be mean to my sister" and "I will get good marks if I don't change my clothes during exam week." They live at the hub, where everything is freighted with meaning. They see signs and correspondences everywhere—in the phases of the moon, the wind in the trees, the cries of animals, common household objects. They grow out of this mystical stage, for the better, although Henry wouldn't agree with me. Their world widens, grows intricate and unmanageable. Other people enter into it.

I read and reread Henry's notes while daylight turned to dusk. There was nothing like a fact in them anywhere, nothing solid to stub your toe on. By the time I was finished I had used up my patience for make-believe. Henry's "flash of gold," that palaver about the future rape victims, got high marks for creativity. Fantasy was tiresome. I wouldn't pay to see it in a theater. If their visions were real, or experienced as real, why didn't they run for their lives? I heard the churchbell ringing the end of the vesper service. When Henry came home, I'd be busy making bread in the kitchen. With my hands on dough, I was always even-tempered and tactful. I resolved not to ask annoying questions. Although his notes made it clear he was not quite so skeptical as I was, he would never take this brand of moonshine too literally. A man who had heard God's voice could hardly mistake it for the growling of a specter.

PART III

Christ Within Us

Chapter Seven

There is nothing unusual about sexual drought in marriage. Every couple goes through such periods. These dry spells may last for weeks or months at a stretch and have nothing to do with the age of either partner. We have little information about the frequency of sex in marriage. When we wed, we expect to have intercourse at least three times a week. If you conducted a survey of sex in long-term relationships, your subjects would assure you that their expectations have been met. Everyone lies about sex when questioned directly. They lie about numbers, duration, and satisfaction. Only a fly on the wall or a camera in the woodwork could expose the truth and rectify the statistics.

In the majority of cases it is men who lose their sexual appetite. When their natural aggressiveness is blocked in some other quarter, such as work or money-making, their libidinous drives are often dampened accordingly. When this happens, the wife will protest but the husband will deny it. She will nag and prod and worry the subject past bearing. The more she attempts to draw him into a dialogue, the more she is faced with a stricken, mulish silence. During these seasons of indifference every wife feels alone in the universe, as if no other woman had ever been sexually orphaned. Henry and I had been inactive for nearly a year, not a record, by any means, but still in the upper percentiles.

If I had known from the start how many women were likewise afflicted, the knowledge might perhaps have brought me some measure of comfort. Ironically, these wives began coming to Henry for help. A modern pastor is trained to act as a psychotherapist, to deal with issues far removed from the articles of faith. He learns to listen objectively and compassionately, no matter how embarrassing or close to home the topic. Jane Morse, Sally Bissell, Ruth Hiram, Gail Croft, myself—a meaningful proportion of the wives in our small church membership. Henry told me afterward that it seemed like a new strain of virus. Much later, when I interviewed Clark Harmon, the Congregational minister, he reported the same epidemic with higher figures, since Congregationalists outnumber Episcopalians in New England. We are entitled to presume, on the basis of these sample communities, that the affliction was not limited to churchgoing Protestant matrons. We can estimate that roughly a third of the women in Dry Falls suffered at that time from some degree of sexual deprivation.

In the animal kingdom spring is the breeding season. On the farms that surrounded us, the females were ready to multiply. That April and May there were signs of disturbance in the reproductive cycle. Our weekly newspaper, the Windham *Runner*, reported widespread stillbirths and false pregnancies. Out of fifty pregnant dams at Michel Roque's sheep farm, only nineteen produced a healthy, normal lamb. Monstrous births occurred at the Ashby farm—calves with two heads or with limbs represented by stumps. Septic fever claimed a good number of the Marstons' nursing sows. Evan McNeil's prize bitch rejected every pup in her litter.

Around Easter the *Runner* printed an alarmist editorial on the subject of the lowest animal birth rate in county history. Questions were raised about improper fermentation of silage, pollution in the groundwater, the competence of local veterinarians, the need for an official inquiry by the state agricultural commissioner. The *Runner* covered a meeting at the Dry Falls grange hall, where one dairyman stated that his cows had been frightened by something getting into the barn. One night he heard them bellowing and stamping in their stalls. He turned on the lights and found they had kicked out some of the slats. He thought it must have been a weasel or a fox. Michel Roque described a similar incident, but he put it down to a spell of freak weather—thunder and lightning with no rainfall. Will Marston himself, who had a doctorate in animal husbandry from Cornell, said the tragedies were an act of God outside the reach of science.

Something in our neighborhood was hostile to females of all species, interfering with their natural function. Like their human counterparts, mother cows grieve from lack of fulfillment. They go off their feed or develop patches of eczema. Cows must languish in silence, whereas human females have recourse to psychotherapy, or pastoral counseling as it is called when practiced by a minister like Henry. His appointment book filled up during Lent with the names of married women. Lent is a season when the faithful are bidden to practice self-denial, an odd time for a priest to be dealing with carnal matters. I wasn't displeased to imagine Henry on the hot seat. His clients would be speaking for me as well as for themselves. He was in a dubious situation, like a hypnotist who smokes treating patients who want to stop smoking. What could Father Lieber say to these unhappy women? Did he tell them, as he often told me, to "give him time"? How did he avoid the pitfalls of countertransference, which meant, as I understood it, seeing my features on their faces? Sexually deprived women are labile: their moods change quickly. By turns, they can be pathetic, shrill, or vengeful. Much later I discovered how Henry preserved his neutrality. He kept a pencil stub in his hand, which he sharpened before each session. Whenever he heard their complaints as attacks on himself, he drove the point of the pencil into his palm. Sometimes he broke the skin, although he kept from wincing. The tiny, dotlike scars took many months to disappear.

Like any other member of the psychiatric community, pastoral counselors pledge to keep their clients' secrets. Their vow is respected by judges, lawyers, and policemen, but it rarely holds up under questioning by spouses. Over the years, Henry came to trust my discretion. I never betrayed him, no matter what knowledge I harbored. My behavior toward Eleanor Webb, with whom I served on the library board, did not alter in the slightest after I learned that she'd been caught shoplifting at Woolworth's in Portland. It was harder with Gail, Ruth, and Sally, who were old friends, although only Sally was a bosom pal (I had known the other two so long that "friend" was the only word for them). Often I was tempted to steer our conversations toward intimate matters. No prompting was necessary. They volunteered the humiliating details. Their disclosures were indelicate, but scrupulous in one particular: by tacit agreement they never mentioned their sessions with Henry. I often wanted to make a meal of it with my kinswomen, to throw my hunk of meat onto the common fire pit, squat down and watch the raw flesh sizzling and separating from the bone. When the impulse to join in became too strong, I developed my own way of keeping faith with my husband and the ethics of his profession. I took a strong mint tablet from a tin I kept in my purse, popped it in my mouth, and sucked on it until my eyes watered.

Each of our cases was different. Jane and Frank Morse were in their twenties, while Ruth and Ralph Hiram were in their early sixties. Frank Morse was a carpenter and house builder, a feast or famine business. There was an infant in the house and Frank had lost the bid on a colony of lakefront cabins. Ralph Hiram was the bank's vice president, uneasy about retirement. Sally Bissell's husband had undergone surgery for cataracts. Gail and Tommy Croft's daughter had been put on probation in high school for cheating on a test. Each woman claimed to remember a full, rambunctious sex life, although their memories were probably exaggerated, given their current inactivity. My ladylike friends, whose clothes matched their reserved New England manners, began to show an aptitude for pornography, like women in labor who shout foul words no one dreamed they knew the meaning of. It was hard to imagine wispy, runny-eyed Ralph Hiram as having a "big, juicy cock," or, indeed, any cock at all, except perhaps the kind of generalized nub found on anatomically correct boy dolls. This description fell from the lips of his wife, our head librarian, who read only the classics, by her definition books written before the First World War.

Sally Bissell, my gardening and cooking buddy, childless like myself, was the president of the Abenaki Association, a private trust that gave money to needy families in our county. Ford (or Haverford) Bissell had no ambitions, or, if he once did, had decided to table them. I thought he was a happy man, managing their large estate on Notched Stick Hill, over five hundred acres of woodlands, leased pastures, ponds, and stocked trout streams. Ford was something of an expert on fly-fishing. He had patented a lure that fish mistook for a damselfly nymph. I learned from Sally one overcast day, while we were trying to come up with a humidity-proof recipe for meringues, that he was also something of an expert at cunnilingus, which is delicate work, like fly-tying, though not chiefly performed with the fingers. "Yankee men," said Sally, measuring out the cream of tartar, "are usually squeamish about it." She gave me a questioning glance, which I evaded by opening a cabinet to get out the cookie sheets. "He can't come into me," she said, "but you'd think he could still do that." "Can't means won't," I retorted. "Are you saying it's a matter of will? That he could if he wanted to?" "There's nothing wrong with him," I said. "His eyes are fine. Laser surgery isn't painful." Fortunately, Sally misinterpreted me. She thanked me for taking her side with such loyal vehemence. The weather defeated us that day. The batch of meringues we produced was flat and gummy.

Like a person who is dying, the female partner in a sexless marriage goes through several phases: self-condemnation, rage, denial (including scheming and "fixing"), and, after a lingering time, acceptance. Self-blame came naturally to most of Henry's clients, except for Gail, who jumped straight to Phase Two and dug in there. "My breasts sagged after the baby came," Jane told Henry. "It was late in the day to start painting my face," said Ruth. Sally ripped up her favorite nightgown, worn smooth and comfortable, full of little holes darned with colored thread. Every contented wife owns a similar nightgown, as much a symbol of emotional security as a costume for sleeping. Before the Dry Falls emergency I slept with no clothes on, but I had other ways of flaunting the stability of my marriage. Perhaps I let my hair go, tied it back too severely, waited too long between washings and cuttings. My mouth went in need of reddening, my lashes of blackening. My fingernails were blunt. My underwear was white and serviceable. The same could be said of all of us. In New England plainness in women was still equated with decency.

Among sexual intimates, no matter how unbridled their activities, there is one last taboo. Sex is inhibited by discussion—before, during, or afterward. Lewd words have their place between partners in the throes of union; but nothing lowers the temperature like instructing, petitioning, or rehashing. As Henry's clients reported it, sex did not die a sudden death. It dwindled away, its end no doubt hastened by the wives' predilection for talking. Recent sexual reformers have spoken out for women's rights in the bedroom. They advise us to let the man know what we like and how we like it. According to their scenario, the sex act would come to resemble a crew of movers lowering a piano out of a second-story window: "Take it up! Stop. Take it down. Slowly. A little to the right. Now the left. You got it. Hold it steady!"

Although my friends and acquaintances did not practice playing traffic cop during intercourse, they had no qualms about holding post-mortems when the act was unfinished. Each of us delivered the same lines in the same gentle, neutral tone of voice: "Is there something on your mind, Ralph (or Ford, or Henry)?"; "Are you feeling all right?"; "Didn't the pork chops (chili, sauerkraut) agree with you?" No matter how carefully the inquiry was conducted, it came out accusatory. Most men have a large investment in their mechanical skills. All over the county at this season, when the grass starts greening, they are struggling with lawn mowers, weed eaters, electric hedge clippers, and power saws. These recalcitrant appliances will eventually have to go to the shop, where their owners confer with the expert in technical language, reviewing discarded theories and advancing new ones. In the meantime they fill the air with commotion and curses. From the depths of basements and garages in every household you can hear their battle cry resounding: "I'll fix it if it kills me!" Any sensible wife blocks her ears and keeps her distance, knowing better than to get in the way of a man and his implement.

When the sex drive is on the fritz, there is usually no specific remedy, no spark plugs to clean or replace, no loose wires between the motor and the ignition. Men can't fix it, so they lose their status as amateur mechanics. The shame and frustration of failure puts a dent in their spirits. As long as they can act, or be allowed to act, as if nothing were wrong, time will recondition them. As long as they are not reminded, every night and at every meal, that their engine is stalling. "It helps to talk about it, Frank (or Ford, or Tommy). We can't sweep it under the rug. It's too important." "I haven't mentioned the subject for a week. I hope you'll give me a little credit." "Why am I always the one to bring it up? Don't you want things to be normal?"

After a dozen—or several dozen—of these one-sided dialogues, we stopped pouring our substance down a dry well. We lost faith in one of our most precious feminine resources. Men fix things with their brains. Women solve problems by uncovering feelings, using speech as their instrument. For us, talking is intimacy and silence is estrangement. By keeping silent, the Fords and Henrys believed they were preserving the status quo, while we felt they were destroying it. Since words were forbidden, we acted out our bitterness indirectly. Gail Croft tried to find some evidence of a rival, poring over her husband's appointment book in search of a recurring mark or squiggle, his personal code for the name of, or a meeting with, his mistress. Sally Bissell, who had a diploma from a Paris cooking school, began to make mistakes that would have disqualified her in her student days, adding sugar to a *pot au feu* instead of salt, burning the onions for *soupe à l'oignon* instead of caramelizing them. Her soufflés didn't rise and her béarnaise sauce curdled. When she turned to simpler dishes like egg custard and baked stuffed potatoes, the potatoes exploded in the oven and her custards wouldn't set in the middle. Ruth Hiram developed a rash on her calves and ankles, scratching herself raw until the sores became infected.

My symptoms were less dramatic—only intermittent bouts of sleeplessness, a kind of blank white insomnia with no content. I had no thoughts, but my body hummed and vibrated. Ordinary sounds were magnified—the radiators, the clock, and, above all, Henry's breathing. I shook him awake four or five times a night: "roll over," "blow your nose," "you're wheezing," "you're puffing," "you're gurgling." After more of these bouts I took myself out of our bedroom, dragging my pillows. I had the choice of many flat surfaces. There were beds in the guest rooms and the attic and two well-sprung living-room sofas.

At first we didn't know we were angry. We called it "nerves" or "hurt feelings." Henry identified the anger for his clients. Naming it released it. They kept on coming to Henry because he acted as a stationary target. He tried to schedule these women on separate days or with an empty hour between them. I saw him leaving one of those sessions, breathing hard and walking unsteadily. Our new faces shocked him. Every one of us, myself included, the pastor's helpmeet, looked in the mirror and saw the reflection of a harpy—taloned, powerful, hideous, and famished.

Anger can explode or implode and none of us could risk the aftermath of an explosion, the rubble of our homes, the torn, scattered limbs, the brushfires that flared up in the wreckage for a long time afterwards. At this point, we managed our anger by the simple expedient of denying it. There was no problem with our sex lives, only lack of creative effort in finding a solution. In retrospect, the denial phase seems comical. I think of Jane Morse poring over the back pages of men's magazines, clipping ads for Oriental products that roused desire, dragon seed pills, "male toner" tea, rubber sheaths with ridges to stimulate the penis. Ruth changed the Hirams' meatless diet to include rare beef. Sally perfumed the backs of her knees with a dab of musk oil. She dug a bed near the kitchen door, where she seeded summer savory, an herb with a reputation as an aphrodisiac. When the plants came up, she dried the leaves and sewed them into "love pillows."

In other words, each of my friends started to practice witchcraft, that branch of the medical profession dominated by women. Like any researcher engaged in an experiment, they learned to temper hope with patience. Failure became a meaningless term, since there were so many variables to play with: regulating the dosage, changing the time of day it was administered; deciding when to harvest herbs, whether at full moon or in the morning before the dew dried. Ruth kept watch over her husband while he was sleeping, recording the number and strength of his nighttime erections. She believed she was well on the way to proving that steak for breakfast produced more and longer-lasting results than steak for supper. She had yet to put shellfish to the trial, or leaner meats like veal, lamb, and chicken.

For myself, I made Henry seek help from various practitioners, both alternative and conventional: a hypnotist, a bioenergeticist, and a marriage counselor. He went to Portland in civilian clothes, guilty and obedient, keeping his appointments at first, canceling or forgetting the later ones. He found hypnosis relaxing, a pleasant, unfreighted interlude. The doctor, a young Israeli, gave him a suggestion to increase his sensual awareness—an image of a sun-soaked beach, the heat washing over him in waves, pretty girls in bikinis oiling their supple bodies. During this time Henry began to approach me, making overtures with his mouth and his hands. One night I misjudged the state of his readiness. Any progress brought about by hypnosis was lost in an instant. The penis is a finely graded instrument, too complicated to be gauged by a lustful woman. There are many degrees of stiffness and congestion. Neither verticality nor engorgement necessarily constitutes a viable erection.

The bioenergeticist, a hairy, short-legged man in his fifties, ordered Henry to strip off his clothes. He lunged at him until Henry, buck naked, started to retaliate. The man parried Henry's blows with a rolled-up towel stretched between his hands. As they fought he encouraged Henry to grunt and bellow, to open his throat and release the sound from his abdomen. These mock battles gave Henry the idea that he needed more exercise, though not the kind of workout I had intended. For a while he went jogging on the track behind the high school. He bought a metal chinning bar, which he installed in the rectory basement. He invited me to come on a daylong hike through Rankins Woods. We took the canoe to a stretch of easy white water on Crooked River. Every one of our shared activities took place outdoors, in the daytime, wearing regulation sporting gear.

I called Doctor Swan myself and accompanied Henry, since marriage counselors begin by seeing people in pairs. Ethel Swan, Ph.D., received us in her office on Harbor Street, a suite of rooms with white walls and bare, uneven floorboards. A chesty dyed blonde wearing a fuchsia scarf that clashed with her red blouse, she greeted us with a smile, giving each of us a firm, two-handed handshake. She singled out the identified patient while we were still in the reception room. Henry followed her inside and I sat down to wait until she summoned me. After a quarter of an hour she opened the door and I went in.

She got right down to business. "Was it your idea to seek treatment, or your husband's?" "It was mine," I answered. "And your husband agreed?" asked the doctor. I caught Henry's eye. "Well, he didn't disagree. He went along with it." She turned to Henry. "You asked your wife to make the appointment?" Henry shifted in his chair. "I don't remember asking. She wrote the date and the time on my calendar." "Mrs. Lieber, will you face your husband? Dr. Lieber, face your wife. Now, let's begin at the beginning. Ask your husband again. This time answer her directly, Dr. Lieber." I felt like a child who hadn't prepared her lessons. "We should go to see a marriage counselor," I recited. "That's a statement, not a question," said the doctor. I tried again. "Will you go to see a marriage counselor?" "No, I won't," said Henry after a moment. We gaped at each other and at the therapist, who got up from her chair and came toward us. "Come back to me," she said very pleasantly, "when you reach an understanding on this subject."

Chapter Eight

My sister came home for the Easter holidays with her bag of troubles. Once I was married and provided an alternative to staying at Emily's, she showed up every year or so, sometimes announced, sometimes unannounced. The drive from Albany took a good six hours, seven without pushing it. Anyone else would have made a start well before noon to be certain of arriving before her hosts had gone to bed. Hannah roused us at four in the morning of Good Friday. Her muffler had conked out in the Effinghams, near the Maine–New Hampshire border, disturbing the sleep of every household along her route through the lower Sebago region. When she pulled into the rectory driveway, she was dragging her tailpipe.

For a churchman Easter week is as busy as foaling season for a horse breeder. Henry had two early Communion services, one at six-thirty at St. A's and one ecumenical service at the Fourth Congregational at seven-thirty, followed by a meeting with the members of the Easter Vigil committee, who wanted to hold the Saturday night vigil at the Violette Brook Campgrounds. There was no sense in going back to sleep for an hour and a half, so Henry and I unloaded Hannah's gear and took her duffel bags upstairs. Hannah's van was packed to the roof with scrap lumber, weathered pieces of red and gray barn siding. Jammed behind the lumber was a rusty wood stove, four kitchen chairs with the seats missing, a pair of wooden cross-country skis, and a carton labeled sheets / towels / blankets. "I'm thinking of staying awhile," Hannah said. "You have plenty of room in the garage. You can store all this junk until I find a place."

By now my mother had lived alone for nearly fifteen years, if I don't count her annual trips to France with the Huguenot Society. Since the Huguenots gathered and were persecuted in every province in the country, Emily's pilgrimages came to resemble ordinary tourism. When I married, she gave away every stick of the Beaulac furniture, along with all the curios and knickknacks, the beadwork pictures, stuffed songbirds under glass domes, tapestry footstools mounted on deer hooves, three-tiered revolving centerpieces. She made her house as spare and clean as a wilderness cabin. Every object it contained had to pass the test of usefulness, whether for sitting, eating, writing, or storage. Some of my father's pieces were there (a chest of drawers, a bench, a trestle table), the few he had not willed to the museum in Portland, the ones he called his "Shaker plagiarisms." The brightest color in the house was the terracotta glaze on some pottery soup dishes. All the color was in her garden, where she sided with Nature against good taste, planting reds with oranges, hot pinks and yellows with purples. Garden books tell you that white flowers tone down vivid colors. Emily discovered quite the opposite: she used white to intensify them.

My mother observed partial mourning, *demi-deuil*, as the French say. She favored neutral shade in her dress, browns and grays with no light in them. We wear mourning for the dead, not the living, but my mother was grieving for her elder daughter, who was lost to her. There was no longer any open rift between them, which might have forged a vital connection, even though a negative one. Feuding parties can be sure of always being in each other's thoughts. Perhaps it would have been kinder if Hannah had kept on using Emily as her whipping boy, as she had when she was in her teens, spiteful and defiant. For the last ten years she had treated Emily with a casualness reserved for old acquaintances, names in her address book who got notices of art shows where her sculpture was on exhibit, or a postcard out of the blue from the western provinces of Canada: "You can breathe here—everything on a massive scale—we live like ants in the East—Roger (Phil, Gary, Mark) and I back next month if the van holds up—Be well, Hannah."

When Hannah blew into Dry Falls, I usually got a few days' warning, but Emily had no word from her. Left to herself, Hannah might or might not drop in on her after a few days, squeezing in her mother between visits to her high school woodworking teacher and Bobby Court's sister, Helene, who owned the Dexter Shoe franchise on the strip in South Freeport. I made it my job to get everyone together for the evening meal, as if we were a closely knit family reunited after an unwelcome separation.

Emily was quiet and unobtrusive on these occasions, like a first-time guest or a governess or companion who has been invited to eat in the dining room with her employers. Hannah smoked cigarettes between courses, giving us her opinions on the art world (dominated by a handful of powerful collectors and dealers), the probability of nuclear war, the reasons for the failure of her latest experiment in communal living ("it doesn't work if everyone's an artist"; "I was the only artist in a bunch of farmers"; "there's such a thing as too little structure"; "they had too many rules"). She tried to get a rise out of Henry: "You work for a big corporation. What's the difference between you and a VP at Procter & Gamble? Nothing but the wages." I came in for my share of it: "I love this fifties food, sis. Lot of wonderful passé things going on in your kitchen."

Early Good Friday morning I told Emily about Hannah's arrival. It was best done in person. I rang the bell and let myself in the front door, although Emily was probably in the garden. I saw her from the screened-in porch, carrying a tray of seedlings in peat pots. I called out to her. I wanted to talk to her before she started tucking the pots in the earth. Emily was touchy and withdrawn when she was planting, as unapproachable as a nursing animal. My eccentric mother, weak-eyed from childhood, who "saw men as trees walking," refused to wear her spectacles in the garden. Inside the house she bumped into furniture without her glasses, but I have never seen her put a foot wrong outdoors. She came toward me, or toward the direction of my voice, stepping over a pile of bamboo stakes lying in her way, skirting a pitchfork plunged upright in the ground. She gave me that luminous smile of the poor in sight, an unfocused smile that embraces much more than its object.

"Ma mère," I said. "She's here."

Although the path was level, Emily seemed to lose her footing. I took her arm and guided her to the steps.

"We'll sit down for a little. You should wear a hat when you work in the sun."

Her hands, small and freckled, were covered with scratches, the nails ringed with dirt.

"Where are those gloves I gave you? Have you already lost them?"

"I knew she was coming," said Emily. "I always know."

"Now listen, mère," I said. "This time she talked about staying."

The hope and dread in Emily's eyes were painful to see.

"I'll get the barn ready for her," she said.

"No, no. Pay attention. It won't happen. It's just one of her notions."

Emily lifted her eyes and stared out at the back of the garden. If she had been wearing her glasses she would have seen the Smalleys' tiger cat climbing the dogwood.

"Before she comes I always have the same dream. I'm chasing her across a field full of flowers. There are hills in the distance. I'm so out of breath I lose ground. She runs into a cave and I follow her in the dark. I never catch up with her."

I put my arm around her shoulders. "It was only a nightmare, darling. Were you sleeping on your back?"

"Let me speak, Cora. This time the dream changed. There was someone else in the cave. I can't remember. I keep trying. She screams. I can hear it in my mind. The scream was very high. It had notes, like a piece of music."

"It doesn't mean anything. You know what dreams are. They're a kind of mental sewage system."

"She was in danger. She may be in danger."

I laughed at her. "From what? There are no caves in this neighborhood."

Emily stood up abruptly. "I must finish my beans. The pots are drying out."

"You're dismissing me, mère."

She kissed me on both cheeks. "I wonder where you came from," she said. "You're my sunny daughter. It's the dark child who's usually the changeling."

When my dark sister came to stay with us she preferred to sleep in the attic, which Hoyt Furman, the previous rector, had insulated at his own expense as a dormitory for visiting grandchildren. We stored a few things up there—boxes of photographs and canceled checks, a rack of dressy clothes and winter coats in their storage bags, some rolled-up remnants of carpeting, Henry's father's collection of fishing rods, and the Beaulac bed.

Brought by clipper from Nova Scotia in the 1850s, the bed was fashioned out of oak by an ambitious amateur carpenter. With a high plain headboard surmounted by a broken pediment and a footboard too low in proportion to the height of the headboard, it stood a foot and a half off the floor on thick, clumsy legs. It still retained its original paint, a rusty-red color achieved at that period by mixing cow's blood with whitewash. A motto was stenciled on the headboard in fading black letters, N'ESPÈRE RIEN, "hope for nothing," the marrow of the Huguenot religion: only God knows which sinners will be saved; therefore hope for salvation is an illusion.

The bed reminded its occupants that death could arrive at any moment. Perhaps its dark red color stood for the flames of hellfire. I have seen portraits of some of my ancestors, black-garbed, sharp-featured, unsmiling men and women named Raquin, Daillé, and Beaulac. It was easy to imagine them preparing for death while they composed themselves for sleep, as if each night were their last one. My father had banished the bed to the garage on the grounds of its monstrosity. Any bed that ugly, he claimed, would drink up human energy as thirstily as linseed oil. It ended up in our attic when Emily redecorated her house. Walter Emmet, who took a look at it last October, told us such pieces were beginning to be valued for their "primitive vigor."

We had furnished one corner of the attic like a proper bedroom. There was a nightstand, a reading lamp, an armchair, and an oval hooked rug by the bed. It was hospitable enough if the room was aired beforehand, although there was no closet, only space on the clothes rack, and the bathroom was on the floor below. On previous visits Hannah never unpacked her luggage or hung up her belongings. She let her clothes lie where she shed them, until the floor was covered with a patchwork of fabrics, a kind of makeshift carpet.

Late Good Friday morning, while Hannah was in town waiting for Aaron Schmidt to replace her muffler, I took some extra blankets up to the third floor. Hannah's jackets, jeans, and good trousers were hanging on the clothes rack, with her boots and sneakers arranged in rows underneath them. Her bags were stowed neatly under the bed. She had filled the night-table drawers with other necessities—museum postcards, sketchpads, colored pencils, a compass, a slide rule, cigarette papers, and a can of loose tobacco. She had thumbtacked a poster to the wall opposite the bed, an image that echoed the message on the headboard: a naked, gnomelike man handcuffed to a nuclear missile, biting his wrist in despair, drawing crimson blood, the only color in an all-gray palette. Unless she had changed her habits, we were in for a long one, a month or more of her smoke and spleen drifting down from the attic, infecting the household.

The van came back from Schmidt's Auto Shop at two-thirty, bounding up the driveway. The exhaust system was silent, but Hannah was leaning on the horn, startling the worshippers next door out of their meditations. Which of Christ's last words was Henry up to by now? Was it "Father, forgive them, for they know not what they do"? I ran outside to try and persuade her to put a plug in it. She saw me coming and honked again. I pointed at St. Anthony's.

"All right, all right. I forgot. Get in. We're going house hunting."

"Where?" I asked. "Henry wants an early supper."

"I ran into Lorraine Drago at Aaron's. Some client has a cabin on his property. Free till October if I do some repairs."

"Where?" I repeated. "Is it far?"

"Boy, I'm glad I'm not somebody's wife. You're on a short leash, kiddo."

I paid Hannah back with the best shot in my arsenal.

"We're taking Emily with us. She'd enjoy the outing."

If I expected an outburst from her, I was disappointed. She looked at her watch, then leaned over and opened the passenger door for me.

"Let's move it," she said. "Drago's going to meet us there with the keys."

Emily got into the back seat of the van next to a pile of canvas tarps sending out fumes of paint thinner. Hannah told her to open the window and let in some air. "No, no," said Emily. "I'm fine. It's a good, clean smell." She sat straight up in the seat with her head and spine in perfect alignment, her hands resting loosely on her knees, alert but reposeful, like a yogi. On the way out the Poland Road to Moose Meadow Road, past the entrance to Violette Brook Campgrounds, up an unmarked dirt road rising steeply, she kept perfectly silent. Unlike Emily, I have a dread of empty air. I asked all the questions. "Where are we? Are we near the Rolfe place? I've never been up here. Have you, Hannah?"

On our left we saw a clearing with an alley of Norway pines leading up to a rustic building on the scale of the great wooden "camps" in the Adirondacks. According to Lorraine, it had been built by a businessman from Texas, whose heirs rarely used it. The cabin Hannah wanted to see was on their property. Hunting parties had stayed there, and an occasional caretaker. An antlered buck and a doe, grazing on the winter-browned grass, stopped to glance up at us. Beyond the clearing the road became narrower, rough and pitted, a hazard to Hannah's new exhaust pipe. Low-hanging branches brushed the sides and top of the van. Traffic passed this way seldom. White pines, larches, and hemlocks had reached their full height, eighty to a hundred feet tall. So little sun reached the forest floor that it was bare of undergrowth.

I have lived in Dry Falls since my eyes first opened. I thought I knew every piece of land inside its boundaries and the name of every landowner. The house in the clearing was built years before I was born. By the date of my birth these trees had stood here for close to a century. I like to take hikes, go out by myself with a day pack and walk until I tire. If I had any favorite trail it was following Violette Brook upstream, climbing steadily for a mile or more, through deep woods that seemed, in contrast to these woods, skinny second growth. Did the streamside trail rise as far as this venerable forest? Had I failed countless times to reach it because my legs ached or the dinner needed cooking? The van startled a hunting hawk, which flew low in front of us, carrying a small creature in its beak. "Where are we?" I repeated. Hannah braked as the road dipped downward across a washout. "It's not on the map," she answered. "All I have is Lorraine's directions." Emily spoke from the back for the first and only time. "How dark it is," she said. "I don't feel welcome here."

The road ended abruptly at another long-neglected clearing. For the last fifty yards we drove over tussocks of uncut grass, still frosted with unmelted snow, rutted before us by the tracks of Lorraine Drago's jeep. At the far edge of the open space stood a one-story hand-built log cabin with a fieldstone chimney. An overhanging roof supported by timbers covered a narrow porch that ran the length of the structure. I could see from a distance that some of the porch floorboards were missing.

Lorraine emerged from the doorway, holding a padlock. She was wearing a Tyrolean hat and leaning on her knobby walnut walking stick. Her hair, dyed a flat mahogany, concealed the secret of her age. One of her legs was shorter than the other, owing to a childhood bout of polio, but she was as plucky as a tomboy. Limping over acres of rough terrain with prospective buyers, she took frequent spills, righting herself in an instant like one of these plastic clown toys that are weighted on the bottom. One of her bright brown eyes was larger than the other, an outward sign of psychic abilities, according to the researchers at Duke University, who had put her through a series of tests for extrasensory perception. Lorraine volunteered for these tests in the 1950s after a number of unreasonable experiences, such as "seeing" one of her listings consumed by flames and calling the volunteer firemen, who were already at the scene, putting out a blaze that had started with an oil leak. These days her extrasensory powers were lying fallow, unless they accounted for her success in the real estate business. She was known throughout the upper and lower Sebago regions for her talent at matching a client with the property of his dreams.

Nothing captivated me like empty enclosures—houses, lofts, barns, silos, chicken coops. When I stood in these spaces my life began all over again. In my mind's eye I took down a partition, added a window for light, chose a wallpaper pattern, placed the furniture. I was out of the van and inside the cabin ahead of Hannah, filled with expectancy, elated by new possibilities. Dirt and rubble were rarely obstacles to my daydreams. I could see past swags of cobwebs, rodent corpses or their skeletons, a pile of stained blankets in a corner harboring the smell of a vagrant who had bedded down there. I could overlook a trail of raccoon droppings studded with seeds and a patch of green moss on the ceiling where the roof had leaked. This time my imagination shut down. There were signs that the cabin had been vandalized—deep black scores in the floor planks, x's or crosses, unrelated to the grain and condition of the wood, as if someone had taken a red-hot poker and gouged them out. When an empty building has been willfully damaged, it no longer seems uninhabited. The vandal's presence lingers on like an unwanted guest.

Hannah was pacing the length of the cabin with a light in her eye. Her excitement mounted as mine subsided. My virtues were purely domestic, but my sister had a carpenter's skill and an adventurer's spirit. She crouched on the hearthstones and looked up the chimney, emerging with a veil of soot on her cheekbones. She climbed on a wooden crate and scraped away the moss with her pocket knife. She spanned a section of wall between her hands, measuring to accommodate some object, probably a worktable. I pointed at the ugly black gouges. She turned around, annoyed by the interruption. "The boards are two and a half inches thick. Rent a sander and sand them down.

What's the matter with you?" I said I could see daylight though the logs in any number of places. "I'll mix up a little mortar. It doesn't take a brain surgeon."

Whether she is showing a mansion or a shack, Lorraine Drago left clients alone to explore the premises, free to make negative comments, argue among themselves, or go into raptures without fearing they will compromise their bargaining position. I expected to find her outside chatting with Emily, but she was parked on the lower step relacing her shoes, an ungainly pair of black walkers designed to follow the natural shape of the foot. My mother was absent from the scene. I thought she must have gone into the woods to look for wild plants. Emily was always equipped for collecting specimens. She carried waxed paper sandwich bags and a miniature trowel in the pocket of her skirt or jacket. I sat down by Lorraine. Daylight was waning but our legs were still in sunshine. "I hope Emily doesn't roam too far afield," I said. "Unlikely," said Lorraine. "She's sitting in the van." "She won't get out?" I asked. "She hasn't. I didn't make a fuss about it."

I went over to the van and opened the passenger door. I gestured toward the cabin. "I don't know what you're up to, mère. Can't you show a little interest?" Emily bowed her head. Her hands were clenched in her lap. In distress she became unresponsive, almost slow-witted, giving no clue as to whether the matter was urgent or trivial. I was irritated to distraction by this habit. "You don't like the cabin. You think it's too isolated. You think it's too ramshackle?" Emily hunched her shoulders and bent her head even lower. "Please get out. You'll have a scene with Hannah. Come inside and pretend you like it." Moving painfully, as if she were stricken with arthritis, Emily allowed me to hand her down. She leaned heavily on my arm as I walked her across the grass and up the steps. At the doorway she balked like a nervous racehorse at the starting gate. I put my arm around her and pulled her the last few inches over the threshold. Hannah was struggling to open the left front window, which was painted shut. She said, "One of you get over here and give me a hand." I left Emily standing motionless in the center of the room. Hannah continued to pound on the window jambs, trying to loosen them.

Conscious of family tensions, Lorraine had faded back into her jeep, well out of earshot. She was reading a newspaper. The sun had also retreated, to the spot where the van was parked. I was making my way toward the light when Emily came out again. I had taken her inside hunched and feeble, aging before my eyes. She walked down to join me with a brisk, decisive step, shoulders back, head erect, eyes front, the same woman who could move rocks unaided to build a stone wall. She had stayed in the cabin a matter of five or six minutes, a very short time to work such a change, too brief to allow for a ruckus with Hannah and a reconciliation.

Emily spoke with an authority that matched her stride. "Lorraine will take me home. Hannah has the key and the padlock." "Can't you wait and drive with us? We won't be long." "I can't prevent this," she said. "It's beyond my powers." "She can fix it," I said. "She's like Francis. She knows how to fix anything." "There are other cabins. There are several on Proud Lake. I'll leave it up to Lorraine." My mother was not a meddlesome person. If she had tried to influence people and events, she might have cut short years of sorrow. "You can't go behind her back. She won't stand for it." "I have no choice," said Emily. "Something is wrong here."

I watched Lorraine turn the jeep around and drive away, playing a farewell volley on her horn. Sometimes Emily had these prophetic fits, delivered in peremptory terms with no substance to ground them. Her utterances always concerned the prodigal daughter, never the stay-at-home. Perhaps she resorted to premonitions because Hannah had banned any other form of communication. There was no reasoning with psychics, maternal or professional. Their knowledge was superior, outweighing your hidebound demands for proof and results. Emily's track record was not only poor, it was nonexistent. None of her dreams or "strange feelings" had ever come true, yet she was willing to gamble her fragile connection with Hannah on one of these forebodings.

Any number of things were "wrong" with this decrepit log cabin planted in a virtual wilderness. It rotted. It sagged. It let in the wind and the weather as well as human and animal intruders. The only atmosphere emanating from it was one of neglect and maltreatment. Our accredited sensitive, Lorraine Drago, had inspected the premises often in the course of business without picking up any unusual vibrations. Some real estate agents will suppress disagreeable information to expedite a sale, but Lorraine bent over backwards in the opposite direction. She described the condition of a property before the first viewing, handing clients an itemized list of defects, along with estimates from local contractors for the cost of repairing them. It goes without saying that I, Cora, the earthbound daughter, mired as I was on the material plane, felt and saw nothing but dirt and breakage, a housewife's nightmare. When it came to the paranormal I was tone-deaf and color-blind. Perhaps I was put here to check and balance the excesses of others—a husband who heard the voice of God, a mother who believed in dreams, a sister who renounced her kindred in the name of Art.

That very sister—the squeaky wheel, the thorn in the flesh, the vixen in the henhouse—came out onto the porch with dirt smeared like war paint across her face. She positioned the padlock, but left it unattached. She waved at me, gave me the V sign. The palms of her hands and the knees of her trousers were coal black. When she was pleased, or merely unirritable, she brimmed with mischief.

"I can work here," she said. "Look at all the free lumber. And did you notice? Emily really hates it." I hadn't seen her look so self-satisfied since the age of fifteen, when she sneaked out of the house at midnight to meet a boyfriend and came back at four-thirty in the morning, undetected. I said, "I'm not in love with it myself. I'd rather live in a tent." "That's an idea," said Hannah. "I'll cadge Henry's pop-up while I'm working on it."

Hannah had the bit in her teeth. She jabbered all the way back to the rectory, ticking off extra items she needed to borrow (tools, dishes, gas camp stove, a cot, a kerosene heater), reminding herself to ask Lorraine about the depth of the well, figuring out which buddies from the old days she could weasel into helping her. Questions about how many trips her van could survive on that potholed, axle-busting road she brushed off as obstructive and unfriendly. She didn't like hearing speculation as to whether the intruder might be a local or an out-of-town hunter who thought he'd established squatter's rights to the cabin and might take out his resentment at her presence in some unlawful fashion. She accused me of trying to get rid of her. She said I was afraid she was "bad for Henry's career." I told her she thought the world owed her a living. She got in a dig about "preliberated women," and their slave mentality. Compared to her, I told her, Francis was a paragon of selflessness. She said I wanted to keep Emily to myself. I said she could have Emily, since Emily was obsessed with her anyway. If we had been children instead of acting like children, she would have gone for my hair and I would have aimed at her stomach with both fists. These days we settled our conflicts by punishing each other with silence. When we got home I went into the kitchen and began slicing onions for soup. Hannah disappeared upstairs. She came down while the onions were caramelizing, walked straight past me, and slammed out again. I heard her drive off, scattering gravel.

Chapter Nine

Accepting a sexless marriage is a gradual process, subject to lapses. Every night brings a fresh opportunity for regression, reviving the hope that two bodies lying side by side will catch fire spontaneously. When proximity fails to work its remembered magic, every night is a new occasion for disappointment. There were nights when I slept close to Henry in our usual fashion, with my head on his shoulder and my right arm across his chest. There were others, and their number was increasing, when I waited until he fell asleep and pulled away from him. On Friday night, Good Friday, with Christ still hanging on the cross, I pulled away from him—the least erotic date on the calendar, when this clerk of God had been on his feet for fourteen hours hawking the gospel. I lay awake on my side of the bed very close to the edge. I threw off the covers. His body gave off too much heat. The bed was too small. I couldn't sleep unless I left the bed.

I had nowhere to go when Hannah was in the house. I couldn't camp in another room and let her find me there. I heard her going upstairs just after we turned out the lights, walking with a heavy tread, missing a step, dropping something she was carrying, swearing. It was one of those nights when the bathtub began to seem appealing, except that our tub is high-sided and curving, too short to stretch out in. I could make up a bed on the floor with a pile of comforters, a nice, ostentatious solution designed to give Henry the message. I was strong and fit. I could go without sleep for one night without breaking my health. I needed a glass of milk, a plate of crackers spread with butter and peanut butter, or a British detective story. Reading in bed never disturbed Henry.

Propped against extra pillows, with a heating pad warming my back, I opened one of Patricia Wentworth's Miss Silver mysteries. The girl in the book thought her husband had hired someone to kill her. His family estate was exorbitantly taxed and she was an heiress. When Miss Silver was called in there had already been three attempts on the heroine: brake failure, a trip wire on the staircase, a misdirected bullet. On each occasion the husband's cousin had been the first on the scene. Was he Johnny-on-the-spot because he was the killer, or because he was keeping watch over her? With each murder attempt my body grew more relaxed. I was reading through half-closed eyelids, lulled by the mechanical motion of the plot unwinding. Another member of the house party drank hot milk intended for the heroine. The milk was doctored with a tasteless poison. I never reached the end of the story. I fell asleep with the light on, *Till Death Us Do Part* slipping gently out of my fingers.

I had nights of insomnia related to sexual anger; but once I passed out I was a perfect sleeper, a eusomniac. Lying on my back, rarely changing position, I sank to a level where my dreams were not retrievable. Unlike my mother and my sister, and Henry with his combat experience, I had never had a nightmare, even as a child with a fever. The most graphic and urgent of dreams, nightmares force themselves on our attention. They remind us that our grasp of the world is insufficient, that we need to consider the demands on the unconscious.

I often envied people who dreamed, who had an open channel to the unconscious. They might be troubled by their nighttime visions but they were connected to the greater mysteries. The unconscious was both personal and impersonal. It contained forbidden desires and shocking memories, the debit side of the ledger of the conscious mind; but there was far more below than buried injuries to our childish psyches. It was as if there were a tunnel in each of us, a shaft leading down to the center of the earth and back in time, to when our ancestors adored and feared the sun and moon and lived as equals with the animals. The tunnel opened out onto stormy infinity beyond space and time, where human history had its ending. Even the most experienced travelers in the unconscious lost their compass and the last shreds of identity in this termless region. Christians believed infinity was a realm of white light; but I thought it must be black, blue-black, booming with the thunder of colliding atoms, a theater of energy. Out of this chaos particles formed and reformed into shapes of dread and desire, evil and enlightenment. We called them angels, elementals, demons, ghosts, gods and goddesses. They approached us spirit to spirit, taking physical shape because our understanding was limited to the material. They had messages for us, which we received as scrambled images or riddles, since our material minds could not take the truth directly. They told us, if only we would listen, that Reason was the sleep of fools and the Self was a mirage.

Experienced dreamers came back from the unconscious trailing clouds of darkness. Until they readjusted to the light, they might see the natural world in shades of gray, as moving shadows. Sometimes the twilight prevailed. The unconscious can produce casualties, diagnosed by the experts as depressives and schizophrenics. The rest of the dreamers, the safe returners, learned to straddle two worlds. They learned to give house room to the invisible. According to individual temperament, the world around them became magical or fearsome. Empty spaces were filled and resonant. Every stone was made up of secrets as well as molecules. Every tree might address them familiarly.

In the years before the Dry Falls emergency, when I had no dreams, I felt inferior to these night travelers with their open tickets to other worlds. Of course I had dreams of a sort, all related to physical functions, such as dreaming I was in a rowboat that was filling up with water, a signal from my body that I needed to go to the bathroom. In those years it was enough of a miracle that yeast made bread rise and that cream, when churned, turned to butter, that a foal came out of the womb and could stand immediately. I believed that Lorraine Drago's brain cells were organized in a pattern different from mine. I believed my mother's garden flourished during hailstorms, heat waves, and insect blights because she worked so hard tending it. Henry had heard God speak to him in Belgium because he needed to find a refuge from the shelling, if only in his mind.

Henry used to charge me with having a joyless view of the universe. I answered that his view was the bleak one, the anemic one, that belief in the supernatural drained the sap from creation. Why look further than your own home county for meanings and justifications? Outside our wood and stone shelters everything was in order, in the sequence of the seasons and the tides, the movement of the stars, the health and disease of all species. I told him human beings should try to emulate plants and surrender to the life cycle. All our woes came from thinking, from imagining we were better than life. Mystics and meditators did nothing but subdue their bodies and fool with their brains. Their spiritual certainties were the purest invention, products of mind. Henry asked me why I'd married a priest instead of a farmer if I was such a materialist. Since I'd chosen a man who traded in invisible currencies, I must have a hidden spiritual agenda of my own. I asked Henry why he'd married a skeptic instead of a believer. I suggested that he enjoyed lording it over a less evolved creature, a metaphysically obtuse female.

My sleep was so heavy that I wakened on Holy Saturday half blind and half conscious, weaving as I walked. I stood in the middle of the rug on my way to take a cold shower, trying to remember why I was getting up or what life I led outside the bedroom. I saw by the clock that it was eight a.m. Christ was in his tomb and Henry was already in church for morning Communion. I pulled up the blinds, wincing at the bright morning light. The Great Easter Vigil at the campgrounds began at seven this evening. I had promised to organize the food for the community supper. At noon several women from the parish—Ruth Hiram, Mariette Roque, and Adele Manning—were coming to help me assemble the meatless casseroles and the dried fruit compotes. Minnie McNeil was baking her unyeasted Lenten raisin rolls. The men's committee was supplying cold drinks and coffee. Who had volunteered to take charge of glasses, dishes, silverware, napkins? I sat down in the armchair and leaned back to rest my eyes, a rash undertaking, since I quickly dropped off again.

What was making that unholy racket? A truckload of coal was being poured down the coal chute—except that the rectory furnace had been converted to oil in the late 1940s. It took me some moments to trace the source of the noise to the attic instead of the cellar. Hannah was yelling, taking the Lord's name and mine in vain, running across the floor. She had a heavy tread at the best of times. I had no intention of hurrying to the scene in my nightgown because she had stubbed her toe or knocked something over. She could deal with the breakage while I washed my face and put on a sweater and trousers. I wanted with every fiber of my being to make her wait until I had drunk a cup of coffee.

When I opened the attic door I found her huddled in a corner wearing a pajama top. She was crouching behind a dozen packed cartons that had been piled three or four to a stack and collapsed in a jumble, forming a kind of barricade. The cartons falling had made the noise I'd heard. I lifted and restacked some of the boxes so I could get to her, asking her if she could move. As I bent over, I saw spots of blood on the back of her pajama collar.

"You've hurt yourself," I said, thinking she had fallen and hit her head on a corner of one of the boxes. I tried to lift her to her feet but she nearly dragged me down with her, clinging to me. "You're cold," I said. "You have to put some clothes on." She shook off my hands and jerked away from me. She was coming back to normal, scowling, blaming the first person who was handy. "I'm not going near it. I'm not going to sleep here. I won't spend one more night here."

Generally the wisest course with Hannah was to let her rant until she wore herself out. I went over to the chair by the bed to get the blue jeans and sweatshirt she had dropped there, the low lace-up boots with her socks jammed into the toes, yesterday's underwear.

So soon after waking I often saw things but could not interpret them. Until I approached the Beaulac bed, I had failed to take stock of it. One pillow lay on the floor some five feet away. The second one was mashed against the headboard as if fists had pounded it. The top sheet and blankets were tangled into a coil. The bottom sheet was rumpled in a pattern like choppy water. The mattress had slid out of place, on a sharp diagonal. The bed itself had moved forward, a foot from the wall. Anyone, including myself with my bleary vision, could have drawn the conclusion that more than one person had slept there, that several people had engaged in a fight for available room, or even, by the look of it, in some kind of sexual scrimmage.

I backed away, wary of drawing nearer, waiting, perhaps, to be sure all activity had subsided. From my post I observed that the sheet was stained with wetness, patches of damp drying with a faint brown outline, from a discharge that might be heavy perspiration. A patient with pneumonia who had undergone a crisis in the night, or a dreamer held hostage by a nightmare with a violent plot line, might have created this exceptional and repellent disorder, as could a pair of lovers who had swallowed an exciting substance, such as grated root of mandrake. All this had happened on the night when Jesus hung dead on the cross and Joseph of Arimathea, a good man and a just, was petitioning Pontius Pilate for his body.

I knew I should strip the bed and change the sheets, but I resisted the prospect of touching them. I had an idea that the mattress should be replaced and an even more peculiar impulse to burn the bed linen. I wanted to turn my back on this lurid scene, which was none of my doing. I felt like that stock-in-trade character in detective stories, the backpacking hiker who stumbles on a corpse in the woods, goes out of his way to inform the local authorities, and finds himself inconveniently detained throughout the course of a murder investigation.

When I was cooking, I needed my full attention. Since I had no children, I had never learned to prepare food with other people milling around me, wanting to talk to me. Most of the time mothers were required to do several things at once, which is why their cooking suffered and their interest in cooking waned until the children left home. I could sympathize with all mothers and their perpetually fractured concentration, pulled as I was between Hannah and the vegetable casseroles. She sat hunched over her coffee mug, using it as a hand warmer. She didn't want to be alone and I was confined to the kitchen until the dishes for the church supper were prepared. I lent an ear to my sister while I separated heads of broccoli and cauliflower into florets of uniform size.

Hannah kept repeating herself, requiring little of me except murmurs of reassurance, small change for the jukebox. Over and over she said, "I didn't do it," as if she were defending herself against criminal charges. "It didn't get that way by itself and I didn't do it." She couldn't have done it, because she remembered having a nightmare "about not being able to move."

"I knew there was something wrong with the attic," she said, and I didn't like to remind her that she usually called before her visits, asking me to get the third floor ready for her. I told her the rectory was clean. There were no legends connected with it except the story that Father Kurtz (two rectors ago) used to bring his laying hens inside for the night when the temperature fell below zero. Hannah said she would have to borrow my clothes unless "somebody" brought her belongings down to the blue guest room. Irritating people are rendered no less so by hardship and distress, and so it was with my sister. She was milking the incident, if it was an incident, and not just her own rambunctious sleep behavior. Down here in my warm kitchen with my hands busy, I had demoted the chaos in the attic to the level of a nasty housekeeping chore. I could hire Mary Fran to deal with it. I could get Ollie Swope at Yonderhill Galleries to take the Beaulac bed on consignment and put it up for sale at the first auction of the season, on Memorial Day weekend.

I started making the white sauce, using chicken broth and milk instead of plain milk or milk and cream. I could have made white sauce in my sleep, even in large batches, but this time I kept forgetting how many tablespoons of flour I had measured out and was obliged to start counting over again. Hannah was distracting me. Her aggrieved, insistent voice was a little too loud to be background noise. Then I began to realize that she was interfering with my thought process, simple as it was, because of what she was saying and not how noisily she was saying it.

She was describing her dream, but now she thought she had been awake instead of asleep. She said she heard footsteps coming across the room, "whooshy" footsteps like several pairs of feet in felt-bottomed slippers. A moment later the bed "went down," as if a knee were pressing on the outside edge of the mattress. "Then my head went down. I thought I was going to roll out. I wanted to scream but my voice got stuck in my throat."

"It was a nightmare," I said. "Nightmares often seem real."

"The awful thing was I couldn't move. I couldn't even move a finger. There was a weight on my chest forcing me into the mattress."

"Well, of course," I reassured her. "That explains it. You were hyperventilating during the nightmare."

"Are you a doctor?" asked Hannah.

"Oh, shut up. I read about it somewhere."

"Find me the book and show me the page."

"They call it sleep paralysis," I said. "It happens from overeating and with people who have heart conditions."

"I know you," said Hannah. "You get all your medical information from women's magazines."

"It's true," I laughed. "They condense it into such dainty, digestible portions."

By the time I had finished the white sauce and grated the Swiss cheese, Hannah was talked out and sensible again. Talking was a miracle cure, far more effective, say, than helping me chop the scallions and parsley. She was full of spunk, raring to go to the cabin and spend Easter Saturday prying up worn-out floorboards. Now that it was daylight, with the sun attaining its zenith, the attic was an ordinary room to her. I assured her that the beds in the middle guest room were always made up, in case she had another bad dream. I asked her to join us at the campgrounds for supper around seven-thirty, or ride over there with me and Henry and the casserole dishes at exactly six o'clock. "I'd rather be hung by the ears," she answered from the dining-room doorway.

I kept my eye on my wristwatch while she was upstairs. She came back down again in nine and a half minutes. She was buttoned, zipped, straightened, tucked in, and laced up. None of her clothing was on backwards. Her hair was uncombed, but restrained by a nylon headband. She had even brought down the sheets and stuffed them into the washing machine; so she had stood by the bed, bent over it, touched it, without a panic attack or any other evil consequences. Hannah departed by the back door, pink-cheeked and smiling. There were many incidents like the bed scare in my sister's life, opportunities for emotion and high drama, shit fits in teacups. She took them in stride; in fact, they seemed to pep her up. On the whole, she took them much better than her unwilling audience did.

Hannah was setting out for a day of invigorating manual labor, leaving me indoors to perform more gender-appropriate tasks. She would be working alone in the cold, using her muscles and getting stronger. I would be one of a nest of women working together in a snug enclosure, no one of us taking the credit for our culinary achievements. My sister had this effect on me, that she could bring on discontent like a spreading rash. She was a lone gun and I was a herd animal, penned and tethered. Her inner life as well was more enterprising, more freewheeling. Other people's nightmares were usually diminished in the retelling: nothing remained of their power but a rambling anecdote. My sister's nightmares left behind actual evidence of their passing. Awake, she could carry stacks of two-by-fours on both shoulders; asleep and dreaming, she could apparently move a bed that weighed several hundred pounds. When envy was upon me, I forgot that she was also something less than an Amazon: she was a person who suffered; who saw her hope for recognition eluding her; who had no close companion; who set impossible trials for her friends and family, like a king testing suitors for the hand of his daughter. I forgot that she told herself lies to make things come out the way she wanted them to, that she covered hurts with sarcasm and fears with bluster, as she was probably doing now. I forgot about the small, fresh wounds behind her ears, marks she'd dismissed, as I had, as self-inflicted.

I had helped Hannah belittle her fears. She had had an unusually vivid dream, so "real" she believed she was awake and perceiving the attic bedroom in accurate detail. I supposed it was common for sleepers to incorporate their real setting into their dreams. For all I knew, half the adult population wakened from bad dreams and routinely discovered little bleeding cuts at the base of their skulls on the mastoids, exactly the way Hannah had. She had seen the blood on her collar and looked in the three-way bathroom mirror. She said there was only a little blood, that the cuts "smarted at first" but seemed to heal very fast. By the time she showed me the cuts, they were two pink lines about a half an inch in length, running horizontally, or parallel to her shoulders. Hannah was sure she had scratched herself in her sleep before the nightmare started. Once the nightmare was under way, every part of her, she claimed, was immobilized. The cuts were so straight and fine they might have been made by a scalpel. My sister's fingernails were by no means precision instruments. They were bitten flat across and down to the quick, incapable of leaving a mark on any surface.

I was making fresh bread crumbs for the tops of the casseroles by my own whipstitch method, grabbing hunks of crustless bread and rolling them between my palms. Looking down, I saw that half the crumbs had piled up at the edge of the counter and the rest had sprinkled onto the floor. In all conscience I couldn't use the ones on the floor, although I would have if I'd been cooking for only Henry and me. Hannah had left, but she was preying on my mind, as much as if she were still sitting in the kitchen droning at me. I needed a container for disposing of renegade facts, something roomy and respectable, like the mind-body explanation. Suppose the wounds were a hysterical reaction to the horror of the nightmare, the psyche seeking to escape by bursting through the skin? If the cuts were nothing more than dream stigmata, there was no need to imagine an outside agent or evildoer.

What sort of agent? In those days I was not a particularly imaginative person. I thought shadows were made by solid objects intercepting the light. The play of light and shadow over surfaces enhanced the beauty of things. I failed to observe that light and shadow were well-matched antagonists. I never considered that shaded areas might be doors to the underworld, through which legions of the unbodied slipped in and out at pleasure. As far as I knew then, there was no underworld, or if there were, it was wholly housed in the unconscious.

. . .

My volunteer ladies were arriving and I hadn't even started on the compotes. Mariette Roque could easily plump the dried fruit in boiling water, and Ruth was equal to the task of making a light syrup flavored with cinnamon. I would tie an apron on Adele Manning and set her to washing pots and pans, even though she did let the water run continuously. It was best to give Adele a simple task, since she could keep her mind on only one thing at a time. I had made a brief attempt to discourage her from serving on the supper committee, but it was always a bad idea to look a gift volunteer in the mouth.

I heard car doors slamming and the sound of voices. I went to the window. Naturally they had all arrived at once in separate cars, in spite of the gas shortage. Mariette Roque wore no hat, coat, or gloves. She never did, even when she was working outside or in an unheated barn. Her face was roughened and cracked from the cold the same way a sailor's is weathered by the sun and wind. Ruth was muffled up to her nose in her down coat and six-foot scarf. Down coats flattered no one, especially Ruth, who had short legs, a thick waist, and an overhanging bosom. Although Easter was on the late side this year, we were having a cold snap, which might very well put an end to Henry's plan for holding part of the vigil service outdoors around a bonfire.

At odds with the weather whatever the time of year, Adele followed Mariette and Ruth wearing a purple cotton skirt, a blouse with billowing sleeves (soon to be soaked in dish water), a black cloak cut from a limp, unseasonable fabric like silk or rayon velvet, and a pastel knitted cap with earflaps. On warm days you might find her sporting construction worker's boots and a tweed vest. She was twenty-six years old and had come of age in the 1960s, when fashion was taken out of the hands of the special interests and given back to the people.

With her pale, oval, eyebrowless face set on a swan's neck, her slanted eyes, high forehead, and fair hair skinned up and knotted at the crown, Adele was the image, in repose, of some late medieval princess—Henry the Fifth's fair Katharine of France. In fact, she was the daughter, granddaughter, and great-granddaughter of Episcopal parsons. Typing and filing for the Reverend Henry Lieber, she was, in a way, going into the family business, from which women would be excluded for a number of years to come. We were living in unstable times for the younger generation. Adele's arrangements with Henry were changeable also. She settled down to work for three or four weeks at a time and then was apt to take off for a week or so, seized by some enthusiasm—a workshop, a seminar, a marathon retreat weekend that promised to reveal the secret of life. When she was in harness, Adele was so good she read Henry's psychology and theology journals and wrote abstracts of the articles so Henry could decide which ones he could skip, without having to plow through all of them. Adele was able to make peace between Michel Roque and Hubby Drago, vestrymen who were always squabbling about how to invest the church's tithes and pittances; and she had come up with more than one idea for a sermon. She had trained the ladies of the altar guild to funnel all requests for Henry through her. Henry remarked that Adele had been sent to him as a form of spiritual discipline, a constantly renewed reminder that all good things must come to an end. The Lord giveth a perfect secretary, and the Lord taketh her away again.

During one of Adele's "sabbaticals" from Henry's service, she had spent two weeks on an estate in the Catskills, sitting at the feet of a wrinkled Indian guru, Sri Bandha, about whom no harm was known. Adele was a seeker as much as a nonconformist. Her generous nature embraced many people, and some of these people had odd beliefs. She, in turn, would want to broadcast the word about her latest inspiration. I have many little gifts that provide a record of Adele's experiments—a square of red silk in which to wrap my tarot deck (always supposing I owned one), a ceramic statuette of the goddess Isis from a museum gift shop, a tape recording of the marriage rites of the Nemo tribesmen of West Africa, a packet of dried mushrooms I keep meaning to throw out, since I've forgotten whether they're culinary or hallucinatory.

When she first arrived, fresh from a summer job at Stanek's in Portland, the region's occult bookstore, Adele asked my advice about putting in a garden on the sunny side of the Bissell garage, over which she was living. She had found a book or a pamphlet called *Floral Therapy*, and she wanted to grow flowers and extract the flower essences for her personal pharmacy. "Apparently what I need, Mrs. Lieber, Cora, is something called 'mugwort.' Is that easy to grow?" "It grows like a weed," I said. "What does it do for you?" Adele picked up the booklet, which at that time was always on her person, and began reading: "O.K. It gives you 'greater psychic sensitivity in crossing the spiritual threshold, especially during sleep.' " I asked her to translate, and she said it meant she would have more coherent dreams instead of baffling fragments.

The rest of the flowers on her list were hardy in New England: pink yarrow for emotional clarity, iris for opening the soul life, Shasta daisy for archetypal understanding, black-eyed Susan to cure self-blame and self-censorship, phlox for distraction. I told her I thought she was a wonderful person and why did she go in for all this fiddling and fine tuning? "I wouldn't want to be a priest," she blurted out. "Even if I could. You don't have to be a priest to see God." That was her intention. She was making herself ready. She wanted to be worthy of seeing a vision, while some fully accredited male cleric was bypassed in her favor. I asked her how she could be sure, when the time came, that it was God she was seeing. "At this point I don't know that it matters. I don't care if it's a man from Mars. I'd settle for anything out of the ordinary."

I watched by the window, waiting until my volunteers started coming up the path before I opened the door and let in the cold air. They were still standing in the driveway, listening, as Adele unfolded a tale. I could see her only from behind, but she was making a production of it, flapping her arms, looking like an animated clothesline. She was almost six feet tall, as tall as any man who was privileged to take holy orders. When she was growing up, her height had embarrassed her and made her awkward. I smiled to think of Adele at the Easter Vigil supper, carrying one of those hotel dining-room trays large enough to hold thirty dessert dishes. As she moved back and forth between the tables, every diner in the room would be keeping an eye on her inadvertently. Adele had never actually dropped anything while she was waiting on table, but her saves and near-misses were heart-stopping.

My ladies broke out of their huddle and started up the walkway. The walk concealed a triple hazard: wet moss, patches of black ice, and bricks heaved askew by past frosts. Adele slipped only once and righted herself by grabbing Mariette's shoulder. I came out to greet them. I said, "When you got here you were five minutes early." Mariette kissed me on the cheek. "Adele was telling us about a nightmare." "I hate hearing about people's dreams," said Ruth, "but this one was as good as a ghost story."

"There was someone in my room," said Adele, breathless and starry-eyed. "I heard it coming up the stairs, swish, swish, swish, what a funny sound, like a dust mop. I knew it was there across the room. I could hear it breathing. I heard it all night. It was strange for a dream. I could see every part of the room the way it is in real life." Adele hugged me strenuously. "I know I was probably asleep. But what if I wasn't? Wouldn't that be something?" I think she expected to be congratulated. She was hungry for manifestations, if not full-scale miracles; and she needed the support of her cheering section. I got her inside along with the other two and showed them where to put their coats. I deflected the conversation away from nightmares by offering to make a sandwich for anyone who hadn't eaten and asking if they wanted coffee or a glass of raw milk from Arnold Crowley's cows.

I was sick of dreams for one day. I was tired of reassuring fanatical dreamers that I believed what they said, every word of it. I did pause to note that two women in one night, living less than five miles apart, had had dreams with very similar motifs: the "whooshing" or "swishing" sound, the presence in the room, the uncertainty as to whether they were asleep or awake. Since I was a nondreamer, I knew little about dream symbolism except that flying was supposed to mean orgasm and empty boxes, suitcases, or trunks stood for the uterus. Perhaps it was as common to dream about a specter swooshing into your bedroom as it was to dream about finding yourself in a public place with few or no clothes on. In my opinion, there was nothing particularly symbolic about these dreams. Neither Hannah nor Adele had a current sexual partner or even an admirer. If I had been endowed with foresight instead of the useless hindsight that burdens me now, I would have taken the time to question Adele meticulously.

And what could I have done with any stray bits of lore I gleaned? Appointed a round-the-clock watch on her? That afternoon my perspective was typically feminine and mole-eyed, close to the ground. I looked no further than my kitchen. All I could see were mounds of vegetables wilting on the counter, piles of cheese losing moisture, pans of white sauce clotting on the stove—all these elements needing, while life was still in them, to be blended and changed by the transforming power of fire. My foresight extended only as far as the lodge at Violette Brook Campgrounds, an oversized shed with a wall of windows facing away from the road toward the woods, that shed full of expectant people, waiting for the dawn of Easter Sunday, whose stomachs would be filled and palates charmed by dishes of my own concoction. Cooking was the most esoteric discipline I practiced or believed in. Jesus Christ said, "Take no thought for what you shall eat or what you shall drink," but it was not his heavenly father who kept him and his disciples from starving on their lifelong road tour. It was the Marthas like me who came out of their houses to wait on the dusty performers and lead them to the table.

PART IV

Christ Beneath Us

Chapter Ten

In the middle of April 1974, Dry Falls had an August heat wave. It began the day after Easter and ended ten days later on the feast of the hermit saint Declan, who kept poisonous snakes as pets and was able to read men's minds. The weather systems that moved across the rest of Maine, bringing cool, sunny days, chilly nights, and regular rainfall, bypassed our eastern section of Cumberland County. This localized hot spell, with temperatures in the high eighties, went totally unreported on radio and television. For ten days and nights Dry Falls slipped through the nets of the weathermen. According to their maps, we showed daytime lows of 40 and highs of 54. At first no one bothered about the discrepancy, although Ralph Hiram called the Portland University classical music station to complain. Everyone expects the weather report to be inaccurate.

I had to put shade netting over the seedlings in the kitchen garden, the cool weather crops—lettuces, spinach, and peas. They drooped and died and I reseeded them when the climate returned to normal. Henry started to sand and paint the wrought-iron garden furniture, a task he usually performed a month later. I outlined a column on various ways to brew iced tea (steeped in the sun, steeped in cold water in the fridge overnight, steeped in boiling water with the addition of raspberries) until I realized my topic was premature. Most of my readers were still wearing coats and sweaters.

Unless they were farmers or gardeners, my fellow townspeople seemed to believe that hot, dry weather was unconditionally good and cold or wet weather evil. They were especially overjoyed when temperatures turned warm out of season or in time for a weekend. All over Dry Falls people were congratulating one another, taking our heat wave as evidence that Nature had lost this particular round and Humanity had won it.

There were dissenters, of course. On the fifth day, a Friday, I had occasion to go to St. Anthony's around noontime. Bishop Hollins had called, asking Henry to take over Dean Cortesi's guided tour of English cathedrals, scheduled to leave June first, because Cortesi had broken a leg and would still be on crutches. The Bishop always wanted a same-day (if possible, a same-minute) answer. I stepped into the nave, looking for Henry, and there was my mother kneeling in the first row of pews and Arnold Crowley seated at the back with his head bowed, since his knees gave him trouble. They were praying for rain—at least Emily confessed to it later.

All the hurtful years with my father had never driven her to church, nor had a lifetime of countless other barometric hardships—late frosts, premature thaws, droughts, nor'easters. What was different about this spot of eighty-seven-degree weather with summer just six weeks away? It was happening in the spring, after all, not in January, the stronghold of winter. Emily had always relished all weather, even when it brought some devastation to her garden.

When a squall was brewing, I have seen Emily take a chair to the window and sit there, watching until it blew itself out. It was a form of entertainment for her. The storms she liked best were the violent ones, the ones that would be suppressed if they were cop shows on television. If it was merely pelting rain instead of threatening to tear the roof off, Emily often went out in it, hooded and caped if it was cold, bareheaded and unprotected in summer. She would stand there way past the saturation point, until her clothes and pores could not absorb another drop and she was streaming with water like a fountain figure. She took us out with her when we were little, holding us by the hand, but we soon grew restless and ran back indoors. Emily stood too long in one spot and made us observe complete silence. Her behavior never seemed odd to me until Mrs. Smalley happened to witness one of these drenchings and expressed concern for Emily's health, when it was clear from her tone that it was Emily's mind she was worried about.

Emily passed on to me her love of the changing seasons and to Hannah her ability to take the weather one day at a time. Hannah never learned to love weather in all its variety, but she was, unlike me, inured to it. To her, it was usually a negative presence, an obstacle or problem, causing paint to dry too fast or too slowly, tools to rust, boards to split, or an artist's fingers to become numb and clumsy. My sister carried on in spite of the weather, and developed a remarkable tolerance for physical discomfort. I welcomed change, that stately progress of one season to another, birth to death to rebirth, in a timely, orderly round, but I hated deviations from that round. I hated meteorological events that were out of order, unless they were provided for by long-established tradition, like Indian summer or the January thaw. When it hailed in July or snowed in mid-September, I was disturbed unreasonably, and most of all when it grew hot in the colder months, since I was among those who believed the world would end in fire. Disorderly weather seemed to me to be a sign of some calamity approaching. It meant the universe was out of kilter and our earthly habitation with it.

I followed Emily home from church and let myself in without knocking. She was already in the kitchen, cutting up some store-bought broccoli to cook in the steamer and eat with lemon juice and margarine. I knew because I had seen it so often—she would steam the broccoli for twenty-five minutes, until it was khaki-colored and waterlogged. It was a great mystery to me that a woman whose own garden produced such abundant, unblemished vegetables would consistently overcook them and anoint them with a tasteless butter substitute. She asked if I would stay to share her lunch, and I could truthfully say that I was meeting Sally Bissell at Ernie's in the village.

When I saw how Emily looked, gray and puffy, pushing up her spectacles to dab at her eyes, I felt a pang of worry. I hoped that she was only fatigued from sleeping badly on these hot nights, or that something in the heavy, unmoving air might have revived her allergies. I was still childish enough to want her unimpaired, sound and competent, in good working order like the natural cycle of the seasons. Some part of me imagined that my mother's demise would render the earth sterile and upset the balance of things. We are so primitive with regard to our parents. We cannot help making gods of them.

Pulling up a stool to the counter, I made ready to consult the oracle, an oracle with chapped, red hands, frog-eyed behind her thick glasses. Like most oracles, my mother was inclined to be obscure and roundabout. I expected riddles for answers. I should have brought along an offering of chocolate truffles, Emily's only weakness.

"With all due respect, mère," I ventured, "you don't look rested. Did you have Bill Washburn take down the storm windows?"

"Cluck, cluck," said my mother. "I know how I look. I've been having those infernal cave dreams again. It's impossible to get back to sleep afterwards."

"Is that why you came to church?"

"You have such a curious attitude for a minister's wife. You don't trust the religious impulse."

"I certainly don't where you're concerned."

Emily laughed at me. "Well, I'll tell you why. It's the coolest place in town."

"That means you're bothered by the heat."

"Of course I am. It's very strange for this time of year. What will be left by August?"

"By strange, do you mean abnormal? You think there's something wrong with it?"

"Cora, you're hanging on my words. What are you pressing for? I can't imagine where you got your rigid notions about the weather."

"Don't be evasive, mère. Remember how squirrelly you got at Hannah's cabin. Is this 'wrong' the way that was 'wrong'? Explain it to me."

Emily checked the flame under the steamer and lowered it a little. She turned to face me, or her own oblique version of facing me. She was incapable, optically speaking, of staring you directly in the face. With glasses on, her eyes were so magnified and, without them, so myopic that she seemed to be looking around you and some distance beyond you.

"These dreams about your sister are a burden to me," she said, pressing her hands together, summoning her dignity. "I would like to be able to talk to you, but you won't let me. You dismiss the subject and badger me about the weather."

"I am honored to be a listener," I said, "but you can't expect me to be a believer."

"There may be nothing to believe in but the extent of my anxiety for your sister."

"You mean the dreams have changed for the worse."

"Now she is standing at the mouth of the cave and beckoning me. I try to follow her inside but the opening closes over, like a sliding door."

"You heard her scream before. Did she scream?"

"No, she doesn't scream. She seems joyous. Last night the door to the cave slid open and she came outside for a moment with another person."

"Who was it? A man or a woman?" I was caught up in Emily's dream in spite of myself. It was like the fairy stories she had read to me at bedtime out of books with covers in every color of the rainbow. I almost called out, "Don't stop! Don't stop!" just as I used to each night in childhood.

Emily cut her recitation short, breaking out of that trancelike mode common to people who are telling their dreams. She turned off the flame under the steamer. I refrained from warning her that leaving the broccoli in the pot with the lid on would only make it browner and limper. She rummaged in a drawer for a knife and fork, making an angry clatter.

"I need sleep. I have to keep fit. What would happen to the garden if I lost my health?"

"I can give you three hours a week. Would that be a help right now?"

Emily ignored my offer and went on with her grievances, like an actress complaining to a director about repeated script changes.

"I'm tired of dreaming. Dreaming all night and deciphering dreams all day, when there's no sense to them. I'm just reliving the day Hannah left us. That's what they're about. Why do I have to contend with caves? Why bring in that strange girl, Henry's secretary? I can't remember her name."

"Adele Manning. What about her?"

"That's who was standing with Hannah at the mouth of the cave. They hardly know each other."

"Dreams are supposed to be symbolic, mère."

"Well, it's an aggravating detail. It preys on my mind. I have no relationship with her. Why should she be there?"

Emily lifted the steamer from the pot and turned it over. The broccoli was so soft it flattened out when it hit the plate. Unappetizing as it was, it reminded me that I wanted my own lunch—Ernie's sour cream and cottage-cheese omelet, or his scallop stew with green peppers. I kissed Emily on the cheek. She turned her back to me. She never liked to say goodbye, even at a bus station or an airport, where farewells are the principal agenda. At the last moment, with departure well under way, she ducked her head and lost the power to speak. While you were waving and calling to her, she had already begun to walk away. As a child (bound for camp or to Portland to visit my grandparents) I found this habit of hers unconsoling, but I gave up trying to change it. Leave-takings affected her so strongly that she was literally unable to go through the amenities.

If we slipped through the nets of the weathermen during that ten-day heat wave, Adele Manning somehow slipped through our nets on Easter Eve. She was lost to us or stolen for an interval not longer than two hours and a quarter, between ten p.m. and fifteen minutes after midnight. I did not credit my mother's dreams with any magic, since some word of the incident might easily have reached her, then escaped her memory. There were fifty people at the Violette Brook Campgrounds lodge on Holy Saturday, sharing a meal and waiting for the break of Easter morning. Only fifteen or so of the hardiest lasted until sunrise, but there was still a full house around midnight when Adele burst in from outdoors in the middle of the service. "He hath set me in dark places," Henry was reciting. "As they that be dead of old," the congregation responded. Those in the front row of folding chairs heard a murmur of voices on a rising inflection coming from the back. I looked around and saw Adele being helped, or, rather, compelled into a seat, several gray heads bent over her, blocking my view of her, trying to stamp out the disturbance before it spread.

"He was unto me as a bear lying in wait," Henry continued. Sally Bissell, who was seated in the next to last row, forgot to join in the response because she heard Adele, unsubdued, asking her guardians where all the food had gone. She demanded to know how they could have "hidden" it, as she put it, in the five or ten minutes she'd been absent. Sally left her seat and moved swiftly to the back. Waving away the three elderly vestrymen (one of them her father-in-law), she put her arm around Adele and held her hand, patting and soothing her, whispering in her ear, keeping her quiet through the "Christus Factus Est," the psalm ("The Lord Hear Thee in the Day of Trouble"), the final prayer, and the lighting of the candle on the serving cart that doubled as an altar. Every hour until dawn, a short service would be conducted. Only as the sun rose, giving light enough to see the risen Lord by, would we be permitted to sing the canticles and psalms instead of speaking them.

Sally found Tim Webb, the park warden and a St. A's communicant, and asked him if she and I could take Adele to his office, the only private space in the lodge. Tim got his key and unlocked the door for us. By rights, he should have backed out discreetly, leaving us alone; but Adele had started to talk and he stayed on, caught in the torrent. He heard Adele tell us she had gone outside after her crew had served dessert, just long enough to bathe her face and hands in the brook, a matter of a few minutes. She was certain she had left at exactly ten o'clock. She wanted to know how long it would be before the services started, so she had asked Ruth Hiram for the time. Tim saw her grab Sally's wrist, push up her shirt cuff and stare at her watch, a sporty, very legible job with a gold-and-stainless-steel bracelet. She asked to see my watch, with its fraying leather strap, and Tim's heavy chronometer, the kind used by pilots and submarine commanders. Each of these timepieces told her the same unacceptable story: over two hours of her life were missing, one hundred and thirty-five minutes by any clock.

Tim made a good warden because he had a cool head. In other words, he was a person of little or no spontaneity, whose feelings went numb in a crisis. It was a useful trait when dealing with a camper whose gas stove has just exploded, and just as efficient for pulling Adele back from the brink of hysteria. While she spoke his expression was blank, although his square-cut beard may have concealed a tremor. His very woodenness reassured her, and soon she was talking only to him, grasping his sleeve, begging him to listen and believe her. Tim questioned her with about as much concern as an allergist investigating the cause of a patient's sneezing fits: had she felt ill; been imbibing alcohol; tripped and hit her head; heard or seen strange noises or movements, anything threatening; ever been subject to blackouts; taken mind-altering drugs that could repeat without warning; gazed at the moon or especially the reflection of the moon in the water and brought on a trance? Was there any item she could remember, no matter how small or irrelevant?

At last Adele was getting into the swing of it, enjoying the attention, the appeal to herself as an expert. Tim was helping her to view the experience from a slight remove. "I saw a fly," she said, as proud as an amateur magician who pulls a quarter from behind your ear without flubbing the trick. Tim allowed that it was still too early, officially, for the black fly, which appeared the first week in June. "I know black fly," said Adele. "This was a large housefly. It buzzed me. I thought it was trying to sting me. I swatted at it but it kept on coming. Then I tried to throw water on it."

Unfair as it was, I suspected Adele of playing to the gallery. I was fond of her; I endorsed every molecule of her except her fey streak, which had widened as the spirit world went on cold-shouldering her year after year. I knew what she was after with the housefly: she was trying to pin a supernatural tag on the missing two hours. Any Christian knows that the Host and Ruler of Many, the Lord of the Dunghill, the Prince of Darkness was a shape-transformer whose principal disguises were a ram and a fly. It was obvious to me that Adele's problem was either (1) temporary or permanent amnesia or (2) whimwham. If she was in flight from reality, what trauma was she fleeing from? The sound of a coyote killing a grouse? A bone-chilling sound, in fact, a concerto of snarls and screams with some rich, hog-like grunting for a coda. Another red-eyed cloud, like the one seen by the girls from Burridge Academy? Or something much more terrible, a human lurker with sexual intentions? According to Tim's records, the park was empty. No campers had made reservations or signed the logbook. If we had called in Mark Centrella, our resident state trooper, he would have opted for sexual assault before Adele had finished giving her statement. Trooper Centrella, like myself, was a materialist.

If Adele was inventing reality instead, wouldn't that be more alarming than escaping from it? It was typical of Adele and her elfin fancies to "bathe" rather than "wash" her face and hands in the brook, when there was a sink with running water (brook water) right outside the lodge door. Following the advice of Dr. Mary Yerkes, author of *Resacralizing Your Life*, Adele made up all kinds of rituals. Adele hoarded rituals like a magpie. Somewhere she had learned that steeping nasturtium flowers in the bathwater invited a visit from your guardian angel. Whenever she went to Lake Sebago, she brought away a stone from its shores and put it in a growing pile at the foot of the stairs to her apartment. "You're only allowed to take one stone at a time," she told me, making reference to some unidentified higher authority. Water figured prominently in her rituals. She made a distinction between still and running water. The former was for revelation, divination, communication with the all-in-one and the one-in-all, while the latter was for cleansing both the physical and the etheric body. Adele regarded running water as a kind of karma wash.

I have mentioned that Adele bathed in moonlight as well as water. By preference she took a blanket outdoors on nights of full moon, but the yard behind the garage was exposed to the Bissells' neighbors, a pair of tax lawyers (husband and wife) who came up from Boston some weekends and a month in the summer. When it was cold, or the Coolidges were in residence, she let moonlight wash over her body through the windows, left open as often as possible so the rays could reach her unfiltered and undiluted. Adele was as methodical as her daytime equivalent, the sun worshipper, turning from her back to her left side to her stomach to her right side at intervals of fifteen minutes in each position. Although she claimed these immersions did not affect her sleep, I noticed that her vitality was low at these dates of the calendar. Her eyes were glassy and her movements languid. Ancient peoples bared themselves to the moon in adoration, but they knew, while we have forgotten, that the moon rules over death as well as fruitfulness—the moon waxes but it also wanes, dwindling to black before it can appear again.

Adele collected rituals the way she adorned her person or her apartment, picking and choosing from various eras and styles, some of them conflicting. Hunks of amethyst quartz, spears of crystal, and fat black candles sat on her counters and windowsills. The black candles, used by witches and magicians in their conjuring ceremonies, were draped with strings of rosary beads—very pretty beads, made of millefiori glass, and such a nice effect, the brilliant colors contrasting with the black. Instead of lunches, dinners, concerts, or movies, her appointment book was marked with the feast days of many cultures. She celebrated Midsummer Eve by keeping a bonfire going all night (with Sally Bissell's reluctant permission) and August 15, the Assumption of the Virgin, by wearing a Mary-blue dress. Adele said that the Blessed Virgin and the goddess Persephone had a lot in common because they had both been kidnapped. The fact that one of them had been snatched up to Heaven and the other down to Hades was completely unimportant. Christian, Greek, Celtic, Norse, Egyptian: all traditions were one and the same to her.

Adele was leaning back in Tim's office chair with her eyes closed. Tim held her right hand, pressing the acupuncture point for acute anxiety, Heart 7, located on the crease of her wrist in line with the little finger. He was concentrating hard, frowning slightly as he set about his task, rotating the point first clockwise, then counterclockwise. If only Adele could find a decent, practical man who would bring her down to earth. Tim knew how things worked, and when they broke, he could mend them. When a family of goslings lost their mother, Tim raised them himself. From my point of view his brows were too heavy and his nose tilted so far upward that you were faced with more nostril than you cared to be, but Adele might not mind that. Usually it was women who grounded men, instead of the other way around, but Adele needed ties and obligations or she, too, might be snatched away to some never-never land. Adele was a walking target for the paranormal, just as a person can be marked for sorrow or even murder. Adele and her unconscious were already drumming up uncanny happenings, of which this time-loss incident was just the first and the least notorious.

All victims, whether of crime, fraud, accident, loss, or lovelessness, are compelled to tell their stories many times over, in puzzlement at first, and then with increasing conviction, a touch of the soapbox. They have to repeat them to give their ordeal some meaning. Adele had finished with Tim. She sat up abruptly, releasing her wrist, turned to Sally and me and beckoned us closer. In case we had missed something, or let our thoughts wander during her recital, she was giving us a chance to pick up the thread and fill in the gaps. It was a generous impulse, in part, but it derived from the assumption, shared by a majority of victims, that her story was interesting. Her story was worthy of sympathy or, rather, she was, so we gave her our respectful attention.

"Those trays are so heavy, you know how awkward they are; the dried fruit thing was delicious, Cora; it's too bad we didn't have heavy cream; oh, no, was it me? Was I supposed to bring it?" I said no, it was my fault entirely; and she continued in that vein, inconsistently, with digressions, entreaties, and unessential detail, such as the fact that Ruth Hiram's watch was a brooch that she wore pinned to her sweater. Adele's progress to the lodge door was so lengthy that I wondered if she were going to drag out her story for as many hours as she had lost, by way of compensation.

At last she stepped outside into the chill night. We were told that she tripped on her way to the brook, she couldn't imagine how, since the path she took was smooth and well trodden. She told us how silent it was when she reached the edge of the brook, only thirty paces from the lodge. She wondered why she heard no voices or clatter and reckoned that the storm windows acted as soundproofing. It seemed to her now, no, she was certain, now that she thought of it, that she had seen the brook running but couldn't hear the water, had watched the tops of the white pines swaying and heard no wind, no branches creaking.

Sometime during the narrative Henry had eased the door open and let himself into the office, just out of Adele's line of vision. He had taken off his starched white surplice to keep it fresh for the next performance. I noticed that his cassock was a little frayed at the sleeves and short in the skirt. He wore all his clothes until they were shabby, including his clerical vestments. His face looked strained from the effort of getting Our Lord resurrected single-handedly. He had taken all the services in Holy Week himself because his sometime assistant, a young itinerant pastor who served Episcopal parishes in both Cumberland and Oxford counties, had been granted compassionate leave after the death of his mother. Henry had come by to find out if Adele was in need of help. His reasons for staying were not so altruistic. I could tell he had caught a whiff of the unaccountable, of something beyond the pale, something he used to find in the rites and sacraments of the church. He was watching Adele as if she were a reliquary containing a martyred saint's dried blood that was reported to liquefy, or a statue of the Virgin Mary that was supposed to shed real tears on Good Friday. When Adele became aware of Henry, she dropped my hand and shifted her gaze to him.

It was all coming back to her, she said. The more she concentrated on the scene the more details she recaptured. She remembered testing the silence, not wanting to admit she was testing it, "accidentally" dropping a penny from her pocket onto a rock. Then she picked up a sizable stone, let it fall on the same flat surface, and watched as it too landed noiselessly. Enveloped in silence, "fogged in," as she described it, she kneeled down and put her hand in the brook water somewhat tentatively, as if it might have suffered a change into another element. The water was shockingly cold on her hands and face and it steadied her nerves. She tried one more experiment, shouting the vowel O into the night, projecting her voice upstream as far as it would carry. She could hear the sound in her head, but not outside around her. The darkness absorbed every wave and reverberation. From this point on her memory failed her until she found herself back on her feet and walking toward the lodge, disconcerted as she looked through the windows and saw people assembled in prayer instead of at table, where she had left them.

I hated these subjective reports. Even now, as a psychical researcher, I have trouble with unsubstantiated personal testimony. The notion that a subject can be a reliable witness eluded me then and still eludes me, in spite of my later tribulations. There were two English ladies who visited Versailles in the early 1900s. They heard music, with no musicians in evidence, and saw people dressed in antique costumes, whom they took to be Marie Antoinette and members of her court. Afterward they wrote up their adventure (which makes the most wonderful reading), a case of what we now call "walk-in retrocognition." It doesn't take much to shred their story to ribbons. It doesn't take scientific training, only common sense, once you know that they composed their first account three months after the event and later brought out several other versions, which expanded and improved on the original. The "dreary, unnatural depression" that seized them on their tour of Versailles was evidence of nothing more paranormal than a heavy French lunch. What the ladies probably saw, according to a recently published study, was a dress rehearsal for one of the historical tableaux put on at the Petit Trianon by Count Robert de Montesquiou and his bohemian friends.

If I had been put in charge of Adele's case, I would have said she was probably free-associating, constructing a rationale to account for the alleged time lapse, which was causing her intense anxiety. I would have hypothesized a blow to the head (she had fallen when she tripped), which had brought on temporary deafness, then loss of consciousness. I would have had her examined by one, or several, neurologists, to see if my theory squared with their expert opinion. Unlike me, Henry valued personal, anecdotal testimony. He was interested in Adele's experience as well as her account of it. While I was mainly concerned with whether Adele was believable, Henry saw her as a storehouse of priceless information. Unlike him, my inclination was to sift subjective reports of all their impurities in order to determine what gold might remain, if any. All that was left of Adele's story after faulty memory, narrative embroidery, and the process of perception itself had been sifted out was her claim that she had "lost" the hours between ten p.m. and midnight.

Here at the Center for the Study of Anomalous Phenomena, Henry considers our main task to be description, not evaluation. He believes our role should be that of self-effacing scribe and listener. We must be like the tillers of the soil, patient and plodding, gathering a harvest of insignificant details. The keystone of our work is the person who has the experience—the subject, the participant, the "experient" (to use the term currently in fashion). The subject is our supreme authority, along with those subjective reports I so mistrusted. There would be no supernatural phenomena without a subject-observer, nor any paranormal experience without an experiencer. Can hauntings go on in houses that are uninhabited? Aren't Bernadette and Our Lady two halves of a single phenomenon, like Joan of Arc and her voices, or the corn-belt farmer and the flying saucer? Henry finds himself at odds with many investigators in our field, who think that emphasizing personal testimony is either bad science, or sensationalism, or both. This contingent of researchers is apt to leap ahead to theory, preferring abstract speculation to the pedestrian chores of interviewing and data collecting.

If Adele Manning's time-lapse case were on our current agenda at the Center, I would have to charge Henry with jumping to conclusions as fast as his opponents do. As soon as Adele had finished telling her story in Tim Webb's office, I noticed a change in him. Performing the rest of the services, the last of them at six in the morning, on his feet without sleep for twenty-four hours, he had never been more charismatic. Evan McNeil came up to me afterwards and in his forthright way voiced what I was thinking, "Just between us, Cora, your man's been riding on empty and now the tank's filling up again."

Between the services Henry kept looking in on Adele, offering each time to have someone drive her home. From four-thirty to six-thirty a.m. she was asleep in Tim Webb's swivel chair, using his bunched-up parka as a pillow. Tim sat on a straight-backed chair in the corner, leafing through a stack of back issues of the *Ranger*, guarding her rest. During the breaks, Sally and I joined the clean-up committee, helping to scrape plates, rack the rinsed dishes and glasses, pack the leftovers, bag garbage, and load everything into the McNeils' covered pickup for delivery to the kitchen in St. Anthony's parish hall. Monday would be time enough to deal with it, since we were already well into Easter Sunday, with three services on the docket for Henry (eight a.m., eleven a.m., and five p.m.) and a choice of three for his parishioners.

I had some time alone with Henry a little before six. The hem of his cassock was coming unsewn and I wanted to tack it up. I carried needle and thread in my purse for such vestimentary emergencies. To save time I began to hem it with Henry in it, sitting tailor-fashion on the floor while he stood facing away from me.

"This is ready for the rag bin," I said. He shifted his weight, interrupting my stitching momentarily. "I wonder what she saw," he said, "what she's blocking out." "What makes you think she saw anything?" "It must have been something tremendous to require drastic measures like amnesia." "Hold still," I said, refraining from more pointed comment. "It's all there in the literature," he said. "Sensory dislocation. The cessation of sound. 'The approach of the numinous' is what Hoskins called it." "I don't know what that means," I said, trying to rethread my needle in the dim lighting. "Oh, yes, you do," said Henry, "when you're not trying to get my goat." "You don't have enough to go on," I said, "it's too soon to be calling it supernatural." "There is nothing wrong with her hearing." "You have only her word for it," I said. "Whose word do I need? She's the expert. She's the one who went through it."

Henry went on to accuse me, as he still accuses me, of trying to attribute all supernatural events to incorrect perception or defective reasoning. I snipped the end of the thread with my nail scissors. I told him he was married to a lowly worm without wings to soar. Then Haverford Bissell, Senior, rang a bell to call us back to worship, a silver bell borrowed from his own dining room, used by Edie Bissell, when she was still alive, for summoning the maid.

Chapter Eleven

After the episode of Easter Eve we tried to keep Adele close to us. By now she was starting to forget whatever it was she couldn't remember. The intervening weeks had taken the edge off her ordeal. The only residue was an occasional bad dream in which she was paralyzed from the neck down. Otherwise, she had come around to thinking that her experience had been more remarkable than frightening. She talked about it freely and colorfully, as if she were telling a story about someone else. People who wanted to get in to see Henry were so entranced they never noticed how long they'd been kept waiting in the outer office.

Since Adele worked next door and had lunch with us in the rectory kitchen every day, we began asking her to stay for supper too, and to spend the night, and to give some thought, if she liked the idea, to moving back in with us. When Hannah abandoned the attic, taking her belongings and her vibrations up to the mountain, Mary Fran and I gave the room a good turning-out, washing the floors, walls, windows, and wooden furniture, putting a dash of ammonia in the wash water. I ordered a new mattress for the bed, an expensive and famous brand. Adele had once lived in the attic contentedly for several months, draping the chairs and book cartons with Indian cottons, hanging strings of beads from the sconces and the standing lamp. This time, however, she declined our offer abruptly. I was aware, in any case, that I had invited her as much for our sake as for hers.

When a marriage is sexually empty, it helps to fill the house with extra people.

If Adele did not want to stay with us permanently, she was perfectly happy to let us drag her around with us as if she were a daughter or a younger sister. We took her almost everywhere we went, to the shopping plaza in Windham to stock up on paper goods, to my mother's on Sunday evenings for vegetable soup and gin rummy, to Walter Emmet's veranda, where he set up a telescope and showed us how to find the three bright stars that make up the summer triangle—Altair, Deneb, and Vega. Like the family dog, who hops in the car the minute the door is opened, Adele went along with all our plans. She enjoyed riding in the back seat with her head out the window and the breeze blowing in her face. Riding in the car was the best way to keep cool for all of us. The only breezes blowing at that time were mechanically generated.

Throughout the month of June 1974, the temperature was always the same, sunrise to sundown, as if the needle on some cosmic thermostat were stuck at an unwavering 87. The skies were still and windless. Perhaps I am exaggerating. There was some fluctuation: at night it might go down to 85 and in the daytime creep up to 90. (After that short-lived heat wave in late April, we had gone back briefly to seasonable conditions, clouds and sun in perpetual competition, with fleeting victories on either side. The weather we were used to in Maine was, above all, variable.) As the days went by and the novelty of constant hot temperatures wore off, the residents of Dry Falls gave in to grumbling and uneasiness. The hot "spell" we were having began to seem permanent, not temporary. Ernie Silver told his captive audience at the lunch counter that it was on account of the government launching rockets and satellites, and Mary Fran Rawls said she heard it was caused by using hairspray. We had to drive only seven miles south to Oak Hill or ten miles north to Bancroft to discover we were living under some kind of climatic glass bell. The rest of the county put on layers of clothing and shed them again several times during the day, shivering or sweltering at the whim of the barometer.

If heat had been allied to drought, our grumbling would have turned to paranoia, but we had regular periods of rainfall during the month, enough to keep the farmers happy and let our lawns go without watering. These rains were also unusual for our part of the world—teeming downpours, as if a tap had been turned on full force, with the sun shining through the whole time and the cloud disappearing as soon as the tap was turned off—very much like rains in the tropics, or so I was informed by Walter Emmet, who had visited Cuba and the Bahamas. Ruth Hiram called these downpours "waterfalls from the sky" and thought there was something spooky about them, but Ruth needed a bit more local folklore to round out her new anthology and she went looking for it under every rock and toadstool. In Bancroft and Oak Hill and elsewhere in the Lake Sebago region, foul weather ran its course as God and Nature intended: rains threatened before they arrived, darkening the sky; showers lingered after a drenching; and rain clouds took their time scattering.

When does a heap of earth become a mountain instead of a hill—at a hundred feet? At five hundred? I would have called Hannah's mountain an oversized hill, but we found it on a topographical map in the town surveyor's office, where a local cartographer had dubbed it Mt. Pughole. I was in the process of baking sesame wafers, eighteen dozen of them. On the premise that any elevation, including a stepladder, would be cooler than my kitchen, I decided to bake one more batch and then take off for higher ground. Every year I did the canapés for the Burridge Academy graduation, for which I was paid the equivalent of four newspaper columns. Burridge graduation fell very late, around the summer solstice, since the girls were required to take a job off campus during January and February.

I went over to the parish house to collect Adele—an automatic reflex by now—and found she had nothing to do for the rest of the afternoon except the place cards for a dinner honoring Haverford Bissell Sr.'s retirement from the vestry, which she was writing out in elegant cursive script. Henry was in Portland for a meeting of the diocesan ethics committee, so we left Casco Answering Service to pick up the telephone. I was carrying towels, bathing suits, and a thermos jug of iced tea flavored with lavender. Adele laughed at me. "Why did you bring suits?" she asked. "Are you still modest in front of your big sister?"

Adele prided herself on her easygoing attitude toward nudity, but Adele was not a native of Maine. Mainers are not prudish; they are chilly, which may appear to be the same thing, a set of reflexes that resemble inhibition or bodily shame. When you walk on Maine's beaches, you have no need to avert your eyes in case nude sunbathers have taken refuge behind the dunes. A glimpse of nudity in the open would be as rare as the sighting of a moose on the Dry Falls common. Sunbathing is a meditative pursuit requiring total relaxation. Just as you cannot relax while sand flies are stinging you, you cannot tan naked in the sun if the sun keeps going into hiding. In Maine the sun clouds over so often that nude sunbathers would be constantly jerking upright, snatching towels or robes to cover their gooseflesh, shivering until the sun reappeared, hoping there might be some truth to the notion that you can burn just as quickly on an overcast day as on a clear day.

The tribesmen of Central Africa are more self-assured with their clothes off; but northern people lost a measure of confidence with every item they removed. Nakedness left us exposed to the elements and to the wrath of God, who was reminded by the sight of our worm-white bodies how He had driven us from the gardens of Paradise for our disobedience. What would happen if natives of Maine liked having their clothes off? I wondered if Dry Falls would prove to be a test case, now that we were three weeks into a spell of hot temperatures and our climate was beginning, in its own small way, to approximate conditions in Zambia and Zaire.

Already there were signs that the heat was an agent of change. There was no real need for Jimmy Hawes to be pumping gas bare-chested, runnels of sweat crisscrossing his torso, blue jeans held up by pure willpower, like the juvenile lead in a Tennessee Williams play. I have never seen the common get so much traffic, as if everyone who lived in town had moved outdoors. Young mothers loaded strollers with diaper bags, baskets of food, and babies, a household on wheels, headed for the greensward each morning, and pitched camp until after sunset. Employers and employees took their lunch hour under the trees, loosening collar buttons, rolling up shirt sleeves, lifting skirts to mid-thigh or higher, knotting blouses or jerseys over the sternum, revealing the midriff. In an effort to serve his country during the ongoing energy crisis, Hiram Baldwin at Baldwin's Hardware turned off the air conditioners and let his salesclerks come to work in shorts and sleeveless shirts. Hiram himself, a man over sixty, went only so far as to leave off his jacket, but I'm sure he winked at me as I was accepting change from a ten-dollar bill for a package of large staples, and Sally said he had winked at her too.

If there is anything Mainers are not, it is touchers. Yet I saw my neighbors putting their hands on one another, patting a shoulder, a forearm, a cheek; ruffling a head of hair, tweaking a ponytail; exchanging kisses with "Hello" and "Goodbye," like city people and foreigners. We northern New Englanders used to make fun of this kind of behavior. We called it "southern." In my own family, the term was stretched to include bad taste of any kind, as in "did you notice that southern cozy on the toaster/beading on the bridesmaids' dresses?" No one had appointed me official town censor, nor did I want the job. I was not being censorious, although I preferred a decent reticence in public interaction. I was only stating the facts when I told Henry that if the heat went on much longer it would be the end of civilization as we knew it.

On top of Mt. Pughole a little breeze was stirring, but the current was warmer, instead of cooler, than the surrounding air. I had honked the horn as we entered the spacious clearing, but Hannah was not one to dash out and wave you a joyous welcome. We were climbing the porch steps when she appeared at an open window. "Oh, good," she said. "You can help me do some sandpapering." We told her we had come to laze around and we expected her to join us. Hannah liked Adele. She was amused by the way her parts didn't work together. We sat on the porch and sipped iced tea. Adele and I passed the thermos cup back and forth; Hannah drank from the bottle. "You didn't bring food," said my sister.

Although Adele intended to sunbathe without her clothes on, she undressed inside the cabin and wrapped a beach towel around her, Tahitian-style. We watched her as she walked down across the clearing, stepping as high as a stork over thick tufts of grass that might have tripped her, clutching her towel in front, carrying her gear in a paper sack, impairing her already precarious balance by denying herself the use of both hands. "Suspenseful, isn't it?" said Hannah. "I can hardly bear to watch," I said. "Oops," said Hannah, "there she goes again."

Near the edge of the woods, Adele began circling the grass, looking for a place to lie down. When she found the right spot, she groomed it carefully, picking up twigs and stones and throwing them away, flattening the long grass with her feet before taking off her towel and spreading it on the ground. Naked in the sunlight, she stamped back and forth on the towel, flattening the grass further. "I wish I could draw," said Hannah, appraising Adele's small, high breasts and sloping hips. "I wish I could catch that Botticelli/scarecrow quality." It was true that my sister could carve wood and model in wax and clay, but her drawings on paper were formal and lifeless. Naturally, she wanted to draw in direct proportion to her lack of talent for it, just as great comedians yearn to play tragedy, and popular novelists write poetry in secret. Adele's bosom and bottom had no aesthetic significance for me. All I saw was youth and smoothness—as well as bad posture, which would take its toll in ten years or so.

Until now I had been watching Adele, whose movements, as always, were hypnotic. She was lying flat on her back, as quiet as she ever got, a twitch here, a scratch there, a yawn, a stretch, an adjustment of sunglasses. Then my eye took in Adele's surroundings. How could I, a gardener, my mother's daughter, have failed to see the bed of daffodils blooming just south of Adele's large but slim-ankled feet? A planting as garish as a picture in a bulb catalogue, too many colors and too many varieties, planted too close together: twenty-four-inch-tall giants; six-inch miniatures; light yellow, dark yellow, pink, white, and bicolored; large cups, split cups, trumpets, doubles, multiflowered. I wondered why they were in bloom so late in June and who had put them in, chosen to plant them at the edge of the woods so far from the cabin, crowded them into a narrow patch instead of sowing them in natural drifts.

I asked my sister, although I didn't expect her to know. She was ignorant enough of gardening to think that daffodils could spring up like wildflowers, without human agency. Narcissi have long-lived flowers, lasting two or three weeks unless the weather is very blustery, and many of these specimens had already begun to wilt (petals first, cups last). "How many times are you going to ask me?" Hannah said. "I don't care how long the damn things have been in bloom. I didn't see them." To hear her side of it, the flowers had appeared overnight, as if by magic, as they did in fairy tales or Greek myths. We got down to some sisterly wrangling about how I thought I was better than she was because I could cook and make things grow and how she thought I was a brain-dead housewife. Bickering was thirsty work, so we drank all the iced tea and left none for Adele. I looked down to see if she was showing signs of dehydration.

Adele was lying on her stomach. She must have been asleep or she would have felt the presence of the large black dog sitting just above her head. Unmoving, barely three feet away, he seemed to be on guard duty. He sat so still he might have been one half of a pair of statues. Smooth-coated and glossy, like a Labrador retriever, he had the heavy head, long muzzle, and powerful frame of a mastiff, a breed as old as the wheel and the plow. Adele changed position, flopping over on her right side, facing the woods. As she turned the dog turned with her, so he was pointing in the same direction.

"Jesus," said Hannah, "he's gigantic." "Have you seen him before?" I asked. "Does his owner live around here?" "In case you hadn't noticed, there isn't anyone else 'around here.' " "All right, don't snap at me. What if he's dangerous?" "Well, if he's been lost in the woods," Hannah said, "he must be hungry." "Do you have anything he could eat? Even bread. We have to go down there." "You do," said Hannah, "I'm not going anywhere near him."

We went indoors to inspect Hannah's larder. Her food supplies were hanging from a beam in old-fashioned pie safes, cages made of wood with wire mesh between the slats. There was a hunk of cheddar sweating in its cellophane wrapping, a can of corned beef, a can of cocktail frankfurters, and a box of Ritz crackers, unsealed. These salty foods were no better for the dog than they were for Hannah, but the only other items in her stores were two spotted pears and a bunch of limp carrots. I opened the little wieners and arranged them on a plate. I anticipated the dog's relish, as I did with any creature I was feeding. If he were aggressive or nervous, food would tame him. I left Hannah unwrapping the oozing cheese, ruminating about whether or not it was still good to eat. I had crossed the porch and descended the steps before I saw that the black dog was gone. I thought I should take the plate down to Adele anyway, in case he came back. I turned and called to Hannah, whose answer was unintelligible. I expect she was tasting the cheddar.

When I turned around again, the dog had reappeared; only this time he was facing in my direction. I felt a pang of uneasiness but I continued forward, holding the plate out in front of me, hoping the sausages would guarantee my welcome. There was something wrong with that dog. He was much too deliberate. His behavior was not dog-like. Never once, as I made my way toward him, did he shift his gaze, scratch a flea, become distracted by a movement in the grass. He met my gaze with a fixed, vacant glare, as if he were in a trance. Halfway there, I put the plate on the grass and walked as casually as I could back up to the cabin, where I intended to shut the door, no matter how hot it was.

Hannah came out to meet me and asked if I had fed the dog. I looked back and saw the plate where I'd left it. The plate was full but the meadow was empty except for Adele, who was lying flat on her back with her arms and legs extended, like Leonardo da Vinci's drawing of a man in a circle. I said, "You've got to put an ad in the paper and a notice at the post office. He must belong to somebody." "Let's wake her up," said Hannah. "She'll be red as a lobster." We agreed to give her ten more minutes, and in the meantime my sister wanted to show me her tomato plants and the cucumber vines she was training against the back wall on kitchen string, which I told her at once was too weak a support unless she was growing the miniature pickling varieties. When I warned her that tomatoes were heavy feeders, she said they'd have to survive on junk food, the way she did. It was time to call

Adele. We thought we could make her hear us if we stood ten paces or so from the cabin porch and both yelled at once.

The black dog was sitting next to her head, staring down into her sleeping face. If we had gone ahead and shouted, we might have caused a terrible accident: Adele opening her eyes and screaming, frightening the dog, the dog attacking her, sinking his teeth and holding on as mastiffs have been bred to do since man walked upright. Hannah stood looking down for several minutes—silencing me with a gesture when I tried to speak—at the picture made by the rosy nude and the coal-black dog on a rectangle composed of colored squares against a sweep of green. It was an intimate, enigmatic image, canceled all at once when Adele rolled away from the dog and rose to her knees, lifted her arms and stretched as high as she could, unkinking her back. She moved on all fours to the edge of the checkered beach towel, where she had dropped her underwear and an oversized tee shirt with the slogan "U.S.A. Out of North America" in blue letters. The dog followed her as she crawled, sat behind her while she dressed and tied her hair back with an elastic.

Finally, Adele stood up and began to gather her belongings, which were scattered all over the towel—sunglasses, baby oil, library book, hairbrush, tarot pack. Hannah grabbed my hand. The black dog was standing four feet to the right of Adele, level with her waist. If she leaned over to retrieve her bandanna, she would be nose to nose with him. Either the dog managed to stay just out of eyeshot or Adele was in a torpid condition from the heat and the sun. Several times she brushed by him, but she seemed to be entirely unaware of him. "She can't see him," said Hannah, gripping my hand even tighter. "She needs glasses," she added. "Those sunglasses aren't prescription." "She needs glasses for distance, not for close up." "Cut it out," Hannah said. "He's there. He has to be there. Both of us can see him."

Adele started up the meadow, carrying her sack and her towel. The dog followed behind her. From our vantage point Adele was so tall that she hid him from sight, except for an occasional flicker of haunch and tail when he stepped out of line. "She's bringing him up here," said Hannah. "She's acting like a magnet." We spent a few minutes arguing about which of us was frightened of dogs; whether mastiffs were supposed to be gentle or fierce; whether a dog was attracted to the smell of menstrual blood, the way bears are; whether our grandmother's cocker spaniel's name had been Brandy or Biscuit. By the time we left off, Adele was almost upon us. She was swinging her sack as an expression of high spirits, then swung it a little too far to the front and managed to trip herself with it, a remarkable achievement. She apologized, as she always did after these antigymnastic feats of hers. I ran out to help her up, forgetting about the big black dog. There was nothing to remind me of him. At some time during the ascent, he had disappeared. We didn't mention him to Adele. It seemed pointless to frighten her.

Later that afternoon Adele asked me to drop her at her apartment over the Bissells' garage. She said she hadn't done her laundry for two weeks and couldn't stay for supper. It was over two weeks since Henry and I had been alone at the dinner table. I found that I missed him intensely, as if he had been in Australia. The mushroom crop was short-lived that year, but I managed to gather enough morels under the apple trees in the churchyard to make a mushroom fondue, which I liked to serve over slices of fried bread. From the kitchen garden by the back door I picked several sprigs of marjoram, the freshest-smelling herb and my favorite. Some chopped marjoram and a clove of garlic sautéed briefly and removed from the pan were all the seasonings wild mushrooms required. For our salad I picked red lettuce, sorrel, and rocket, which I had planted in the shade. For dessert I had strawberries from the Marston farm. The meal so far was too dainty for a man Henry's size, but I had no intention of turning on the oven. He would have to be content with whipped cream and sugar on his berries.

Ethics Committee meetings always ran late, since they were chaired by Bishop Hollins. The Bishop had usually read a recent inspirational bestseller like *To Thine Own Self* or *Soulcraft* and liked to quote passages that fit the cases under review. That day's case was an odd one—a minister in Red Beach on the St. Croix River who had taken a job as one of the second-string movie reviewers for the biggest paper in the area, the Calais *Gazette*, in order to supplement his clerical income. Apparently his flock objected less to their pastor moonlighting than to the fact that he had been spotted watching *The Exorcist* nine times at the drive-in theater; and they were convinced that number was only the tip of the iceberg. "Did you send him to a shrink?" I asked Henry when he walked in, as hot and dusty as if he had driven a Conestoga wagon to Portland instead of the Dodge. "Actually, yes," said Henry, a little sharply. "The poor bastard thinks the demon was using his father's voice."

I kissed Henry and told him he had plenty of time to take a shower. I wanted to set the table on the screened-in porch, pick a few flowers for the centerpiece, put out candlesticks and votive lights, serve the morels, which were as precious as gemstones, on Tante Rosalie Beaulac's porcelain plates, which were rarely used and needed washing. When everything was ready, and myself combed and powdered and zipped into a scoop-necked cotton dress, I filled the wine bucket with ice and brought it to the table. The porch was flickering with lights, filled with the sweetness of moss roses in a bowl and the evening fragrance of nicotiana blooming just outside the screens. I was startled by my own unawareness. I believed I was creating a setting that would be worthy of that aristocrat of mushrooms, the morel, when in fact I had been staging a seduction scene.

The air at supper was charged with the possibility of sex, but it was also saturated with heat and the fumes of wine. Somehow I never told Henry about the black dog because he got me laughing so hard at his imitation of Bishop Hollins, who had never seen *The Exorcist*, trying to grasp the plot from shorthand descriptions fired at him by the five committee members. Bishop Hollins had a lot of trouble with the idea of evil, anyway, especially the idea of a supernatural source of evil. According to Henry, the Bishop believed that the root of evil was the lack of summer job opportunities for high school students. Laughter gives rise to intimacy, so I spent a certain amount of time on Henry's lap, with his hands taking liberties, until it was incumbent on me to serve our dessert. I don't know if I left his lap because Henry loved strawberries or because I was perspiring and making him sweat, the exchange of calories beginning to reach the discomfort level.

Once we might not have been so punctilious about dessert. The berries could have waited on the counter, softening in sugar, turning a darker and darker red, for as long as it took, sometimes until the following morning, when they would be swimming in juice. We might not have cared about the heat, perspiration serving as a lubricant for moving body parts. As it was, we picked at the berries, dunked a few in sugar, forwent the cream altogether. Henry washed the dishes while I cleared the table. He went upstairs first because I had to transfer nineteen dozen sesame wafers from cooling racks to airtight cookie tins. If I left them till morning, they would lose their crispness. In a long-term marriage, chores often seemed to take priority over carnal impulses.

There was nothing left of Henry by the time I went to bed. He lay sprawled on his back with his arms and legs flung sideways, as if he had fallen from a great height, his mouth gaping, his penis stretching limp across his thigh. His penis was transparently pale and thin, almost tubular, the instrument of a boy in early puberty. I made preparations for bed carelessly and quickly, spot-cleaning with a damp washcloth, neglecting the bottoms of my feet. All the windows were open and the electric fan was revolving; but it was still a night for sleeping uncovered. I took off my bra but left my pants on. I saw no reason to remove them, since there was no danger of anyone approaching me. I slept in my underwear as a way of showing Henry that I expected nothing. I climbed into bed, keeping well to my side, another signal to Henry, if he were interested in reading my signals.

Henry was snoring, a gravelly sound interrupted at intervals by a gasp or a hiccup. He had already reached the farther shores of the river of forgetfulness. At such times, my mind produced fantasies of subjection, of stroking him upright, mounting and riding off with him. I always imagined him awake and participating at the climax, which is all that differentiated this fantasy from necrophilia. I jiggled his shoulder to make him change position and stop the snoring. As I watched him turn over so dutifully, I saw the flush on his cheek and the back of his neck, and I kissed the place behind his right earlobe, remembering that I loved him in a human way—poor overworked brute who carried a whole congregation on his shoulders. Our sexual estrangement was an endless mystery and a source of sadness.

At first I thought it was a dream, but my eyes were open. As soon as they adjusted to the dark, I could see that everything in the room was in its rightful place. Nothing was happening the way I remembered it, but after so long, my sexual daydreams had begun to have a gothic quality—floating chiffon, swooning rapture, the eagle flying off with a dove in its talons, motifs from what my grandmother Beaulac called "housemaid's literature." Instead, he was lying on top of me, pinning me down, he who was always so careful to prop himself up on his elbows. His breathing was heavy and disordered, rising periodically to a grunt, with an alarming pause before the next breath, as if it were the last he might ever draw on earth. When I tried to free my arms, I found they were immobilized. I wanted to ask him to shift his weight but he was cutting off my breath, so I could only whimper. He felt cold, and smelled as if he'd been spending the night under the bed where the dust balls gathered. After almost a year of abstinence, his technique had altered drastically. There was only one explanation for his loutish behavior. Although he had no prior history of sleepwalking, he must still be asleep—and we know the unconscious is ignorant of sexual etiquette.

Were we engaged in sex at all, when you came right down to it? How could I be sure he had entered me? By now my lower body was anesthetized. Sooner or later the partner on top should begin to make back and forth movements, but he lay there inert as a stone, growing heavier and heavier. Maybe he had been awake at the onset and fallen asleep during the act, a fit commentary on my attractions and the condition of our sex life. It was anger that was suffocating me as much as his heaviness. I swear if I had been able to move any part of me—hands, teeth, knees, feet—I would have used it to injure him. For this shambling, careless parody of love I had been waiting a year, or close to it, keeping myself like an acolyte in the temple, praying to be delivered from bitterness, striving to be worthy when the time came. I thought how much I wanted to throw him off, pictured him falling and hitting the floor, cracking his head; then, suddenly, I found I could jiggle the little finger, then all the other fingers, one after another, of my left hand.

As soon as I moved the pressure was gone. I gasped with relief, waiting until I could breathe normally. He must have given up on me, rolled back over to his side of the bed, gone to sleep again. If, in fact, he had ever been conscious. Then I heard the sound of his slippered feet on the stairs, slap/glide, slap/glide, and I wondered why he would wear his slippers, even backless ones, on such a hot night. I imagined he was headed for the porch to seek fresh air and finish the night on the wicker chaise longue.

I was too worn out to follow him. The nape of my neck and the small of my back were soaked with sweat. I believed I could go to sleep, after all; and on the way I reviewed a parade of thoughts, about rape, attempted rape, and rape in marriage; about how cold he had felt while he covered me, so cold I had never even begun to perspire, in spite of the heat, until after he left me. I did not like to sleep on my back. Reluctant to make even so small an effort, I flopped onto my left side, yawning and stretching my arms and legs, extending them into the empty space on his side of the bed.

I thought it was empty. I hit a barrier of flesh the size and shape of Henry, who said, "What?" in Henry's voice when I bumped into him, who was warm and damp and smelled of soap. He muttered, "Go to sleep, Cora." Then I knew with the greatest sense of relief, as well as accomplishment, that I had had a nightmare, my first nightmare, the kind practiced dreamers describe as being so real you wake up and think it's still going on.

When did I wake up from the dream? Before or after I heard the slippers flapping down the stairs? As an unskilled dreamer, I needed a frame of reference for interpreting dream images, and Henry's bookshelves were stocked with Freud, Ernest Jones, and Jung. However, I was not so ignorant as to believe that the cold, heavy-breathing man on my chest was the real Henry, except on one level. I was even aware that the backless slippers were a "Freudian" symbol and the dark heavy man was more "Jungian." I also knew that some psychologists believed that every element in a dream is an aspect of the dreamer. That being the case, the oppressive figure must be the embodiment of some inner complex or cultural convention that was stifling my growth, and if Henry was implicated it was only in the general sense that a husband is a man—and society, up to the present, has been dominated by men.

I had been blooded, as they say in fox hunting of a novice rider who was in at the kill. First kill, first nightmare—they all landed you at the gateway to Hades, the nether regions. Proud as I was of being an initiated dreamer, I rather hoped this business of dreaming would not become a nightly habit. I was attracted and repelled by the prospect, as the maiden Persephone must have been while she was being abducted. I did not share Adele's enthusiasm for the sport of dreaming, or my sister's either. They had come to believe you could "get good at it," play a more and more active role, learn the answers to questions, program yourself to dream the solution to a problem. I'd have to say they were pretty far gone in that department, given their recent very similar dream. They were beginning to think that the action was right in the room with them, like a 3-D movie with surround-sound.

I was pretty far gone myself, feeling sleep come upon me, when one last idea sneaked across my darkening field of consciousness. Both Hannah and Adele had heard footsteps accompanied by a "swishing" or "whooshing" sound. I myself had heard slapping and gliding—not exactly the same, but near enough. All of us had dreamed of being crushed by a weight that seemed to have gender. What if we had "caught" the dream from each other like a flu virus—in other words, were "giving" it to one another? Perhaps Adele or Hannah was sending tonight, and I was receiving? In that case, there was nothing to be frightened of. All we were doing was using telepathy, which was nothing more than an undeveloped power of the human mind. I could hear Henry breathing deeply and regularly, with a slight rasp at the end of each exhalation. If I had been able to keep awake for another sixty seconds, I would have summoned my latent telepathic powers and started sending him nightmarish images of an overweight female pressing down on top of him, trying to suffocate him.

PART V

Christ Above Us

Chapter Twelve

Two days later, on June 23, I drove over to Burridge Academy with a trunkload of party foods for the graduation reception the following day—boxes of sesame wafers; five hundred cheese puffs frozen into marble-sized balls and stored on plastic-wrapped cookie sheets; mushroom caps stuffed with mussels, shallots, bread crumbs, and parsley, stored ditto; the makings for curried stuffed eggs—whites and yolk mix packed separately. Burridge's kitchen staff took care of the assembly and cooking, although I often hung around to make sure they baked the cheese puffs while they were still frozen and remembered to dot the mushroom caps with specks of anchovy butter before running them under the broiler. The staff also set out platters of ham, turkey, breads, and mustards, as well as the inevitable baskets of raw vegetables served with the head cook's sour cream–and-onion dip. I liked old-fashioned foods at parties, onion dip and all, and would hold out as long as I could against newfangled items like miniature quiches, caviar eclairs, and deep-fried brie nuggets. Because of the heat I had driven over the Sinkhole Road too fast. I made the four miles in seven minutes, honking my way past Arnold Crowley, who was driving his tractor with the manure spreader attached. Mary Fran Rawls, who earned extra money working at Burridge functions, helped me unload the car and rush my trays and boxes to the nearest source of refrigeration. "You ought to take a look before you go," whispered Mary Fran, who had been educated by nuns. "They're out by the rose garden rehearsing in their *bathing suits*."

The founder, Miss Nancy Burridge, had planted the rose garden herself, with an able-bodied helper standing by. She did not dig the serpentine beds (that took a crew of four), but she made deep holes in the well-prepared earth with her own spade, hilled up the soil to support the bare roots and filled in the holes, watering at intervals with rich manure tea. Every spring she had the beds mulched with chopped corn husks. Her garden helpers did the work of protecting forty bushes for the winter, hauling earth to mound it up into cones around the base of the plant, wrapping the cone of earth in several layers of burlap.

Miss Burridge had taken it into her head to grow old Bourbon roses, which should, by all rights, have found winters in Maine too harsh. Did Miss Burridge grow roses because they had so many traits in common with her adolescent pupils—softness, dewiness, sweetness, occasional thorniness? Or did she start a school for girls because they bore a resemblance to her beloved roses? The Burridge mansion, whitewashed brick with dormer windows and a raised brick terrace in back, was the academy's main building now, used for offices, receptions, concerts, lectures, prize day, and, in case of rain, graduation. Beyond the terrace ran the upper lawn, and down a flight of steps dividing a fieldstone retaining wall lay the lower lawn, where beds of roses flanked the wall in staggered triple rows.

I smelled the roses before I saw them, flourishing in the heat, which reminded them of their ancestral home in the Indian Ocean. Their branches arched to the ground with heavy clusters of blooms, a predominance of white, pink, and magenta. As plain and compact as a sparrow, dressed likewise in grays and browns, which made her skin colorless and her small features more insignificant, Miss Burridge was drawn to roses with extravagant coloration—marbled, spotted, striped, variable, or unstable; roses with contrasting centers, edges, and reverses. Her allegiance to the Bourbon roses lasted all her life, although she had a brief, unrequited fling with the modern hybrid teas, especially color innovations in the orange area of the spectrum—beiges, apricots, and coppers.

The human counterparts of Miss Burridge's favorite flower—twenty graduating seniors ages seventeen and eighteen—were standing in line in order of height, waiting to rehearse the processional. Well-formed, fully rounded, creamy white flushed with pink, they added charm to the landscape, pearling with sweat as roses bead up with dewdrops. I saw redheaded Mercy Locke, one of the girls Henry rescued from the cemetery, wearing a smaller bikini suit than any on her classmates, the smallest bikini, I think I may venture, ever to be seen inside the Dry Falls town limits. Mercy's cohort, Helen Akers, the tallest girl in the class, brought up the rear of the line. Since she was lame, she was the only one to whom the processional gait (step/slide/pause; step/slide/pause) was natural. The others teetered on the pause, as girl graduates and bridesmaids have done for generations, adding an element of suspense to an otherwise predictable ceremony.

Now the young ladies were filing toward their seats, white wooden folding chairs set up on either side of a speaker's platform, which tomorrow would be draped with a Persian rug and decorated with pots of Madonna lilies. They remained standing for the last chorus of *'Tis June*: "Lift up your voices clear and strong / Hope guides the future's wa-ay / Love lights the path we've known so long / Hail to Commencement Day!" They sat down decorously, as if they were actually wearing coronets of white roses and long white dresses.

Before Miss Leatherbee, the art teacher, could say "Well done!" they had broken ranks, slumping down in their chairs, leaning across one another, taking off sandals or tennis shoes to inspect their feet for blisters, whispering, laughing, beating time on the tops of their thighs to some unsung tune. "Anarchy is in the air," said Miss Leatherbee, whose own frizzy white curls had declared mob rule, breaking out of the net she wore to keep hairs from falling into the art supplies. "This group is precocious," said Myra Littlefield. "They began misbehaving back in March." Myra was wise enough to turn a blind eye to most outbreaks of senior restlessness—oversleeping, cutting classes, keeping food in their rooms, which attracted mice. When she smelled smoke wafting through the spring nights, she confiscated the cigarettes but imposed no other punishment.

It was not Miss Littlefield, however, but bashful Miss Burridge who had started the tradition of lighting a bonfire on graduation eve. After supper, at twilight, the girls would build a fire in a sand pit near the edge of the woods, where the full-moon celebrations were held. It was an amateur bonfire, started and fed with lumber scraps, twigs, and the students' report cards. Lecture notes and term papers also went on the fire, depending, I suppose, on how the papers had been graded. Miss Burridge, and Miss Littlefield, drew the line at books of any kind, even textbooks. Every so often a girl threw her gymsuit into the flames before anyone could stop her. Of course, copies of their report cards were on file in the secretary's office, but symbolically, at least, the fire wiped their slates clean, giving good ones, naughty ones, brainy ones, and lazy ones the feeling of escape from the stereotypes that had dogged them all through their school days. Some years it rained; then they burned their report cards in the dining hall fireplace—an anticlimactic alternative in spite of the fact that they turned the lights off and did it in the dark. Even outsiders like me had heard the rumor, pooh-poohed by Myra Littlefield, that "bonfire girls" did better in college than "fireplace girls."

In the old days bonfires were lit all over Europe on St. John's Eve to celebrate the summer solstice. Priests asked the gods to protect the ripening crops and increase their yield, while lovers wandered into the forest away from the firelight to act out private fertility rites. Miss Burridge, who was a student of mythology, must have known all about these beliefs and practices, but the Burridge seniors seemed unaware of the importance of this night. I watched Mercy Locke absentmindedly biting the skin around her thumbnail and Helen Akers shoving two girls out of their chairs so she could put her bad leg up. The two girls, snub-nosed and pigtailed, began to practice headstands. All the girls were waiting for Myra Littlefield to dismiss them or begin another run-through, but she was talking to a tonsured, fat-cheeked, plaid-trousered father of one of the seniors, a chunky brunette who rushed forward to claim him.

I turned and saw a group of mothers, aunts, and sisters coming down the upper lawn, a healthy, homogenous group, with their tanned skin and their pastel dresses, looking cool and appropriate despite the heat. Young and older, their faces were defined by deep crow's feet, caused by squinting too often into the sun to track the progress of a golf or tennis ball. Every female among them wore her hem at the middle of the knee. As they drew close enough to see the bikini-clad graduates, their facial expressions became even pleasanter and more noncommittal. I could picture them emerging from the water at the yacht club in their one-piece suits with modest skirts or shorts attached. In any case, the bikinis on the seniors would be gone by late afternoon. The students were required to be fully clothed as they capered around the bonfire.

Therein lay the difference between a ritual and a tradition: in the latter the clothes stayed on while in the former they might all be shed as the spirit dictated. If events took their natural course, young animals, perhaps even young girls, might be thrown into the fire. A tradition, if you like, is an expurgated version of a ritual. I would classify Holy Communion as a tradition, although I would think twice before saying so to Henry. With its sweet wine and its gluey wafers, the Lord's Supper was the palest shadow of the ancient Greek mysteries, where raw flesh was eaten and blood was sprinkled on the initiates. People came out changed after a ritual. The function of traditions was to guarantee that nothing ever changed.

I believe Miss Burridge truly intended to create a ritual, a rite of passage to adulthood. Why else would she have chosen such a powerful day for it? The summer solstice was not only a time when Nature holds our fate in her hands, when she can blight the tender crops that will see us through dark winter, or make them flourish. It was also the eve of the feast of St. John the Baptist, Christ's herald and understudy, whose life ended in a sacrifice, the same as any bullock on a bonfire. In paintings John was depicted as a head on a golden charger, eyes staring open, the neck cords played up or played down according to the style of the period. John the Baptist was a medicine man who lived in the desert outside the walls of Jerusalem, dressed in animal skins and subsisting on locusts and wild honey. He was Jesus Christ's rival for the people's allegiance, about whom Jesus sometimes spoke in a tone of irony, "What went ye out in the wilderness for to see? A man clothed in soft raiment?" There was a time, just before he was sent to prison, when John the Baptist pulled larger crowds than Jesus. He was a wild version of Christ, who could make Our Savior come across like an establishment smooth-talker. A roll of the dice, a spin of the wheel, a piece of soot in God's eye, a sandbag falling from the fly gallery—and St. John might have found himself playing the leading character. All the millions who might have been Christians would instead be called Johannites.

Like All Souls Eve, or Hallowe'en, St. John's Eve was one night of the year, according to legend, when supernatural beings came out in the open. All the nature spirits were about—elves, trolls, wood nymphs, and water nixies, and some which must not be named because naming them summons them. These spirits were the survivors of a fairy race who inhabited the earth before men began usurping their territory. I like to think of John the Baptist as a Nature spirit, more empathic than Christ to forms of life other than humanity. At solstice time, the veil between the upper world and the underworld was thin and permeable. Miss Burridge would have been better advised to plan graduation ceremonies at a more neutral period, one without so many echoes of the primitive past.

The very first year several graduates went to extremes, breaking out of the circle to jump across the fire pit while the flames were still knee-high, lifting their skirts above their under-britches. The second year, a girl ran across the glowing coals in her bare feet and received her diploma in a wheelchair. Miss Burridge grew frightened of the ritual she had established. She began to impose rules and regulations, trying to keep it in bounds: proper attire—shirt and trousers; long hair tied back or braided; no bare feet; no jewelry; no food allowed, with the exception of marshmallows; no chemical fire starters WHATSOEVER; a faculty member present at all times.

Miss Burridge whittled it down until it became a tradition, and still it had an atavistic tendency. Each year the proceedings slipped out of gear in some unpredictable fashion. I wondered what would happen at this year's bonfire. What could possibly top last year's, when Flora Hamlin, Miss Burridge's own grandniece, had a group of girls trying to brand initials in one another's biceps with metal skewers smuggled in for the purpose?

As I was walking back to the car I heard shrieks and cheers, an indication that the rehearsal was breaking up. I turned around and saw the entire class, except for Helen Akers, making a running dash across the lawn and around the far side of Main Building, headed in the direction of the pond. Even Helen was moving faster than usual, and I wondered if the hot weather was good for the pain in her bones and muscles. Heat and exertion had heightened her color, so that her flat cheekbones looked more prominent and her slanted eyes seemed wider. I waved to her and she acknowledged my wave, unembarrassed, as if my knowing about her antics in the churchyard made her feel more at ease with me rather than less so. I called out a greeting and she began limping toward me. I walked over briskly to spare her the detour.

"You're off for a swim," I said. "Don't let me hold you up." "I only want to dunk my feet," said Helen. "I never go all the way in. There are fish and turtles in the water." "How's your leg?" I asked. "You seem to be walking better." "I am, really. It's not the break any more; it's a nerve or something." "I'd like to congratulate you, Helen. I wish you success." "Thanks a lot, Mrs. Lieber. I'll be glad to get out of this place. I don't think I like the country." "What's wrong with it?" I asked. "It's too isolated," she said. "It makes me jittery." I smiled at her. "Is this the person who decided to spend a night in the cemetery?" "You don't understand," she said earnestly. "People frighten me more than spirits. There was a break-in at West Dorm last night. The kids next door saw a shadow and screamed, so whoever it was ran off. I think it was the handyman, but Mercy and the others are sure it was some local boys."

We were standing at the edge of the lawn near the parking area. A car pulled in and three young men got out—brothers, cousins, friends, or beaux—trim, square-jawed fellows wearing faded polo shirts and khaki trousers, varsity athletes, from the breadth of their shoulders. Instead of going directly to Main Building to request an audience with their female relations through official channels, they crossed the driveway and strolled past the dormitories toward the woods. The freckled one was whistling a tune, while the buck-toothed one kept leaning over to pick something up—a stone, a wildflower—

and show it to the towheaded one. They were making an exaggerated attempt to move slowly and casually, lest anyone question the right of three males to roam freely about the grounds of an all-girls' school. They disappeared into the trees some twenty yards before the footpath leading to the pond. Either they were there by prearrangement or they hoped to be witnesses to some skinny-dipping.

"They could be your pranksters," I said to Helen, and asked her if she recognized them. She said no, not really, although Pickle Raines had gone to the Rumsey dance with a guy who looked like the freckled one. "I hope they don't do it again tonight, if that's who they are." I said, "Remember to tell Miss Leatherbee. Isn't she your housemother?" "They look so ordinary," said Helen, "like lots of other boys." "They're no beauties," I said, "but at least they have clear complexions." "I don't like boys," said Helen. "They work in packs." I laughed and hugged her impulsively. "Get down there and warn your friends," I said.

I watched her move away, taking long strides, walking alone and thinking for herself. Of course, her reaction to the band of male visitors was overstated. What harm could the three young men inflict on a group of twenty girls who had the home court advantage? In their freshman ancient history and mythology class, these same young women had acted out the death of Dionysus, impersonating the delirious nymphs who had killed the god—in this case, a straw dummy—by tearing him limb from limb and floating the pieces down the river.

Chapter Thirteen

Among the records of the Dry Falls emergency, our file on the events of June 24 is one of the largest. Some of the relevant documents came from the police files, copied by permission of resident state trooper Mark Centrella. Among those he interviewed, the school handyman, Helen's candidate, was sixty miles away at a revival meeting, a monthly all-nighter run by Brother Caleb Mercer of the Hallelujah Fellowship in South Fryeburg. As for the three suspicious-looking young men, one of them was Lally Ellsworth's brother. The other two were his roommates at Bowdoin. "We went swimming with the girls," said Bud Ellsworth. "O.K., I did try to duck Mercy but four of them jumped me and held me under. Then they made us leave because they heard one of the teachers calling. We were out of there by four o'clock anyway."

The owner of the riding stable, John Crowley, had spent a blameless night helping a Morgan horse to foal, in the company of Charlie Gerstel, our local large-animal veterinarian. John was questioned only because he was a single male and a newcomer. I hoped we were not approaching a time when people's names would be picked by whim or malice for persecution. There were no vagrants or escaped convicts in the area, nor any townspeople with a record of assault. Trooper Centrella had no need to call for reinforcements from the barracks at Windham. All the leads began at the school and ended at the school.

Within twenty-four hours he had declared that the incidents were not a police, but a medical, matter.

What were Henry and I doing that night, when we might have been of help? After supper I walked Henry over to church, carrying a freshly starched and ironed surplice on a hanger. I hung it in the vestiary and waved goodbye to Henry, who was standing on the chancel steps. Henry claimed he was going to weed out any battered hymnals or prayer books, but I knew he wanted to be alone to think. He did some of his best thinking stretched out in a pew with a kneeler under his head. The soaring lines of the columns carried his eye upward to the vaulted ceiling painted dark blue with gold stars, like the sky at night. He found it beneficial to stare at the ceiling, letting his mind go as blank as a lobotomy patient's. On the evening of June 23 he was not as much thoughtful as preoccupied, wondering how to tell Bishop Hollins he wanted a break from parish life, and how to get out of the Bishop's office before he suggested they pray together. He also wondered if resigning from the parish was just a childish way of paying God back for his near thirty-year silence.

Usually I felt lowered in spirits myself when Henry was dejected or in conflict. That night I gave myself over to ignoble cravings and paltry pastimes. Henry was doing his worrying in a building made of stone, which locked in the cool. I had no way of keeping cool except to sit in the garden in my slip finishing off a pint and a half of vanilla ice cream with flecks of the bean in it. I ate very slowly, using a silver demitasse spoon I had chosen for the purpose. Except for man-made sounds (a car going by with the radio playing), it was a noiseless night, like all the nights during the heat wave—no crickets, no owls, no raccoons at the garbage, no creatures hunting or being hunted. All the dogs in the neighborhood were quiet, and so was Harold Schwartz's German shepherd across the road.

I might have sat brooding on the unnatural silence, but instead I went back to the screened-in porch, angled a lamp toward my feet and spent an excessive amount of time clipping and filing my toenails. I noted that my right big toenail was in danger of ingrowing and my little toenails were too thin and lacked several protective horny layers. When I was done, I leaned against the back of my chair and stared through the screen at the shapes of plants in the garden, until my vision became imprinted with the pattern of the fine wire mesh. Mentally, I was operating below subsistence level. Part of me yearned for absolute stasis; another part knew, far away and dimly, that I must gather myself to combat this lethargy, which properly belonged to the realms of sleep and death.

Nothing would have roused me before the sun rose if Henry hadn't come in banging the kitchen door, grumbling that the lights had gone off at church and he was damned if he was going to break a leg groping his way down to the crypt to find the fuse box. I said it might be an answer from God. If the church needed rewiring, Henry could leave once he'd raised the money to cover the cost. He said God was far more likely to be using electrical failure as a metaphor for his, Henry's, spiritual darkness. We went up to bed and slept soundly until we were awakened at six-thirty in the morning by a call from Myra Littlefield, asking for Henry.

All twenty members of the class of '74 at Burridge Academy graduated in good standing, but only fourteen put on long white dresses to receive their diplomas. The other six, all residents of West Dorm, had been confined to the school infirmary on graduation morning. Miss Littlefield told their relatives and friends they had eaten bad food, the blame being cast on a supply of canned smoked oysters, consumed on saltines and washed down with root beer. Myra Littlefield and Nurse Shufelt conspired so successfully to prevent suspicion from arising that none of the parents became alarmed and none insisted on visiting the infirmary. The graduation guests assumed that state troopers were present at the festivities because they were directing traffic. I don't know how they kept the lid on Jean Leatherbee, who "found the bodies," as Myra put it.

Reading the June 24 file fills me with pity for Jean, who was unsuited to play a role in any crisis. Like so many boarding-school teachers, she needed to be near young people in order to recapture the lost glow of youth. Adulthood, with its burdens and its muddles, was uncongenial to her. In spite of her prematurely white hair, long earlobes, and creased brow, she had kept some of the look and mannerisms of a schoolgirl into her late forties. She was apt to laugh suddenly and too loudly; bound forward to greet people like a large untrained puppy; play with a strand of her hair during assemblies, dreamily twisting it around one finger. At graduation Myra Littlefield kept Jean as close to her side as she could without using physical restraint. Instead, she used Betty Barnes, the gym teacher, who coached games and supervised any young woman who wanted to increase her strength and develop her muscles through weight training. Myra and Betty were able to rein Jean in until the ceremonies were over, but not very much longer. Jean left Dry Falls on graduation day without giving notice. Several months later Myra heard through the prep-school grapevine that she had joined the faculty of the Berwick Rise School in Lisbon, Connecticut.

As far as we can make out from Jean Leatherbee's hiccuped narration to Mark Centrella, it started with a howling dog. The howling woke Jean at six-thirty a.m. on the twenty-fourth, half an hour before the alarm clock was set to ring. There was no school dog at Burridge Academy, although there was a fat, affectionate school cat. Jean stumbled to her feet and put on her bathrobe and slippers. She dreaded coming to the aid of an animal in distress. It took all the courage she could muster to overcome her fear of finding a half-severed paw, a gouged eye, emaciated ribs. Every lost or hurt animal was a testimonial to human cruelty. She must be forgiven for dawdling a little, putting off the confrontation while she combed her hair, debated whether to brush her teeth, started making the bed. Her room was at the rear of West Dorm, one flight above the fire exit. She went down the back stairs slowly, gripping the handrail, wishing she could go back to bed and cover her ears with a pillow to shut out the howling.

Jean opened the fire door and poked her head out. The noise had stopped. Made bolder by the fact that there was no dog in sight, she ventured along the brick walk as far as the tennis courts. The howling had come from that direction. Relief at being spared the necessity of caring for a maimed animal warred in her breast with the obligation to search the bushes surrounding the court in case he had collapsed of his wounds and was lying there, weakened and voiceless. Cowardice got the better of her. She stood where she was for several long minutes listening for the smallest sound—labored breathing, a whimper. She headed back to the house, taking care not to hurry, expecting the howling to break out again. The dog was quiescent, so she darted inside. Instead of going upstairs the back way, she wandered through the sitting room, straightening cushions, putting newspapers and magazines into a basket provided for the purpose, making sure the house was fit to be seen by visiting relatives. She went up the front stairs this time, noticing by her wristwatch that it was almost time to ring the wake-up gong.

There were four rooms on the second floor—three doubles and Helen Akers's single. Wouldn't it be nicer, she thought, to waken the occupants individually? A gentle tap on the door instead of an ear-splitting bong? A gesture in honor of the day, person to person instead of warden to inmate? On the way down the hall to her own room, crisscrossing from right to left, she knocked four times and called each of the occupants' names liltingly. Ten juniors lived on the third floor, but they were all going to Barcelona with the American Friends Service Committee and had been given permission to leave before graduation. She went up anyway, opening all five doors to check for forgotten belongings, books, stuffed toys, and mateless sneakers. On the bathroom floor she noticed a puddle of pink acne medicine, identifiable by its sulphurous smell, and in room number five she discovered Helen Akers. Helen had slept in her shorts and tee shirt on top of Connie Jessup's bare mattress. The bed was next to the window, which was open to its full height. Helen was curled on her side with her knees drawn up to her chest, but her eyes were open.

"What are you doing here, Helen?" asked Miss Leatherbee, forgetting her democratic impulses of a moment before. She was so unsure of herself that she saw any behavior not strictly by the book as an attempt to undermine her authority. "It was too hot in my room," said Helen. "Heat rises," said Miss Leatherbee, ready to pounce at the least sign of mendacity. "It would be cooler on the second floor." By this time Helen was standing at attention, tucking her grubby white tee shirt into her waistband. "I don't like my room," said Helen. "The ceiling is too low." "Come on, Helen," Miss Leatherbee insisted. "That makes two different reasons you've given me." Helen slid her feet into a pair of unstable-looking clogs. "I like being alone on the floor. I'd rather be by myself, anyway." "You're being very evasive, Helen," Miss Leatherbee retorted, "and I can only say I hope you'll be more straightforward in your dealings with people at Hampden College."

Jean Leatherbee had entered her own room and closed the door behind her before she realized there should have been some signs of life from the seniors. On graduation morning they often woke up rowdy. In years past she had been required to break up toothpaste fights. Always one to borrow trouble, she had a fleeting vision of smuggled liquor and six girls with hangovers, for which Miss Littlefield would hold her responsible. She marched up the hall to the first door on the left (on the right was the bathroom), rapped first with her knuckles, then banged with her open palm. Without waiting for a response, she opened the door and said loudly, "Everybody downstairs in five minutes."

When there was no answer, she advanced several feet into the room and found Mercy Locke lying on her back with no clothes on, sleeping or unconscious. Face upward on the other bed, one arm dangling over the side, hand trailing on the rug, Pickle Raines was lying motionless and as naked as a newborn. By this time Helen had joined Miss Leatherbee, and together they opened the two remaining doors to find four more versions of the same incomprehensible scene. Jean told Trooper Centrella that at first she thought they were dead and of course it would be her fault. When the trooper pressed her for a full description, she became extremely agitated and accused him of wanting to use her as a camera. She supposed he thought a "visual person" like herself would be able to provide more "grisly details." Myra Littlefield, who stayed with her while she was being interviewed, asked the trooper to come back later when Jean was calmer. After he left, Jean kept begging Myra Littlefield not to "make her go near them."

. . .

Jane Shufelt, R.N., the school nurse, was fifty-six years old, gray-haired, blunt-featured, and blunt-spoken. Nothing stopped her from speaking her mind and nothing embarrassed her. It goes without saying that she was capable of embarrassing others. When Nurse Shufelt stood up in assembly to announce revised infirmary hours or the availability of flu shots, she also congratulated any girl who had had her first menstrual period. Her lack of delicacy extended to her description of the six students, whom she examined in their beds at West Dorm before taking them to the infirmary.

Jane Shufelt had been director of patient care at Penobscot General Hospital in Bangor. She had taken postgraduate specialties in pediatrics and gynecology. She maintained she was in retirement, but she supplemented her work at Burridge with two voluntary duty periods a week at Portland General. She was a dedicated, highly trained practitioner, but she seemed to view the incident at West Dorm—at least in some aspects—as a kind of Rabelaisian joke. Jane gave a statement to the state police and a much more unbuttoned account to Henry, who had already begun keeping notes on curious occurrences. What relish she took in Jean Leatherbee's discomfort! "You can imagine old Jean," she told Henry. "All of them lying there naked with their legs open and everything showing. She didn't know where to look. I'll bet she doesn't even know she has one and she sure as hell doesn't want to think these kids do. I asked her to stand by while I took some samples. She lit out so fast it made your head spin."

When Henry saw the girls, they'd been covered with sheets right up to the chin. He was not sure why Myra had summoned him, except to be a reassuring clerical presence. When he got to West Dorm, Myra was talking to Trooper Centrella on the telephone. Jane Shufelt was wrapping a package to be delivered to the pathology lab in Portland. Jean Leatherbee had started defrosting the refrigerator, and Helen was sitting on the front stoop hugging the school cat, a tortoiseshell tom, ignoring his struggles for freedom. None of them talked to Henry, although they thanked him profusely for being there. He knew only one way to make himself useful. He went upstairs and paused by each girl's bedside, repeating the first blessing that came to his mind: "Almighty God, be our strong defense against our enemies;

grant that this child may be purified and cleansed by your abiding grace."

Looking down into their faces, he saw that they were deeply asleep, breathing almost imperceptibly, deaf to his words. It was only on the way home, after promising Myra he would show up for graduation an hour early, that he remembered the origin of those words. Instead of taking them from the service for the visitation of the sick, the most logical source, he had borrowed most of the language from a prayer for the reconsecration of churches and objects inside churches. It was surprising that that prayer should have sprung to his lips so readily. He had performed the service just once in his career, when the baptismal font at All Souls had been profaned by teenage vandals in the predictable fashion. The rest of the prayer began to come back to him: "that whatsoever has been stained or defiled may be purged from all pollution to the glory of your name." At the time Henry believed that such language was too strong to fit the circumstances.

What exactly were the circumstances? The day after the Burridge graduation there was still no general agreement, and no explanation. By the simplest reckoning, six girls had been discovered prostrate on their dormitory beds, naked and stupefied. The blood and vaginal samples analyzed on a rush basis at Portland General as a favor to Jane Shufelt revealed no traces of alcohol, drugs, or semen. The law, in the person of Trooper Centrella, was satisfied that the young women had not been molested sexually. As an added precaution, the bloods had also been tested for less obvious substances like poisons and viruses. Whatever the narcotic agent had been, it had kept six teenagers in various stages of lethargy for nearly sixteen hours.

The first to snap out of it was Mercy Locke, whose system needed very little rest under normal conditions; and the last was Abigail Hardy, a big, soft girl who happened to suffer from a mild thyroid deficiency. Once the girls were awake, they were not in the least groggy or upset. In fact, they were bubbling with high spirits and ready for a little postponed carousing. When they heard they'd missed graduation, they cheered and whistled, all except Pickle, who had wanted to show off her custom-made white dress. In a gesture rare to headmistresses, Myra Littlefield brought two bottles of French champagne over to West Dorm and poured everyone a glass to drink while they packed their belongings. Miss Littlefield was so eager to see them gone and the winds of scandal dispersed that she helped fold their clothes, hunted up extra cartons, and carried many of their boxes and suitcases downstairs herself to groups of parents waiting on the lawn, chatting in the sunshine.

All of us hoped the girls themselves could explain their long sleep. Of course, they were questioned delicately, in order not to alarm them or dampen their spirits, but they were as unconcerned and forgetful as hypnosis subjects obeying some kind of post-trance suggestion. Since Henry was a pastoral counselor, Myra asked him to be present while she and Jane went from bed to bed in the Burridge infirmary. Each of the six, in more or less the same words, said she hadn't worn anything to bed since the heat wave began; she had fallen asleep pretty early for graduation eve; she had slept straight through without even getting up to go to the bathroom.

Only Mercy Locke and Jill Bloom had anything different to add. They had fallen asleep smelling meat or had dreamed about smelling meat. Jill said the meat smelled "slightly rotten," whereas Mercy remembered wondering where the meat had come from. She and Helen had gone down to raid the icebox around eleven p.m., while Miss Leatherbee was in the shower. There was nothing to eat except yogurt, bran cereal, a jar of tahini, and a few rinds of cheese. Jill added that she had dreamed the meat was in the room with her and she was afraid she might be forced to touch it. When Henry pressed Mercy further, she said maybe one of the kids next door to her had brought some cold cuts home from the pick-up supper before the bonfire and the heat had made them go bad very quickly. "I don't see how I could have dreamed it," said Mercy. "I never heard of dreaming about a smell."

Henry decided to pursue another line of inquiry. The collective slumber had followed the bonfire by only a few hours, so perhaps there was some connection between them. On his second trip to the school, he had to wait until the patients had their temperatures and blood pressure taken. He started with Pickle Raines, a scrap of a freckled girl wearing red pajamas, sitting with her legs stuck out straight in front of her like an unjointed doll. "I guess I expected a little magic," Pickle said. She went on to describe the ceremony that was kept so secret from year to year: laying the bonfire, feeding it as high as the supply of kindling would allow; grabbing hands and dancing around it until it died down; appointing one person (Helen) to pour water on the embers; watching the faculty supervisor (Miss Barnes) poke around with a stick to make sure the fire was really out. "That's all there was to it," said Pickle. "It took about an hour. I think they make too big a deal of it." Other West Dorm seniors expressed the same disappointment. Jill Bloom said, "When you think how long I'd been looking forward to it, it's a little depressing." Mercy Locke said she was sure Henry would understand, if anyone could. She thought the bonfire would be like the cemetery, "where something really did happen, Dr. Lieber—didn't it?"

Since adolescence is the most feverish and idealistic time of life, Henry believed every adolescent was a potential visionary. At that time there was a window in the soul looking out on another realm, until experience of the world fogged the glass and darkened it with soot. Perhaps by seventeen or eighteen the visionary streak was all but extinguished. None of the graduates, Jill and Mercy included, had awakened with any sense of awe, curiosity, or even fear about their deathly sleep, the hours that had been stolen from them. What interested them most was finding a car, driving to Chester's in West Raymond, and ordering mixed drinks with funny names. Chester's had a dance band and a fleet of motorcycles parked outside on any given evening. As he walked down the corridor toward the reception room, Henry overheard Mercy trying to bribe Pickle (who was the smallest and nimblest) to sneak over to West Dorm and bring back her frosted pink nail polish.

Chapter Fourteen

Henry was perfectly content to stick to phenomenology—the broadest, most flexible system for his purposes, but he was running out of phenomena. Provocative incidents kept cropping up and coming to nothing—nocturnal invaders, red-eyed clouds, time lapses, collective slumbers. It seemed to him that his life was a sequence of tantalizing vistas and dead ends. He was becoming more and more of a materialist in matters of the spirit. He wanted apparitions and manifestations, rains of blood, rocks splitting asunder, unscheduled eclipses of the sun. Instead, he was presented with highly colored statements by immature female witnesses, interesting but inconclusive. Perhaps God was testing him, waving dross in front of his eyes to remind him of the color of the real thing. In June of 1974 Henry was still telling himself that the paranormal was merely an intellectual challenge like any other branch of learning, and in no way a serious rival to his vocation.

For this stage of life he needed the counsel of someone wiser. When Henry was at the seminary, trying to reconcile the sights of war with God's infinite mercy, he called on Gilbert Barber, the head of the theology department, a bird-beaked man with a pin in his hip and, as he put it, "a relationship with pain." Gilbert would have known when to listen quietly and when to bring him up short, to show Henry how things might look from a longer perspective; but Gilbert had been dead for ten years and Henry had only me and Walter Emmet to confide in, a cook and an antiques dealer.

Walter Emmet was unacquainted with any of the events since Easter because he had been "on the road" most of the spring, going up and down the East Coast from antiques show to antiques show, in a van packed as intricately as a Chinese puzzle. Henry thought he might drive over to Battle Hill Road, which was less than a mile from the school, and unfold his tale to Walter. Walter was an excellent listener, but he could listen properly only if he was doing something else at the same time. In cold weather he might be polishing wood or cleaning metal. In the summer he would be out by the shed, pot gardening. He planted bulbs and seedlings in shapely old clay pots and brought them up to the terrace as they came into bloom. On Walter's terrace garden plants were always in their prime. Nothing was ever allowed to die back, except inside the roofless greenhouse to which all pots were banished once their flowering was over. Walter treated perennial plants like annuals, making no attempt to bring them through the winter. This method of gardening suited him because he went south every January and February and did not feel flush enough to spend money restoring the greenhouse. His approach to horticulture, which was really a form of stage design or set dressing, horrified my mother, who told him Nature would rise up against him for breaking her laws and treating her so arbitrarily. Walter laughed and brought Emily pots of lilies and foxgloves to adorn her property, but the plants ended up in the ground and the pots in fragments—even pots that Walter assured her had once been the property of one of the great English country houses.

Before Henry could leave the school to see Walter, he ran into Jane Shufelt in the infirmary waiting room. At first glance the room appeared to be empty, but Henry saw Jane Shufelt in the far corner putting a quarter in the vending machine and pressing the button for a ginger ale, the only drink the machine had been programmed to dispense. Jane took her drink over to a seat by the window, where Henry joined her. He told her he wanted to confer with Walter Emmet, who had helped Judge Harvey's widow find her lost sapphire engagement ring.

"Why don't you ask Lorraine Drago?" asked Jane, always the champion of her sex. "I don't want to put her on the spot," said Henry. "Walter has no personal stake in his so-called powers." "Of course Walter could find a ring," Jane said. "He's better with objects than he is with people." "I like that impersonal quality," said Henry. "I tend to trust it." "I don't know the name for our little epidemic," said Jane, "but it's not in the same department as a piece of lost jewelry." "All right, then," said Henry. "I'll leave Walter out of it." "Oh, count him in, by all means. But there are a few items that might be a little strong for his delicate stomach."

Jane's honest, square face was best suited to serious expressions, not broad, knowing grins. She seemed to enjoy the idea of offending Walter as much as she had relished shocking Jean Leatherbee. Aesthetic sensibilities were just asking to be violated, in her opinion. For some reason, she put Henry in the same category as doctors and nurses, who embraced life in its crudest state and strove to triumph over death. What Henry witnessed of moral corruption and spiritual torture entitled him, in Jane's eyes, to stand shoulder to shoulder with the surgical staff of a hospital. "You're tough," she would say to Henry, as if his ministry were conducted amid the blood and stench of a downtown emergency room instead of a quiet village. The trait Jane most admired in other people was a lack of squeamishness. Her faith in Henry was justified. Far from wincing at the material she proceeded to give him, he made her repeat it a number of times, until she no doubt regretted her intention of using it to test male fortitude. Henry asked her to put everything down on paper as soon as possible, before it faded. She dropped her typewritten account at his house before he was back from Walter's.

Jane's revelation was baffling, embarrassing, appalling. It also met one of the standards of objective truth: two different witnesses confirmed it. Myra Littlefield had taken Jane to examine the sleeping bodies. What Jane saw, Myra saw—although Myra would have given her shares in Littlefield Shipyards not to have seen it. Although she was willing to confirm Jane's report with "yes" or "no" answers, Myra did not want to commit herself further—but Jane was able to express herself in straightforward, neutral language, the language of case notes:

We found them lying naked on their backs with their knees bent outward, six girls in the identical position. The inner thighs were wet from the pubis to the middle of the thigh, glistening with fluid. The vaginal secretion is volatile and dries so fast that I was forced to conclude that they were having some kind of sexual experience on the spot, with no external stimulus to account for it. The quantity of fluid being produced was unusually heavy and would create a personal hygiene problem if it were habitual. However, there was no odor connected with it. We could not establish the onset of the secretion, but we observed it had stopped by nine-thirty a.m., or shortly before we moved the girls to the infirmary. It must have been going on for some time, since it had soaked through the sheet and the mattress pad and dampened the mattress. Aside from the fluid, other signs of sexual arousal were also apparent: hardening of the nipples and the clitoris; swelling and reddening of the labia. If they hadn't been so deeply asleep, I would have expected to see rapid breathing and pelvic activity.

These are the facts as I perceived them. It is not my place to offer any theory. Someone is bound to suggest, however, that each of the girls was dreaming an erotic dream. From what I know about sleep physiology, dreams are always accompanied by rapid eye movements *and there were none*. The girls had reached—and remained in—a stage of sleep far below REM sleep.

Signed in full
Jane Elyce Shufelt, R.N.

Battle Hill Road dead-ended at Walter Emmet's property. Walter's house rose up where the road stopped, so in winter a town snow truck was obliged to plow Walter's driveway and turnaround unless the driver wanted to back down the hill half a mile to Cass and Albert Nolan's. The front of the house was plain—unpainted, unshuttered, with only a strip of molding around the doors and windows. The back of the house was fancy. Walter's balustraded terrace, with its enormous paving stones and semicircular marble steps, might have been attached to a Renaissance villa. Henry was mercifully free from the sin of envy, except when he stood on Walter's terrace gazing across at dark wooded hills and a green upland meadow, set like a jewel in the center of the view, where Michel Roque pastured some of his sheep.

Walter was planting September-blooming lilies, the glorious Green Dragon, six feet tall, ivory tinged with chartreuse, in a pot that weighed seventy pounds when it was filled with soil. Walter hauled pots this size and larger every day, rarely using a wagon or a dolly. Walter's strength was not apparent from his looks. He was slight, narrow-chested, a little taller than the Green Dragons, with a close-fitting reddish beard, sunken cheeks, and deep-set brown eyes. Because he was so thin, he gave a false impression of frailty. As far as anyone knew, Walter did nothing to build his muscles the rest of the year except lift heavy illustrated reference books on the decorative arts. With one long, slender, dirt-stained hand Walter waved Henry to a seat and told him to have some iced tea. As usual, Henry poured himself a glass from the thermos jug on the white iron table and asked Walter if he could do anything to help him. Walter thanked him, as he always did, and said he was nearly finished. Knowing Walter was most attentive when his hands were busy, Henry settled back in a white iron chaise longue against the striped canvas cushions. "I'm going to start talking," he said, "and I'm not going to stop until I've finished.

With his eyes on the distant hills, he began to bring Walter up to date month by month—March, April, May, June. Even for a friend and former member of the psychical research group, Henry felt obliged to coat his discourse with irony, implying that he would be the last man to swallow such a mountain of hearsay and unlikelihood whole, in spite of his profession. He had a three-quarter view of Walter at his work table, enough to take account of his reactions. Walter was stirring compost, sand, and crushed limestone in a washtub, making his favorite recipe for potting mix. Henry expected a smile from Walter when he got to the "red-eyed cloud" described by Mercy and Helen, but Walter's face wore a distracted look, as if he were imagining the ideal location for the potted lilies. A flicker of annoyance did cross his brow as Henry summarized Adele's experiences at the Easter Vigil—or perhaps he had merely encountered an undecayed avocado pit in the compost. The incident of the West Dorm seniors, so fresh in Henry's mind, made Walter mutter something under his breath. Later that day I started to ask my husband if he'd mentioned the black dog to Walter, only to recall that I'd neglected to tell Henry about it in the first place; it had seemed both too outlandish and too trivial.

Henry began to recite the nightmare that had driven Hannah from our attic and been "picked up" by Adele, then by me. Henry was attracted to dreams because their source and their message were mysterious, but he discounted three-quarters of everything my sister said, and he presumed the same skepticism on Walter's part. Before he finished his recital he noticed that Walter had stopped stirring.

In a moment he spoke, asking Henry to run through the dream again. Afterwards, he said, "All three of them thought the weight was a man? Or somehow masculine?" "I should tell you," answered Henry, "that my wife thinks she had a nightmare. It's the other two who think it might have been something else." "What about you, my friend?" asked Walter. "Do you have an opinion?" "I don't see the point of having opinions in advance of the facts." Walter smiled. "I'm surprised at you, Henry. You never struck me as one of those modern pastors—one of those mental health professionals in cassocks."

Henry began to feel like a backward schoolboy, as if the answer to a question were lying under his nose and he was too thick to see it. "That's the way we do it, Walter. If a parishioner comes to see us with a vision or a revelation, we have to clear away the psychiatric rubble first. An authentic spiritual experience should be able to stand up to the closest scrutiny."

Walter turned to face Henry, gesturing with his trowel, letting fly a spray of dirt. "What if you're throwing the revelations away with the rubble?" Henry started to defend himself—his character, his ministry, the relatively new field of pastoral counseling—but Walter interrupted. "It's not only a question of discarding some scrap of divinity. People come to you with visions of light, but there are others—more, I would guess—who bring you visions of darkness. What happens to discarded demons? Do they die a peaceful death on your rubble heap?"

Henry answered, "They surface in some other form. So do the angelic ones." "They have a course on Freud at your seminaries," Walter persisted, "but I understand they've dropped demonology." Henry suppressed a snort of laughter. He said, "I think demonology was dropped from the curriculum in the 1700s."

Walter dragged the hose over to the workbench so he could wet down the potting soil. He was red in the face and more out of breath than the job entailed. "But we still perform exorcisms," put in Henry, as if to reassure Walter that the Episcopal Church was medieval enough for him. "You don't study demonology," Walter repeated. "So you go out into your parishes unprepared. You make mistakes. You misdiagnose. You underestimate."

Henry lifted his big frame out of the chaise and began pacing back and forth, glass in hand. He had several inches on Walter and felt at less of a disadvantage standing up. It very nearly made a comic scenario—an antiques dealer haranguing a doctor of divinity about the education of the priesthood. Yet who was more concerned with tradition than an antiques dealer? More concerned, in truth, than the Bishops of the Anglican Communion, who approved the rewriting and modernizing of the Prayer Book, an act equivalent, Henry felt, to installing Coke machines in Chartres Cathedral. Henry submitted to Walter's scolding patiently. It seemed that Walter had something to teach him about his blind spots and deficiencies. The most serious of these, apparently, was his tendency to favor the transcendent and ignore the abysmal, forgetting that the human soul is composed of depths as well as heights. It wasn't his fault, according to Walter, because Christians were brought up to believe that the Dark and the Light are two separate kingdoms, instead of two halves of a whole, each requiring the other. Walter implied that "mystics like Henry" could be dangerous to other people.

Henry protested this unfairness. How had Walter suddenly become his spiritual director? He said, "I wouldn't have sought you out in the first place if I weren't uneasy." Walter put down the hose. He took a handful of wet potting soil and squeezed it to make sure it held together. "You're right to be uneasy," he said. "I'd suggest an even stronger reaction might be appropriate."

Henry had taken enough condescension for one afternoon, especially from someone who was only an amateur in occult matters, whatever impression he tried to create to the contrary. "May I get off my knees now?" Henry asked. "Be my guest," said Walter, who was pleased with himself and feeling expansive. He had accomplished what he'd set out to do, although he deplored using shaming tactics. He had put Henry on the scent. Henry would track these events to their source, never wavering in his commitment, spurred on by the idea that it depended on him to save his fellow creatures from some as yet unspecified harm. Walter was willing to serve as a consultant as long as he did not have to leave home. He had traveled all winter, ending up in Palm Beach. It had been a stressful visit. During a séance with a well-known British medium, held in an empty, neo-Moorish villa, he had witnessed some disturbing manifestations, including a fireball with a zigzag flight pattern, and he had the singed eyebrows to prove it.

It was true that Henry went around with his eyes raised heavenward, seeing all human experience as an opportunity for choice, change, growth, and/or redemption. "When in doubt, go for the transpersonal" was his motto as a pastoral counselor, and he always managed to elicit a statement of something positive, even from patients who painted the bleakest pictures of their lives. In the middle of a tale of disaster and misery, a patient might cock his head and say, "You know, I did have a good laugh yesterday" or "I was driving home from work and I noticed how beautiful the light was," and Henry would go for it. From one faint spark of hope he and his patient went on to build a blaze. Henry was never one to let a patient stew very long in his own pathology, although a more distinctive and zesty mixture might have resulted from the simmering process.

Henry knew the names of the demons that persecuted his patients and his parishioners—Anxiety, Depression, Lust, Anger, Self-Loathing; and he knew these demons by their ancient and medieval names as well, from Asmodeus to Zizzubabel. In the consulting room he gave demons short shrift, since to him they were nothing more than stumbling blocks on the way to self-realization. However, he remembered very clearly that there was a time in the history of the Church when demons were perceived as something denser than neurotic figments. According to many generations of churchmen and inquisitors, demons could assume a certain earthly reality in order to appear to us. By borrowing from energies in us and in the atmosphere, they could create a kind of semi-body, a spurious organism. Just as human beings longed for union with the spirit, so incorporeal beings, both angels and demons, yearned for contact with matter. Angels contented themselves with exerting a benign influence over men's bodies—snatching them out of the path of a boulder during an avalanche, guiding the surgeon's hand during a long and difficult operation—but demons had no such ability to hold their natures in check. Their desire to be familiar with flesh was ravenous, insatiable, the more urgent because they possessed no generative powers. Night after night they assaulted human beings in their beds, striving to produce life—but all that came of their efforts were empty wombs swollen with air. Night after night they persisted, taking the topmost position with women and the lowermost with men, in a sterile parody of passion.

"Speaking entirely theoretically," said Henry to Walter, "there is a name in the annals for a demon who disturbs women's sleep." Walter was planting the first Green Dragons, five bulbs to a pot, with a mothball at the bottom of each hole to keep rodents away. "An incubus," Henry continued. "Plural 'incubi.' " Walter smiled and nodded encouragingly. If he hadn't been holding a spoon and a bag of bulb food, he would have patted Henry on the back. "I don't like being led by the nose," said Henry. "If you already knew all about it, why not name it yourself?" Walter held a good-sized bulb up to eye level and flicked old dirt off the roots with an artist's soft-bristled paintbrush. "And why are you cleaning the damn thing if you're going to stick it right back in the dirt again?" Walter began to laugh, a big laugh for such a scrawny man. "Ruffled your fur, didn't I?" he said. "That's all right," Henry said. "I asked for it."

Their comradeship restored, Henry stayed on a while longer. It was six o'clock and the afternoon was over. Henry lingered pleasurably, declining the offer of something stronger than iced tea. They discussed the evidence for and against an incubus, as if demonic assault in our neighborhood were as matter-of-fact an occurrence as infestations of tent caterpillars. Walter had been given to understand that demonic forces were much more potent away from towns. Such attacks were most likely to take place in the country or in the mountains, where human settlement was sparse. "That Burridge student," he said. "The one who didn't fall asleep. I hope someone is keeping an eye on her." They argued about whether the West Dorm seniors were dreaming or under attack. Walter reminded Henry that an incubus-devil may or may not elect to manifest to onlookers. Walter had become so animated that he paused in his labors, turning away from his workbench to speak to Henry face to face. With a gleam in his eye, he predicted we weren't "out of the woods": the dreams would become more lascivious, and the line between dream and waking reality would be blurred past recognition.

If Henry minded hearing that his own wife, among others, was going to be besieged by recurring erotic nightmares, he was soon distracted by the view of the hills changing color in the golden light, and the sight of several sheep playing tag on the upland pasture. He was always soothed by high places and reluctant to leave Walter's terrace for the Dry Falls flats. He was only half listening to Walter, who was holding forth on the subject of "bedroom invaders" from vampires to extraterrestrials. Walter was exercised because authors and scholars ("pseudo-scholars, Henry; the field is a magnet to them") tended to lump all nighttime intruders together under a single broad heading: "hauntings." A phenomenologist by instinct—although he would have called it "training your eye"—Walter felt that strange happenings should be classified with at least as much attention to detail as furniture. If it was possible to distinguish an eighteenth-century chair carved in Newport from one made in Providence, then there was no excuse for mixing up one kind of paranormal occurrence with another. First and foremost, ghosts merely *appeared* to people, whereas vampires, demons, and aliens *interfered* with them. "Everything on its own terms," said Walter.

Henry settled deeper into his chair. Here on Walter's terrace it was possible to ignore the unchanging heat for a little while. It was pleasant to lie quiet, aspiring to inertness, but he was failing in his conversational duties. His host was looking at him impatiently. "Sorry, Walter," he apologized, and went on to say that psychologists were just as bad as psychical researchers. They, too, filed all nocturnal visitations under a single heading: "hallucinations." Walter and Henry continued conversing until Walter invited his guest to share his supper—nothing but sandwiches; he usually ate standing up while he potted. With great reluctance Henry left his chair, the view, and his friend. Later he would remember what a luxury it was to be discussing anomalous events from a vicarious distance with no special urgency—like two undergraduates at the end of term lying by the river and arguing about whether the cow on the opposite bank existed in her own right or only when they were looking at her. That evening, and for a short time to come, all secret, black, and midnight agencies were still just airy abstractions deriving their existence from men's footloose intellects.

Chapter Fifteen

Sometime during the fork luncheon served on the Main Building lawn after graduation, Jean Leatherbee stole away without collecting her paycheck or leaving a forwarding address. I had nothing to do with the food except make a sporting attempt to eat it, and I wondered if Jean had decided to leave before or after tasting the chicken salad, so dry from overpoaching that no amount of mayonnaise could moisten it. The tension behind the scenes must have communicated itself to the kitchen staff, accounting not only for the chicken but also for the choice of dessert—bricks of vanilla ice cream garnished with multi-colored sprinkles. The cook had simply given up and taken the easy way out, just as Miss Leatherbee had. Jean's departure affected Helen Akers particularly. She had agreed to be with Helen throughout the day and to stay the night. Poor Helen had no claque in the audience at the ceremonies. Her father and mother were dead, and there was only a brother, who'd been posted by the foreign service to Capetown, South Africa. The day after graduation Jean was to have put Helen on the bus for Boston, where she lived with her grandmother, who was confined to her bed with bouts of crippling arthritis. Apparently Helen's story—almost Victorian in its accumulation of pathetic detail—made no appeal to Miss Leatherbee's conscience. Myra Littlefield thought it would be distressing for Helen to stay at the school, so she asked us to take her.

Before I knew Helen was coming, I'd already started to prepare an old-fashioned farm supper: chicken stew with a biscuit topping; three kinds of vegetables (green beans, wax beans, and mashed potatoes); sliced beet-and-red onion salad dressed with oil and vinegar; stewed rhubarb with whipped cream for dessert; and a pitcher of iced mint tea to wash it down. Sometimes I began to free-associate in the kitchen and forget I was cooking for only two people. Having another mouth to feed gave me fresh incentive. I dashed off a batch of ginger cookies, which were still in the oven when Myra and Jane dropped Helen off and handed me Jane's report. By the time Henry came home, I had given Helen a tour of the bedrooms. She had chosen to sleep on the third floor because her room in her grandmother's house was in the attic. "There's no room to stand up straight except in the middle," she said with a grin, as if that were an ideal arrangement for someone who had hurt her leg.

If Henry could be said to have a favorite dish, it was a mound of buttery mashed potatoes with a well of chicken gravy in the center, but he was ready to give up the sight and taste of it in an instant for the chance to question Helen at the dinner table. During the crisis at West Dorm Helen had been overlooked. No one saw to her psychological welfare. If she had managed to stay awake, she must be all right. The sleeping seniors were "sick"; therefore, Helen was "well." Since she had slept on the third floor, she had been questioned only perfunctorily. She had been neglected as a source of information. Henry wanted to correct this oversight as soon as possible, before Helen could take another portion of green beans (rich in vitamin A, which helped rebuild broken bones), before she was distracted by the sweet/sour flavor of the salad, before the rhubarb fool (two cups sugar to three cups of fruit) made her drowsy and inattentive.

He began by asking her if she had applied for a single dorm room or had been assigned one. I changed the subject by reminding Henry that the adult confirmation class had been put off for a week because its only two members, Cass and Bert Nolan, had Bert's eighty-year-old mother visiting. Next, Henry wanted to know if she had gone to bed before or after the other seniors. This time I tried several wifely gambits all at once: frowning at him, kicking him under the table, interrupting him to ask Helen if I could refill her iced-tea glass. After that, he stuck to questions that concerned her intention of majoring in ancient history in college and her ardent desire to go on a dig with a Professor Fennerman, who was excavating the ancient city of Sardis. When supper was over, I served coffee in the living room instead of at the table, as I usually do. I lingered behind, clearing away the dishes, leaving Henry and his subject seated opposite each other.

Before I heard Helen's story, I was a curious bystander. After I heard it, I was less secure in my skepticism. When I asked Henry how she had told it, he answered "stoically"—as befitted a girl who had sat two hours in the emergency room waiting for her leg to be set after the bicycle accident and then insisted, when her turn came, that the feverish child sitting next to her be attended to first. Above all other virtues, New Englanders prize self-control. Henry and I were impressed by Helen's testimony right away because she tried to hide her suffering. If we put less stock in Adele and my sister, it was because they made a display of their pain; and there is an element of pleasure and release in the process of self-disclosure. We credited them less than Helen, even wondered if they might not be "getting a kick out of it." Adele and Hannah told their stories from start to finish without brooking interruption. They had no use for captions, headlines, flash bulletins, or any other synoptic devices. Once under way, the story flowed like a river, carrying the listener helpless in its waters.

The Trojan prophetess Cassandra was locked up in a tower as much to spare her hearers the style of her delivery as its gloomy substance. In order to make sure no one would believe her, far-seeing Zeus gave her a grating, high-pitched voice. Cassandra and her kind are remembered best as bores and windbags, no matter how high their scores for accuracy. Looking back on it now, Helen's story was taken seriously not on its own merits but because Helen herself had a high degree of credibility. If it hadn't been for that steady gaze, that brave tilt of chin, that artless, sober way of speaking, we would have attributed her experiences to any number of reasonable causes: fatigue, fear of the dark, a bid for the spotlight, the increasing burden of virginity.

. . .

There were two single rooms in West Dorm. They were both on the second floor and one belonged to the housemother, Miss Leatherbee. At the end of spring term Burridge students drew lots for roommates and room assignments for the next academic year. Helen wanted the single, although the rest of her dorm mates thought it was undesirable, even bad luck. After she drew it, she found out where the misfortune lay. When laughter from the twin-bedded rooms seeped under her door, her heart froze with loneliness. She had looked forward to being by herself—reading, studying, doing research on the arrowheads she found in plowed fields. After a year of sharing a room with Abigail Hardy, she was ready for solitude. The notion of privacy was threatening to Abigail. If two people were sitting in a room reading instead of conversing, that meant one of them was mad at the other.

Helen was especially aware of her own isolation on weekend nights and special occasions like the Rumsey School dance. She had no one with whom she could endlessly review any number of trivial incidents, such as how long exactly Pickle and her freckled partner had been missing from the dance floor; and whether the punch tasted weird and what was saltpeter anyway? Mercy used to say that if something was worth discussing once, it was worth discussing a hundred times, but Mercy hadn't been her roommate since sophomore year. On Saturday nights Helen fell into the habit of sneaking into Mercy and Pickle's quarters after room check until she began to catch tireless, good-time Mercy stifling a yawn and Pickle making no attempt to keep her eyes open.

On the eve of graduation Helen kept to her own room, in spite of an invitation from Mercy and Pickle to "try and stay up all night." The world seemed to be organized into couples and she was sick of being the leftover person. She and Mercy did go down to raid the icebox and found its contents disappointing. They parted in the kitchen, Mercy taking the front stairs and Helen the back. Helen's trunk was packed, but her suitcase lay open on the bed, waiting to be filled. She was folding sweaters when the sounds of merriment reached her—giggling, music, and chatter muted by solid oak doors. At one point she heard doors opening and closing. She peeked out and saw Pickle Raines gliding up and down the hallway, showing off her white graduation dress. She visited every room except for Helen's and, of course, Miss Leatherbee's. Helen grabbed her favorite book, *Jane Eyre*, a self-pitying choice, turned out the lights, and stole quietly upstairs to the juniors' floor. She let herself into the room nearest the stairwell, the room Connie Jessup had shared with Nancy Cole. She stretched out on Connie's bed, propped her head up with several pillows, and began to read by the light of a forty-watt bulb. Up here, with the door closed, she could hear an occasional thump from downstairs, but no merry voices. She read only as far as Jane's first morning at the Lowood School, when the porridge is burned, before her eyes closed.

"I think I dozed off with the light on," Helen told Henry. She heard the door click open, too small a sound to wake her out of a deep sleep. She heard the click—and the next thing she knew the door was wide open, but she never saw it opening. When she looked around, she couldn't see much. The light was dim, as if the bulb was dying, and it was brownish, or yellow-brown. She thought a fog had come in through the window, but it was a dirty city fog—not the silver-white fog you see in the country. She thought Miss Leatherbee must have looked in, seen her sleeping, and decided not to wake her.

She turned over on her stomach and composed herself for sleep again. On the point of nodding off, she became aware that the low-lying brown fog was issuing from the door, not the window. It was moving, swirling, gathering itself into a shape that filled the doorway, a mass of vapors imitating a solid material body. She couldn't see through it. It was taking form, a restless, amorphous form about the size of a man, now hooded and caped, almost realistic; now a circular blob; now a tall, narrow rectangle, something on stilts. It had no face as such. There were two dark holes in the place where eyes should be. "There was no face," she said, "no facial expression. But I'm sure it was staring at me."

Lying on her stomach with her face turned toward the door, she was able to see the murky presence through half-closed eyelids. Her body was paralyzed, except for her eyelids. When Henry asked why she couldn't move, she said something was weighing her down, a uniform, all-over pressure, not terribly heavy but strong enough to hold the threat of suffocation. Who was pressing on her, or what? Could she feel the imprint of hands, a knee, a foot? She said no, it was only weight, but a weight with a purpose, a will of its own, related to the presence in the doorway—"split off from it" was how she put it. The shape moved as she watched it, billowing across the threshold, then receding into the corridor. How far beyond the threshold it moved depended on her. Helen was sure of two things: she knew she was fully awake because everything in the room was in its place, and she knew that if she tried to struggle it would penetrate the room.

Therefore it was her job, as she construed it, to stay alert as long as the shadow stood in the doorway. It never occurred to her that there might be only one of him, that he was "acting on his own." She saw him right away as a kind of sentinel, warning others of his kind against the approach of danger. But why were these "others" mounting a guard on her? In what way could she represent a danger to their plans? While the night wore on, Helen lay there breathing as shallowly as someone in a faint. She fell heir to numerous small afflictions—stiff neck, itching nose, jumping nerves, numbness and tingling in the limbs, an urgent bladder. It took all the willpower she had to keep from trying to change position and alerting her warder. In fact, these sources of discomfort were a godsend. As long as she was trying to combat them, she was protected from an experience of fear. She said, "I think if I had known I was afraid, I would have died of fear." Sometime before full light, her eyelids closed from exhaustion. When she opened them again the form was gone and Miss Leatherbee was bending over her. "I never saw him leave," said Helen. "I was hoping when daybreak came I could see him better."

It was Helen herself, without any prompting from Henry, who noticed she had been referring to a faceless, bodiless collection of gases as "he." This late in her story, her shoulders were drooping and her cheeks were a hectic, patchy red. From the back of the living room I tried to catch Henry's eye. I pointed at the ceiling, to indicate that Helen needed to go to bed. He had no intention of sparing her at such a juncture. His questions began to come faster. If she vacillated, he pinned her down relentlessly. I advanced into the room until I was standing a few feet behind the sofa where Helen was sitting. Watching Henry in pursuit of knowledge made me apprehensive. I could see Helen sitting up straighter, bracing herself for the onslaught. Why did she think it was a he? Did it make some typically masculine gesture? Did it communicate in any fashion, in speech or by thought transference? Did any sound emanate from it? Was there an odor? Had she perceived the pressure on her back as sexual? As pleasurable? The opposite of pleasurable? When Henry paused for breath I got his attention. I made the arm movements an umpire makes when he calls the base runner "out." I believed my usually kind and sensitive husband had been about to ask an orphan and a virgin if she had been afraid of (1) anal penetration or (2) entry from behind, using the vagina.

As much as Henry pushed her, Helen could produce no good reason why the shape in the doorway was masculine. Her conviction seemed to be based on the degree of menace it generated: the fact that it was in control, that it was "bigger and stronger" than she was, that she "had to do what he wanted" or suffer the consequence. These statements revealed more about her image of masculinity than they did about the presence. But when it came to the question of odor, she was very specific. "I smelled meat," she said. "No, wait. It wasn't meat. It's the way the butcher paper smells when you leave meat in the fridge and you don't change the wrapping. It smells like blood, stale blood. It makes you think the meat is bad but it's really the blood on the paper."

If Helen was clear and precise about the odor, she was less satisfactory when it came to describing the pressure. She said it was like having too many covers on, layers of quilts and blankets of different thicknesses. As she described it, the "covers" were heavy but not hot. From time to time a layer would be added, or one would be taken away. Toward the end of the night she felt she had fewer covers on than she had at the beginning. "It seemed like a reward for good behavior." Who or what was rewarding and/or punishing her? Helen was certain it wasn't the sentry at the threshold. "He was only a minion," she said. "I don't mean he wasn't dangerous."

So far, Helen had been doing her best to give complete, thoughtful answers, as if she were a graduate student taking her orals and Henry one of her examiners. All at once, she got irritable and began to show some spirit. She wondered how Henry could possibly imagine the sensation of pressure as pleasurable. It was one more trial in the mass of discomforts she had endured. And she didn't think that whatever was pressing down on her was trying to rape her, if that's what Dr. Lieber meant by "sexual." Helen leaned forward, challenging Henry. "You think my friends were raped," she said, as if the idea had struck her for the first time. "Is that it? Is that what happened?"

If Helen was forced to keep going over her experience, she would soon be too agitated to fall asleep. We had to get her up by seven the next morning. The bus to Boston left at nine o'clock, and the bus station was twenty minutes away in East Windham. Henry motioned to me, inviting me to join them. Seated to either side of Helen, we managed together to calm her down, reassuring her—truthfully enough—that clinical tests had proved none of her classmates had been raped. As to her own ordeal, Henry told her there was a name for the strange, shifting images you see just before sleep: they were called hypnagogic hallucinations, and they often occurred in connection with sleep paralysis. Helen was an intellectual girl, who aspired to a career in scholarship. In spite of her experience, so fresh in her mind, she was able to hear an appeal to reason and be influenced by it. Before accompanying her up to her room, I made her swallow two tablets with a glass of water. Clear thinking combined with aspirin would guarantee her rest.

That same prescription had the opposite effect on her hosts. We sat up until the small hours, trying to solve the puzzle by approaching it logically. Four people had dreamed the same nightmare with certain differences that might be significant: Helen was lying on her stomach, not her back; she never heard the presence coming or going, or the footfall described by Adele as "someone using a wet mop." Three out of four preferred to believe they were awake through it all. At what point did a series of dreams form a pattern that deserved a name? When the dreamers numbered in the hundreds? In the hundreds of thousands? For a few minutes Henry allowed himself to think aloud about a new way of life in which he was no longer a corporate functionary but a free agent, practicing at the secular end of the mysticism business, conducting private research projects and supporting his research with scores of interviews, interviews with dreamers, hallucinators, out-of-body travelers, automatic writers, seers of ghosts, angels, and demons—anyone reputable, or disreputable, who might have some information about the existence of God and other incongruous phenomena.

Henry shook off this reverie by reminding himself that the shadowy invader was probably nothing more than an archetypal figure, a symbolic formation of the collective unconscious. Jung's archetypes were disappointingly human in origin—patterns of behavior and responses inherited from the cave man, well-worn grooves in our primitive memory. The shape in the doorway derived from an ancient fear of the darkness and from a deep-seated instinct to safeguard the integrity of the body. No matter how powerful an archetype like Helen's "form" might seem, it was not an independent entity. Archetypes did not, and never would, constitute grounds for believing in the spirit world. After several hours or discussion we came up with nothing but questions—such as why had Helen merely been restrained instead of sexually stimulated, like the others? Colored by fatigue and frustration, our speculations on this and every item were as vaporous as the sentinel in Helen's doorway. Perhaps Helen was inviolable by nature, we conjectured, a born spinster, a kind of prep-school Joan of Arc. When we finally went to bed, Henry was suffering from dejection as much as fatigue. "We don't know what happened," he said. "We don't know if anything happened."

The nine a.m. bus to Boston left without Helen Akers, and so did the eleven o'clock. We didn't have the heart to wake her up. At noon Henry decided to drive her down himself, seeing no reason why he shouldn't be back in time to meet with the church festival committee at six-thirty. I stayed behind because I had promised Ruth Hiram to provide canapés and a cheese board for a little cocktail party at the library in honor of several outgoing volunteers. Ruth had enough money in the budget to pay for my services. I was pressed for time, but

I packed picnic lunches for Henry and Helen—egg-and-watercress sandwiches, tangerines, and some of the ginger cookies I'd made. I tucked my red sleeveless tee shirt and a copy of *A Girl of the Limberlost* in with Helen's things—she had admired the one and asked to borrow the other.

I wanted to do what I could for her. For no medical reason, Henry and I were childless. Most of the time it suited me fine, but occasionally I felt regret, as I did that morning at the sight of Helen fighting back tears. I wanted to be the one person in the world who was allowed to see her weeping and to hold her until the sobs passed. As it was, I could only hover in the background, refilling her glass of milk at breakfast, finding her an extra toothbrush and a comb because she'd left her own at the dormitory, fetching her suitcase so she wouldn't have to climb the stairs again. Helen had come downstairs at ten-thirty, while Henry and I were having a second breakfast. Henry turned off the coffee grinder when he saw her. I put down the bread knife. She walked into the kitchen with her hands clasped behind her back and her head bowed, like a child expecting a scolding. She looked up and met our eyes without a trace of resentment in her expression. She said, "He followed me. How did he find me here? Is he going to follow me to Boston?"

Henry told Helen's grandmother that a group of Burridge seniors had been put in the infirmary just before graduation. They were fully recovered, but no one knew what they'd come down with—probably an intestinal bug. Henry hoped Mrs. Reid would watch Helen carefully over the next few days for an outbreak of symptoms and instruct her staff to do so as well. Mrs. Reid was a bright-eyed, fine-boned old woman who was exasperated by her inactivity and welcomed any diversion. If anything, Henry wagered, she would supervise Helen too closely. She thought she might ask Helen to sleep on the folding cot in her dressing room for several nights. "I'll make up some excuse. Give the night nurse time off to visit her daughter." It seemed that Mrs. Reid's flair for coloring the truth in a good cause was at least as well developed as Henry's. What else could he have said? That her granddaughter had been frightened by a hypnagogic image? That she believed she was being pursued by a baneful specter? That her fears might be well founded?

Since Helen had been my guest, I was distressed that she'd spent a bad night under my roof. It might have been more solicitous to insist she take one of the guest rooms on the second floor, but to have done so would be the same as conceding that the attic was contaminated. In my opinion, Helen would have conjured up her phantom pursuer no matter what bedroom I had put her in. Her encounter in our attic, however, had tallied in several particulars with testimonies by Adele and Hannah. She claimed she had heard him climbing the stairs. He walked slowly. His footfall was soft and gliding. She said, "It flashed through my mind that his feet were wrapped in rags." Thereafter the encounter replicated her experience in the dormitory: "He" remained at the threshold, willed her into immobility, and disappeared at sunrise.

Henry came back from Boston energized rather than depleted. The five-hour trip had not tired him. When the church festival committee meeting was over, around eight o'clock, he went straight to the telephone to call Walter Emmet. He told Walter he had decided to let Lorraine Drago have a whiff of our third floor. Dazzled by opportunity, he also wanted to waltz her through the bedrooms in West Dorm. Walter fell in with his plan. They would be using Lorraine the way miners used a caged canary when they were checking underground passageways for poison gases. Torn between fear of failure and a desire to play a part in this enterprise of Henry's, Lorraine agreed to be used.

The following morning Henry went off to meet her at the Borden Cramer house (1760), where she was conferring with the building inspector on behalf of interested clients. From thence they would proceed to the school, ending up at the rectory. I had no stake in what they got up to as long as I was not obliged to give them lunch. I had July's columns to finish and mail to the paper: "Fireworks Picnics," "An Old-Fashioned Ice Cream Social," "The Summer Vegetarian," and "A Choice of Cobblers." I walked Henry out to the car. He kissed me goodbye and said, "I think we have enough to go on." I forbore to tell him he had nothing to go on except coincidence and wishful thinking. Instead, I stood in the driveway waving until his car turned out of sight.

Lorraine's performance at West Dorm was "less than amateurish," according to Walter, but he had never seen Lorraine in trance before. Most psychics appeared to be undergoing some kind of torment. Lorraine went into a stupor, glassy-eyed, mouth hanging open, speech thick and off-key, as if her tongue were swollen. Some psychics remembered nothing when they came to. Lorraine Drago was alert and sensible right away, with excellent recall and an unusual ability to be objective. All she had picked up on the second floor of the dorm was something she called "room noise," a kind of humming perceived as silence by the unaided ear. Then, out of the blue, she asked Henry who was living in the dormitory. Was it possible Miss Leatherbee had come back? Who was roasting a cut of meat that early in the day? Lorraine was certain it was beef. The odor was distinctive, sharp and sweet and a little sickening so soon after breakfast.

At Lorraine's insistence they explored the dorm kitchen and the housemother's suite, both of which were clean and empty. From the kitchen they could see the back end of the infirmary, sixty feet away. In Jane Shufelt's apartment on the second floor the windows were wide open. A figure, Jane herself, was moving back and forth in one of the rooms. She reached up to open a cabinet, turned around and stooped down out of view, then stood up and walked out of the frame, carrying a pot or a dish in gloved hands. From which they deduced, all but Henry, that the room they were observing was Jane's kitchen; that Jane was in her kitchen, cooking; and that Jane's cooking was the source of the odor Lorraine had reported. But why, Henry asked, was Lorraine the only one who had noticed it? Walter's sense of smell was well developed and Henry's was perfectly normal. Walter played the part of the rationalist. "You and I were too focused on Lorraine to notice it," he said. Henry reminded Walter that the windows of West

Dorm had been closed while Lorraine was in a trance, and that several students had also smelled meat. He could see that Walter was losing interest in the idea of a manifestation that took the form of cooked, or cooking, flesh. Walter had tightened his mouth into a firm line and was rubbing an imaginary spot on the knees of his trousers.

Waiting silently on a straight-backed chair, Lorraine Drago was embarrassed by her lack of success. She had brought back one small pearl from the depths and now its authenticity was being questioned. She was more than ready to believe her perceptions were false. Her gift had begun to dwindle in the last few years, perhaps from lack of practice, perhaps because she was too successful in business. She had been foolish and vain to respond to pressure from Henry and Walter. Except for those few sessions in the Duke University laboratories, she had never performed well when she was the center of attention. However unreliable her gift, Lorraine was too fair-minded to back out before her task was finished. She had promised to examine our attic and she always kept her promises. I was typing at the kitchen table when the front door opened. I heard Lorraine say, "Let me just nip upstairs for a minute. I'll go by myself."

Lorraine was gone a short time, only twenty minutes or so. She came up dry, for Henry's purposes, although I learned she had seen the figure of a woman in a long-sleeved nightdress and ruffled nightcap on her knees by the Beaulac bed, saying her prayers. A young woman with a pronounced nose and heavy, dark eyebrows that met in the middle, she resembled the miniature portrait, inherited by my mother, of my great-great-great Aunt Sévérine. There was nothing to account for Sévérine's appearance on this occasion, or any other. Her life had been fruitful but humdrum. She lived seventy years, bore nine children, and died in her sleep in the early 1850s. Of course, it is possible she was praying for the soul of her youngest daughter, Laure, who had eloped with a dissolute French Catholic.

What was Henry left with after all his sleuthing? A considerable deficit, in my opinion. His recruits were showing signs of vacillation. Walter began talking about how tied up he'd be with the antiques show in Portland, for which he'd been commissioned to supply the flowers and do the arrangements. Lorraine pleaded that summer was the busiest season for real estate agencies. She was unlikely to want to risk failure soon again. She was too mortified to take heart from the fact that she had seen a real ghost, if I may put it that way. Her sighting delighted my mother, but it disappointed Henry. Henry had lost a measure of confidence in Lorraine. Any other time he wouldn't have felt he had to double-check her findings. Since she had proved herself to be an ineffective lightning rod, he offered himself up instead, "just to see if I get anything."

It was a genuine sacrifice to sleep in the attic in the current heat wave. All an electric fan could do was push the hot air around. Henry came down the next morning with black circles under his eyes from tossing and turning, but not from encounters with specters.

PART VI

Christ to the Left of Us

Chapter Sixteen

Ever since the First World War the church festival had been held on August 15, the feast of the Assumption of the Virgin Mary. The wartime incumbent and his vestry picked that date because the festival was, in large part, a celebration of women's work—needlecraft, cookery, gardening, flower arranging. Contributions from the kitchen, the garden, and the Dorcas Guild still produced most of the income from the fair, although we had added booths to display and sell local arts and crafts. Headed by Ralph Hiram, the men of the parish ran the lunch room and the pancake tent. When I married Henry, I immediately put myself in charge of the bake sale, which was now so well stocked and so superior it attracted people from the summer colonies along the coast. Our standard was high: no cakes with the top layer slipping sideways; no items made with packaged mixes; no recipes that called for the inclusion of jelly beans, gumdrops, or any other candy sold in movie theaters; piecrust made with Crisco only; a large selection of breads, rolls, and muffins. As a spur to vanity as well as enterprise, ribbons were awarded in five categories: yeast breads, quick breads, cookies, pies, and cake decoration.

This year—like most years—I was one of the judges, along with Jane Morse, Sally Bissell, and Ruth Hiram. I had scarcely seen my friends since the Burridge exigency. In early July I called a meeting of the bake sale committee, hoping it would give us a chance to spend time together.

At the small-town level, all committee meetings were two-thirds gossip and one-third work. This meeting was a disappointment in both respects. Everyone was late and no one apologized for it. When we were all assembled, it took them a while to settle down. Sally made a telephone call. Ruth got up twice to get more ice for her glass of lemonade. Jane leafed through the magazines on the coffee table. At last they sat back in their chairs and looked at me expectantly. Instead of jumping in and all talking at once, which was our custom, riding over the ends of one another's sentences, reading thoughts, they were waiting for me to take the lead.

"What do you want us to do?" asked Sally. "I can't think in this heat," said Jane. "I haven't slept for weeks," Ruth said, with that hint of smugness common to insomniacs. I went down the agenda as briskly as possible, divided up the list of women who had baked last year and ought to be approached again, stuck Sally with the job of designing the booth and the printed labels, asked Jane if she was ready to launch her *savarin*. Their lack of interest was obvious. Sally and Ruth kept asking me to repeat myself. Jane was taking notes with her right hand, while her left hand was always touching some part of her body, stroking her neck, kneading her upper arm, removing one sandal and rubbing her foot.

They left as soon as our business was concluded, another departure from custom. Usually we refilled our cups or glasses and did some catching up. Today they were unwilling to linger long enough to fix a date for our next meeting, so I would have to round them up by telephone. As I cleared away the glasses and plates (no one had eaten a single one of my shortbread hearts), I wavered between hurt feelings and irritation. I had a large—you might say an exaggerated—stake in the success of the bake sale, but it had never alienated my friends before. In fact, they used to tease me about it. Perhaps I was taking their coolness too personally. It was not as if they had presented a united front, all three radiating a concentrated hostility toward me. On the contrary, each of them had seemed to be in a private world of her own. Sally's behavior was especially distracted. I don't believe she heard a word we said. Her expression flickered on and off between a smile and a little frown, as if in response to some troubling inner dialogue. If we were teenagers and still in high school, I would have said my friends were keeping secrets from me.

Two days later Sally stopped by to make excuses for her behavior at the meeting. I had difficulty accepting her explanation but was trying not to show it. She had brought me some pots of Roman chamomile, which was reseeding itself too liberally in one of her borders. If the plants were intended as a peace offering, I would have been better pleased by a few divisions of her expensive red daylily, the only variety that came close to a true fire engine. Sally took off her battered straw hat. Her short blond hair was plastered to her head and her right eye was bloodshot. The heat was having its toll on our looks as well as our spirits.

Sally had come to bring news that was not very welcome to me. "I'm happy for your sake," I said. "For all of your sakes." "I wouldn't be so generous in your place," said Sally. I gestured at the flower beds. "Can I give you anything of mine?" "All right," she said. "Do you have any lavender to spare? It loves this weather." I picked up a trowel and a six-inch plastic pot. "No, not now," said Sally. "Sit down and talk to me." "Stay where you are. I'll get us some ginger ale." "I don't want any," she said. "You're trying to dodge me. I've upset you." I perched on the edge of a bench, ready to bolt if the conversation took an offensive turning. With envy and spite and all uncharitableness I told Sally she didn't look like a woman who was having a second honeymoon. "You look as if you're coming down with something," I said.

We had never formed a club for wives of sexless marriages. If we had, I would be its only surviving member. According to Sally, the rest had fallen by the wayside. I was obliged to hear that Jane believed she was pregnant, while Ruth reported that her Ralph was "making overtures." It seemed Ford was approaching Sally every night, and completing his approaches. If she looked hag-ridden, it was because he feasted on her from the small hours until daybreak, robbing her of rest. As a sop to me, or so I thought, she permitted herself to complain about his new insatiability. Although Ford had always been "athletic," she confessed, he was good for only one round a night, at least until now. Once she was asleep, he would never have dreamed of rousing her for sex. As concerned for her pleasure as for his own, he had always encouraged her to ask for what she wanted. His manners, social and sexual, were beyond reproach, as were his habits of personal grooming. Ford could work outdoors all day without getting dirty or sweat-stained or ruining the crease in his khaki trousers. He kept his work clothes as immaculate as his dress clothes, his nose hairs clipped and his chin free of stubble. He exuded a constant reminder of his most recent ablutions, of soap and spicy shaving lotion.

If I were inclined to believe Sally's story, Ford had begun to forget his manners along with his deodorant. Once, he had given all her sensitive areas equal attention, so that her earlobes were never less privileged than her nipples. Now his target was exclusively genital. She woke up to find him pinning her down. "He doesn't care if I've finished," she said. "He keeps pushing at me." They had always reached climax with their mouths fastened together in a kiss. She was grateful he no longer tried to kiss her. She inhaled his sour breath on her neck and remembered when his mouth had tasted of mint. He used to whisper to her while he aroused her, borrowing love words from classical pornography. Now he was silent except for occasional "snurfling" noises.

It was the paramount duty of friendship to be an ungrudging listener, to remove one's ego as far as possible from the equation. I wanted to blame Sally for abusing my generosity, when all she had done was reach its limits. Either to spare my feelings or stave off my resentment, she was downgrading her own good fortune—a common but ineffective female tactic. I cut her lamentations short and said she should be talking to her husband, not to me. She hung her head. "I can't do that. You can't do that to a man."

All at once I wondered if my friendship with Sally was a friendship of convenience. We lived a few miles apart. We were the same age. We loved cooking and gardening. Now I found there was a gap between us. I felt honesty had a place in sex; she believed it was on a footing with emasculation. She was excited by old-fashioned dirty words. If Henry ever tried referring to my "tickler," "quim," or "pouters," I would have died laughing, unless he started laughing first. Were the differences between me and Sally drastic or manageable? Was I inventing a rift where there was none because I was envious of her? On the whole, I would rather have neighbors than friends. The lines between neighbors were clear-cut. You fed their cat when they were away for the weekend. They watered your houseplants ditto. You were not required to follow them into the bedroom, or listen to tales that should be told only to a sex therapist.

In order to regain the initiative and salvage my friendly feelings, I decided to ask questions. While Sally was making her confession, I had been pacing up and down, unable to meet her eye. Now I sat down opposite her, knee to knee, and patted her hands, which were clenched in her lap. A yellow jacket was browsing in her sweat-soaked hair. I brushed it away. She went on explaining how she couldn't talk to Ford but had tried to send a message indirectly. "I let him fall asleep, then I left the bed and went to the guest room. Sometimes I did that when I had a cold. I had a night to myself, but the next night he followed me. He stayed a long time, then I felt him leaving. When I got up he was still asleep in our room." She anticipated my next question. "I couldn't," she said. "Besides, we never had keys to the bedrooms."

I had shown none of Sally's wifeliness. I'm sure I broadcast my frustration every night by some unconscious gesture—a brisk "goodnight" unaccompanied by a kiss, an abrupt withdrawal if one of Henry's extremities brushed one of mine. I was only getting what I deserved. Every other husband was back on the job, except for Henry. I wanted to know what Sally had done to make Ford feel desire again. What actions had she taken? What wiles had she practiced? What perfume had she been wearing? I asked her to think back to the day itself and review the circumstances that led up to the renewal of his ardor.

Sally said that day had been busier than usual, full of extra chores. In the morning she had interviewed housekeepers for her father-in-law, and picked up the thank-offering envelopes from the printer in East Windham. At lunchtime the orchids had arrived, delivered in boxes with labels all over them warning OPEN IMMEDIATELY. She unpacked them and put them in her window greenhouse, recently installed.

I knew how it went with orchid lovers. Eventually she would build a separate glass building to house her new hobby, then several additions to that building. Orchids were the one horticultural topic on which Sally and I disagreed. Orchids hypnotized people. They were creatures of air, not earth, overpowerful and sinister. Their breeders neglected the earth for their sake. You could tell the gardens of orchid fanciers by their lack of bloom. They didn't bother to prune the shrubs or cull dead flowers. These gardeners had transferred their allegiance to the greenhouse, a temple where they worshipped little gods that grew on sticks and blocks of wood. Sally was bound to follow their example, and I would be left without a companion to share the driving on day trips to flower shows and nurseries.

For the present, however, she was still devoted to dirt gardening and all it entailed. That afternoon she drove the station wagon to a beauty shop in Naples, where the owner had collected several bags full of hair clippings for her. Human hair was supposed to be a deer repellent, and Sally's lily beds were under siege, especially on the wooded side of her property. She left two of the sacks in the shed and brought the other one into the kitchen. She spread sheets of newspaper on the floor around the table where she had assembled her equipment—a pile of old nylon tights, sharp scissors, and a ball of garden twine. She went to work stuffing wads of hair into sections of stocking, tying them at both ends to make neat balls. The hair balls could be hung from branches, attached to stakes, or distributed over the ground. As she worked, hair sprinkled to the floor or fell in clumps, covering the newspaper with a patchwork of colors—red, yellow, gray, black, brown, and white.

Before long she regretted her decision to work indoors. Hair was everywhere, visible and invisible, clinging to her knees, layering her socks and sneakers, drifting off the paper toward other rooms, as silent as dust. She found she did not enjoy handling it. "It felt alive," she said, "especially the gray hair." Since her hairdresser cut heads dry, before the shampoo, it followed that the hair he had given her was dirty. Piling up on the paper beneath her, it gave off "a kind of warmth," as she described it, not a smell but an atmosphere. Hair was prized by practitioners of magic because it retained a magnetic link with the person from whom it was taken. Sally wondered how many souls had to be shorn before you could fill two thirty-gallon garbage bags, and whether she had, in some way, invited all of them into her kitchen.

Putting these notions aside, she began the job of cleaning up. She swept the floors and wiped off the counters—but hair reappeared where hair had been banished, as in a bewitchment. That evening she found hair in the bowl of the food processor when she began making béarnaise sauce for the filet steak, Ford's favorite dish. When she turned down the bed later on, she saw a scattering of reddish-brown hairs on the bottom sheet. They had gained passage to the upper story by stowing away on her feet or her clothing. She ripped the sheets off the bed and made it up with fresh ones. That night, while Ford was poised above her, ready to enter her after a year's abstention, she was suddenly aware of an itch between her shoulder blades, and another on the back of her knee traveling down to her ankle, an invasion of itches, caused by sharp, sticky hairs on the loose in the bedroom. Sally vacuumed every day for a week, but she still came across them now and then in intimate places—on the skin beneath her watchband, in the pages of her prayer book, on her powder puff.

Looking back over Sally's day (orchids, housekeepers, printers, hair balls), I saw nothing to suggest she had baited a trap for Eros. Her activities seemed irrelevant to sex, if not positively antierotic. At the end of such a day, Ford should have found her irritable and unkempt, in no way an object of lust for a man whose fires had been heaped with ashes. That night after supper I gave Henry an account of this cycle of sexual revival among our friends, having first ascertained that he was in a good humor and that the vestry had voted to buy a more efficient copying machine with Judge Harvey's bequest. We sat outside at the very table where Sally had unburdened herself, surrounded by bug candles sunk in tin buckets, flavoring the air with citronella. I provided us with hot tea, sometimes more cooling in the heat than iced drinks. Throughout the narration my manner was as detached and comradely as possible, as if we were two professors enjoying a brandy in the faculty club lounge.

Henry was wary at first, but my behavior soon reassured him. He did not suspect for a moment that I might be pointing a moral about our own infirm sex life. Instead, he imagined I had brought him more data for his paranormal research. During these summer doldrums he seemed inspired to find data wherever he looked, like an ancient soothsayer who used anything at hand—gizzards, bones, pebbles, straws—to make his predictions. I never knew what details he might seize on. I was surprised by his interest in the human hair. I thought he would be far more intrigued by the change in Ford's style of lovemaking. His response to her method of repelling deer seemed to be based on Scripture. He wanted to know if the beauty shop in Naples had male clients as well as female. I assured him that the hair in those sacks had been taken entirely from women. Distracted by his thoughts, Henry poured himself a fresh cup of tea, letting the liquid brim over into his saucer. I knew my Bible well enough to recognize that he was quoting from Corinthians when he said, "Is it comely that a woman pray unto God uncovered?" St. Paul went on to say that women must put something on their heads in church "because of the angels."

I was always late to church as a child, trying to find a covering for my head, a hat that wasn't too embarrassing, a scarf to match my dress, a clean, ironed handkerchief. I didn't understand if wearing hats was a sign of respect or a mark of shame. My grandfather Beaulac, who had no religion, explained that angels looking down from heaven were supposed to fall in love with women's hair. I asked him why we covered just the tops of our heads. Couldn't the angels see the rest of our hair beneath our hats, and our bangs sticking out of our head scarves? In more primitive communities, said my grandfather, women were required to wrap their heads. Perhaps my husband could explain, since my grandfather couldn't, what sort of angels these were that human women were admonished not to tempt them, as teenaged girls of my generation had been warned not to lead boys on. I was taught in Sunday school that angels were God's messengers, arrows shot from His side. They partook of His goodness and loving kindness. They had no bodies. They appeared to children who were lost in the forest and guided them home. According to St. Paul, however, angels were not only lustful but also somehow blameless, since women carried the blame.

For a consecrated priest, Henry had some curious ideas about angels. In the Book of Genesis, at the time of Noah, angels hovered close to earth, consorting with human beings. "The sons of God saw the daughters of men that they were fair," recited Henry. "The sons of God came in unto the daughters of men, and they bare children to them." This union produced a race of giants, superhuman beings whom God destroyed out of jealousy, with the exception of Noah, who found grace in His eyes. Over the centuries, angels were relegated to higher and higher spiritual planes by the theologians. Theologians unsexed the angels and censored the chronicles of their deeds, lest they threaten the absolute power of the One True God.

Christians and Jews banished the angels but could not exterminate them. They have kept coming back, yearning to recapture their former intimacy with human beings. Striving to assume human form, they were sometimes successful, as the Renaissance painters have testified, but often they got it wrong, producing a faint flickering outline or simply an inchoate mass, the rude suggestion of a human presence. In their partial or imperfect manifestations, there was nothing to distinguish them from demons, hungry in their own right for fleshly contact. Henry pushed his argument as far as it would go, ending on a question: was there one primal entity? or many entities? one supernatural force that had collected many names in different eras and different cultures? Thus the Greeks labeled gods and goddesses what the Celts called fairies and nature spirits and Western Europeans named angels and devils. I took Henry's cup and saucer, which were sitting on his knee and about to slide off. He was all wrapped up in the notion that the supernatural needs human beings to acknowledge it. "We have visitors here in Dry Falls," he said. "I wonder what we'll call them." He said he thought a name would eventually be forced upon us.

"We were talking about Ford and Sally," I reminded him. "We seem to have wandered off the subject." Henry gave me a frown. He was surprised I could have missed the connection, and so was I. If I had been slow to keep up with him it was because I disliked his ideas and resisted putting them into words. I did not want to think of Ford Bissell as the puppet of an unclean spirit who had been lured from another dimension into ours. I did not want to have to worry about the threat to Sally, or the threat to Ruth, if it came to that. Ruth used hair in her garden too, but she spread it loose around the plant, like a mulch, instead of tying it up in nylon. There was no link between Sally's sexual beleaguerment, Hannah's fear of our attic, the Burridge seniors' drugged sleep, and Helen's optical illusions. Henry needed to spin these webs in order to compensate for feelings of emptiness, to fill the hollow place where his priestly vocation used to be.

I detested the scenarios Henry was imagining. In all of them, the supernatural invaded our domesticity, fastened onto the details of our everyday lives, and sucked the color out of them, like aphids on the leaves of African violets. There were so many things we did in all innocence: simmered beef for stew; grew the tallest sunflowers and the fattest tomatoes; soaked in the tub; crafted hair balls to keep deer away; burned candles, as Adele did, instead of turning the electric lights on. Would there soon be a time when we would have to censor the smallest act of sensual gratification, the most natural, automatic gesture: dabbing perfume on our pulse spots, picking peaches and letting the juice run down our chins? A time when sexual release would be taboo, and all the stages leading up to it? When sexual thoughts and feelings would also require suppression, because they were capable of attracting the Unembodied by the swarms, like the scent used in Japanese beetle traps? Under this regimen of fear the human race would die out for lack of breeding, as did the Shakers and the members of the Oneida community.

I rose abruptly and began to load the tea tray, taking Henry's half-filled cup out of his hand. "I wasn't finished," he reproached me. "I'm going in now," I said. "Stay out as long as you like." That night I sat up until Henry had gone to bed, claiming that I had reading to do, a book of recipes from Maine inns and restaurants for possible review in my food column. I slept in my clothes on the sofa. I wanted to distance myself from Henry and his love of shadows.

Years ago Henry had performed an exorcism at a house in Poland Springs, where sounds of weeping could be heard. By the power of his faith he had reprieved the unhappy spirit and allowed her to move on. Exorcism is a form of psychic healing. Both exorcist and healer run the risk of taking on pain or even injuries that belong to their subject. Henry experienced no ill effects that time, unless you counted a slight case of laryngitis—hoarseness, really—that lasted less than a week and didn't prevent him from preaching on Sunday. Recently Bishop Hollins had asked him to do another exorcism, this time on holy ground, or very near it. At a small community of Anglican nuns outside of Bridgton, there was a wandering cold spot on the second floor of the retreat house, only fifteen feet away from the tiny chapel. Henry refused because the dates conflicted with his rotation at the psychiatric hospital. He was wise to turn it down. Face to face with a malicious spirit, a doubting priest had about the same chance as a cornered mouse with a cat. How could Henry protect the women of his own parish from the encroaching shadows, real or imaginary? Figuratively speaking, he was holding the door open for them, welcoming them in, when he should have been developing a sound immigration policy. As Henry had counted on God to guide and sustain him, I counted on Henry to distinguish truth from illusion. Did losing your faith in higher authorities mean losing your devotion to them? It was always so with God. I hoped it was not the case with a husband.

I woke up to find former mentor and lover bending over me. To my great relief, my heart still opened to him. On his face I could read both hurt and perplexity, as well as a deep reluctance to talk about them. I sat up and rubbed my cheek. During sleep the pattern of the slipcover had been embossed on my skin. Henry smiled and offered to bring me a mirror. He said next time he was going to come down and carry me upstairs bodily. The smell of coffee wafted in from the kitchen, along with the aroma of freshly made toast. I didn't doubt for a second that he had also squeezed oranges for juice and emptied the dishwasher. By just such delicate adjustments are human connections restored to stability before they swing permanently out of balance.

Chapter Seventeen

We were approaching the Feast of Mary Magdalene, July 22, a red-letter day on the church calendar. Since the risen Jesus appeared to Mary Magdalene before he showed himself to his disciples, she is honored at a special service of evening prayers. At St. Anthony's the flowers on the altar were always red on her feast day, although these may not include roses. All the red flowers came from my mother's annual garden—salvia, snapdragons, cockscomb, dahlias, and zinnias. As a favor to the altar guild, I offered to pick them a day ahead and keep them in water. Mariette Roque and the other guild members were intimidated by Emily, who followed close behind them as they picked and often took the clippers out of their hands. Mariette in particular was apt to pick too many. Emily had also caught her breaking stems with her fingers, nearly pulling up an entire plant. Although her flower beds were characterized by profusion, Emily could be oddly ungenerous about sharing their harvest.

In her fastness on Mt. Pughole, Emily's eldest child might as well have moved back to Albany, for all I saw of her. Emily drove up the mountain to visit her, uninvited, walking the last part of the way to spare her old car. When she returned she passed on bits of information to me, so I was not surprised when I saw one of Hannah's black obelisks installed in the tiny garden adjoining the historical society. Hannah did not communicate with us directly. When Henry decided to clean out the gutters over the July 4 weekend, he looked everywhere for the extension ladder. I took it for granted that Hannah had swooped down in her van and taken it, but we found it leaning against the back of the church, where the roofers had left it. I had expected I would keep running into her in town, like it or not. I assumed she would be dropping by our house for showers and free meals, and using my cupboards and icebox as a convenience store. When a thorn in your side is removed, the place where the thorn was lodged smarts for a while. At first I missed the irritation. Then I forgot about my sister, as I had long been accustomed to do, knowing that at some inopportune moment she would take center stage again.

In Dry Falls the rumor mills grind slower than in some villages. The flow of information was sluggish, encountering numerous blockages such as Yankee skepticism, lack of imagination, and overriding personal concerns or crises. News of the Burridge seniors' mysterious disorder trickled into the public awareness through an obvious conduit, Trooper Centrella's answering service. The daytime operator lived in Windham, but her nephew was married to Ernie Silver's daughter, Carol, who called her father from her home in Waldoboro. Ernie listened with half an ear. He was calculating the amount of cold cuts, rolls, and macaroni salad the Chamber of Commerce would eat when they came in for their monthly lunch meeting. Mary Fran Rawls was out front refilling ketchup bottles and salt shakers. Something she overheard Ernie saying piqued her curiosity and she asked him to explain it. While he was telling her, she accidentally knocked over a napkin dispenser, which brought a glass bud vase and two plastic sprigs of lily of the valley down with it, driving Ernie's story out of her head until after quitting time.

When I finally got wind of the rumor, the school had been closed for vacation for several weeks. Peggy McClintock, who came up from Philadelphia to spend the summers, invited me to tea to discuss "the Burridge scandal." Thirty years ago, Peggy had been expelled from Burridge for running a three-volume lending library—*Forever Amber*, *Lady Chatterley's Lover*, and Casanova's memoirs. She still relished any incident that brought discredit to the school. From Peggy I heard the accepted popular version. The girls had let some boys into the dorm after hours and "things had gotten out of hand." Peggy added an ornament of her own to the story, to the effect that the head nurse had been paid for her silence. Some people believed the school was covering up for rape, and others merely for promiscuity. The gossip increased the town's resentment against a wealthy institution that paid no local taxes, opened its tennis courts to the public for the month of August only, and its swimming pond not at all.

The gossip reached my mother through her next-door neighbor, Marion Smalley. Emily was horrified for Myra Littlefield's sake. She imagined Myra coping with lawsuits, trials, reporters, the ruin of Burridge Academy. In a well-meaning fluster, she appeared on Myra's doorstep, offering to help in any way she could. Myra gave Emily the uncensored version, but begged her not to try to set the record straight. Boys in the dormitory were preferable, on the whole, to the inscrutable facts.

When my mother took fright, she never feared for herself or, I might add, for me. Her fears centered on my sister. In her imagination Hannah was always imperiled, either by fate or because of her own wayward nature. A volcanic eruption in Hawaii sent Emily racing to the map, to see how close Hannah lived in Albany to a range of high mountains. The tale of the six drowsy seniors reminded her that Hannah in her cabin was isolated and vulnerable. I recited a list of potentially lethal weapons available to Hannah on her premises—ax, sickle, fire poker, pocket knife, chain saw, automobile jack. Emily became even more agitated, picturing these instruments and tools being used against Hannah instead of by her. She wanted to set off for the mountain right away, but her car was in the garage until the next day, Friday, for work on the transmission. I did not offer to drive her. I had no intention of being roped into this expedition.

There were downpours on the morning of the Feast of Mary Magdalene, torrents of water cascading from the skies—brief in duration but heavy enough to decapitate my delphiniums and wash a second planting of lettuce seedlings out of their furrows. I wondered what the rains had done to the Pughole road and whether Emily had been forced to turn back, her mission aborted. I had never been fond of Mary Magdalene, this saint who was two different people—a psychotic whom Christ exorcised of seven devils and a woman honored above the apostles, to whom the risen Lord said, "Go to my brethren and say unto them, 'I ascend unto my Father.' " It was appropriate that my mother was rushing to my sister's side on this particular day. "Mary" was derived from the Aramaic word for "rebellion," and Hannah was marked by her resistance to authority, one of her private devils. In spite of her devils, or because of them, she was an artist who was true to her art and did not work for worldly gain. Perhaps she was reserved for some extraordinary fate, like Mary Magdalene. Certainly she was honored above all other daughters.

It was Aaron Schmidt himself, of Schmidt's Auto Shop, who found Emily walking on Route 243, a mile beyond the turnoff to the mountain road, six miles in all from Hannah's cabin. "She was weaving," he told us later, "wandering into the road. I thought she might be heat-struck." Emily was headed away from Dry Falls in the direction of Poland Springs, unaware of where she was going, unable to see through a rage of tears. It was more than Aaron could handle, a gray-haired woman moaning in a broken voice and beating her breast within the sight of passing motorists, who slowed down at first, perhaps to help, then sped off when they observed her disarray. Aaron's first thought was for Emily's transmission, so recently repaired but in need of replacement before the winter. He reasoned astutely that a breakdown miles from her house was not the cause of her moaning. He had many female customers, some of whom used tears to persuade him of an emergency—but none had been reduced to so woeful a state by mere vehicular failure, even in the passing lane of the Maine Turnpike.

With a sense of relief Aaron recalled that Dr. Bayer's office, always open on Saturdays, was on the road back to town, only a few minutes' drive. He led Emily into the waiting room and let Gail Croft, Dr. Bayer's receptionist, take charge of her. By the time Dr. Bayer saw her, she was dry-eyed. If she had been weaving as she walked, she told him, it was because she'd broken her spectacles and he knew how blind she was. Her car wouldn't start so she'd been obliged to walk, quite a long walk in shoes that fit badly and gave her blisters. Of course she had tears in her eyes. The blisters had broken and her heels were rubbed raw. Emily's version contradicted Aaron Schmidt's report, but Pete Bayer was a busy doctor, not a detective. He didn't have time to get to the bottom of it, so he prescribed a cortisone salve and five milligrams of a widely used tranquilizer, to be taken as needed. Emily asked Gail to call the town taxi. Gail said Matt Redmond charged an arm and a leg and suggested she call me. Emily refused, so I didn't see her until three days later, when I was scheduled to pick her up and take her to one of her Huguenot Society meetings, held in the library's rare-book room. When she opened the door, I was rendered speechless by the sight of her.

Emily reeked of loss. Every aspect of her appearance proclaimed her inconsolable. Her coarse gray hair, flattened in back and wild on the sides, had not been groomed since she'd slept on it, and it was obvious she hadn't done much sleeping. Her face was drained of all color except for the lines in her forehead, which were etched in red. Her short-sleeved shirt was creased and stained and her faded denim skirt was darkened by dirt at the hem. The right lens in her eyeglasses was cracked. I couldn't let her go to the meeting looking as if she'd been shot in the head and smelling, I soon perceived, somewhat organic. If the state of the kitchen was any evidence, she hadn't eaten, although it was clear she had intended to. Dishes of food sat untouched on the counter: sandwiches curling up at the edges; salad greens turned dark from lying too long in dressing; a bowl of beet soup that had fermented, as I could see from its unquiet surface.

Emily followed me into the kitchen and stood at the screen door looking out at her garden, shaking her head, as if the sight of so much gaiety and color offended her. When she turned to face me I saw her mouth was set in anger, a jangling note in such a show of sorrow. Emily's appearance betrayed her emotion, but her manner was calm, even stately. Her composure so impressed and humbled me that I forgot to question the source of her suffering. I only felt a desire to attend to her. I heated broth from a can and sat with her while she sipped it as a courtesy to me. Afterward I thew away the uneaten food, washed the dishes, and swept the kitchen floor. I persuaded her to skip the meeting and stretch out on the sofa. I advised her not to try to sleep, just to rest her eyes. I sat in an armchair at her head and waited until I heard a gentle wheezing and saw her eyelids quiver. Only when she was safely asleep did I begin to wonder what had injured her. I concluded that only the person she loved most could have hurt her so deeply, and that person was my sister.

Chapter Eighteen

Emily got all the way up the Pughole road in her rusty car, skirting crevices and washouts, parking on the meadow below Hannah's cabin. It was seven o'clock in the evening, with two hours before the light faded completely. There was no sign of life in the cabin or behind it. She pressed the horn timidly to announce her presence and started up the rise with a bag of treats and groceries—licorice ropes, giant olives with pimiento centers, cheese tortilla chips, as well as new potatoes and chard from her garden, and the pick of her raspberries. In the trunk of the car were a hooked rug in a pattern of blocks (old, valuable, and my grandmother's) and a long-handled dustpan and brush, purchased from a catalogue. She made several attempts to carry everything at once, but she couldn't manage it. It was a good thing she had forgotten the carton of art books from Hannah's old room.

Emily was not made welcome, in spite of the gifts she bore. Breathing fast after two trips up the meadow from the car, she tried the cabin door and found it locked. Cupping her hands around her eyes, she peered in the window. All she could see was Hannah's unmade bed. She peered in the window on the other side of the door and scanned the room. At one end stood the fieldstone fireplace. The hearth, stacked with paint cans, was being used as a storage bin. On the opposite side of the room was a wooden table with a battered book propped under one leg. The surface of the table was scarred, as if someone had been stubbing cigarettes out on it. Around the table were four decent Windsor chairs, old enough to be called antiques. In one of the chairs, writing or sketching, sat Hannah with her back to the window.

Emily rapped on the pane. Hannah failed to turn around, so she knocked on the door. Emily knew her habits. When Hannah got a new idea for a piece of sculpture, she was deaf to the world, unaware, even, that she was working in a stifling room with the door and windows closed. She was so removed from the world that its demands made no impression on her. Thus she could hear a knocking on the door perfectly well, but it conveyed no more urgency than one of the sound effects on a television set. Emily knocked again. She called her daughter's name loudly. Her voice broke on the high note. She stopped to clear her throat before she tried again. She could not produce enough volume to achieve her purpose, although she did summon up an echo down the meadow. Through the window she could see that Hannah was no longer moving an implement across a sheet of paper. She was leaning back in the chair with her arms folded over her chest.

There were windows on the long sides of the cabin. Hannah was facing one of the windows. If Emily went around back and looked in, Hannah could not fail to see her. There was an opening, large enough for Emily, between two overgrown honeysuckle bushes. The ground behind the cabin was littered with dead branches, and sawdust and logs piled haphazardly. The hand saw was lying on the ground where it would attract rust and where anyone could trip on it. Hannah had borrowed the saw from Henry, but she was as careless with other people's possessions as she was with her own. Emily picked her way over to the window. She had a clear view of the room and its occupant. Now Hannah had her chair turned in the other direction, facing the porch. She was smoothing a piece of crumpled paper over her knee, presumably a discarded sketch she had decided to salvage. Emily clenched her fists in frustration. She rounded the cabin for the second time, moving cautiously through the log-littered yard, snagging her sleeve on a honeysuckle branch.

As she approached the front window she expected to see Hannah's back, as if this were a bad dream in which she was the loser in a cruel parlor game. The chair had not been moved. Gazing inside, she looked straight into her daughter's eyes. Filled with elation, she waved, tapped, and called out, then stood back and waited for the door to open. When it didn't open, she peered in again. Hannah was looking at her without seeing her, or without acknowledging the fact that she saw her. As the expression goes, she was looking right through her. Emily caught her breath. For a moment her emotions hung in the balance, suspended between embarrassment and misery. This private snub was more painful than a cut administered in a social setting before an audience of sharp-eyed gossips. With no real hope that she might be mistaken, Emily raised her arm to signal her once more. She froze in mid-gesture. Hannah stood up and moved closer to the window. Her cold stare could not be misinterpreted.

Either a masochist or a philosopher, Emily did not take suffering personally. If Hannah had chosen to deny her existence, there must be a reason for it. When the family was living under one roof, Hannah had seen her father ignore her mother, pass by her or occupy the same room without speaking to her any more than he would have greeted a piece of the furniture. She had watched Emily accept his behavior without questioning it. Emily had sanctioned Francis Whitman's conduct years before, and, by extension, her elder daughter's. Emily blamed herself for arriving at a time when Hannah resented an interruption, or when she was expecting someone else. She might be expecting a man. Emily had never met one of her men, but she knew they lived in a culture from which family ties had been banished.

Emily walked back over the meadow to her car, putting one foot in front of the other by an effort of will. She got into the car and turned it around, coasting slowly toward the road. A little way down the road she braked abruptly and turned off the engine. From this position the cabin was invisible. It stood to reason she was invisible from the cabin. There was food and drink in the car, another bag of packaged snacks and a bottle of ginger ale. She could lie across the back seat to sleep, or tilt the front seat backward. In the morning Hannah's mood might have changed. By morning she would know if Hannah had had a visitor. Emily wanted to be in Hannah's vicinity rather than alone at home, cut off from the sight of her. As long as she was near her, the pain she felt was the pain of waiting, not of abandonment.

. . .

The light was fading fast. The moon was in its last quarter. When her eyes had adjusted to the gloom, Emily opened the car door slowly, leaving it ajar lest the sound of its closing should carry. She crept up the road, faltering where her feet met loose stones. Her rashness so appalled her that she felt her two legs might not support her. Step by step she ascended, until she saw the roof of the cabin above the rise. She turned left at the edge of the meadow, picking her way toward a stand of dog rose, *Rosa canina*, a tall, dense shrub well armed with hooked thorns, no place to seek cover. A little farther on was an old lilac, surrounded by unpruned shoots growing up from the base, which formed an adequate barrier to hide behind. From here she could see the whole outline of the cabin against the sky. Behind the windows flickered light from candles as well as the steadier glow of a kerosene lamp. Were the candles auxiliary lighting or a signal? Or was someone inside already, who had approached from the opposite direction through the woods? Emily sank to the ground, bracing herself against the trunk of an oak tree. In this heat, the ground had dried quickly after the downpour. She felt genuinely light-headed from so much indulgence in conjecture, from Hannah's mistreatment, from the fact that she had staked herself out to spy on her daughter. Every minute brought the chance to turn back. In her lethargy she argued that she had until sunrise to make the decision.

It may be that Emily fell asleep or, in the turmoil of her emotions, failed to perceive time passing. She could not otherwise account for the hours between midnight and four a.m. When she came to her senses, she was first of all aware of hunger and a crick in her neck; then she noticed that the lights in the cabin were burning no less brightly than before, as if the candles had been replaced or added to. The flickering light evoked human shapes moving restlessly about, an effect, it seemed safe to suppose, of Emily's state of mind. Any idea of stealing up to look through the windows deserted her. Hannah was not sleeping. She was awake for a purpose not intended for a mother's knowledge.

From her infancy Hannah had pulled away from Emily, wriggling out of her arms, refusing the breast. By the third day of her life she had her mother feeding her entirely by bottle. She started to walk so early that she is mentioned in the medical literature, but Emily knew she was impelled by a need to escape from maternal embraces. She tried to run before she walked. Emily watched her topple over again and again, screaming if she tried to pick her up. Once she rolled down the staircase. Blood was pouring out of her nose, but she wouldn't let Emily near her until she had tried to walk again, and succeeded. Thus Emily was conditioned to believe that Hannah was always in danger. For forty-one years that thought had oppressed her mind. The greater danger, however, lay in acting on the impulse to rescue her. Then as now, Hannah would react to her mother's concern by rejecting her.

The night died slowly, like a person with a wasting disease. Emily watched it linger past all hope of remission, fading into transparency. The lights in Hannah's windows were burning lower, fading along with the darkness. When the sun rose, it would still be several hours before bright morning. If Hannah had been working all night, she might sleep all day. In that gray predawn hour every symptom of aging was more acute. Emily's neck was in spasm. The joints in her fingers were inflamed. Her knees and ankles were swollen. She lowered herself to the ground and lay flat on her back on a rough surface scattered with twigs and acorn caps. This time she slept deeply and awoke with the sun on her face.

During the heat wave, which had lasted so long we thought of it as a new weather pattern, the sun felt as hot at nine a.m. as it did at noontime. Until she consulted her wristwatch, Emily was panicked, thinking she had overslept. As it was, she might already have missed various comings and goings up at the cabin. In broad daylight she saw that the door was half open. She was instantly aware that her lurking place was more exposed than she had realized. She ducked behind the oak tree, whose trunk was more than twice her girth. She wondered how long it would be until she could venture back to the car without being detected. A sense of futility overcame her. If Hannah decided to drive into town, she would see Emily's car. Emily had created a trap for herself. No matter when she went up to the cabin, she was certain to be humiliated and cast out. There was no right moment.

Emily stepped out from behind the tree and looked up at the cabin. The door was open wider. A paint-stained canvas tarp was spread out on the porch, perhaps to dry. Emily tucked in her shirt and shook grit out of her heavy leather sandals. She couldn't see the twigs in her hair or the leaf mold on the seat of her skirt; nor was she aware that she carried her hands clasped in front of her as she walked, like a communicant advancing to the altar rail. Hope of forgiveness always lay close to the surface with Emily. If Hannah was awake and moving about, she had broken out of her mood of frozen concentration. Hannah might deal with her roughly, but Emily would welcome interaction of any kind, including discourtesy. As she waded through the tall grass, accompanied by jumping crickets, she was startled by something gliding across the top of her foot. She looked down at the ground and saw a garter snake making his escape. When she looked up again, she saw Hannah coming around from the rear of the cabin. The cabin had no back door. She had climbed out a window.

Before Emily could call out to her Hannah was heading downhill in the direction of the woods, breaking into a run, running faster and faster until it seemed as if she were being flung downward. Emily started after her, but she was so far behind and her knees were so stiff that she had no chance of overtaking her. At times she actually lost sight of her. As she tottered forward, arms held out straight from the shoulders for balance, her spectacles bounced as high as her eyebrows, momentarily blinding her. In order to see at all she had to pause in her pursuit, giving Hannah a greater and greater advantage. When she halted again, lungs bursting and heart skipping in her chest, she was forty feet or so from Hannah and a little above her. Hannah was racing toward a pool of scarlet, a growth of red flowers with blotched papery petals, some variety of poppy.

Poppies belonged to a fleeting period in June. By this time in July there should have been nothing left of them but their blue-green seed cases. Among the poppies were yellowing stalks, the foliage of daffodils. In all her trips to the cabin Emily had never noticed a planting of daffodils, sown so close to tall trees that they'd have received less than half a day's sunlight and should only have bloomed sporadically. On her visits she'd stayed indoors, performing services Hannah hadn't asked for—changing sheets, fighting cobwebs, sweeping sawdust, arranging pieces of lumber in neat stacks against the walls. When she had finished these tasks, she was not encouraged to prolong her stay, to share refreshment or walk the land. Otherwise there would have been many times during the past month when she could have admired these same poppies toward which Hannah was rushing headlong, as if she were flying to the arms of a lover.

What kind of attraction propelled her, she who in her youthful tantrums had pulled up her mother's flowers and trampled them? Nearing the bed of poppies, she reached out with both hands, like a child who is trying to grasp a lovely toy. Before Emily could take a step forward, Hannah plunged into the bed of poppies up to her knees and disappeared from sight. The forest and hillside rang with her shrill voice. Her mother heard her, and their cries intermingled. Later, Emily said, "It was as if the earth had swallowed her alive."

When Emily summoned us to hear her story, Henry, Walter, and Lorraine made more objective listeners than I did. Emily sat on the sofa where she had lain for several weeks, refusing to speak, neglecting her person and her garden. For our meeting she had bathed, put on clean clothes, and prepared a tray of coffee. I could see through the living-room window that she had begun to take the garden in hand. The wheelbarrow was full of weeds, dead blooms, and grass clippings, ready to be added to the compost heap. It was unlike Emily to issue a summons or make any demands on others, but she was greatly altered, like someone who has had a brush with death. Grief had imprinted itself on her deepest nature; grief was her universe.

While we were sipping coffee, waiting for Lorraine to arrive, I tried to commiserate with her about the heat, which had climbed into the nineties throughout the last few weeks, with no respite at night. Since July 22 no rain had fallen. The corn in its husks was parching before it ripened and the pasture lands had withered. Michel Roque dropped bales of hay from a small plane on the far fields to keep his animals from starving. There were such tight restrictions on the use of town water that lawns browned and gardens were perishing. The ivy climbing the bank building had turned yellow, and the marigolds at the base of the war memorial were burned and blackened, like fragments of metal. Emily looked at me indifferently, unconcerned by any circumstances but her own. Once a faint smile crossed her lips, as if she were gratified that the earth which had seized her daughter was being punished in turn.

Those of us who were gathered around her found her manner unrecognizable. Her bearing was queenly, unbending. It was so painful for me to hear her recital that I believe I blanked out many details and some of the connecting parts. Henry took my hand and pressed my arm against his chest, as much to keep me from running away as to comfort me. Everything she told us comes back to me in pictures without sound or captions. I see my mother crawling on her hands and knees through the bed of poppies and around it in wider and wider circles, frantic to find a crack in the earth, a pit, the mouth of a cave, exposing herself gladly to the fate that might have claimed Hannah. I see her stumbling through the forest in the gloom cast by giant trees. Her mouth opens and closes, but I cannot hear her calling. Exhausted and desperate, she leaves the woods and returns to the bed of poppies, where she finds a fine-toothed black pocket comb, a masculine accessory. I see her panting up the meadow to the cabin, sagging with fatigue onto Hannah's cot, pressing a fist against her heart. She picks up her daughter's paint-stained shirt, buries her face in it. She sees Hannah's watch on the bedside table, a cheap man's watch in a steel case with a flexible metal band; she puts it in her pocket, a keepsake, a talisman.

Then I see her approaching her car, reaching out to grasp the door handle, letting her arm fall back to her side, knowing she is incompetent to drive. I see her slip on a scattering of pebbles in the road and stay down for several moments, the only time she paused for rest during her descent. As she makes her way down she is so given over to grief she wraps her arms around herself, leaning forward as she walks like a person battling a headwind.

When I was eight years old, I swam too far out and was caught in a crosscurrent. As it carried me past the rocks that formed the cove, I saw my mother go over to the lifeguard, who grabbed a life jacket and jumped into a kayak. While he paddled out to me, I kept my eyes on my mother, afraid to lose sight of her. Other people were racing up and down the beach, waving their arms excitedly, but she stood at the edge of the water, in up to her ankles, waiting impassively. When I was delivered to her in the arms of the proud young lifeguard, she stood me up, wrapped me in a towel, and gave me a cup of hot soup from a thermos jug. After lunch I was allowed to go back in the water, where I played and swam all afternoon until my skin puckered. Had she reacted hysterically, I would have been frightened of the water for life, but I would have known how much she loved me.

Emily's narration answered none of our questions. She leaned against the back of the sofa, depleted by the effort. Walter, at least, had no scruples about putting pressure on her, however weakened her condition. His thin face was flushed with temper. Emily's daughter had been missing for two weeks and she had done nothing. Her inaction was criminally irresponsible. "You have two choices, Emily. Either you go to the police or I will."

Henry was torn between several reactions. He was concerned for Hannah's safety, but he felt Emily needed protection from further shock. He had seen patients at her precarious level of distress take refuge in total withdrawal. The parapsychologist in him took a more detached view of the situation. Already Emily's memory of the scene was so clouded by emotion as to be unreliable, but he was obliged, in the interests of science, to try and jog it. He went over to the sofa, sat down next to her, and took her hand.

Unable to withstand this sympathetic gesture, Emily broke down and wept, bitter sobs that arose from her belly and shook her whole body. Henry held her close, stroking her hair until she subsided into hiccups, like a child who is overtired.

Walter was pacing, narrowing the distance between himself and the telephone on a table by the fireplace. Henry ordered him back to his seat in a tone that was so threatening it momentarily halted Emily's sobbing. I had been about to intervene myself. Surely we could operate on two planes at once—initiate a practical course of action as well as delve into the mysteries. Emily had made two statements that clashed absurdly: "She has left me," she said; a little later, "she was taken." Anyone who knew Hannah and was aware of her chaotic relations with Emily could imagine a scenario in which the daughter ducked out of sight and stayed hidden in order to torment her mother and punish her for spying on her. I would make it my business to call Bobby Court's sister in South Freeport, Hannah's high school buddies who still lived in the neighborhood, her last set of housemates in Albany. I believed Hannah would show up eventually, if only because she was working on a commission for a private garden in Biddeford and her patron wanted the piece before Labor Day.

Walter might be intimidated by Henry, but I excused myself and slipped upstairs. Henry glanced in my direction without trying to stop me. I closed the door to Emily's bedroom and called Trooper Centrella. When the dispatcher put him through, I gave him a watered-down description of the events, implying that the time frame was very recent. Hannah had quarreled with her mother and run off; it had happened before, would he send a man up to Pughole to look around; Hannah might have met with an accident. Emily—and Hannah—would be furious if they knew I was raising the alarm, but Mark Centrella had met Hannah often enough to know she could be acting out of spite and cussedness. "Your sister's a great woman," he said, "but I wouldn't want to be on her bad side."

Lorraine sat apart from the others on the cushioned window seat. Her eyes were closed and in her open palm lay the black rubber comb Emily had found in the bed of poppies. Her eyelids fluttered, but her brow was free of strain. I recognized that she was practicing psychometry, attempting to divine knowledge of the owner of the comb through contact with it. There was a feeling of excitement in the room and a definite odor of complacency such as you might find at a séance or a prayer group, wherever mortal subjects try communing with a higher reality. I don't think Henry saw me come back in or heard me drag my chair a few feet forward, closer to the inner circle.

They were addressing the question of whether Hannah had been "taken," as Emily had put it. Perhaps they had reviewed the evidence of an earthly kidnapping while I was out of the room. If so, they had made short shrift of it. They had wandered quite far from such prosaic considerations as the number of felons, their description, their possible connection with Hannah. They were in the realm of pure speculation and wishful thinking, where dire feelings carried as much weight as observation. "I heard a sound like thunder or an oncoming train," said Emily. I broke in to remind them that there had been no thunderstorms in the region during that period, nor any railroad line closer than the one through Portland.

Rather than cast doubt on Emily's impressions, the facts I advanced seemed to give them added meaning. If nothing in the world accounted for the sounds she had heard, then they must have an otherworldly explanation. "I have never felt such terror," said Emily. "I was paralyzed by it. I couldn't get to her." Henry and Walter nodded in agreement. Apparently the degree of fear experienced by the subject was another indicator of supernatural agency. "I remember looking down," she continued. "I thought my foot was caught in a root. When I looked up, she was gone." Emily had omitted this particular detail the first time around. It seemed to rule out a kidnapping. While Emily's eyes were averted, Hannah would have had time to dash behind a boulder or a tree, but there was scarcely time for a full-dress abduction complete with pouncing, struggling, binding, gagging, and bearing away. If Emily had heard any sounds, she would have looked up instantly.

I was about to donate this bit of logic to the company, but Henry raised a hand to stop me. Emily had something more to add, another item she had left out of her original statement—a genuine oversight on her part, or an embroidery? "It grew dark," she said, "as if a cloud were passing over the sun." As swiftly as any kidnapper stalking his victim, Henry snatched this piece of information and held on to it, leading Emily to make a fuller description of the sudden darkness. She blossomed under his guidance, growing more and more confident. Her story flourished likewise. It was not a cloud across the sun, after all, but a fog that had settled directly in her line of vision, screening the poppy bed. A mass of fog with discrete dimensions, about the size, she proposed, of an old-fashioned wardrobe, like the huge armoire, inherited from Emily's maternal grandmother, that grazed the ceiling of Hannah's girlhood bedroom.

Walter and Henry exchanged a glance. Each of them had been counting the various reports of cloudlike fogs or foglike clouds that had been littering up the case, vagrant data in search of a shelter. Emily's report, plus Mercy's and Helen's, plus Helen's alone, added up to the number three, one integer above coincidence.

Emily's next statement recalled one of Helen's. The fog moved as she moved, "billowing" forth if she advanced and back when she stopped or retreated. "It was warning me off," she said. Henry stood up abruptly, turning his back to the room. Walter put down his pen. I found I was holding my breath. We were no longer discussing a natural, if freakish, event. We had been confronted with an "it" that displayed independent volition and a hint of malice. This single piece of evidence had the power to alter Henry's future. Up to now he had been a dabbler, playing at parapsychology to allay his disappointment with the priesthood. If he accepted a supernatural explanation for Hannah's disappearance, he would be well on his way to changing his professional allegiance.

Henry turned toward us. His face was alight with the flame of certain knowledge, transfigured as it must have been in the trenches of Belgium, when God had addressed him. The Christian god was only one aspect of the supernatural, one Entity among many. Henry's outlook had expanded to include all its other manifestations, however clownish, impure, or ill-conditioned. He had converted, you might say, to polytheism. All at once he was charged with purpose instead of duty. He brought up the matter of keeping careful records. With more enthusiasm than she had shown in many days, Emily agreed to write down everything she had seen in as much detail as she could manage. Walter could transcribe her handwriting into typescript and take notes when Henry conducted formal interviews. Henry described his own notes as a shambles, which had to be decoded. He hoped I would help him collate the witnesses' statements, paying special attention to similar features and similar wording. "We're looking for stable elements," he said. "We still don't know if we're dealing with one phenomenon or more than one." He reminded us, somewhat didactically, that so-called "irrational" events often happen to rational people, whose perceptions can provide us with solid empirical grounding. The more fantastic the event, the greater the need for exhaustive observation and description.

From her seat by the window Lorraine began to shift uneasily. She gripped the comb so tightly it was surely making teeth marks on her palm. Her eyes were open, fixed on some object located in her mind. There was nothing in her line of vision but a patch of cracking plaster on the wall. Rough sounds came from deep in her throat, as if she wanted to speak but had not yet acquired the use of language. Her chest rose and fell in spasms. Still holding the comb, she pressed her fists to her chest, as if to relieve some pressure. Walter rose from his seat to help her, but Henry held him back. Emily was breathing shallowly, in response to Lorraine.

She began to speak in an unfamiliar voice, the voice of a frightened young man with a rustic accent: "I'm in a phone booth. They set me up. I'm gonna make a run for it. You never heard from me, O.K.? You tell them I walked out on you . . . I don't know . . . Get out. Go to Carrie's . . . Jesus. Shit. I'm out of change . . . You hear what I said? *Go to Carrie's . . .*"

Lorraine heaved a sigh, toppling sideways with a grunt onto the window seat, unconscious or asleep. Henry picked up her wrist and felt for a pulse. When he found it was normal, he dropped her arm roughly, irritated by the brevity of her performance and, more so, by its total irrelevance. "That does it," said Walter. "That should teach us." Emily rose from the sofa unaided, left the room, and did not come back again. I heard the kitchen door slam; she was retreating into her garden.

Lorraine was still out, fatigued by her psychic exertions. Poor Lorraine, unfairly denied the credit that was due her. She had tuned in to the owner of the comb—some petty crook double-crossed by his cohorts, but her genuine perception did not conform to the group's agenda. As I saw it, she had done us a favor, by braking this parapsychological freight train, with its cargo of chimeras, before it built up to breakneck speed and ran off the rails.

. . .

I'd been checking in on my mother frequently, bringing staples from the grocery store, jars of soup, and covered dishes. She ate what I brought and cleaned up afterward. Her house and garden were in pretty good order, as was her person. We exchanged few words. She thanked me for the food; but she didn't want my company. One day, on my way out to see her, I got a call from Mark Centrella. My prodigal sister, or someone fitting her description, had been spotted thumbing a lift on Route 5, a few miles south of Cornish, near the Maine–New Hampshire border. Hannah had an artist friend in Fryeburg, a short distance northward. "I called your Mom," Mark said. "Maybe you'd better go see how she's taking it." I arrived at Emily's unannounced, carrying an offering of freshly baked bread. When she opened the door, she stared at me, bewildered. I could see from her expression she had hoped against hope I was Hannah. Before I could speak, she closed the door in my face.

PART VII

Christ to the Right of Us

Chapter Nineteen

On the front and side lawns of St. Anthony's the booths and tables for the church festival were draped in baby-blue sheeting, the closest shade to Mary-blue the fair organizers could come up with. Mary-blue, the Virgin's emblematic color, was darker and clearer, without the grayish overtone. On this date, according to church doctrine, Christ appeared as the apostles were taking Mary's body to the grave and carried it with him up to heaven, where it was reunited with her soul. It must be said that Mary's assumption, so sudden and peremptory, bears some resemblance to an abduction, recalling abductions from older traditions than Christianity, when gods and fairies snatched mortal beings for their pleasure. Unlike Roman Catholics, Episcopalians were not required to believe that Mary was lifted to heaven. The Feast of the Assumption was not an article of faith, but a token recognition of the feminine principle, suppressed by the Church over many centuries. Mary was the only goddess we had in the Christian pantheon, a saccharine, watered-down version of a goddess, someone simple men and woman could turn to as a last-ditch measure.

On Assumption Day, 1974, the feminine principle was suffering a visible setback. Under skies bleached white from the heat, the vegetables at the produce stands browned and puckered. The flesh of Ruth Hiram's prize beefsteak tomatoes split open, oozing sallow juices. Jane Morse's rhubarb lay as limp and rubbery as leftover spaghetti. Peppers and eggplants wore their skins loosely. Like dishonest retailers, we kept rearranging the displays, placing the freshest vegetables topmost, hiding the bad ones underneath. We were understocked to begin with. Late crops of lettuce and spinach had bolted before they matured; and the corn was inedible. Our local peaches had succumbed to the heat, rotting on the branch, although you had only to drive as far as Raymond to see tree after tree bowed down by the weight of the ripe fruit. The flower arrangements, on the theme of "Lazy Summer Days," were exhibited at the back of the church, wilting in their containers, from which water was rapidly evaporating. Onlookers shook their heads at the judges' selections. By what standard had Edna Merrifield's entry been awarded a blue ribbon? In a toy canoe three feet long, lined with green florist's clay that hadn't been wetted down for several hours, cattails, pond grasses, ferns, and pink Joe pye weed hung lifelessly over the gunwales, brushing the tabletop.

Like the chief mourner at a funeral, I stood behind the baked goods table until closing time. Any other year, our stores would have been depleted by noon. This August our only customers were church members, who bought token items from a sense of obligation. Out-of-towners, summer people, and tourists approached our table and edged away, feigning interest in the Attic Treasures booth behind us, stocked as it was with nonperishable goods made of china, wood, and metal. As the heat wore on, our table began to resemble a visual catalogue of culinary failures. Sponge cakes collapsed in the center. Meringues softened gluily. Angelfood cakes sank to half their lofty height. Icings melted and separated, lazy droplets of butter trickling onto the platters. There was nothing to tempt a buyer but our loaves of plain bread, which had held up nicely but were perceived to be guilty by association.

Henry passed among the booths, inspecting the cash boxes. His hopes for installing a new furnace were dwindling rapidly. My mother made a short appearance after lunch to pick up a supply of Arnold Crowley's honey. I watched her at the produce table, smiling as she handled a wrinkled green pepper and a spotted tomato, deriving some secret amusement from their inferior condition. I saw Sally Bissell going into the church with a watering can, too late to save the flower arrangements, but I had lost sight of Adele, who was usually on duty at the crafts table, where some of her own work was on sale: beach stones painted with mysterious faces, matted and framed collages of feathers and dried flowers, lopsided baskets woven from grapevines. Mariette Roque said she'd gone home to get more of her beach stones, which were enjoying an unaccountable popularity, but Henry claimed he'd seen her in church, praying on her knees, head bowed over the pew in front of her, undisturbed by loud-voiced visitors to the flower show.

Adele worked at a church and came from a long line of churchmen, but her attitude toward religion was pantheistic, not to say heretical. If she was worshipping indoors, when the vast temple of nature was available to her, she must be prey to some misfortune or disturbance of mind. Over the last three weeks I'd been taken up with my mother, my lost sister, the festival. I had disregarded my young friend, whom I hailed in passing at the parish house without stopping for prolonged conversation. Adele had been absent for several days during this busy period, leaving Henry stranded. When I asked what was wrong, he said, "She didn't give a reason and I damn well didn't ask." Adele may have looked paler and droopier than usual, but she tended to wear loose summer clothes in greenish shades that washed out her complexion. I left Jane Morse in charge of the bake sale and made my way through the thinning crowd to the church building.

The church was empty and a scant degree cooler than outdoors. Over an exhibit of miniature roses arranged in a child's tea set ("Meet Me in the Playhouse"), one of the spotlights was flickering, about to die. I climbed on a chair and removed the bulb. The roses had shed most of their petals anyhow. From my higher perch I glimpsed the toes of a pair of feet protruding into the aisle, feet wearing sandals with wide straps and shaped soles. I stood the folding chair against the wall and approached the feet cautiously, in case, by some chance, they belonged to a stranger. I was halfway down the aisle when Adele sat up in her pew, like a reanimated corpse from a coffin, startled to be awake and to find herself in such surroundings.

Unlike a figure in a horror story, she began by apologizing. "I'm sorry you had to come looking for me. I know I should be on duty. They must be furious at me."

I sat down in the pew behind her. "No one sent me," I said. "Henry saw you. He said you were praying."

She flopped down on her back so I had to lean over to talk to her. "I was resting my head on my arms. I'm so tired I can't describe it. I thought if I didn't lie down I'd fall down."

"You should go home. There are plenty of hands to spell you."

"I suppose so. As long as it's light. I can't fall asleep at night."

"Emily makes a good herbal tea. It might help you."

Adele sat up abruptly, trying to gather herself together, smoothing her hair back, digging into her duffel-sized purse for a handkerchief to mop her forehead. "I have teas. I have tinctures. I have herbal pillows and white-noise machines. Nothing helps."

"Are you sure you want to drive? Can't I take you?"

She turned on me in anger, as if I were the author of her insomnia. "You can't expect me to last without sleep. There has to be an end to this."

I watched her march out of the church, her version of a stormy exit, the effect somewhat marred by the fact that she dropped her heavy bag and it tripped her. She saved herself from falling, but several items rolled out of the bag—a jar, a pencil, a checkbook. She ended up on her hands and knees anyway, rooting under a pew for her runaway possessions.

If the feminine principle was losing ground in our neighborhood, crops succumbing by degrees to the heat and drought, our women were also being subverted from within. The female character was under assault from its lower side. In every household to which I had entry there was a woman suffering from helplessness or phobia, diseases of dependency. Friends and acquaintances displayed symptoms for which fatherly physicians usually suggest daily doses of tranquilizers. Earlier in the season I had watched them growing sleek from sexual attention, blooming and ripening along with the fruits of summer. Now the glow of fulfillment had left them. Ruth Hiram's cheeks, chest, and forearms were covered with a rash diagnosed by Pete Bayer as dermatitis, a purely descriptive term meaning inflammation of the skin, in which the emotions were often implicated. Every salve she applied aggravated the itching, until the inflamed areas were dotted with blackish scabs. At the library, where she presided on Tuesdays, Thursdays, and Saturdays, she refused to look the borrowers in the eye, offending many of them by her changed, gruff manner. Jane Morse discovered her pregnancy was imaginary. She took the news hard, as if she had brought some disgrace on herself and her husband and was no longer fit to show her face in public.

Something was inimical to women in the Dry Falls vicinity. For the first time in parish history there were more men than women in church on Sunday mornings. Father Darren reported a similar imbalance, as did Clark Harmon, the Congregational minister. Female parishioners filed into their consulting rooms, but these same women were skipping worship services. Most of them were active members, the kind of women known as "pillars of the church." Fortunately, none of these good women abandoned their parish duties. They neglected their spiritual welfare, but they continued to look after the church. Each week Sally Bissell picked up the vases, filled them with greenery and blooms from her estate, and returned them, or asked me to return them, to the altar. She dashed in and out of the sanctuary without making a reverence in front of the cross, as if she were a delivery person from the florist's instead of a Christian believer. Jane Morse taught Sunday school in the parish house common room, as she always did, but she did not accompany the children into church at the end of the service, when they were allowed to sit and watch from the back pew and take part in singing the rousing recessional hymn. Mary Fran Rawls had stopped going to Mass at St. Mary's, but she still cleaned St. Anthony's for us. She knew God was not a Protestant.

From Henry's perspective, these women appeared, at first, to be going through a crisis of faith. Like the other disaffected churchwomen, his own constituents were frightened and angry. They were angry at God, more or less consciously, for being a man. They took out their bitterness on Henry. "Yes, I know," snapped Ruth Hiram. "I know He has no gender. Or so you say. Just don't tell me you'd be a priest if He was a woman." Sally Bissell was querulous and tearful. She didn't like being rude to Henry, who was her pastor and her closest friend's husband. "I'm sorry, Henry. That's exactly the point. God can't protect me. He's utterly useless. And so are you."

Adele didn't make an appointment. She poked her head in early one morning and asked if he had a minute. She was defensive and on edge, as if she had come at Henry's insistence instead of on her own. Some of her remarks echoed Sally's. She referred to the Deity as "your God" and "my father's God." She lashed out at Henry, "How can He protect us? He's one of them." Since he thought I was in her confidence, Henry asked me what man she was lumping in with God. Who was her current or recent lover? What had he done to her? I said it worried me sometimes that Adele had no men in her life, hurtful or otherwise.

After the first session, Henry predicted they wouldn't come back. He hadn't made a dent in their resistance. An ethical counselor never tried to hook a client into returning. He let them go with his good wishes, like thistledown blown on the wind. Henry knew his therapeutic instincts were slipping because his baser curiosity was aroused. He was hooked himself. He wanted to know why all of them had raised the subject of protection. He wanted to know what had made them so angry—angry and cosmically defenseless all at once, a blend of feelings he hadn't witnessed since his fieldwork courses at divinity school, when he was assigned to St. Luke's Women's Infirmary, doing the intake forms on rape victims.

One by one his clients reappeared, except for Adele. By then Henry had made the connection. Each of them had come to him before, complaining of sexual frustration. Now they alleged they were oppressed by sex. They needed protection from the demands of overeager partners. "We got what we asked for," said Sally. "You think it's funny, don't you? It's a joke on women." "I'm going to leave him," whispered Jane. "I'm going to my mother's." Mariette took more forceful measures. She moved into the guest cottage and bolted the door from the inside. "I don't know how he got in," she said. "I'm sure

I locked the windows. He left before it was light. Of course he denied it." Ruth challenged Henry with bleary eyes. "You have to do something, Henry. This is an indignity."

It was not the first time in his work as a counselor that Henry had felt he was out of his depth. Now he found himself once more at a juncture where his compass wavered and all signposts to the truth were weatherworn and unreadable. Any insight into a marriage stopped at the bedroom door, but it was impossible to associate these husbands, his friends of long standing, with acts of such crudity. Perhaps Ralph Hiram was a little humorless, and Frank Morse, to put it kindly, wasn't very complicated. Ford Bissell had a materialistic streak and the money to implement it. Michel Roque castrated sheep and slaughtered them, all in a day's work. But these were tendencies, not characteristics. How could any of them have built such strong, monogamous marriages on a foundation of sexual callousness?

Henry had grown more cautious since the fiasco of Lorraine and the plastic comb. He thought his clients were probably having erotic nightmares. Out of a sense of scientific responsibility, he interviewed the husbands, although he knew in advance what their reactions would be. "I haven't touched her," said Frank Morse. "I haven't been near her for months." Ralph Hiram broke down. "What can I do? Why does she keep accusing me?" Ford Bissell begged Henry for medication. It was unclear whether he wanted it for Sally or for himself. Like the others, Michel took the blame. "I lost desire and now I have driven her to this hysteria."

Henry had satisfied himself that the husbands were blameless, but he was not so confident about the nightmare theory. It raised more questions than it answered. Why were so many women having nightmares at the same time? Dreams that were so similar? Had they told one another their dreams, spreading them like gossip, programming one another like people who claimed to have been abducted by aliens and whose accounts were identical to stories circulating in the tabloids? Dreams occurred during sleep. Why did these dreamers insist they were awake throughout, or had been awakened? None of them presented their dreams as a series of distorted visual images; they offered them as lived experience.

Bogged down in uncertainty, Henry was clear on one subject. His parishioners showed the clinical signs of sleep deprivation: unreliable reflexes, short attention span, lapses into incoherence, irritability. For weeks Adele had been tardy, absent, careless, or inattentive. Henry's clients lost their bearings in mid-sentence. They forgot one-syllable words and proper names. Their volition was diminished. When he asked if they wanted coffee, they were as stumped as if he were waiting for the answer to a calculus problem. Lack of sleep compromised the immune system. Sally had swollen glands and a low-grade fever. A superficial cut on Mariette's arm kept getting reinfected. Ruth's rash was, if anything, worse. If people were deprived of good sleep long enough, they misperceived things. They formed paranoid ideas.

Henry was faced with a conundrum. Were these nightmares depriving them of sleep or was sleeplessness engendering delusions of sexual menace? Whichever came first, the bad dreams or the insomnia, he was no closer to finding the cause of either one of them.

If Henry asked himself why his own marriage was still untroubled, he never did so in my presence. He came home from his office and sought me out in the garden. While I inspected the damage from the heat and drought, he followed me up and down the rows of vegetables, reviewing every detail of his client sessions, treating me like a disinterested colleague who had no personal stake in the subject. He followed me so closely that we collided when I stopped to bend over, hunting for a single sound green tomato to ripen on the windowsill, or a few viable chard leaves. Henry seemed to take my unresponsiveness for like-minded clinical detachment, and to congratulate himself on it.

In fact, I had no emotion to spare for my friends' marital upheavals. I was mourning the loss of my garden. It was over, a month before its time, devastated by unnatural August heat instead of Maine's late September frosts. Even crops that weathered frost were finished: the leeks were as thin as pencils; the parsnip roots had forked; the Brussels sprouts had cracked and split open. When I went inside, Henry pursued me to the kitchen, still talking at me, blind to the tragedy in the garden, sensitive only to human dramas. I had picked a basket of crab apples from our tree, hoping to salvage something of the summer by making apple jelly. As I handled the fruit I could see I had cherished false hopes. Each apple was spotted and riddled with worm holes. The few unblemished sections had gone mealy.

Henry was standing beside me at the counter, too close to me. He had seen Ralph Hiram that morning. Ruth canceled at the last minute, so Ralph took her session. I was treated to a heartfelt portrayal of Ralph's stricken innocence, his dismay over Ruth's vindictiveness. Ralph broke down and wept in front of Henry, who took his tears as proof of sincerity. In his anguish Ralph was ready to admit to any wrongdoing, whether he remembered it or not. Like Lon Chaney's pitiful werewolf, he begged to be placed in confinement so he could not get out at night. "If I am doing these things," he cried, "I should be locked up."

Absorbed in his story, Henry reached for an apple from the basket. He brought it to his mouth and bit into it. I watched him swallow several bites before he noticed its condition. He spit a piece of apple into his palm and looked at me reproachfully, as if I had offered him the rotten apple instead of merely allowing him to eat it. Several times that afternoon I caught him glancing in my direction. At tea and at supper he looked closely at the food I put before him, breaking a cookie into several pieces, spreading mashed potatoes around on his plate in case they happened to be concealing something. It had crossed his mind for the first time in our marriage that he took my good will too much for granted.

Chapter Twenty

On these stifling nights we sat out in the yard on reclining chairs, sipping ice water with lime. Our conversation was lethargic. Every so often one of us remarked that the temperature seemed lower (or higher) than the night before. In late August the northern lights were visible in our latitude. We had watched them for several nights, suspended across the sky like hanging draperies, glinting white with a tinge of blue, the color of glaciers. It was a cooling spectacle. The aurora was brighter and closer this year, as well as more pictorial. Supposedly it coincided with magnetic storms in the upper atmosphere. We had no reception on our home and car radios, only blaring static, but as soon as you drove past the Dry Falls town limits, the stations came back loud and clear. When Michel Roque went up in his plane to drop hay for his animals, he was out of contact with the local airfield at Danville for most of the run.

We were still outdoors at eleven-thirty. The later it grew, the more we were convinced it was cooler, a wishful perception based only on the fact that it was sunless. Neither one of us had the energy to check the thermometer. Henry had turned its face to the wall some weeks ago. It was more unsettling to know the temperature than not to know it. When the telephone rang, I got up to answer it. Hannah might be trying to call me instead of my mother. By the time I struggled out of my chair, the ringing had stopped. It began again while I was still upright and kept on until I reached the instrument, as if the caller were well aware I was dragging my feet.

When I heard Sally's voice, I assumed she was canceling our date. We were going to a conference in Portland tomorrow, the subject of which was gardening with native plants.

"I know she's in there," said Sally, without apologizing for the lateness of the hour. "Her car's there, but she hasn't turned the lights on." At first I thought she meant the lights in Adele's car, not the garage apartment. Sally scolded me for not listening. "For God's sake, Cora. She's been home for six hours!" "She's exhausted," I said. "She probably flopped down for a nap. She'll sleep straight through."

Sally reminded me that the garage apartment was dark, even in the daytime. Originally intended for a live-in housekeeper who would spend her days in the main house, it faced north and had small windows. The efficiency kitchen and the bathroom were inside rooms, both windowless. I had visited Adele often enough to remember she automatically flipped the light switch when she opened the door. The switch governed a standing lamp next to the sofa and a reading lamp on a table between two armchairs. Without illumination, you stood a good chance of tripping over piles of books for which Adele had no shelf-space. Adele managed to run into them even with the lights on.

"A fuse blew," I suggested. "The fuse box is in the garage and she was too tired to deal with it." "I checked the fuses," said Sally. "There's nothing wrong with them." "When did you check them?" "Just now. That's why I called you." "I don't understand. You were in the garage but you didn't go upstairs?" "I almost did," she said. "I started to." It was unlike Sally to be so hesitant. "Hang up and call her," I ordered, "unless you'd rather sit and stew about it."

There was a pause at the other end. Slowly and deliberately, she explained that the phone had been busy, but "the wrong kind of busy." After several tries she had called the operator, who told her there was trouble on the line and thanked her for reporting it. They would send someone over in the morning. "I'm running out of ideas," I said. "There's no way around it. You'll have to go in. Don't forget to take your key with you."

While I waited for an answer, and an end to this roundabout conversation, the answer finally struck me. She wanted us to leave our backyard and our cooling drinks, spring out of our deck chairs like volunteer firemen when the bell sounds, and drive hell-for-leather to her aid. By the time we arrived, roused Adele, and calmed everyone down, it would be close to one-thirty.

Sleep came in cycles. If you violated one cycle, you had to wait for the next one to begin. I clocked our chances of getting to sleep at no earlier than three a.m. "Do you want us to come over?" I asked. Sally consented without thanking me. She was way past caring if I had made the offer in earnest. "Give us fifteen minutes," I said. "I have to break the news to Henry."

Sally was waiting for us in the driveway. As hot as it was, she was sitting inside her car with the windows closed. She held a battery-operated lantern on her lap, which lit up the interior with a pallid glow. As we drove by and parked in front of her, she turned off the lantern. I expected her to come out to meet us, but she stayed in the car. Henry tried to open her door, jiggling the handle. She had locked herself in. He jabbed a finger at the glass, pointing at the lock button, until she finally released it. She almost fell getting out of the car. Henry caught her in time. "You go first," she said, handing him the lantern. He led the way across the gravel drive to an enclosed stone staircase on the far side of the garage. The steps were uneven and gritty from unswept particles deposited by shoes. I was halfway up when Henry reached the landing. Sally hung back, one foot on the ground and one on the bottom step.

The light over the door wasn't working. Henry flicked the switch several times, then reached up to unscrew the bulb. He held it to his ear and shook it. "It seems all right," he said, and screwed it in again. This was taking too long. I pushed past him and opened the door. I tried the light switch on the wall. Nothing happened. The lights were out of order, but the refrigerator was humming. The appliances and the lights must be on different circuits. It was Sally's fault. She said she had checked the fuse box. At this rate we'd be lucky to get to bed before dawn.

The living room was blanketed in darkness. Nothing was visible from the door but the outline of the sofa. Henry came up beside me with the lantern, playing the beam around the room, deepening the shadows. There was a carton of milk on the table and an open jar of peanut butter with a spoon in it. Adele's duffel-shaped shoulder bag, flap open, spilled crumpled tissues and coins on the kitchen counter. Her long green dress was lying on the braided rug in front of the sofa, where she must have stepped out of it. Henry shone the light along the opposite wall, looking for the bedroom. The bedroom door was slightly ajar, a matter of an inch or so.

Sally had ventured over the threshold. She was less anxious in the dark with us than alone outside. Henry moved toward the bedroom. Sally followed me so closely she tripped on my heels. We were right behind Henry as he grasped the knob and started easing the door open. I discovered I was holding my breath. This stealth was absurd. We were acting like lawbreakers. What would happen if we barged in and startled her? At worst she might scream and take a moment or so to recognize us. I put my shoulder to the door and shoved, breaking Henry's grip on the knob. The door swung inward, stopping short of the wall. It was a long, narrow room with a window at the farthest end set close to the ceiling, like the windows in basements. A mattress on a wooden platform, the double bed was beneath the window, head to the wall.

Adele was lying across the bed. She had been there all along. The lantern lit up her form in its entirety. She was so tall that her feet would have touched the floor if her knees had not been raised and spread apart. She wore a white slip drawn up to her navel and no article of clothing below it. The straps had slid off her shoulders. Her knees opened wider. Her pelvis rose and fell in a broken rhythm, faster and then slower. The motion drove her backward, until her head hung over the side of the bed. I had seen her naked in the meadow below Hannah's cabin, too far away to observe that her mount was so prominent or its hairy covering so tropical. In the lantern light we could take the measurement of her clitoris, as fat as a human thumb from knuckle to tip. Her arms were flung sideways, hands outstretched, fingers digging at the bedclothes. She was taking pleasure without touching her body, using secret muscles or imagination, some brand of masturbational yoga. Transported by impending orgasm, she seemed oblivious to our presence. The only thing worse than watching her would be having her catch us at it.

Sally seized my arm and tried to pull me back. Henry's lantern wavered, dropping its beam to the floor, leaving Adele in modest darkness. We had no need to see this or ever speak of it. It would take all our compassion to forget it. I turned aside, assuming we were of one mind, when the beam moved back to the bed. I put out my hand to appropriate the lantern, but Henry stopped me. He pointed the light directly at Adele's face. Her lips were trembling. Her brow was contracted. Her eyes were closed but her eyelids were in spasm. We had misjudged her. She was not in charge of the workings of her body. She was deeply asleep and dreaming, a dream that was giving her pain as well as pleasure. The lantern moved back and away from her face. Her pelvis strained upward, mimicking copulation. Lashed to an invisible partner, a lover endowed with the stamina women dream of, she was nearing fulfillment. I watched her with envy, since I had no erotic life and no ability to dream one. Now it seemed a dreamed encounter and a waking one were equal in intensity.

By every standard of decency we should have taken our leave, but we stayed for the climax. When it came, it was accompanied by convincing vocal music—sighs, trills, panting. One moment she was as taut as a bowstring and the next her body collapsed, inert and ungainly, as if she had been thrown on the bed like a bag of laundry. Release came so suddenly we feared her heart, overtaxed, had given out. Henry took a step forward to see if life was still in her. Sally clung to me, whimpering. I tried to break loose, but her embrace restrained me.

At that same moment, clearly visible in the lamplight, a column of black vapor rose up from between Adele's legs. About the stature and shape of a man, it dissolved from the bottom upward, until all we saw hanging in the air was the contour of a head and shoulders. When the last wisp of black had vanished, Adele stirred and moved her lips. Very slowly, as if underwater, she turned herself over on her side, facing toward us, pushing her fists into her groin as if to bar access. Her breathing was regular and her eyelids were motionless, signs that she had passed into one of the stages of dreamless sleep. A wave of sickness came over me, forcing me to choose between vomiting and losing consciousness. I want to think I staved it off until I knew Adele was uninjured. As I went down I remember trying to understand, as if the matter were of great importance, why it was I, and not Sally, who had fainted.

Three of us saw it, by lantern light. It took us by surprise. Researchers or thrill seekers who set up watch in a haunted house are conditioned by past reports and local legend. They expect to see something, and what they see bears a strong resemblance to previous sightings. We had no expectations. We thought we had intruded on a dreamer and succumbed to a voyeuristic impulse. Otherwise we might have come prepared—brought infrared cameras, spectrometer, and recording equipment. (Had that smoky black shape produced sound? We would never know.) If we had any inkling, we would surely have come protected, armed with crucifixes and holy water. With a little warning Henry might have had the wit to pray, uttering formulas of exorcism.

Did Henry castigate himself because his priestly reflexes had failed him? Quite the opposite. He could not believe his own good luck. He was as keyed up as an investor who had a hot tip on the stock market. He bustled about, organizing all of us, bringing me around with a good shake and a dose of black coffee. The lights had come on as he was carrying me out of the bedroom. I heard him say, "You see that? Would you call that coincidence?"

He closed Adele's door, announcing that one of us would look in on her every twenty minutes. He put Sally to work at the dining-room table, writing a description of the apparition while it was fresh in her memory. He sat me up sooner than I wanted to and made me do the same, urging us to close our eyes and form a mental image before we committed words to paper. He sat across from me with a pad on his knee, following his own orders. It did not occur to him that Sally and I might not want to relive the experience. When I tried to picture the scene, I saw nothing but black. My head ached, and I was afraid of bringing on another faint. I was no better at visualization than I was at dreaming, but I didn't want to admit it to Henry. He would never let me lie down until I got the job done.

Thanks to Henry's persistence we completed our eyewitness reports within thirty minutes of the sighting, record time in an atmosphere of crisis. We neither emoted nor exchanged impressions until we had finished, so our reactions were as free as possible from collective influence. It was true that Henry had used the term "apparition" in our presence, but "apparition" meant anything that appeared, usually something remarkable. What else could he have called it? In any case, his slip of the tongue did not seem to have contaminated our perceptions. Our accounts, when compared, differed in some particulars. Sally called what she had seen "a darkness" and claimed it "billowed outward," increasing in size until it enveloped the figure of Adele, obscuring her from view. Henry described a pillar of black vapor, too dense to see through. His account tallied with mine, with one exception. He saw the head, but did not see the lighter spaces where eyes should be (unless I had tacked on this sensational item after the fact). Details aside, we had reached a status quo that satisfied Henry. A black shape had materialized from between Adele's legs, towered in the air, and evaporated. Henry was certain it had wanted us to see it.

We forgot about Adele, unguarded in her room as the sky turned gray and the moon dropped low on the horizon. When we reached her bedside she was sleeping on her stomach like a child, her rump uncovered. As Henry started to draw the sheet over her, he noticed part of it was drenched with wetness, stiffening as it dried, as if it had been laundered with starch. He pulled the top sheet back and felt the bottom sheet, which was wringing wet, soaking through the pad into the mattress. Telltale sheets, betraying the flow of sexual fluids, too copious for a single act of intercourse. When had Henry come across another example of such abundant liquefaction? The Burridge sleepers had drenched their beds with feminine secretions, light and watery like the sap from flowers. The viscous substance on Adele's bedclothes resembled seminal emissions. To my disgust Henry bent down and sniffed. He said the sheets had that whiff of the ocean consistent with semen, something briny or seaweedy.

Henry had been talking in a whisper. Now his voice rose high enough to disturb Adele. Like a doctor on rounds at a teaching hospital, he was too absorbed in the problem before him to mind what the patient overheard. Did we have proof right under our noses that a specter could ejaculate? Were we safe in supposing that a nonhuman entity had completed an act of coition with a human partner? The amount of semen emitted was in itself prodigious. Even more surprising, the fluid was, or was like, a man's. You would think it might somehow be more "spectral," black and inky, like the entity's coloration, or so volatile no trace would be left of it. During the witch-hunts many inquisitors believed that incubus demons "borrowed" semen from men, collecting and hoarding the fluid men spilled in sleep during nocturnal pollutions. The proof lay on the sheets and inside Adele's body. Henry pulled out the top sheet and made a project of folding it, in half, in fourths, in eighths and sixteenths. He got no help from me and Sally. We wouldn't have touched it under threat of torture. He intended to ask Jane Shufelt to have the sheet analyzed. For humane reasons, getting a smear from Adele was, of course, out of the question. You could see his mind working, still wrestling with the issue, the scientist trying to argue the priest out of his scruples; then he left the room to find a plastic bag to protect the evidence.

Sally and I went back into the living room to resume our vigil, and found Henry letting himself out the front door. "You're not leaving us alone," said Sally. "I have to get this to Jane," he said, annoyed that an explanation should be necessary. I reminded him that it was five-thirty in the morning, too early even for Jane. He shut the door and walked over to the window, peering out at the whitening sky as if he could hasten the sun's progress by force of concentration. I looked in Adele's icebox for something to fortify us, but found only apple juice, soy milk, and an empty box of granola. Her shelves yielded an open package of Fig Newtons, which went down easier dunked in coffee. Henry ate and drank standing up. He kept his eyes on the horizon, half listening, while we tried to interest him in the victim instead of the perpetrator. What was to be done about Adele? Should we stay until she stumbled out of bed into the living room? Compound the shock of finding us there by telling her the whole story? If we left before she woke, we would spare her distress and embarrassment. She was safe now that night was over. "They can't stand the daylight," said Sally. Henry tuned in briefly to tell her she was thinking of vampires.

Swayed by numerous self-serving arguments, we decided to leave Adele. We would approach her later in the day, after a few hours' sleep. Sally could pretend the garage apartment needed construction work. Henry would insist she move in with us. I could see the idea appealed to him. It would give him a chance to observe her at closer range. I found I didn't want her in my house, although I couldn't say so. I wanted Henry to send her home or recommend her to another parish. With the heightened awareness induced by lack of sleep, I thought I saw events plainly.

An entity had been grazing in our precinct, sampling the fodder, foraging in one pasture after another—my sister, my married friends, the Burridge seniors. Had it found my sister tough, my friends stale, the Burridge girls green? As cattle prefer alfalfa to grass and corn, it had savored Adele above the others: she was fresh but not raw; plucked but not bruised; mature but not overripened. It had shown itself to us to mark her for its own. If she left, her spirit raptor would follow her, even into hiding. Get her out of town and the women of Dry Falls would have their lives back. If I was ready to sacrifice Adele for the common good, I was no worse than Henry. He saw her as the cornerstone of his new faith, as Christ's miracle had been for the congregation at Capernaum. Like the Galileans in the synagogue, Henry had seen an unclean spirit departing from a person, and been converted. Would he be content to bear witness to the supernatural or would he covet Christ's role? Stand amazed while demons were banished, or play a part in banishing them?

I wanted nothing to do with the spirit world or its middlemen. Let Henry delude himself that psychical research was an extension of the healing ministry. I refused to regard Adele as a victim or a patient. Couldn't she take some responsibility for her affliction? Show some nerve and fight back? I rejected her claims to my attention, as all healthy people reject sickness or misfortune, no matter how irreproachable their behavior toward those in need. My impulse was selfish, but selfishness is not purely callous. It can also be energy mustered in the service of life. Sally was so tired she clung to Henry's arm on the way down the outside staircase, but I had my second wind. It seemed imperative that I get to Portland for the native plant conference, as necessary as nourishment for hunger or antiseptic for a wound. In this drought, whether natural or unnatural, I wanted to know all I could about wild and native species, like our roadside bergamot, which could thrive in dry conditions. I needed to be with other gardeners, that thin blue-denimed line barely holding its own in a world overcast by the shadow of abstraction, a world increasingly ruled by numbers and machines, mathematical entities.

I drove us back to the rectory so Henry could pick up our second car, the battered station wagon. I don't know if I didn't talk to him or he didn't talk to me. He held the white plastic kitchen-can bag with the soiled sheet in it on his lap. He seemed completely absorbed in its custodianship, untwisting the tie to open the bag, flattening and smoothing it to eliminate air pockets. When we arrived, he carried it across to the station wagon, holding it out in front of him with both hands, minding where he walked, as if it were made of some breakable material. I watched him back out of the driveway and into the street. As he drove off, he played two beeps on his horn, remembering belatedly to say goodbye to me.

PART VIII

Christ When We Lie Down

Chapter Twenty-one

Even parish priests were entitled to a yearly vacation, two weeks with full pay like any unionized laborer. We usually spent our leave at the Lieber family camp in the North Woods. The camp, built in 1923 to accommodate a party of twelve, consisted of a log house, a mess hall, guides' quarters, and a boathouse. We chartered an amphibian aircraft in the settlement of Frenchtown, landed on Big Black Brook Lake, and taxied to the dock, when Ed Hawkfoot, the caretaker, met us. Ed stocked the main house with provisions, which Henry supplemented with fish from the lake and its feeder streams. I enjoyed a respite from cooking. We grilled salmon and trout and ate salad while the fresh lettuce lasted, then we opened cans of beans, peas, and artichoke hearts.

Every day Henry took the rowboat with the outboard motor and left me the canoe. I slapped a sandwich together for lunch and explored the shores of the lake, tying up when the sun was high to go swimming off the rocks, many of which were long and flat enough to stretch out on full length and warm up afterward. The lake was cold, but never as cold as the ocean. Its waters were so smooth and still that swimming seemed effortless. By late afternoon, when a breeze blew the surface into ripples, it was time to paddle home.

Henry would have cleaned the day's catch and started the campfire. He would tell me my lips were blue and rub me down from my head to my ankles with scratchy camp towels. I sat by the fire, all wrapped up, until I stopped shivering. He pulled me down on those same rough towels and made love to me, my hair damp and tangled, while the fire burned down to embers, too low for cooking. I went up to the house and put on trousers and a long-sleeved shirt to protect me from mosquitoes. By the time I returned, combed and dressed, carrying a bowl of salad or a pot of peas and a bag of marshmallows, he had built up the fire again.

What I remembered with most regret was not making love, but shivering—being cold enough to shiver. Violette Pond and Sally's swimming pool were tepid and afforded no refreshment. From forty feet underground our well pumped lukewarm water. Fall was almost upon us, with its seesawing temperatures. When autumn came, winter was supposed to follow, although there were grounds for believing that Nature had suspended the seasons. This year, when I needed it most, Black Brook Camp had been denied us. Henry's cousin, Maury, the one who ran the smoked fish business, had mixed up the bookings and given our two weeks to cousin Jason's son, Alex. Maury begged for our understanding and cooperation. The Alex Liebers lived in Cleveland and had four young children. The camp was ours any time in October, if we wanted it. The snows might have started, of course, but no serious accumulation. It would be quite an adventure for us. By the time the conversation was over, Maury had convinced himself he was doing us a favor.

Henry saw it that way, although he was careful to pretend disappointment when I raised the issue. During our annual furlough, young priests who were waiting for their first assignments were dispatched by Bishop Hollins to take over the services. This summer's recruit, Sam Borders, commuted from Portland on Sundays. Daily services were read by lay people. The new head vestryman, Ralph Hiram, was in charge of parish business. The office was closed, and the answering service referred callers to Ralph's home number.

Adele had been packed off to Baltimore so fast she hardly knew what was happening to her. Her mother was in Europe. Adele's father was rattling around in the deanery writing a paper on ascetic practices of the Cappadocian Christians, living on crackers and tea, forgetting to turn off the burner when the kettle had boiled. Adele was needed at home, or so Henry persuaded her. Short of a crisis (a rock through a stained-glass window? Sam Borders's car breaking down on the turnpike?), Henry could count on being left alone so assiduously that it might have the paradoxical effect of luring him back to his duties.

Henry was enjoying his civilian status. He didn't shave, went shoeless and bare-chested, poked around in his library for clues to the identity of the Dry Falls ravisher. Jane Shufelt dropped off the report on Adele's sheet from the hospital laboratory. "Bad luck, Henry," she said. "Negative for semen. Nothing but female secretions and traces of a popular brand of laundry detergent." Instead of being depressed by the news, Henry was elated. There had been a starchy, yellowish liquid on the sheet. He had seen it and touched it. The fact that it had disappeared was in itself miraculous.

Henry spent a lot of time talking to Walter Emmet, who was at loose ends. Walter's pot garden was so far gone he had given up on it. It was too hot to make the effort of getting together, so they gossiped on the telephone. I decided to clean the storage closet on the landing outside Henry's office. I could have organized picnics at the beach instead of closets, but I had no intention of making the best of things. Beyond the Dry Falls town limits the days and nights would be cooler, but whether we escaped for a day or a fortnight, we would always be faced with returning.

The closet was a morgue for old winter clothes, moth-eaten lumber jackets, grease-stained down vests, a hooded black cape, rusty with age, that had been my grandmother's. Henry would never agree to get rid of his army uniforms, but I had no attachment to the polo coat I had worn in college. I emptied two cartons from the closet shelf directly into a lawn bag. One carton was filled with knit caps and ski masks; the other with unmated mittens. The cartons came in handy. The floor was heaped with decrepit boots and outgrown ice skates. Propped at the back was a collection of snowshoes with broken bindings. I decided to keep them. The bindings could be replaced. While I worked in this inferno of wool and dust, every item I handled a reminder of cooler seasons, I caught snatches of Henry's talks with Walter, and some of their drift.

Henry was sitting in his swivel chair with his naked feet on the desk, relaxed and cheerful, little knowing what fate awaited his hockey skates. Teenaged girls held the honors when it came to long telephone calls, but Henry and Walter were setting a record for middle-aged men. Occasionally, the chatter stopped for a minute or two. Henry looked up a reference while Walter stayed on the line, or Walter left Henry holding to get more iced tea. They were having as much fun discussing biblical demons as girls did trading lore about clothes and hairstyles. "Listen to this," said Henry, quoting from one of the texts on his desk. "Asmodeus is the 'bringer of erotic fantasies, the genius of matrimonial unhappiness or jealousy.' Hold on. Here it is. In Persian, the name means 'lustful.' "

I had packed the contents of the closet into eight lawn bags and three cardboard boxes. I spared the cape and the uniforms. Before I swabbed the closet floor and shelf I had to use the vacuum cleaner. When I switched on the machine, Henry and Walter were rehashing a Bible story. I knew the legend of pious Tobit, who went blind because sparrow droppings fell onto his eyes while he was sleeping in the courtyard. Tobit's troubles were compounded when his son, Tobias, fell in love with a girl who had been married to seven husbands. The wicked demon, Asmodeus, killed each of them on his wedding night before the marriage could be consummated. The archangel Raphael instructed Tobias to marry the girl anyway. When he entered his bride's chamber, all he had to do was put the heart and liver of a certain fish on the embers of the incense. The odor of the fish organs would repel the demon, who would flee to the ends of the earth and never bother her again. I turned off the vacuum cleaner and heard Henry saying he had no idea what kind of fish were found in the Tigris, but he was sure there must be similar species in Maine rivers. He was silent for a moment, then he responded, "Are you sure, Walter? I thought you hated fishing."

I could see what we were in for. An antiques dealer and a minister restored to boyhood, heading off to the nearest stream with their poles and tackle boxes, catching their lines in trees, forgetting the insect spray, coming back with sunburned noses and faces swollen with mosquito bites. I imagined it all, the fish blood on the kitchen counter, the guts in the sink, the charcoal-colored chunks of church incense smoldering in my copper gratin pan. Squawks of rude laughter as the fish organs met the embers and released a stink. Histrionic coughing and gagging as the fumes filled the room and, soon, the whole house. These experiments repeated daily while the boys ranked the fish as to which kind smelled strongest.

Men won't leave things alone. They kept tinkering with fate. Dry Falls had been quiet since Adele was expelled. Marriages were mending. I saw Ralph and Ruth Hiram out walking, arm in arm. Ford and Sally had given a party on Labor Day weekend. Was our town merely in remission, or was it cured? Henry and Walter's experiments might be dangerous, like keeping guns or Ouija boards in the house. They were practicing witchcraft, scripturally inspired or not. Their biblical remedies could boomerang, attracting the identical powers they were meant to repel. They had forgotten, or intentionally ignored, one crucial item. The fish Tobias cut open was a unique, miraculous fish, plucked from the river and dropped at his feet by one of God's angels.

I left Henry sitting at his desk, telephone cradled between his ear and shoulder, reading a map, giving Walter the comparative mileages to the Kennebec and the Sheepscot. Bags of clothes and a stack of cartons barricaded the doorway and clogged the landing. If he wanted to get out of his office, he could haul them downstairs himself.

When Henry was at home we took time out for tea every afternoon. I insisted on it. Tea stimulates the system without jangling the nerves. Before tea, events drive you; afterwards, keener and calmer, you can take back the reins. It was so hot for late September that we were still drinking iced tea, Darjeeling steeped with mint and a lump of fresh ginger.

Since our leave began, I had fallen down on the job. Today the cookie tin was empty. There was a loaf of banana bread somewhere—I was sure of it. I found it in the freezer, rock-solid. If I overdid the ice, I might manage to stretch the tea left in the pitcher to fill two glasses.

Any other day I would have whipped up a batch of brownies, thirty minutes from start to finish. While the brownies were baking,

I'd start the spaghetti sauce for our supper, making do with canned tomatoes. Before the timer went off, I might dice an eggplant, salt it, and leave it to sweat in a colander. Or slice a store-bought cucumber for our salad course; dress it with sour cream, lemon juice, scallions, and dill; and crisp it in the icebox. I went through all these steps in my head, gesture by gesture, from unwrapping the squares of chocolate to tearing off a sheet of waxed paper to cover the dish of cucumbers. Reviewing the motions was tantamount to performing them. The tasks themselves would be repetitive and uninspiring. My skills in the kitchen were reduced to thinking up menus. I was losing touch with the sensuous dimension of cooking, which is nine-tenths of it.

I was suffering from a form of sensory deprivation. The world outside my windows was losing color. I looked out on a landscape of sapless browns and yellows. A shimmering veil of heat changed every familiar object into a pale, two-dimensional counterfeit. Every day this past month I drew the curtains downstairs against the sun, so the house was darker in daytime than it was at night, putting time out of gear. I began to feel like a prisoner in the house, cut off from normal pursuits, condemned to inactivity. I had no heart for cooking. There was nothing to do in the garden but clip dead stalks and prepare the beds for winter, two months early. I couldn't sew and was no great reader.

There was no one to keep me company. My friends were involved with their husbands, and my husband was involved in raising spirits. In bodily form, I had no chance of getting his attention. On previous leaves at the North Woods camp, Henry read morning and evening prayers in a grove of birches by the lake, with me as his congregation. He kept his pocket-sized copy of the prayer book on his person. Some of its pages were foxed with dampness. Its limp leather covers smelled faintly fishy. This year he'd abandoned the ritual, or simply forgotten it. The dry cleaners found Henry's prayer book in the pocket of his windbreaker. I put it on his desk, where it was currently buried under a pile of psychical research monographs, topmost of which was "Witch-Riding: Sleep Disorder or Supernatural Assault?" from the *Occult Science Quarterly*.

There was an atmosphere of oppression in the house, my own projection. My domestic surroundings no longer had the power to confirm me. I felt somewhat detached, light-headed, as if my sinuses were congested. Physical exertion was the surest cure for the doldrums. How long had it been since I'd dusted the living-room bookshelves? I started to sort through my kitchen files, determined to scrap any recipe clippings for dishes that were too complicated (pastry shells filled with minced pheasant, truffles, and wild mushrooms) or not complicated enough (Seven-Can Church Social Casserole). I kept it up for half an hour or so, fighting an urge to sleep. At last I put my head on my arms and dozed off at the kitchen table, like a grade-school pupil in rest period.

Afternoon naps, like breakfast in bed, were linked in my mind to illness and convalescence. When I slept in the afternoon, I slept too deeply. I woke up feeling seasick and hesitant, as if I were in the wrong body. When I finally came back to myself, it was usually time for bed.

That afternoon, something woke me before I touched bottom—a bell-like tone, like the chimes outside the window in a season when breezes were blowing. With the greatest reluctance, I began the long passage upward. Through half-parted eyes I could tell it was still daytime. My cheek was resting on the surface of the table. One arm had fallen into my lap. The other was stretched out in front of me. I registered a crick in my neck, not yet painful enough to prevent me from nodding off again.

I heard another sound behind me, coming from the hallway or the entrance to the dining room, a kind of swishing and crackling, like a large plastic sack being slowly dragged across floorboards. The sounds stopped and started at irregular intervals. Henry must be bringing the garbage bags downstairs, lugging two at a time. The bags were overstuffed and awkward. I knew I should get up and help him, but each of my limbs weighed as much as a sack of woolen clothing.

I heard footsteps on the kitchen floor and felt a hand placed gently on my shoulder and quickly withdrawn. Henry thought I was sleeping. He dropped a kiss on the top of my head and went out the back door. The spell was broken.

I arched my back like a cat, raised my arms above my head and leaned back in my chair, yawning deeply. I got up slowly and took a few steps. I was on solid ground. I went into the dining room to pick up some of the bags Henry had been wrestling with, but the bags weren't there. He must have left them in the hallway or on the stairs. The hall and staircase were empty. I walked up to the second floor, around past the bedroom and down the steps that led to the back landing outside Henry's office. The bags were piled where I'd left them. The stacked cartons blocking the doorway were tumbled on the floor. Henry must have barged straight through them, knocking them any which way. I thought the noises I had heard were softer and closer to me, but perhaps they had been only the echo of Henry's passage as he toppled the cartons and jostled the plastic lawn bags.

Chapter Twenty-two

The next morning after breakfast, while I was staring into the icebox trying to make a grocery list, Ruth Hiram showed up at the kitchen door. She had a child in tow, a girl about ten years old with a pointed chin and wise eyes, a pale-faced city child wearing a dress and ballet slippers. "This is Ralph's grand-niece, Angela," said Ruth. "I hoped I'd catch Henry."

Henry had gone to the post office to send a package by registered mail to Carlos Ring at the New England Center for Psychical Research. After a conference on the telephone, Dr. Ring had asked to see Henry's notes on the Dry Falls incidents, Xeroxed and unedited. Henry had said he might swing by the garage on the way home; one of the brake lights on the station wagon was out.

Ruth was happy to sit and visit until he came back. "I'll take my chances," she said. "Are you sure I'm not disturbing you?" I wasn't glad to see her, but I was embarrassed to think she might have picked up on it. I felt so disconnected that contact with other people was an exertion, friends no less than grocery clerks. I offered Ruth a cup of coffee. Angela refused a glass of orange juice. There was nothing in this house for a child to do. A minister's wife should know enough to have a drawer for young visitors, full of coloring books, crayons, and board games.

Angela was quiet enough. She had brought a kit for making pot holders, a plastic frame and a bag of nylon loops in primary colors.

Ruth was brimming over with talk. I could tell she was on one of her hobbyhorses, bit between her teeth. She had a theory, or one of her notions, and she intended to round up as many supporters as she could to endorse it. Ruth was counted as one of our local intellectuals. She handled books, read books, and had even compiled a few of them. She had a master's degree in education. When her name came up, someone always said she should have been a teacher. The didactic mode was second nature to her. From behind her desk at the center of our little library, she dispensed advice five days a week on what to read, guiding uncultivated minds, young and old, on the path to literacy. If a subscriber wished to borrow a gothic novel, Ruth urged her to take out *Wuthering Heights* as well as its degenerate modern offshoot. No one took offense. Ruth was so positive; she surely had their good in mind.

Ruth, who was also childless, was no more experienced with children than I was. She belonged to the school of thought that favors treating them like adults. In my opinion the subject of Adele was inappropriate for young ears, but Ruth plunged right in, pressing me for details to round out what Sally had told her. "I don't think . . . ," I began, with a nod in Angela's direction. Ruth brushed off my reluctance. "Did she remember any of it? How did she react?" "We weren't with her," I said. "We left before she woke up." "I know that," said Ruth impatiently. "What did she say when Henry spoke to her?"

I didn't like Ruth's interviewing techniques or her proprietary attitude toward the subject. Once she heard a piece of information, she thought she owned it.

"She was very shaky," I said. "She talked about recurring nightmares." "Did Henry set her straight?" asked Ruth. "She could use a dose of reality. I hope he didn't try to coddle her." Ruth's vindictive tone repelled me. "You blame Adele," I said. "You think she brought this on." "It's stopped, hasn't it?" said Ruth. "She's out of the territory. We don't want her back." "You want a scapegoat," I said. "She was a dabbler," said Ruth. "Those silly spells and charms and vegetarian diets. She had black candles in her apartment. Do you think that's harmless?" "She also had white candles and rainbow-colored candles. And candles shaped like bunny rabbits." "You're not involved,

Cora. You were spared because your husband is a minister. The rest of us had no such safeguard."

For several weeks I had been living in retreat, too torpid and discouraged to relish human society. I had withdrawn of my own volition, or so I imagined. I didn't know I was being ostracized, "left out" of an exclusive sorority of victims. Bigotry is blind and unempathic. They thought I was safe with Henry, when it should have been plain to anyone that he was halfway to opening his home and his church as a soup kitchen for vagabond spirits. All comers welcome. Free counseling services provided.

Ruth put down her cup. I rose from my chair, thinking she was ready to go. She assumed I was getting up to serve her more coffee. I reminded her that Henry might be delayed, but she was determined to try her ideas out on me. A captive audience was as good as a willing one. "This will interest you, Cora," she said, with the complacency of someone who rarely met with any argument, and who would ride over it if she did. I poured coffee for myself as well. I felt ominously sleepy, knowing I was bound by politeness to hear Ruth out for as long as she cared to detain me.

She began by reviewing her credits, as if she were both introducer and speaker at a meeting of some scholarly institute. "You're familiar with my books," she said, referring to two short volumes of Maine legends and ghost stories, published by a printer in Windham, who distributed them, along with a line of postcards, to area gift shops, museums, and historic houses. "You may not know," she said, affecting modesty, "that I've been in correspondence with one of the top folklorists at the university. He asked me to donate copies of my books to the department library."

I smiled and nodded, hoping Ruth would get on with it. "I've been going through rejected transcripts, as well as written legends I didn't use for one reason or another. With all this interest in my work, I decided to reassess the discards. I thought I might have enough for a new volume." Even Angela was growing restive at this point. She had put down her pot holder and was drumming on the linoleum with her slippered heels. "Go in the other room, Angela," I said. "You can look at the magazines."

Ruth drew her chair close to the table. "I've found something," she said. "I'm sure Henry will grasp its significance." "One of your legends?" I asked. "The Bethel haunting," she said, implying that any person of average intelligence would know what she was talking about. "I don't write these books for their entertainment value, Cora. I'm a student of supernatural belief traditions. The Bethel woman's case bears some striking resemblances to ours. Conversely, our cases have some of the traditional features of a haunting: the sound of footsteps, doors opening and closing, a threatening presence, paralyzing fear." "I thought hauntings were associated with specific places," I said. "Good for you," said Ruth, "and our incidents have been spread all over town, five or six venues at the latest count."

"Then we don't have a ghost in Dry Falls?" I asked. "They believed in ghosts in the early nineteenth century," she said. "They lumped any unexplainable event under that one heading." "We don't believe in ghosts any more," I said. "That's right," answered Ruth. "We don't know what to call them." In spite of myself, I was caught up in Ruth's line of reasoning. I was surrounded by amateur sleuths of the supernatural. It seemed everyone wanted to get in on the act. Ruth, who had been terrorized nightly, was back in possession of her objectivity. For her, the antidote to terror was scientific investigation. "Bear with me," I said. "Was the Bethel case a haunting or wasn't it?" "We need a new name for both of them," said Ruth. "Our experience and the Bethel woman's."

I folded my hands in my lap and prepared to listen. There are people who enjoy surrendering their will to a narrator. I wasn't one of them. Stories unfolded in time, and I was a clock-watcher. You were tied to your chair for the duration, awaiting release, locked in silent conflict with the storyteller, whose goal was to prolong the tale and delay the ending. Part of my resistance to Ruth's story was based on superstition. By concentrating on the occult, we were sure to attract it. The spaces we inhabited were already darkened by shadows. Behind everyday noises you could hear the rustle of wings.

Ruth had started to speak, pausing slightly at the end of her sentences. I had missed the beginning, probably the name of the woman and a description of the house in Bethel, one of the oldest in Maine and listed in the *National Register of Historic Places*. I have compressed Ruth's tale, which contained inordinate digressions, and set it down in my own words, not hers.

There was a widow, recently bereaved, whose husband had been a volunteer Indian fighter. She was left to bring up their young son, a handsome, sickly child. In the spring of the year 1747, the boy came down with chills and fever. Bethel was little more, at that date, than an outpost in the wilderness. There was a doctor at the fort, but the garrison was on maneuvers. To quiet the child's shivering, she held him in her arms during the day and took him in bed with her at night. Toward the end of the second week, the boy expired. Half distracted by grief, the mother dug his grave herself and planted seeds of deadly aconite upon it to keep wild animals from digging in the soil.

One night, approaching Midsummer Eve, she awoke to hear the bedroom door creaking. Soft footsteps padded over the floorboards. Something climbed in bed beside her, pressing up against her. She lay very still, thanking God for answering her prayers. Her child had returned to comfort her and be comforted. The following night she felt his gentle weight on her chest, but when she tried to embrace him she found her arms were paralyzed. On successive nights, the weight on her chest grew heavier. She welcomed the pressure, knowing her child craved her body heat. The weight increased nightly, until it seemed as if it might smother her. The creature above her weighed as much as a full-grown man.

Then one night, when her lungs were nearly bursting, she felt a hand on her throat, choking her. It came to her all at once that grief had ensnared her. Her nocturnal visitor was not her child. It was a spirit who had taken on his guise in order to deceive her. With her last ounce of strength she managed to move her right hand. The weight lifted off her chest and fell to the floor with a sound like a cat jumping down from a windowsill.

"In God's name be gone!" she cried out. She heard footsteps retreating with the slow, halting gait of a cripple, down the narrow stairs toward the doorway. Fearing its return, she lay huddled beneath the covers, unable to get out of bed to light a candle. At the first rays of dawn she fled the house and took to the road. A soldier on horseback, returning from Indian territory, found her clinging to the trunk of a tree, barefoot and wearing her nightclothes.

It was the soldier who passed on her story, which was relayed from mouth to mouth down the generations. In the mid-1800s the story assumed written form. It is preserved in a letter in the archives of the Lewiston Historical Society.

Attracted by the sound of Ruth's voice rising and falling, Angela had crept back to the kitchen to listen without our noticing her. "I know that story," she said, when Ruth had come to a standstill. "I read it in my purple fairy book. It's the same as the hairy goblin who sits on the princess, only she thinks he's a prince, but the real prince was turned into a rock at the bottom of the pond." "It's just a bad dream," I said, unwilling to be led into a discussion in front of Angela. "Apparently it's a common type of nightmare," I persisted. "You're alone in the house with a prowler. A lot of people have them." "I had one," said Angela, who probably got glowing reports for classroom participation. "He was coming to get me and I tried to call my mother but I couldn't." "I wonder if Angela would like to go outside and play on the porch swing?" I asked. Ruth ignored my appeal. "I can see you're uncomfortable," she said, "but you'll have to take my word for it. It wasn't a dream. In each case the sleeper wakes up and sees the room accurately. Mariette and Sally bear me out. Jane and I live in the village. While it was going on, she could hear her neighbor's television. I heard the Congregational church clock strike the hour and the half hour."

Ruth was waiting for a reaction. I had missed my cue. "You seem distracted, Cora," she said. "I realize this is difficult material. I asked our friends to supply me with dates and, if possible, times and duration. Of course, my task would have been simplified if they had kept journals, as I do. I drafted a table comparing the data. Henry will find it useful. Eighty percent of the incidents took place on the same nights and within the same general time frame. I'm sure you understand the implications." "Telepathy?" I suggested. "Call it a mental operation, if you prefer," said Ruth. "Better than facing the fact that it might be a genuine experience. Easier than coping with the notion that there might be more than one of them."

Angela was standing by my chair, leaning against me the way large dogs do to remind you to pet them. "One of what?" she asked. I put my arm around her little waist. There was no hope Ruth would change the subject, or give a childproof answer. She might condescend to her adult intellectual inferiors, but she never talked down to children. It obstructed the learning process.

"The experience is real," Ruth continued. "Different traditions give it different names—witch-riding, possession, haunting. They attribute it to different agents, such as Pan, ghosts, incubi, succubi, vampires. The legends vary in detail but the gist is the same. None of us had puncture marks on our necks or loss of blood. All of us were pinned to our beds by a force that overpowered us."

Angela pressed in closer and grasped my hand. I couldn't tell if she was clinging to me or I to her. "There must be some physical explanation," I said for Angela's benefit. "It only seems to happen when you sleep on your back." "Sleep paralysis," said Ruth. "You'd like that, wouldn't you? There's plenty of research on the subject, but it doesn't account for the basic contents of the experience, or its persistence from culture to culture. All it does is describe a physiological state in which the experience can occur."

Angela had forgotten she was a grown-up young lady of ten, practically a teenager. She was sitting in my lap. Her skinny body was almost weightless, an inadequate buffer against Ruth's onslaught. "You have two choices," Ruth instructed. "Put your head in the sand or live with the questions." "They're not my questions," I countered. "You're missing an opportunity," said Ruth. "Is that how Jane and Sally see it?" I asked. "I regret to say they lack my sense of adventure," answered Ruth. "I came to offer my services to Henry. New blood for his team."

Outsiders see our loved ones in terms that dismay us. According to Ruth, Henry was the leader of a team of researchers. He and his colleagues worked toward a clear-cut purpose. Their work was abstruse, serious, and respectable. I had acquired the habit of belittling his new interest. It was a safety valve for priestly frustrations. It was a fascinating indoor sport. Since it was too hot to go out and play, Henry had invented a game using mind, not muscles, in which he made up all the rules. He was playing this game with other housebound locals, whose jobs were too narrow for their spiritual ambitions. The game had an element of risk, which raised it above the level of armchair recreation. Up to now, only women had been at risk, and Henry was attracted to the role of knightly champion and rescuer. In recent years his career had afforded him no outlet for heroics, except on the occasion of the Baldwin baby's baptism, when the hefty infant squirmed out of his godmother's arms. Henry had caught him by his diaper as he was falling, head first, into the font.

Ordeals and tests of mettle were missing from Henry's life. Where he saw an occasion for gallantry, he might be capable of miscalculating the dangers. It was possible to love someone and, at the same time, doubt his wisdom. The rift in our sexual connection had brought with it a degree of emotional detachment, bleak and unfamiliar. Could I trust Henry's judgment in a crisis, the kind of confrontation he seemed bent on manufacturing? What good had he been that hateful night in Adele's bedroom? Had he saved Adele from defilement? If the Thing had turned on me when it finished with her, he would have been torn between opposing interests, between an impulse to protect me and a desire to verify the spirit's existence.

At least Ruth had no doubts about Henry's leadership abilities. Like a lot of new volunteers to important causes—suicide prevention, population control, world hunger—she was eager to overcommit herself: sign up for extra shifts, offer her home for meetings, get involved in fund-raising. She expected to make a difference from the outset. Volunteers were sometimes plucked from the ranks and elected to the board of directors. Ruth announced they must go because Angela's parents were due to fetch her, but she left a slew of messages for Henry. "Tell him he can use the library documents room for meetings; it's tucked away on the second floor. Does he know I have considerable experience writing grant applications? He should delegate one of us to look into Dry Falls history—Indian massacres, underground rivers, Viking stones. That sort of thing. I'd be glad to do it. Lorraine's talents might come in handy. Has Henry thought of letting her loose in Adele's apartment?" "She's been away," I answered. "They have a shack on Cliff Island." "So Lorraine's not one of us," said Ruth. "I didn't think so."

I lifted Angela off my lap and stood her on her feet. I took her hand and led her over to Ruth. I waved from the kitchen door as they boarded Ruth's van. Ruth leaned out the window and delivered one last message: "Have Henry call me when he gets back. We should get to work as soon as possible."

Chapter Twenty-three

After Ruth left, I carried our coffee cups to the sink, letting the water run long and wastefully, as if it could rinse away traces of her arrogance. I called Ruth a friend, but friendships in a village are less a matter of choice than of proximity. I shut my eyes to her irksome qualities because I had to live with her. Feuds and rifts, with the attendant side-taking, were unthinkable in a small community. They affected every connection, narrowing an already restricted acquaintanceship exponentially. I might resent her officious behavior, but I was required to hide my feelings. It was eleven o'clock in the morning and I was worn out, as much by the content of her visit as by her personality.

The kitchen was so hot I checked to see if I'd left the oven on. I moved from room to room downstairs, testing the temperature. Was the dining room cooler than the living room or only darker? We kept the wicker blinds drawn until sunset on the screened-in porch. They kept out the sun but they also cut off the air. In the front hall, a space wide enough to hold a slat-back settee, there was a cool (or less warm) spot in one corner, related to water pipes inside the wall. The settee was narrow and hard. Could I sleep on the floor with my body pressed against the cool spot?

In search of a better solution, I went back to the living room. There were two sofas, one at the far end near the dining room and one at right angles to the fireplace, both covered for the summer in well-worn linen that didn't stick to the skin. I was wearing long shorts with the cuffs rolled up and a sleeveless blouse. The electric fan, a relic from the forties, was plugged in under the window to the right of the fireplace. By stretching its fraying cord full length, I could lie on the sofa and let it play directly on me.

I gathered up the sofa pillows and piled them on an armchair. I preferred to sleep with a pillow, but all of these were wool or velvet. I lay on my back, listening to the fan as it turned on its base. There was a rattle on its cycle and an irregular stutter, as if it were on the point of breaking down. I began to count the beats between rattles and stutters, wondering if the noise would keep me awake. The last thing I heard was a brand-new sound, a faint moan, no doubt the grating of metal on metal. I fell asleep trying to remember that the fan needed oiling.

When I slept in the daytime I went too far out, so far from my body that the way back was long and difficult. An astronaut is fastened by a lifeline to the mother ship. In day sleep I drifted unsecured, swimming home against outgoing tides, beaching up as exhausted as when I set off. As I came awake, I registered a series of small discomforts—the ache behind my eyes, the stiffness in my neck, the sweat pooling under my shoulder blades. My mouth was dry and I had trouble swallowing. I knew the penalties for napping. When I got up it would be hours before my head cleared. There was every temptation to prolong this state of limbo. I had nothing to do but put two more meals on the table.

The fan was rattling and whining, louder than before. I ought to unplug it. The cord was so old it could cause an electrical fire. I opened my eyes halfway, saw the crack on the ceiling and the overhead light fixture, an ugly brass ring set with flame-shaped bulbs, installed by our predecessors, the Furmans. We never got around to replacing it. I closed my eyes again. Wherever I looked I would see the house beckoning me, pointing out chores, unfinished projects, urgent repairs.

The muscles in my neck might relax if I shifted position. When I tried to turn over on my side, I couldn't move my feet. I felt a sensation of weight, as if a good-sized dog, say a Labrador, had jumped up on that end of the sofa. My feet were asleep. My knees and thighs had no feeling. I would have to stay as I was until the numbness passed. I stretched my neck to release the cramp, with some success. I took a deep breath and prepared to drift away again. With any luck I could sleep through lunch duty. Henry could scavenge in the cupboards or have a sandwich at Ernie's diner.

As I was casting off, letting the current take me, I thought I heard Henry coming in. How slowly he was walking, trying, rather clumsily, not to disturb me. He was putting his feet down flat, one in front of the other, like a driver arrested for drunkenness required by the arresting officer to walk a straight line. The footsteps advanced unsteadily. I had an image of his feet in shoes that were a size too large. I kept my eyes closed, practicing deceit. He was too considerate to wake me for no good reason. Perhaps he had invited someone to the house and needed the living room. Or he wanted to drive to the garage in two cars so he could leave his car overnight to be worked on.

Now the footsteps were approaching from the direction of the open window near the fireplace. He had been in the room all along, before I woke up, so my subterfuge was futile. I opened my eyes and extended my arm for him to lift me up and help me walk off my numbness. I saw the window, and the curtains moving, stirred by the fan. I raised my head to scan the room. There was no sign of Henry. He had come and gone. I had incorporated his footsteps into a dream, unaware I was sleeping. Perhaps I was asleep even now, dreaming the room exactly as it was, dreaming my thoughts, my confusion and lethargy.

There was one way of determining whether I was awake. I pulled a hair from behind my ear and held it up to my eyes, a long yellow strand with a gobbet of scalp attached to it. People scratched a rash in their sleep, hard enough to draw blood, but no sleeping person inflicts and feels pain voluntarily. I rubbed tears from my eyes. The place behind my ear still smarted. The footsteps resumed. They were coming from the window again. What else could be making that sound, slap-slide, slap-slide? A loose slat in the venetian blinds? The pages of a magazine rustling in the artificial breeze?

I tried to move my legs, but my lower body was immobilized. I had the use of my arms. If I had to, I could push myself up to a sitting position, take hold of my legs, and lift them off the sofa. If my legs still refused to obey me, I could drop to the floor and drag myself from the room like a cripple who has fallen from her wheelchair. Across the living-room rug, using my elbows, over the sill and across the dining room into the kitchen. Along the hard surface of the linoleum to the screen door, down the wooden steps head first, overweighted by my senseless limbs, pitching sideways over the edge, landing flat on the ground, stunned and winded.

Why was I planning an escape when nothing was threatening me? The room was empty and silent, except for the fan. In my family Hannah was the sensitive one and I was the sturdy one. Everyone agreed I had no imagination. If I lacked the imagination to make up the footsteps, the sound of them must have been real, against the evidence of reason. From outside the window came a combination of sounds—a thwack followed by a swish, easy to identify. Our neighbor across the street was pruning trees, the lower branches of a stand of white pines along the roadside. Harold Schwartz was in his sixties, the veteran of one heart attack. He had hired someone else to do the pruning for him, some robust youngster, probably working shirtless. Whoever he was, he was earning his wages, already reaching for the higher branches, which toppled with a crash. In the motionless air the sounds re-echoed in the room with me, jiggling the Chinese dogs on the mantel and the fire tools in their iron stand. Were there two young titans working on Harold's trees? One man alone could never chop so fast. At the rate they were going the stand of pines would be decimated. The noise was deafening, abusive. If they kept it up much longer, the neighbors would be up in arms. I had to call Harold and protest. They seemed to be starting on the tree trunks.

I willed my dead legs to move, but the weight on my lower body was moving upward, paralyzing my middle from my pelvis to my abdomen. I could lift my head with great effort. My arms were powerless. I had time to wonder why the workmen were using hand tools instead of power saws before the thudding of their axes and the booming of fallen branches resolved itself into a din that subsumed all loudness: hurricane, cataract, dynamite, forest fire, bombing; avalanche, church bells, foghorns, sirens, war cries; a thousand steam engines roaring along parallel tracks. The universe was noise and I was an organ of hearing, a vibrating surface, a cymbal, a gong, a kettledrum. I was a marble chamber resounding with giant footsteps, massive feet shod in iron shoes. I was conscious of nothing but sound. Sound pressed on my eyelids, forcing them closed. Sound weighted my body, pushing me so deep into the cushions that I felt the springs. Sound was taking possession of me, prying me open, entering me through my clothing, filling the birth cavity. I was swollen with sound—vagina, womb, bowels, lungs, esophagus. The pressure from inside was equal to the force from above, as it happens in drowning. It seemed I must burst into pieces, like a bladder pumped too full of air, little scraps of me flying outwards in every direction, irretrievable, unmendable.

I heard Henry's voice through the tumult, far away, nearly inaudible. "Move your hand," it called. "Cora, move your hand!" He was asking the impossible. When Jesus bid him rise, did Lazarus spring to life instantly? I believe he lay there some time, resisting, thinking, "I can't. He's expecting too much of me." As soon as I began to frame thoughts, Henry's voice became louder. "Try to move your hand. You'll be all right if you move your hand." I directed my thoughts down my arm, to my wrist, to my palm, to my dangling fingers. I imagined them curling, flexing, making a fist. "Try harder, Cora. Just try to move one finger!" Why was he so impatient? I felt I had been trying for hours, for years, for a lifetime. "Move your finger. Just move one finger!"

I gave up. I surrendered to the weight above me. All at once it lifted, rolling back like low-lying mists in a scudding breeze. In that moment of relaxation I had managed to bend my thumb almost imperceptibly. I could open my eyes. The room was thick with a brownish vapor, dispersing silently. At first the absence of noise was overwhelming, as if all sound had been sucked out of the room, creating a vacuum.

In an instant Henry was in front of me, yanking me to my feet, which gave way under me. He caught me before I collapsed, hooked his arm under my shoulders and dragged me as far as the dining room.

"You can walk, Cora. Use your feet. I won't let you fall. Don't quit on me!" He steered me around the room until I grabbed the back of a chair and shook him off. He was forcing my arms out of their sockets. When I proved I could walk on my own, he marched me into the kitchen. I wobbled toward a chair, but he stopped me. He made me walk back and forth, the length of the room, following behind me. When I began to complain, he took me in his arms like a dancing partner, leading me around the table in a lively two-step.

At last he let me sit down while he fixed a cup of instant coffee with hot tap water and ordered me to drink it with two spoonfuls of sugar. Was he treating me for shock or an overdose? I hated sugar in my coffee. I was tired to the bone, as if I had been doing physical work that was too hard for me. Under Henry's eye I sipped the sweet coffee and conjured up images of horizontality. I thought of lying in a tub of scented water, of resting on a bank of pillows with another pillow under my knees, of swinging in the hammock on the porch, weightless and languid.

The coffee was acting like a sedative. My head fell forward, startling me awake. Henry grabbed my shoulders and pinned me against the chair-back. He jerked my chin up, squeezing my jaw so tightly my eyes watered. He was angry enough to hurt me. "You can't go to sleep, Cora. I'll keep you awake any way I can. You can sleep when this is over."

PART IX

Christ When We Sit Down

Chapter Twenty-four

The next day the house was full of people making themselves at home. Henry had invited them and I was expected to feed them. There was a day shift and a night shift, composed of different personnel. Some of them took both shifts if they liked what was on the evening's menu. We were having a marathon house party, three main meals, afternoon tea, drinks and sandwiches on a tray at ten p.m. Because of the heat they slept on top of the beds, not in them, dirtying only the pillowcases. I couldn't ask them to be as sparing in their use of towels, but I did make a general announcement about emptying the ashtrays. I overheard Ruth objecting to the use of tobacco and alcohol—and Henry saying we had to cater to the volunteers if we didn't want to lose them. They seemed happy enough to me, gabbing away on the screened-in porch, hanging around in the kitchen, dipping their spoons in my sauces and their fingers in my cookie batters.

I had no privacy. Someone was always on my heels, following me into the garden while I picked rosemary, the only herb to survive the drought; trailing me as far as the bathroom door. They hung around me but nobody helped out, except when Jane Shufelt was on duty—and she was no use. Oddly enough for a nurse, she thought running water over the dishes was the same as washing them. I tried to close the door to the dining room when I was cleaning up, but someone always thwarted me, standing sentry in the doorway and chatting with the people at the table. Occasionally one of the women wandered in with a plate or a couple of glasses; otherwise I passed back and forth with a tray, clearing the dirty dishes—cook, scullery maid, and waitress.

After several days of three sit-down meals, I informed them that breakfast would be self-service and lunch would be soup and salad. I wrote little notes and posted them in major traffic areas: "Jiggle the handle after flushing"; "Silver knives DO NOT go in the dishwasher"; *Please* refill the ice trays." Henry caught me tacking a notice on the pantry cabinets ("Please do not open new jars before checking the icebox"). "I'm sorry you feel so resentful," he said. "They're doing this for your sake."

Apparently I was the "stolid, materialistic kind of person" who could tolerate negative atmospheres that drove more sensitive souls to madness. For this estimation of my character I was indebted to my closest friends and family, who were giving so generously of their time and energy in order to watch over me. As an object of concern and the subject of a psychical experiment, I was discussed quite openly, in my presence or within my earshot. I might even be consulted as to the accuracy of their opinions.

While I was serving breakfast the first morning, Walter said, "It's important to keep her fed every two hours. The stomach should never be empty." "She's always been a good feeder," said Emily. "Haven't you, Cora?" "Just a piece of fruit or a cracker," added Walter. "Who will volunteer to see she gets one?" "I'll take care of it," said Henry. "The bowels should be kept open," said Walter, as I was heaping scrambled eggs on their plates. "If waste is allowed to accumulate in her system, it puts her at a psychic disadvantage." "I've never known Cora to suffer from constipation," said Emily. "I'll keep you up to date," I said. "Should I report to Emily?"

In my sophomore year of college I came down with mononucleosis, the scholar's disease. I had a case of hives along with it, an unusual symptom that puzzled the doctors at the hospital. Every day of my week's confinement they gathered at my bedside with a group of medical students and interns, watching the progress of my blisters. They aired a number of theories right in front of me, some of them alarming, as if I were a cadaver in anatomy class. No one spoke to me, not even a "Good morning" or a "How are you feeling," although one of the younger ones winked at me as they were filing out.

My present situation was no different, except that I was ambulatory and my keepers and minders were novices who made up their strategies as they went along. Ruth Hiram carried around a pile of musty books, the last word, she maintained, on the subject of supernatural assault. She read quotations from them when she was losing the conversational initiative. At tea, Jane Shufelt proposed a fitness program for me—two sessions of calisthenics, morning and evening. "Exercise is good," she said. "Keeps her in the body." "Too hot to exercise," said Walter. "Massage would have the same effect." Ruth picked up one of her books, a psychic self-defense manual, and thumbed through the pages. "When there is a threat of supernatural attack," she read aloud, "it is important to get back to the physical plane and stop there *resolutely*."

Ruth looked up from her book, expecting a vote of confidence, but her audience was listening to Walter. "We're lucky Cora isn't the dreamy type," he said. "We'd have our hands full if she was a meditator." "Not me," I said, filling his cup too full, so that tea slopped into the saucer. "I don't have a mystical bone in my body." "Cora likes company," offered Emily. "Hannah was the solitary one." "Forget about exercise," said Henry. "She'll get plenty doing the cooking and the housework."

"Is there any more cake, Cora?" asked Jane. "I'll go cut some," I said. Jane picked up the cake plate. "Drink your tea, dear. I'll do it." Ruth intervened. She took the plate away from Jane and handed it back to me. "That's a perfect example. Cora doesn't need rest; she needs bustle. We shouldn't try to spare her." "But we're Cora's guests," Jane objected. "Guests ought to do their part." "This isn't a social situation," snapped Ruth. "Rules of etiquette don't apply." "I agree with Ruth," said Walter. "Cooking and cleaning fill the bill two ways. They keep her body moving and her mind focused on mundane things. Cora's natural skills are her best protection."

I drifted out to the kitchen, unnoticed, where I sank onto a chair and applied my natural gifts to staring at the walls, the cake plate on my lap. Perhaps I was alone ten minutes before I heard a commotion of footsteps and Walter's voice raised in panic. "We let her get away. Where is she?" In a moment they were all around me, peering and pawing at me, taking my pulse and checking my pupils for signs of dilation.

"Her hands are cold," said Jane. "I don't like her color," said Walter. "I'm tired," I said. "I want to lie down." "I've explained all this, Cora," said Henry. "We can't let you sleep in the daytime." When I stood up to cut more cake, I could see they were reassured. By now the tea had grown cold. I asked Jane to fetch me the pot while I boiled fresh water. I decided to play by their rules and bide my time. Sooner or later they would be discussing me so intently they'd forget I was there. Then I could give them the slip and steal another interval of solitude.

Henry wanted to keep me awake around the clock, but Walter dissuaded him. The lower my stamina, the greater my vulnerability to psychic attack. The ban on nighttime sleeping had been lifted, as long as someone watched beside me, observing carefully any signs that my sleep was being disturbed—any muttering, twitching, or, most particularly, pelvic motion. Who was more entitled than Emily to be my night nurse? She had seen me through my childhood diseases—measles, chicken pox, mumps, and whooping cough.

Emily had another qualification besides the maternal one. She needed very little sleep. It made no difference to her welfare when she got it. If she went to bed at ten, she was up again at midnight, reading or roaming the house in winter, gardening by flashlight in the warmer weather. At some point in the small hours she went back to bed, or napped where she was sitting. Once I found her outside in a deck chair, covered by a tarp.

As children we slept in an unquiet house, the stillness broken by the sound of shuffling feet instead of owl calls. We woke in the night to hear the clinking of fire tools, the thud of dropped wood, and from back in the kitchen, muffled by distance, a clatter of pots and pans, slammed cabinets, and running water. During her wakeful hours, she often built a fire or made soup. Fortunately for us, she couldn't play the piano or use a typewriter. My sister developed insomnia, and my father moved out and set up house in the barn. I learned to sleep deeply, defensively, covering my head with a pillow.

Unlike our friends, who worked in shifts, my mother was in permanent residence. She went home in the mornings to care for her garden but came back by lunchtime. She brought me presents of Hubbard squash and the striped Delicata, as well as baskets of blue-green kale and bunches of September asters—crimson Adela Martin and Korngold's Pink. We had not seen local produce since the beginning of August. It added zest to my cooking to invent new ways of cooking kale: braised, with bacon and vinegar; casseroled, with Swiss cheese and bread crumbs; in a slaw (far superior to cabbage).

At dinner each night Emily was flattered and cross-questioned, especially by Walter, who seemed to suspect her of some kind of horticultural chicanery. "It's miraculous, Emily," said Lorraine. "How on earth do you do it?" Ruth said. "You ought to be conserving water. Aren't you worried about your well?" "Admit it, Em," said Walter. "You bought it all at Taft Farms in Raymond."

Smiling and blushing, she parried their compliments. "I do the same thing every year," she said. "I mulch with a good, thick layer of salt hay." "I use squares of old carpet," Ruth said. "Everybody mulches nowadays," said Walter. "What's the real secret?" "I do have some shade cover," she added. "Most people grow their vegetables in the baking sun." Walter refused another helping of squash. "I don't believe a word of it," he said. "You're muttering incantations. You're sprinkling chicken blood on the beds." Emily averted her eyes modestly, letting Walter's speculations hang in the air just long enough to make an impression. Jane lifted a forkful of kale, then put it down again. Lorraine patted Emily's shoulder. "Sour grapes, Walter. Stop teasing her." When the main course was over, I noticed most of their vegetables were half eaten. They did justice to the apple crumble, however, coming back for seconds and thirds, secure in the knowledge that Emily's garden contained no fruit trees.

. . .

In middle age, we sometimes get a new mother, or perhaps we see the old mother differently. The Emily of my childhood, tentative but determined, patient in her suffering, had changed in later years into a woman who took some knowing. The shift in my perspective was appropriate. I was an adult, very different in turn from the child she had mothered. I seemed as unfamiliar to her as she often did to me. "You're so brusque/sure of yourself/opinionated, Cora," she lamented, when she saw me running a meeting of quarrelsome church festival workers or answering questions after one of my food talks at a local women's group. She couldn't recognize certain features of my character, any more than I remember noticing, as a youngster, her tendency to coyness, that air of mystery so at odds with her self-effacing ways. She wanted to attract attention almost as much as she tried to evade it, a conflict that distorted her behavior. Believing she had no right to self-expression, she expressed no emotion naturally or directly.

Lately, Emily had been picking up the phone but no one answered. This series of hang-ups convinced her my sister was trying to reach her. "I know in my heart she is desperate to come back," Emily told me, and there it was—that lowering of the eyes, that tilt of the head, that pursing of the lips, body language that imparted self-complacency rather than deep feeling. Her manner so annoyed me that I nearly told her Hannah had been sighted all over the county, from Gray to Standish and as far west as Kezar Falls, where her high school art teacher was part-owner of a gallery, open during the tourist season. In Emily's fantasies Hannah was still being prevented by some outside agency from being at her mother's side.

We could count on Emily in the present emergency, since Hannah was gone from the neighborhood. When I went up to bed, my mother was already settled on the chaise with a pile of fall nursery catalogues on her lap, marking her selections by turning down the corners of the pages. I undressed in the bathroom and put on a cotton nightdress in the interest of modesty. "You've got the Beaulac figure," said Emily. "Hannah is slender like the Whitmans." The standing lamp would be lit all night to accommodate Emily; it was unlikely to disturb my sleep. I was tired out from fetching and carrying, too tired to be afraid of assuming a recumbent position. I took care to lie on my side, but otherwise the memory of the experience that required Emily's presence at my bedside had all but faded. Around the edges I was apprehensive, but not frightened. I didn't want it to happen again; it had been too depleting. If my mother could grow vegetables in a desert, she could surely defend me against the crafts and assaults of the underworld.

My chief wish, as I closed my eyes, was that my home no longer be a guesthouse. Our friends were enjoying the sensation that something might happen. Why else were they here, unless to witness an exceptional incident? Several nights running, I awoke to an exchange of murmurs, one or the other of them peeking in to check with Emily. "Everything O.K.?" they asked. "Just fine," Emily would answer. "She's sound asleep." "Nothing at all?" they persisted. Her response was inaudible, a finger to the lips or a shake of the head. "We're right downstairs if you need us," they said, sounding disappointed.

I was roused more than once during the night, though not by spirits. Emily was beside me, before me, behind me, on my right and on my left, all around me. Her watchfulness enveloped me. Her ceaseless ministrations steered me through the underground waters of sleep past the rocks of nightmare. If in my oblivion I grumbled, whimpered, or knit my brow, she whispered reassuring suggestions into my ear, like stories for children. "You are in a meadow blooming with flowers. The sun is shining. The air is filled with clear bright light. You are basking in the light." If I ground my teeth, I felt her hand massaging my jaw. When I flopped over to lie on my back, she turned me gently on my side. When my nightgown crept up around my hips, she drew it down again.

Half awake while she rearranged me, I sometimes heard sounds from below, footsteps and laughter. Ruth and Walter were night owls. I heard Henry walking past our bedroom to his office, where he was sleeping on a daybed three inches too short for him. When Jane was in the guest room diagonally across the hall, she kept her radio on all night with the volume low, tuned to the classical music station in Portland. How did I manage to sleep with so many disturbances? Luckily I was not like Henry, who thought the only good sleep was an uninterrupted sleep. If he woke up once, he complained of a restless night. In the mornings I felt quite refreshed. It was the days, not the nights, that tired me. My rest was in my mother's hands. She had never cared for me so well since I was in arms. I enjoyed waking up to feel her caressing my hair, shifting my position, soothing me. Surely I was wrong to believe she had room in her heart for only one of us. A mother's love, by definition, was bottomless.

Five days into the vigil, Sally Bissell was invited to spell Jane Shufelt. Burridge Academy had opened its doors for the forty-fourth year, with an enrollment of seventy-five out of a normal one hundred. On the first day of orientation, Nurse Shufelt would be weighing and measuring both old and new girls, inspecting their tongues, testing their reflexes, and taking their temperatures—"nipping an epidemic in the bud" was how she put it. Jane offered to come back when her day was over, around nine or ten p.m., but Henry thought it was too hard on her. He called a council of war at lunchtime to appoint a substitute.

I had laid out a buffet of cold chicken and kale slaw, a basket of sliced bread, a bowl of apples, and the rest of the peanut butter cookies. For once I was sitting in the dining room with the rest of then, eating in peace. My presence at the table inhibited them not at all. Walter was grumbling. "Why do we need a replacement for Jane? She'll be back tomorrow." I agreed with him, and said so. A new person for the night meant extra laundry. "I want six people in the house," said Henry. "Why not eight? Or eighteen?" asked Walter. "Six is a perfect number," Henry said. "A number of harmony." Walter stared at him. Ruth thought it was funny. She snorted when she laughed, amusing herself tremendously. They seemed to think that setting traps for spirits was a perfectly sensible project, while applying numerology to bait the trap was irrational.

Until now no one had challenged Henry's authority. He was their mentor, anointed by the church, their great white ghost hunter, their St. George. In learning he towered above them, as he did in wisdom. It was hardly a serious challenge—an outburst of sarcasm, not a mutiny. Even so, it troubled me. My safety would be disregarded in a power struggle. The atmosphere was informal enough as it was. To pass the hours between my bedtime and theirs, Ruth and Walter played gin rummy in the living room. They had started with matchsticks, but now they were playing for money, albeit for pennies. When I was settled for bed, I heard doors creaking open and falling to—someone leaving the house at night, against specific orders, for an elusive breath of air. Discipline was slack, and slackest when it counted most, around the toll of midnight. As the week wore on, even Emily seemed restless at her post. Several times I woke up to see her sitting by the window, peering out, or standing in the open doorway, straining to hear the banter of the card players.

The clouds of rebellion dispersed as quickly as they had gathered. Not a peacemaker by nature, Ruth smoothed things over by suggesting Sally Bissell, perhaps because Sally was good at card games. "Haven't we been through this?" asked Walter. "I thought we'd ruled her out at the beginning." "You did," said Ruth. "You said she'd be an attractant." "I did not," snapped Walter. "Henry did." Ruth turned to Henry. "Why would she be more of an attractant than me? Or Cora?" Walter answered for him. "Overt sexuality," he said. "Race horse temperament." "She won't do it," said Ruth. "She suffered terribly over that episode with Adele."

Walter rebuffed her. "Let's stick to the point," he said. "Since Lorraine has gone to Cliff Island, why not ask Mariette?" "The county fair," I answered. "They win prizes every year. It's important for their business." Walter shifted in his chair. "I'm doing an antiques show in Baltimore at the end of next week. I can't afford to miss it." "I have commitments of my own," said Ruth, "but I'm pleased to help out in a crisis." "How long is a crisis?" asked Walter. "We've been here for five days and we've got nothing to show for it."

Henry had been waiting for an opportune moment to seize the reins. "I wonder," he began, pausing to capture their attention. "Perhaps we need to stir the pot. Add an unstable element. Call Sally. I think Cora can persuade her."

Chapter Twenty-five

The Unstable Element was delighted to be asked. "My feelings were hurt when you didn't call me," she said, as if we were giving a fancy party and had left her off the list. "Can't I stay two nights? It would be such fun."

Henry agreed that Jane could use a furlough, so I got her room ready for Sally—changed the pillowcase, hung fresh towels, arranged some supermarket chrysanthemums in a vase on the bureau. Sally was fond of duck, so I thought I might make a ragout with olive sauce. Sally loved chocolate, too, but she would have to be content with baked apples.

The purpose of our gathering, originally so serious, had gotten blurred, if not lost for good. People in emergencies always reverted to the ordinary. Trapped in elevators, they powdered their noses, quarreled and complained, shared, or refused to share, their Life Savers. At this stage, Ruth and Walter were here for the gambling and Jane because she hated cooking. Sally seemed to think she'd been invited to some version of a teenage sleepover, the girls making fudge at midnight with their hair in curlers, trying out dance steps and lurid shades of nail polish.

What did Henry think? Was he keeping his eye on the sparrow? I noticed he was rationing the liquor—two bottles of wine at supper, four fingers of whisky, decanted, on the drinks table. The supplies had vanished to the cellar, for which Henry kept the only key. He patrolled the house with a flashlight at two a.m. and at four, the hour of the dead. Between rounds he sat at his desk, writing notes in a journal by the light of an adjustable lamp. What did he find to write about? The days were humdrum and the nights uneventful.

On the morning of Sally's arrival, I went up to tidy his office while he was out running errands for me. I straightened the cover on the daybed, plumped the pillows, retrieved wads of paper that had missed the wastebasket. There was a plate and a mug on the windowsill, and another mug on the desk, half filled with coffee. Cookie crumbs speckled the open pages of his journal. I held it over the wastebasket and brushed them off. Replacing the notebook exactly as I found it, I began reading entries before I was aware of it. I wasn't snooping, I reasoned, because Henry would have given me permission if I'd asked for it. It was clear from the entries that Henry was more observant than the rest of us. He had chosen to suppress his observations, confiding only in his journal. I could see why he was keeping mum. Separately, the items were trivial. Lumped together, they yielded no significance.

Monday. 3 p.m. Crack in the cellar floor over by the clothes dryer. About an inch at the widest point. Cement seems to be disintegrating. Original dirt floor cemented in the '40s? Ask Hiram Baldwin.

Tuesday. 4:15 a.m. Pile of leaves and soot on the fireplace hearth. Flue open. Who would be fiddling with the flue in this heat? Kitchen door wide open. Remind Walter and Ruth to close it and lock it when they go up to bed.

Tuesday after breakfast. Ruth and Walter adamant. She says she locked the kitchen door herself and he saw her do it.

Wednesday. 3 p.m. Unmarked white panel truck parked out front. Two men in white coveralls walk toward our driveway. Stop to confer; turn to look at the house. One of them points at it. They get back in the truck and sit there several minutes before driving off (away from town). Delivery men with the wrong address? (Water-softener technicians?) I should have asked them their business.

Wednesday. 4:30 a.m. The mantel clock has stopped. Also grandfather clock. Wound them yesterday evening as I always do. Both stopped at 3:45.

Thursday. 11 a.m. I've never seen so many mole runs on the lawn. Stepped on one and the earth gave way. Must be connected with the drought.

Friday. 2 a.m. Someone out for a late-night walk across the street. Can't identify him from here. Poor bastard can't sleep either. Not much of a vacation for Cora. Will make it up to her. Sending the troops home Sunday at the latest.

Mole runs? Delivery vans? I could only infer that Henry was feeling the strain, seeing signs and portents in every circumstance. Keeping notes was his way of making work in the absence of real activity. I was concerned about his judgment, not so much about what he had recorded, but what he might have missed with his eyes fixed so firmly on the ground. When I told him I had read his notes, he thanked me, as if I were complimenting him on them. "You can see a pattern developing," he said with a daft, cheerful grin. "Not at all," I answered. "Of course you can," he insisted. "A series of attempted break-ins." I was close to losing my temper. "Now I understand," I said. "You think the lawn is being torn up by were-moles. They're climbing down the chimney and burrowing into the basement. They stopped the clocks with their little claws. They changed themselves into delivery men."

We were alone in the kitchen for a change. The others were finishing their lunch on the screened-in porch. "Keep your voice down," said Henry. "You're hysterical." "I notice things, too," I said. "You're not the only one. There were seven dead flies on the windowsill in your office. Not three, not four, mind you. Seven. The Tapleys' black cat crossed my path when I was taking out the garbage. This morning I woke up with two red bites on my neck. Were they spider bites? Not in this madhouse. *I think they were mole bites.*"

Henry glanced at the door to the dining room, a possible escape route. "Are we having a fight, Cora?" "Don't be silly," I said. "We never fight." "I said you were hysterical." "That's all right. I was making fun of you." "Fun," Henry said. "Never heard of it." I went over to him and put my arms around him. Big as he was, his body felt light to me. "I brought this on us," he said. "I went after it. I pushed too hard." I held him closer. "We don't have to live here," I said. "We could move somewhere else." Henry pulled away abruptly. The group was coming back from the porch with their dirty dishes. The dishwasher was full. I had forgotten to run it after breakfast. Walter was pestering Emily to give him the tray. "It's too heavy for you, Em. You're going to drop it. At least let me carry the pitcher."

Our guests dispersed after lunch to take a siesta, a habit they had formed while under our roof, and one they disavowed each day with the same stock remarks. "I never do this at home" (Emily); "I shouldn't eat such a big lunch" (Ruth); "I think I'll go upstairs and read for a few minutes" (Walter). Henry followed them, at my insistence, although he waited until they were aloft and crept up to his office by the back stairs. I heard his weight collapsing on the daybed from down in the kitchen.

No one worried about leaving me alone in the daytime any more. I was contending with the ducks (three ducks for six people), struggling to cut them into quarters with knives that seemed to have lost their edge overnight. They had been sharp enough when I used them to dice the Hubbard squash for yesterday's supper. A whetstone improved their performance, but after two or three passes they had to be ground again. The job was slow and the result was hack work. I hoped a rich olive sauce would disguise it.

I put the ducks to roast in a slow oven and finished coring the apples, relieved to notice the corer hadn't gone the way of the knives. I was so preoccupied with food preparation that it was past three o'clock before I looked out the window to watch for Sally. Her car was turning into the driveway at that moment, but all I could make out were the headlights. I was slow to take in what I was seeing. At first I thought she'd left the headlights on from the night before; then I realized she needed them for driving.

The world outside the window was encased in fog, so thick it hid the trees, an occurrence unknown in Dry Falls since the Easter season, as marvelous to my eyes as snow to a South Sea islander. Fog was composed of minute globules of water. If there was moisture in the air, the drought must be over, with time enough left before winter for the grass to green up, brooks to fill, and wells to be replenished. I began to revise the death count in my garden. My Betty Priors would survive. I would be pruning dead branches in the spring, not tearing out dead rosebushes, a sickening task, since the roots could be as long and as fat as a human arm.

I ran out to meet Sally. She was carrying her overnight case and a basket of dried flowers—statice, strawflower, and immortelle in the pastel colors referred to in seed catalogues as "art shades": fawn, apricot, mauve, and pale yellow. "Ghastly, aren't they?" Sally said. "But they deserve our respect. They made it through the drought." I flung my arms around her. "It's going to rain any minute. Can't you feel it?" "I suppose so," said Sally. "It's raining all around us. I've just been to Windham doing errands." "They're not for me?" I asked, referring to the flowers. "Of course not. I wouldn't insult you. They're for the church. Will you walk me over there?" I put her suitcase on the kitchen steps. We decided to take the long way, down the drive and along the road. The fog was too heavy to hunt for the shortcut through the shrubbery.

We shuffled forward, making slow progress, concentrating on the ground to avoid wandering into the road. I held onto Sally's arm. We could see about two feet in front of us. The route from the rectory to the church was like uncharted territory; there were no familiar landmarks. The church and the house across the street were completely invisible. At one point we bumped into the mailbox at the foot of the driveway. The fog billowed around us as we walked, filling our nostrils. I smelled a faint, organic odor of decay—rotting vegetables, overripe cheese, spent bonfires. A little farther on we escaped another collision. The sign on the church lawn loomed up in front of us, black letters on gray-painted boards: SAINT ANTHONY THE HERMIT (Protestant Episcopal) ALL WELCOME. With the sign as a guidepost, we found our way over to the gravel walk leading up to the church.

Once on the path, we had no need to be concerned about our footing. We stopped for a moment to rest. Sally put her basket down. The fog in our lungs made it hard to breathe. I felt the top of my head, wishing I had worn a scarf to keep my hair dry. I was wearing a sleeveless shirt without a collar. I touched my bare arms and the hollow of my neck, expecting to find them slick with dampness. In response to my dumb show, Sally patted her cheeks and her hair, taking care not to disarrange her pageboy bob. "Is your hair wet?" I asked her. She paused, open-mouthed, both hands on her head, considering my question. "No," she answered at last. "But why not? Why isn't it?"

We drew closer together, as if for security. Our preconceptions had brought us this far and left us stranded, enclosed by cloudlike masses in surging motion. What kind of fog was this, which carried no moisture? What kind of substance—dry as smoke, its whiteness shot with brown and dirty yellow, like pollution from the city blown inland? If every structure on Main Street were burning, if the city of Portland were a steel town, working at wartime production, the smoke and smog would not so engulf us.

We had been suffering from extremities of weather since early spring—heat and drought, and now this foglike emanation. Who was I to judge by appearances? A fog may be dry and still be a fog. A fog might occur in any color of the rainbow. I had read about blue moons and green suns, black rains and red tornadoes. Meteorology was a wonderful science, a catchall for phenomena unclaimed by other branches of knowledge—fiery wheels of light following ships at sea, showers of sand falling on Naples and Tasmania, transportations of objects by hurricanes (bits of metal, fish, frogs, sprigs of grain). These were actual events, recorded not through hearsay and legend, but in almanacs and meteorological journals. As a gardener, I kept one eye on the skies during the planting and growing seasons. I was dependent on the state of the atmosphere. It consoled me, rather than the opposite, to learn how many unusual incidents had been classified as vagaries of the weather.

What would Henry make of the fog? I could picture his excitement, fatigue wiped away by this windfall for his frustrated researches, so much richer than moles and delivery vans. I imagined him outside in the yard, making passes at the fog with an empty glass jar, trying to trap a sample for analysis. I could hear his mind working, manufacturing a connection between this fog and other suspicious cloud formations at the Easter Vigil, in the churchyard, in Adele Manning's bedroom, in our own living room, linking them inevitably with the assaults on local women.

Since I had been out in the fog for some time, I expected to be cross-examined. I could anticipate some of Henry's questions: did the fog have a smell? a texture? was it luminous or slimy? was it uniformly dense, or patchy? could you make out any shapes in the clouds, any forms that were recognizable? By the end of the session I would feel as if I were trapped inside his theories, like a bait fish in the belly of a whale.

I started up the path toward the church. Some defiance in my posture must have reassured her, because Sally retrieved her basket and followed behind me, instead of hanging on to my waistband or squeezing in beside me on the narrow walkway. The fog was thicker now and almost motionless. In Henry's idiom, it was a manifestation of the Dry Falls assailant, and its thickening a sign that the assailant was gaining strength. In my present temper it was an impediment to visibility, an inconvenience, and—even more—a bitter disappointment.

"It's not going to rain," I said. "It's never going to rain." "I know," said Sally. "I got my hopes up." "Perhaps we should try prayer," I suggested. Sally thought this was hilarious. "You don't mean that," she laughed. "You haven't tried it?" "No," I answered. "I never thought about it." "How odd," said Sally. "You're the preacher's wife and I'm a churchgoer. So much for religious indoctrination." "I'm not religious," I said. "That's Henry's job." "I thought I was," said Sally. "But don't you see? If we were cave people in the Stone Age, we'd be praying. It's a natural impulse, a form of speech. It may be prior to speech, like breathing. We're gardeners, small-time or not. We have a big stake in this. Prayer should have been the first thing that occurred to us." "And the reason it didn't," I added, "is because we've left praying to the priests? Because religion cut us off from nature?" "The Christian religion," said Sally. She burst out laughing again. "Does this mean I can quit the altar guild?"

We had reached the church steps, where the fog was thinner, a fact from which I drew no conclusions. I entered the building ahead of Sally and switched on the wall sconces. It took my eyes a moment to adjust to complete visibility. I half expected to find that the fog had infiltrated the church interior. There were two empty vases on the altar, white porcelain encased in silver filigree, more suitable for irises or lilies than Sally's modest everlastings. She took her basket and walked down the center aisle. I sat in the back pew, watching her go about her work, blending colors expertly.

At a service in a crowded church I felt estranged, unconnected. In an empty church I experienced a sense of relaxation and a quickening of the spirit, as if the curtain were about to go up in a dimming theater. It was a friendly little building, well worn but well kept, hymnals faded and loose at the spines, brasses gleaming and altar linen spotless. Something resided in this vaulted space, however mankind had misportrayed it.

Sally sat down next to me, surveying her arrangements with a critical eye. "They're all vase," she said. "The flowers look anemic." "What do you think?" I asked her. "Should we pray in here or out in the open?" "It's better here," she said. "The fog might act as a sound barrier." "Does that mean we should pray out loud? Should we pray in unison?" "We're giving it too much thought," Sally said. "It's supposed to be instinctive."

She picked up the prayer book I had been leafing through, an edition dated 1945. "Is there something in here?" she asked. "The usual stuff," I said. " 'Send us rain and showers that the earth may yield her increase for our use and benefit.' " "As if Nature were our servant," she said. "It's in the Bible," I said. "Right up front, in Genesis. 'God said unto them, "Replenish the earth, and subdue it; and have dominion over the fish of the sea, and over the fowl of the air, and over every living thing that moveth upon the earth." ' " "You have a great memory," said Sally. "So what do you propose?" I asked. "Shall we wait till the fog lifts and go up Pumpkin Hill with rattles and noisemakers?" "Are you in a hurry?" Sally asked me. "A little," I said. "I have to get back to put the tea on and rescue the duck."

Sally leaned against the back of the pew. "It's nice here with no one around. It's a neutral zone." By unspoken agreement we sat in the quiet nave for a decent interval, eyes open (Sally) and eyes closed (myself). I didn't move my lips, although she may have. What formulas she used, if any, I would never ask her. Neither one of us got down on our knees. At first I listened to the silence and found it was full of sounds, the creak of old boards, a faint buzz from an electric light bulb, Sally's breathing. I thought of rain, or, rather, tried to remember it, slanting rods of gray water, boiling puddles spreading on the ground, flower stalks quivering as the rainwater slashed them, petals smitten and scattered. I pictured gentler rains as well—showers, drizzles, sprinkles, and mists, falling harmlessly. I heard rain making music in my head on rooftops and gutters, splashing, clattering, tinkling. At last I settled like a pool in the woods stirred by pelting rain, till I was cleared all the way to the bottom of mental sediment.

When we emerged into daylight from church light, calm and comfortable in our skins, the fog had diminished to a shimmer, a condition of the everlasting heat wave. Our prayers had not been rewarded, although dispersal of the fog was surely an unsought boon. Prayers were not always answered in kind, in order, in haste, or even in our lifetime. We took the short way back to the house through the hole in the shrubbery. The bushes were so dry and brittle that twigs snapped as we brushed past them.

Walter was waiting for us in the kitchen, mopping his face with a wet paper towel. Accentuated by enormous dark circles, his brown eyes had a glint of irritation in them. "I dare not hope you're going to turn off the oven," he said. "If you're hot," I asked, "what are you doing in the kitchen?" "It heats up the whole house," said Walter. "You should have turned on the ventilator." "You could have turned it on yourself," I said. "It's not working." "Yes, it is." I reached under the range hood and pressed the switch. The fan came on with a roar. "Is that better?" I asked. "I couldn't find it," said Walter, blaming me for the design of the stove as much as for my negligence.

Sally intervened to keep our wrangle from getting out of hand. "Have you been outside today, Walter?" "Briefly," he said. "I heard the weather report from Windham. I thought there might be some sign of rain." "And there wasn't?" urged Sally. "You've just been out," he retorted. "Why are you asking me?"

Ruth appeared in the doorway. "Oh, there you are, Sally," she said. "Did you know it was raining in Windham? This blue sky is an insult." "We went over to the church," I said. "It seemed a little hazy." "Not at all," said Ruth. "I walked to the village for my mail. It was as clear as a bell."

I shooed them out of the kitchen to the screened-in porch, promising them a bottomless pitcher of iced tea. Ruth went to call Henry and wake Emily, who was still napping. Sally stayed behind to help me, putting glasses on a tray while I filled the ice bucket. “I’d say that was fairly conclusive,” I said. “Not a happy thought, is it?” she asked. “I guess we’re the only ones who saw it.” “Don’t mention the fog to Henry. I refuse to let it spoil your visit.” “It’s not a normal visit,” admitted Sally. I finished slicing a panful of hermit bars and piled them on a plate. “Throw this to the animals,” I said. “It may keep them from turning on us.”

PART X

Christ When We Arise

Chapter Twenty-six

One after another we came down to dinner in unaccustomed finery, the men wearing open-necked shirts and linen trousers (Henry's oatmeal, Walter's coral pink). The women were dressed in summer frocks and bits of jewelry. Bunches of blown-glass grapes dangled from Ruth's ears. Emily's neck was encircled by a string of little wooden pinecones, Maine's modest state flower. As with colonials in a half-savage outpost, our attire had seen better days and more scrupulous maintenance. Ruth's green polka-dotted shirtwaist, unbecoming to her dumpy figure, showed the wrinkles from the suitcase. Emily's blue skirt and overblouse, made of some sort of heavy-duty cheesecloth, had been shaken but certainly not pressed. My white sundress had been in the closet for several years. There were grayish hanger marks on the straps to prove it. Only Sally lived up to homeland standards. Her black silk slacks and matching camp shirt were spruce and fetching.

The decision to dress for dinner was entirely spontaneous. Was Sally our sartorial inspiration, with her inborn sense of style and grooming? Or was it the aroma of my succulent ragout wafting from the oven? British foreign officers and their wives, assigned to equatorial Africa, preserved the social rituals of home in their hilltop bungalows, sipping gin cocktails in their yellowing dinner jackets and beaded sheaths. On nights when the native drums were a little louder, the lions a little closer, the houseboys surlier, they played American dance tunes on the wind-up phonograph to drown out their misgivings.

We were having a party, a celebration without a cause. We lacked paper hats, crackers, and favors but we were full of convivial spirit, hearty appetites for food and drink. Henry made more than one trip to the basement during the evening. He kept our wineglasses filled and surprised us with champagne at dessert. Toasts were drunk, both respectful and irreverent, to my cooking, to Sally's elegance, to Jupiter and Thor, who bring lightning and thunderstorms. Walter picked up the saltcellar and shook it over his left shoulder. "Salt for the tail of the Devil," he said, raising his glass to us.

Catching his mood, Ruth got up from her chair and pulled it back from the table with a flourish, as if she were offering her seat to an unexpected guest. "Come join us," she called, gesturing toward the ceiling. For an answer we heard a loud knock, obligatory sound effect at any séance, coming from the living room. The ladies cowered in their chairs, all hilarity stifled. Henry dashed toward the scene, followed by Walter. "Stand back," ordered Henry, who entered the living room alone, still gripping his white damask napkin in his left hand. By now we were huddled together at the threshold. I peered over my mother's shoulder. Ruth was armed with a dessert spoon and Sally had seized the salt shaker.

Henry advanced to the center of the room and pointed at the floor. From one of the bookshelves a sizable volume had fallen and lay face upward, its back out of line and probably broken. Henry picked up the book, holding it a little away from him. Making a kind of stretcher of his napkin, he carried it back to the table and began to unwrap it. "Would you hurry?" I said. "What is it?" "It's a message," breathed Ruth. "What section did it fall from?" asked Walter, whose library, unlike ours, was organized into categories. Henry made a production of closing the book and straightening its spine. We leaned in to read the lettering on the jacket. "Drug what?" asked Sally, pushing me aside to get a clearer look. "*Drug Prescribing for the Elderly*," read Walter, "by Dr. Norman J. Ross and Carol Benedetto, Ph.D."

I heard them carrying on in the living room as I loaded the dishwasher—I could never leave the dishes till morning. They were daring books to fall from the shelves. Walter wanted to start with a paperback. Henry picked a collection of Ogden Nash's light verse because it was "less resistant" than the Penguin *Lives of the Saints*, Walter's earlier choice. There were a few seconds of silence, interrupted by bursts of laughter, scolding from Walter, Sally demanding more champagne. Ruth suggested they each try a separate volume and see who won. Emily said they were working too far from the target. Henry decided to give them a handicap, allowing them to pull their books out two inches from the shelf. Sally was accused of cheating and Walter came into the kitchen to ask me for a tape measure. At one point they were quiet long enough for me to finish washing the casserole and a saucepan; then they all turned on Walter, who was standing too close to his book, "nose to nose," protested Sally.

I smiled with pleasure to hear them so high-spirited. Laughter was a benefit, restoring balance, relaxing tensions, improving the circulation and the elimination of waste products, mental as well as physical. They were laughing so hard they had to abandon the book game. Telekinesis was too competitive. They wanted something they could play together in a circle, not the usual guessing games or card games, something with the same forbidden character as moving books mentally.

"I've got it!" exclaimed Walter, who was always in the vanguard. "Where's your Ouija board, Henry?" Henry said no reputable parson would keep a Ouija board in the house; it was grounds for unfrocking. Walter announced they would make one. All that was required was a piece of brown paper, cut in a rectangle, a black Magic Marker, and a teacup. You wrote the letters of the alphabet at the top, the numbers one to ten at the bottom, and the words "Yes" and "No" in the space in the middle. Everyone had played with the Ouija at some time or another, though not for decades. When the Ouija is brought out at a house party, one of the guests always expresses dire misgivings. "It's nothing to fool around with," said Ruth, piping up right on cue. I was pressed into service to find a large paper bag, some scissors, and a marker. I donated a blue-and-white willowware cup that had long ago lost its saucer.

As I passed back and forth, clearing the salts and peppers, wiping the placemats and crumbing the table, I saw them gathered around the living-room coffee table while Walter lettered the brown paper. Henry and Sally had taken off their shoes. Ruth was kibitzing. "Leave more space between the two rows of letters. Your 'I' looks like an 'L.' " Emily perched on the edge of an armchair, bright-eyed and expectant. Walter said Henry should bring the mirror above the fireplace to their end of the room and prop it against the wall so that it reflected them. "When there are spirits in the room, a mirror darkens."

This brought on fresh laughter and moans of simulated terror. Sally was drumming her heels on the floor. Wiping her eyes with her hand, Ruth managed to smear her lipstick. Emily rocked back and forth, but emitted no sound. They could scarcely contain themselves. Walter started joking about what he would ask. "Maybe it can tell me who stole my snuffbox at the Framingham Antiques Show." Sally gasped, "Let's ask it if Ford has a mistress." Walter said, "Let's give it the acid test. Ask it if *I* have a mistress."

Drying the silver knives, I listened indulgently to their foolishness. None of it was as funny to me as it was to them. I could hang up my dishrag and join them, or I could start polishing silver—the cutlery, the saltshakers, the covered serving dish. I was happier in the role of auditor. It was too late to catch up with them. They were shedding constraints right and left, while my first priority was the housework. Laughter was liberating, perhaps overliberating, a way of tempting fate. Here was Sally hinting at, or wishing for, a rift in her marriage. And Walter, who guarded his respectability as fiercely as any curio in his inventory, making fun of his sexual inclination. Laughter tempted you out on a limb that might not hold you. If it prompted self-exposure, what other forms of rule breaking might it lead to?

They had laid down rules for insuring my protection and already broken most of them: alcohol was flowing; I was in one room and they were in another; they were embarking on a game with an uncertain reputation, considering the circumstances.

The Ouija was popular with teenagers. We used to play it at slumber parties. The questions were usually innocuous: Does Tommy like me? Who will ask me to the prom? Did I pass my algebra test? The plastic message indicator, shaped like a heart, wobbled haltingly around the board, interrupted by recurring squabbles: "You're pushing"; "I am not"; "Well, someone is!" The indicator was slow-witted and obedient. I had never seen it acting on its own, zooming from letter to letter, diving off the edge of the board or refusing to budge, as it was supposed to do when the magic was working. Even to feel its slightest movement was a thrill, which had satisfied me and my girlhood chums and left a lasting memory.

Why should the group in my living room have a more intense experience? Surely the oracle responded to the seriousness—and sobriety—of the players. The lore of the Ouija was full of warnings to dabblers and smart alecks. The oracle, a creature of the light, was only as strong as the good faith of its petitioners. When the latter were frivolous or disrespectful, it could be ambushed and hog-tied by thugs from the realms of darkness, usurpers of its office. According to the evidence, to which the living-room group seemed temporarily oblivious, there were ruffians of this class in our vicinity. Serve everybody right if the Ouija were shanghaied by the Dry Falls entity. In its control, the message indicator would lead the players on a breakneck chase, scaring the wits out of them. I was going to bed to finish reading *Murder at the Vicarage*, unnoticed by my so-called guardians.

At the top of the stairs I heard Sally's voice. The game was under way. She spoke loudly, as if she were calling the oracle long distance. She addressed it by name in a courtly style. "Tell us, O Ouija, if the fog was natural or supernatural." She had let it slip, and now Henry would go after it, keen as a scent-hound. The alarm would be raised, people rushing to the windows to see if the fog had returned, bursting into my room to make sure I was still intact. Emily would be sent up to sit with me, making it impossible to read, spoiling my peace with her cloying watchfulness.

The inquest was beginning. "What fog?" asked Henry. "Where was it?" Ruth interrupted him. "No talking, Henry. We can't concentrate." "You've broken the connection," said Walter. "We'll skip Sally's turn. Someone else ask a question." For a minute or two they were quiet, focusing their attention, a long interval for a rowdy gang of tipplers. I expected an outburst momentarily—Sally protesting the loss of her turn, Walter shushing her, Ruth lobbying to be the next one in line. Then Emily spoke up in a tone of prayerful humility. "Please help me, Ouija. When will I find my lost daughter?"

As I slipped between the sheets my nightdress rode up above my hips. There was some kind of grit in the bed, prickling my bare backside. I got out of bed and inspected the bottom sheet. It was scattered with gray-green crumbs, dried vegetable matter. I picked up the pillows and saw a bunch of leafy stems tied together with white ribbon. I had asked Emily not to put herbs in my bed. The first night I found sprays of mugwort, because Emily had read that John the Baptist wore a girdle of it in the wilderness. This time it was common garden sage, for its cleansing properties, I supposed, and for its reputation as a demonifuge. Grumbling at Emily and her good intentions, I shook out the bottom sheet and remade the bed, propped my pillows against the headboard, and settled down to read myself to sleep.

I had chosen the right book—not enough blood to cause bad dreams, nor human interest to inspire wakeful empathy, a quaintness in the atmosphere suggestive of unchanging values as upheld by the Church of England. Soon my eyes began to close and the book slid out of my hands. I turned off the lamp. The moon was high and almost full, its bright rays streaming through the windows. Moonlight magnified the objects in the room, outlining them with shadow. I fell asleep as I was wondering how I would manage to fall asleep in so much brightness.

In my dream I was lying on my stomach and he was on top of me. He had already entered me. I was waiting for him to begin the lunging motion that would bring him to orgasm. I was both a participant and an observer in the dream, able to stand apart and comment on the action. I remarked that Henry and I had never used this position before. There was no climax in it for me unless he pushed his hand under my belly and found my clitoris. It would be difficult to maneuver a finger with the combined weights of two bodies pressing down on it. The position was the wrong one for a man with an average-sized penis and untrustworthy erections, but Henry was long in the shaft and, once hard, remained serviceable even after he had reached completion.

With him inside me I felt full, stretched beyond my normal capacity. In waking life Henry was always aware of the difference in our dimensions. He would move slowly and carefully at the beginning, waiting while I expanded to receive him before he abandoned himself. In the dream he went off at a gallop, riding me at top speed, bareback, in a contest with no finish. Tireless, unspent, he spurred me into regions of pleasure evoked in sexual mythology, the country of the natural orgasm, accessible only through the male—continuous, self-renewing. He was competing at the height of his form, exceeding human limitations, breaking any previously established records for sexual endurance. I was resonant with pleasure, mindless and ultimately bodiless, a unit of pure sensation.

What woke me? Or was I not awake at all but transported to another dream, flung from one circle of the unconscious to another? All at once my eyes were open. I was lying on my back as if I'd fallen there, arms thrown outward, legs twisted to one side. It was an effort to roll over and face the windows, as if I were shifting many times my usual weight. Then I thought I was back in a dream because my bed seemed much wider, extending halfway across the room. The sheet was rumpled. In the moonlight the creases looked like ripples on a body of water. My eyes were as heavy as my body. I let them close again. I didn't like this dream with its strange, yet too familiar setting. I wanted to tune in to another channel, but I had forfeited possession of the tuner.

I felt a movement at the far side of the mattress. There was someone in bed with me. Was he returning to perform in another episode of my continuing erotic dream? Would it be as strenuous as before? What fresh exertions did he have in mind for me? I reached out my hand and opened my eyes to look at him. I froze in unspeakable shock, unable to withdraw my hand, which lay, open-palmed and inviting, on the wide expanse of sheet.

It was not my husband I saw, but a small-boned, soft-skinned, fair-haired woman staring back at me. Only her head was turned toward me. There was something in her posture that gave an impression of sickliness. One shoulder was hunched. Her arms were draped slackly across her middle. Her pudenda were expunged by shadow. Moonlight painted her features with a shiny, tubercular pallor, pinched childlike features in an almost triangular face. Her hair was fine and quite sparse, like the wig of a balding old doll marred by too much handling.

Her eyes were black and expressionless, huge in that little face. Her condition was pitiful. I wondered how much life she had left in her. Her lips were moving. In her weakness she was trying to form words, and I knew I must stop my ears against them, block my ears with my palms to drown out her entreaties or disclosures, which would somehow be the end of me. My arms were paralyzed. I could no more bring them up to my head than lift the bed I was lying on. Her body was trembling, taxed to the limits of its strength by her attempt to speak. Her fingers fluttered. She was trying to raise her knees. I let my eyes travel down her legs. What was hidden was now made plain. The thing had no feet.

I shut my eyes, the only part of me that moved at my behest, as if I could obliterate the vision of those appendages. Her legs ended in two spade-shaped stumps, undefined by toes and toenails, heels and arches—the raw material for human feet, such as a sculptor might rough out when he was modeling a figure, before he filled in the details. In the annals of defective births there were cases of human infants with the same crude extremities, but this ailing feminine entity was not deformed. She was uncompleted.

I forced myself to look. What I was witnessing was not a demise, but a monstrous birth. Instead of dying, she was coming alive. Instead of trying to recover her powers of speech, she was struggling to speak for the very first time. Already she was learning, stretching her lips and rolling her tongue, making sounds like a child born deaf, all vowels and no consonants. With each sound she grew stronger, gaining a measure of mobility. She was able to lift her arms, as yet no more than several inches. Soon she would manage to turn over, then to crawl, with the mattress as her playpen. At the thought of her approach, of her touch, panic overcame me. What did she want with me or one of my kind? To steal my breath, to feed on me? For a moment I lost consciousness, or dreamed I did.

When I revived I was dazzled by moonlight, but I sensed I was alone in bed. As my vision cleared I saw the room in accurate detail. The bed had narrowed to its normal size. My dress was draped across the armchair, where I'd left it. I could see the scar on the closet door, the fraying edge of the carpet, the motley collection of objects on the bedside table—lamp, mystery book, emery board, hand lotion, traveling clock. The clock was ticking. It was light enough to watch the second hand rounding the dial. The time was still early, ten minutes to one. I heard a loud whoop of laughter and remembered the party downstairs, fooling with the Ouija board. The Ouija was supposed to be a solemn game. Perhaps they had graduated to strip poker. Weak with relief, I realized the nightmare was over. I was wide awake and everything was in its place, exactly as it should be.

I felt something sharp and irritating under my right shoulder. Chips of Emily's dried sage, overlooked when I had brushed off the sheets. Crumbs in bed were self-generating, like those plant lice that reproduce by parthenogenesis. I would have to turn on the lights and conduct another sweep. In my mind I could see myself reaching toward the lamp, but my arm was inert. I was paralyzed, just as I had been while I was dreaming. If I was back in the dream, how could I hear real sounds—the ticking of the clock, the drone of an airplane overhead, a truck changing gears as it picked up speed on the empty road? Since I was fully conscious and still unable to move, I was forced to accept the conclusion that except for the erotic dream, I had never been asleep.

A cloud passed over the moon, plunging the room into blackness. There was a movement from the opposite side of the bed. The mattress went down, as if someone climbing on had put a knee on it. Someone heavier than a cat and lighter than a full-grown person. The little starveling woman had returned, hungry for life. As ghastly as she was to look on, she would be more terrible to contemplate in the darkness. As the cloud made its way across the moon, I envisioned her altered and active, fattened and fanged, with bright, greedy eyes. But nothing I imagined prepared me for what I saw when the cloud departed.

It resembled the corpse of a man shrouded tightly in a thin, gauze-like fabric, a featureless body imprisoned in its wrappings. Like the woman, his state of being was ambiguous. He might have been a candidate for burial or the subject of some fiendish experiment, awaiting revival. He was immobilized, as I was, and therefore preferable, as a bedmate, to the unbound woman. My arm had gone numb from lying too long in one position. There was an ache in my thigh along the sciatic nerve. I resolved that if I stared at him intently, I might keep him at bay. I succumbed to magical thinking, but I had no other recourse. I was powerless to move and I could not use my voice for fear of rousing him. Why was I using the masculine pronoun when the neuter form was more fitting? He could hardly be said to be human. It was not even certain he was a life form. I did my utmost to stare without blinking, but my eyes swam out of focus. I had brought on the symptoms of migraine, a band of pain behind the eyeballs, throbbing temples, waves of nausea. I closed my eyes to let the sickness pass. In my misery I spared no thought for my predicament, hoping only for physical respite.

I cannot say how long I waited, abject and abandoned, while the pain in my head changed sites from the eyes to the scalp to the base of the skull. It seemed worse from lying down and worse yet from the heat, two conditions I was powerless to alter. At last it began to subside, leaving me agitated and sensitive to light. I tried to read the time, but the numbers on the clock seemed to flicker. There was a flickering haze all over the room. Objects pulsated, lost their solidity, as they did under strobe lights. By blinking hard, several times in succession, I could convert these dancing shapes into a single image. I concentrated on the clock, which read one twenty-five; on the lamp; on the framed botanical print above the bedside table—anything rather than fix my attention on the form across from me. Even with imperfect vision I had too clear a sight of it. It was there, and it had shifted position.

It was larger than before, or perhaps only closer. It had moved a foot or so inward, away from the edge. In some respects it was the same as before. It was inert, either lifeless or dormant. It had the outline of a hominid. In every other respect, it was drastically different. It had lost its mummylike wrapping and was clothed in flesh, or some doughy, putty-colored substance intended to imitate flesh. It had limbs and extremities fashioned in this plastic material by an untrained hand, a primitive who lacked experience in working from life. Its legs were as straight as tree trunks; its fingers and toes unjointed stubs. It had been given the rudiments of gender, three rounded lumps where the legs forked. The shoulders were massive in proportion to the haunches. The neck was so short that the head seemed to grow directly from the chest.

My vision had cleared, just at the moment when dim-sightedness would have been kinder. The face was in the planning stage. There were holes representing the ears, eyes, and nostrils, but the mouth was being modeled in front of me. An unseen implement was cutting a slit in the lower face, a lipless gash stretching almost the width of the head, like a grin on a Hallowe'en pumpkin carved by an idiot child. Who was the artist? The life form itself? Or some agency apart from it? Whichever it was, it was arrogant, like all bad artists. Did it hope to deceive me with this bungling forgery of life? Until now I believed I had seen three separate apparitions. In fact, it was one and the same. It was a shape-changer.

"It" or "they"? I think there were hordes of them, like flights of bats, swarming in on us from worlds above the earth or passages beneath it, civilizations beyond the reach of our telescopes and dredgers. I think they landed or emerged here by accident, blown or strayed off course, revisiting singly or in legions across the ages. Like all adventurers, explorers, and space travelers, their motives were probably mercenary. They came for slaves, wives, ores and precious metals; for hunting, trading, replenishing shrinking populations, establishing colonies; to bring back samples for scientific study; to set up research stations. They had territorial ambitions. They fought one another to convert us or own us. They were the rulers of ancient Ireland, the earliest settlers of Peru. Since their numbers were incalculable, it was safe to assume they were always with us, appearing to us in various disguises: as clouds, comets, angels, hooded jinns, giants, pygmies; big-eyed, gray-skinned aliens.

I think they can masquerade as every kind of natural and supernatural phenomenon, leaving our beliefs and observations open to doubt. Henceforth any event or article of faith must be considered suspect, from the fall of a leaf to the feeding of the five thousand. Who appeared to the Mexican boy at Guadalupe? Who rolled the stone away from the mouth of the holy sepulcher? Do volcanoes really erupt because gases build up in molten rock? Are earthquakes caused by fractures in the earth's surface? When we look out the window at our carefully tended properties, how will we know that a rose is a rose or a hailstone a hailstone? I think we have been warned. The age of faith was over, faith in science as well as in religion. We were entering the era of uncertainty.

Were they trying to teach us or condition us? For all I knew, we were puppets. They preferred us softheaded and credulous. They manipulated our beliefs, staging miracles and eclipses, spectacles to abash us and keep us malleable. Perhaps we were useful to them. But useful for what? As guinea pigs? Day laborers? As livestock? They had some reason for interacting with the human race, and we did not know what it was.

Were they assisting in our evolution or our extinction? I had seen with my own eyes that they were trying to duplicate us and making poor work of it. Their capabilities were vast, but they had not yet created a convincing replica of a human being. From now on we must temper our natural instincts with suspicion, withhold our compassion for cripples, paraplegics, victims of third-degree burns, Thalidomide babies, the birthmarked, clubfooted, scarfaced, harelipped, and hunchbacked, until we make certain they have human forebears.

Even by taking every precaution, we may still be deceived. How can we know they don't steal our eggs, implant their embryos in our borrowed wombs? They were masters of illusion and stagecraft. Their powers were absurd, inconsistent with reason, and reason was our only defense against them. Had they come, these gods and monsters, seraphs and specters, to show us the limits of our understanding or ways to develop it? For the present we regarded them as enemies, and they were winning. If we banished one migration, others would follow. I knew Henry had made the right choice. How could he continue to preach a religion that might have had its origin in one of their conjuring tricks? He would devote the rest of his life to studying them, case after case, pattern after fantastic pattern, using the only instruments at his disposal, his critical faculties and his obsolete human intelligence.

If I were more like Henry, I could muster his passionate detachment. Absorbed in the spectacle before me, observing its body redden with the hue of life, I would lose all capacity for fear. I would wish for a notebook and pencil to record the elevation of its penis, the thick, segmented shaft, the absence of a tip, as if the head were still in the making. The unfinished penis rose slowly to a vertical position, accompanied by movement in other sections of the body. One mittlike hand jerked sideways. A spasm shook the corresponding foot, convulsions that portended full-scale animation and its consequences for me. The life form was being constructed for sexual purposes, in so far as its makers understood them. A bubble of hysteria expanded in my gullet. I thought my vocal cords were paralyzed like the rest of me or I might have broken down howling. Was the penile shaft hollow inside? Would the head, when they got around to adding it, be uncircumcised or circumcised? The testicles were still unfashioned, the same crude lumps.

Why couldn't they do better? The little woman was more believable; so was the shadow looming over Adele Manning's naked body. They had terrorized us capably for months, using shadows and sounds, touch and pressure, invisible suggestions of their presence. Why had they chosen this moment to take us backstage and show us how the magic worked—the false bottom, the trapdoor, the sliding panel, these ludicrous mannequins? Why had they abandoned illusion for a primitive attempt at realism? I think they wanted to move among us undetected, a more efficient way of controlling us than improvising marvels. When they created an entity that resembled us in every particular, from our patterns of speech to our means of reproduction, there would be no end to their influence. The morning papers would be full of it.

I was pinned here, adjacent to this monstrosity, because I was part of their program. I was one of their laboratory animals, like the other girls and women in our parish. They needed my body to test their prototype of a male organ. Did they also need my life? Why should they be any more merciful than human beings, who tortured and sacrificed helpless creatures to advance the "healing arts"? I must admit I was in pain. The tendons in my neck were on fire. The cramp in my calves brought tears to my eyes. Wincing and grinding my teeth, I realized I still had the use of my facial muscles. Again and again I tried to move my limbs. Depleted from pain and effort, I felt the chill of exhaustion.

As the sensation increased, I noticed that the cold came from a source outside me, as if the dial on an enormous air conditioner were being turned toward the highest setting. The temperature in surgical theaters was kept cool to discourage the breeding of germs. Were they creating a sterile environment for their trials? Sending cold to anesthetize me during the operation? Or was the cold simply a byproduct of their power and malevolence, as it was in the casebooks of ghost hunters. The freezing air came in waves, taking my breath away. Victims of hypothermia became delirious, then comatose. Was it a sign of delirium that the entity's features seemed to be changing benignly? He had taken on the face of a man, not unhandsome, but stereotypical, like the models for students in popular manuals on how to draw: broad forehead; straight nose; bow-shaped mouth; firm, square chin. A normal face except for the eyes, which had no pupils. Was this bland image meant to reassure me, even to entice me? I think they wanted me alive and responsive to guarantee the success of their experiment.

Its jaw came unhinged, yawning open. Its chest rose and fell, as if it were breathing on its own. Without any warning I was thrown from my side onto my back, arms above my head. The weight pressing down on me had the power to crush me. The weight was on top of me, but the life form was next to me, no closer than before. My legs were pulled apart, my knees bent sideways. They were making me ready to receive him. The mattress pitched and shook underneath me. The life form was in motion. Was it trying to stand? Rolling over to rise up on all fours? I heard it snuffle and wheeze from the untried effort of breathing. I heard the bed frame creaking as if it would come apart. Any moment it would be on me, pushing and lunging in a parody of coition, missing the mark, thrusting home again, battering my hidden parts with an engine made of some inorganic substance excruciating to flesh.

Where was my family? The friends who had contracted to watch over me? Their infatuation with outlawed games had brought this on me. I wanted to scream, as much in anger as in terror. I felt a scream rising in my throat. If no sound came out the scream would implode, rupturing my lungs. I tried to stifle it, choking on it, gagging as it forced a passage. I heard scream after scream fill the room, amplifying each other. I couldn't stop. I was like an alarm bell tripped by a rash intruder or a short in the system. I would keep on screaming after death, the same way fingernails and hair keep on growing when the heartbeat ceases.

They were rattling the doorknob, pounding on the door, trying to break in. They were calling my name, berating me for locking them out. There was no lock on our bedroom door, on any of the bedrooms. The door gave way under their combined weight, pitching them over the threshold. They were shouting to make themselves heard. "Cora, stop screaming! It's all right!" "Why is it so cold?" "I can't turn on the lights!" "Henry, stop her. Can't you get her to stop?" "What is that? Jesus Christ, what is it?"

A woman's scream pierced the air, overpowering. I heard footsteps running and stumbling and my mother crying, "I can't stay here!" A second set of footsteps, lighter-footed, long-strided, belonging to Sally. Ruth sobbing, "I can't walk! I can't move my legs!" "Walter, take her out of here!"

Strong arms were pulling me across the mattress, handling me roughly, yanking me into a sitting position, grabbing me as I fell backward. Lifting me up, Henry started toward the open door. The room was swirling with darkness, black clouds massing against us, gathering at the doorway, all but canceling the light from the hall. The cold was shocking, unbreathable. Doubled over, Henry braved the headwind.

Very soon he could no longer carry me. He dropped my legs but caught me around the waist, hauling me along beside him like a grain sack. He lost his grip on me again, and in the end he had me by the wrists—a tenuous hold, then by one wrist with both his hands, his fingers numbing from the cold and slipping.

I felt the hump of the doorsill graze my spine and I was lying across the threshold, half in, half out of the bedroom. "Walter, help me! Pull her over!" It took two of them to finish the job. Their final effort flung me back against the stair railing, knocking the wind out of me. It was only then that I stopped screaming. Between them they got me downstairs, Henry at my shoulders, Walter at my feet, where a huddle of women waited in the dining room. They drew closer together when they saw me. My mother turned her face aside as if she couldn't bear the sight of me. Henry sat me on the floor, propped against the wall. Without realizing I could move, I settled my head back, squinting at them, bothered by the light. They weren't very friendly. Were they staring at me because I was naked under my nightdress? Henry could stay, but I wanted the others to go away. If they left me alone, I could fall asleep like this. There was some reason I couldn't sleep in my own bed. I tried to think what it was, but Walter was down on his knees, leaning in too close to me, pulling back my eyelid. "Her pupils are dilated," he said.

All at once the lights began to dim and flicker. We were losing power. Here in the country it might be a day or more before service was restored. The group was very upset. Emily was gasping asthmatically. I could see the whites of her eyes. Walter tried to light the candles on the sideboard. His hands were trembling so badly he dropped the flaming match on the rug. Perhaps they would go home now. Henry and I could manage. We had a gas stove. But Henry seemed more upset than the rest. He ordered everyone out of the house, but no one wanted to take the lead. "Get into the car!" he barked. "Wait in the car!" I felt so cold. I wondered if they felt it too. It came snaking under the doorsill, tendrils of freezing air reaching across the floor, phosphorescing in the intermittent blackness. "The temperature's dropping," said Henry. "We're almost out of time."

PART XI

Christ All Around Us

Chapter Twenty-seven

Unlike the rectory, St. Anthony's had full electric power. Every bulb in the church was blazing, lights that were never turned on except when workmen were making repairs. In that garish overhead light, which depleted rather than intensified reality, the nave resembled a terminal at three a.m., a place where life is at a low ebb. The hymn board hanging to the far right of the pulpit was set up for morning worship. It read Sunday, September 29, Feast of St. Michael and All Angels, along with the numbers of four hymns, including 625a, "As thou with Satan didst contend."

This was the last Sunday of Henry's furlough. His locum, Sam Borders, was scheduled to take the services, but Henry had put on clerical vestments, wearing a gold brocade stole instead of the green that was usually worn at Trinity season. The light picked up the gold fibers, canceling the floral pattern, turning the band of cloth into a solid strip of metal, a piece of ritual body armor. In old paintings St. Michael was often shown dressed for battle in a breastplate and loin guard. Had Henry chosen metallic fabric to invoke the aid of the Archangel, commander-in-chief of God's armies, who fought and won the war in heaven? But that engagement was a clash between the hosts of God and the forces of Satan, between good and evil, fealty and treachery. How could tradition serve us in the present emergency? The Christian religion was based on one god, who ruled over one universe. If these invaders came from other universes, other physical or psychic realities as yet undiscovered, neither God nor any of his soldiers could defend us.

Henry's acolytes were dressing the stage for the coming enactment. Robed in white surplices borrowed from the vestry, they consulted with him in hushed voices. Walter lifted the lid of the font, with its reservoir of holy water. Ruth brought a vessel of consecrated oil to the altar, enough to anoint a multitude. The objects on the altar formed an unorthodox still life: a box of name-brand table salt, a carton of communion wafers baked at a monastery in the Catskills, a disposable cigarette lighter, a liturgical candle some five feet long and as thick as a waste pipe, my crumpled, sweat-soaked nightgown. The women had removed it as soon as we arrived and covered me with a modest black choir robe. They led me to the front pew, trusting I was calm enough to be left unattended. I had lost my voice so completely from screaming that nothing came out, not a croak or a whisper. I saw from their pitying frowns that they assumed I was still non compos.

Henry beckoned them. At his bidding they arranged votive candles in glass holders in a circle six feet in diameter on the chancel floor, below the altar steps and in front of the choir stalls. Another gesture from Henry, and Walter carried the nightgown to the font, holding it by one strap between his thumb and forefinger, as if it might infect him. They put their heads together, engaging in a muffled debate. It appeared Walter wanted to immerse it, but Henry chose to sprinkle it. They gathered at the altar. Henry dipped his fingers in the holy oil and traced the sign of the cross on their foreheads, then on his own. They filed down the chancel steps, Henry bearing the vessel of oil and Walter the giant candle.

They bowed their heads while Henry anointed me on my brow and over my heart. Walter placed the candle on the pew beside me for some later function. There was a whispered discussion about the proper size of the candle. According to ancient practice, it should have been as long as the cross or Christ's body. How high was the cross on Golgotha? Ten or twelve feet? How tall was the Savior? No one remembered the exact dimensions of the imprint on the Shroud of Turin. Ruth contended that the average height of a Roman soldier was five feet four inches. Henry said they needed some rope to bind the candle. One of the cords used to belt the surplices would do the job. They intended to fasten the candle to something, or someone, at some point in the proceedings. They looked down at me appraisingly, taking my measurements. "Naked?" asked Walter. Henry shook his head. "Only in the last extremity."

Henry proceeded to the altar with his retinue behind him. They kneeled at the altar rail, waiting to receive the Eucharist. Henry recited the service from memory, almost inaudibly, blessing the bread and wine, taking Communion in both kinds himself before he pressed the wafers in their upraised palms and held the cup to their parted lips. When very elderly or disabled parishioners came to church, Henry went down from the chancel to serve them where they were sitting. He was advancing on me with the chalice and paten, taking me for one of their kind, entitled to compassion because of my infirmity. I shook my head and compressed my lips, resisting him. He dipped the wafer in the cup and made me swallow it the way you medicate an animal, pulling down my lower jaw, thrusting the wafer onto the back of my tongue, massaging my throat.

They had another piece of business to attend to before the curtain went up. They made their way toward the font, where Henry took the box of common salt from Sally and poured a measure in his open palm. Extending his free hand over the salt, he spoke, for once, in a voice that carried throughout the interior. "Creature of earth, adore your creator, that you may be purified." Casting the salt into the water, he continued to pray in language that was new to me. "God our Father, Lord of Angels and of men, bless this salt for health of the body and this water for health of the soul. Drive out from the place where they are used every vestige of darkness and artifice of evil, for Jesus Christ's sake. Amen."

As the group turned away from the font, I wondered where they would go next. How did they know what to do, and in what order? Were they making it up as they went along? Voiceless, I was forced to be a spectator, unable to warn Henry that his framework was too narrow. The kingdom of the Christian god was our planet Earth and the stellar system of which Earth was a part. The devils Henry was preparing to banish were part of the Christian scheme, incubus devils who corrupted women's souls by lechery. But the shape-changers I had encountered came from the multiverse outside our system and, as such, were not subject to the power of canon law. Face to face with them, Henry's magic was irrelevant. It was mummery and nonsense, as pointless as sending twenty thousand children on a crusade against the Saracen infidel or a troupe of French actors into Zululand to entertain the natives with a production of Racine.

The ancient and terrible rite of banishment was part of the Christian ministry of healing. What was its cure rate over time and history? Was it more or less successful than the placebo effect, which accounted for recovery from disease in thirty percent of all cases? In an exorcism everything depended on the faith of the practitioner. Any flaw in his belief, or that of his assistants, affected the outcome of the ritual. Even if these were ordinary Christian devils, who were bound to play by the book, how could I rely on Henry? He had all but decided to leave the priesthood. How steadfast were the others? Walter had no religion. Ruth and Sally were Sunday Christians. Emily's garden was her church. I had left myself out of the equation. I was only a Christian by marriage.

Perhaps it was my own thinking that was too narrow. These Visitors were accomplished iconographers. They had usurped many human symbols for their purposes. If they had made crucifixes bleed and the sun spiral earthward at Fatima, it was certainly within their powers to put on horns and impersonate demons. Some, or all, of the Devil's age-old tricks may have been their doing: cattle sickening, crops failing; springs drying up; bread refusing to rise in the oven; women writhing in sexual frenzy on their beds, copulating with unseen partners. When they assumed the role of devils, with a devil's limitations, might they not be caught in the trap the Church had devised for their prototypes? If this were the case, the odds against Henry were slightly diminished.

It was sometime around four in the morning, leaving us three hours or so until daybreak. Plenty of time for all hell to break loose. What kind of violence was Henry anticipating? What kind of incident would set his awesome machinery in motion? Would he know it when he saw it or be taken by surprise? I thought he was destined for disappointment. It was hard to imagine any drama taking place in this barn-like area with its unatmospheric lighting. At least the hall was empty, except for the six of us. Henry would be spared the ordeal of public humiliation.

They were kneeling at the altar rail, all in a row, like swallows on a telephone line. I was weak in the middle and could barely keep my eyes open. Henry stood up abruptly and turned to face the pews, alerted by some sound that had escaped me. The church door was half open, letting in more sounds—the slap of shoes on stone steps, a grumble of voices, the crunch of tires on gravel, more than one set of tires, cars filling up the parking lot.

Hiram Baldwin was the first one to enter, wearing a raincoat over striped pajama bottoms. When he saw the church was set up for a service, he paused to remove his old canvas fishing hat. He put a cautionary finger to his lips and waved the rest of the crowd in, a procession of neighbors and townspeople, dazed and underslept, frowning at the strong white light. Like evacuees from an area of danger, they had come away in a hurry, putting on whatever garments were closest to hand, grabbing children, valuables, pets, sundry items of food.

Ella Macklin, the postmistress, was clasping her jewelry box. The Schwartzes from across the street had their shepherd dog on a leash. The Tapleys from next door lugged two cat carriers, containing one black domestic shorthair and a thirty-pound Maine Coon. Jane and Frank Morse came in with the baby in a sling on Frank's chest. Between them they could barely manage the baby's carryall, overflowing with cans of formula, diapers, ointments, plush toys, and rubber teethers. Michel Roque had brought a newspaper, thick enough to be the Sunday edition; Mariette, a lunch basket with a thermos bottle and a loaf of her bread. Their teenage twins lagged behind, sulky and red-eyed, their hair rolled up in plastic curlers.

I saw the Dragos, back from their holiday. It had done Lorraine no good. Her limp was more pronounced and her eyes were hollow. I saw Mary Fran Rawls and her mother, holding Mary Fran's little boy by the hand, so tired he seemed to be sleepwalking. I saw the Crofts, the Smalleys, and Ford Bissell, helping his father into a pew. In a short time the church looked like a Red Cross shelter. The townspeople were settling in for the duration, pouring coffee, sharing food, changing babies. Henry moved among them, ushering them to seats, lending a hand with heavy bags and fractious children, passing out candles as he did at evening services (white tapers with a paper collar to keep hot wax from dripping on the fingers), urging them to make themselves comfortable until the night was over.

Still they filed in—Ernie Silver; Edna Merrifield; Charlie and Phoebe Gerstel; John Crowley, who ran the livery stables; Clark Harmon, the Congregational minister, pushing his crippled wife's wheelchair. There were people of many persuasions—from Roman Catholics to unbelievers—outnumbering the lapsed and practicing Episcopalians. There were people of many professions—the lawyer, the doctor, the beautician, the town selectmen, the merchants on Main Street, the crew from Schmidt's garage on Route 243 with their families. Most of them lived in the village, but some, like the Dragos and the Roques, had come down from the countryside. There were friends and acquaintances, newcomers I had not yet met formally, and a half-dozen faces I had never seen before—houseguests, possibly, or transients staying at the White Corner Inn or the Lily Pond Cabins.

We got all kinds of transients in Dry Falls—honeymooners, outdoors people, retired couples touring New England, and salesmen on the road. At second glance, the strangers in the church seemed to belong in the last category. They were dressed for business in dark suits that shed wrinkles, plain white shirts, and thin neckties. I thought I recognized a couple of them, but only because their features were so bland and undistinguished, the kind that elude description and frustrate policemen questioning witnesses to a crime. They sat apart from one another and a few seats away from their neighbors. When his row filled up, one of them moved to an emptier pew. Their faces were expressionless, betraying none of the emotions shared by the rest of the community. A murmur of voices ran through the church, not so loud as to be disrespectful, considering the setting. All eyes were on Henry, who had stepped inside the ring of candles with his white-clad acolytes. He moved to the center and they joined hands around him, forming a circle within a circle.

What accounted for this wholesale evacuation? What had driven our neighbors to seek protection on these premises? Something had unnerved them. There was an atmosphere of apprehension that had the power to ripen into panic. I could see it in the way they sat too close together, craving physical contact in spite of the oppressive heat, in the strangely passive way they waited, focusing on the activity in the chancel, as if Henry held the remedy for their troubles. I could see it in the way they avoided me. No one sat in the front pew on either side of the aisle, or in the pew behind me. When I glanced around, no one met my eyes.

Directly in back of me in the third row were Ella Macklin and Trudy Newell, the town clerk. Trudy's black leather purse was stuffed with papers that looked like legal documents or insurance policies, as if she had emptied her strongbox before she left home. Both women had been widowed in the past year and were unused to living alone. It was generally known that Ella called the state police barracks several times a month to report suspicious noises after dark, and that Trudy slept with all the lights on. They were talking in stage whispers, much easier to overhear than a normal speaking voice.

From what I could piece together they had been awakened from a deep sleep by a loud crack and a sizzling sound, as if lightning had struck a nearby tree. They discovered the power had gone out. They checked their fuse boxes (Trudy's, mercifully, was in the kitchen, not the basement), but no fuses had blown. When they called the electric company's emergency number, the operator reported that there was no outage in their area; all systems were fully operative. Trudy called Ella, then Ella called Jim Tuttle, the first selectman. Jim had already had a showdown with a supervisor, who said he didn't care if Jim was the Governor of Maine; he wasn't sending anyone out to Dry Falls when there was nothing showing on the computer. All over town households were hearing the same message with varying degrees of alarm, until Hiram Baldwin, cruising up and down the streets in his truck looking for a dangling power line, drove past St. Anthony's, all lit up like a Christmas tree.

That wasn't enough to start a general exodus to the church.

Reports poured in, relayed from telephone to telephone, of lights coming back on spontaneously, bulbs naked and shaded burning with a faint dull glow, too dim to contribute to visibility. People turned off the main switch at their fuse boxes, but the lights kept burning. Some of the braver ones unplugged a lamp and unscrewed the bulb. The bulb continued to glow in their hands until trembling fingers dropped it and it burst with a pop! into dozens of gleaming fragments. In every house in the village, television screens lit up by themselves, at first with a pattern of snow, then with the ghost of a picture. With one foot out the door and one eye on the flickering image, Ella claimed she saw something on the screen that wasn't part of any regular program. "It was hateful, Trudy," she repeated, "it was hateful." "It was a ______," she mumbled, dropping her voice to a genuine whisper at the climactic moment.

The rest of their dialogue was lost to me. Captivated by this fabulous narrative of magical lightbulbs and preempted broadcasts, I nearly turned around to question them. What germ of truth was embedded in this snowball of hyperbole? It took many hands to weave a collective fantasy. How many versions of the events were being shared all over the church, adding more and more colorful strands to the fabrication, some taken from movies or the tabloids, some from science and horror fiction, some from hearsay, imagination, or honest misperception? Competition entered into the process: who would win the prize for having the most grueling experience? Between them, they were concocting a modern myth or fairy tale, but with the supernatural agencies as yet unidentified. Until the powers behind these happenings were revealed, the story would remain at the level of local legend, to be transcribed by Ruth Hiram and distributed in pamphlet form to regional souvenir shops.

From the center of the circle Henry stretched out his arms to the congregation. He was beginning mildly enough, with a collect for aid against perils taken from the daily order of evening prayer. "Lighten our darkness we beseech thee, O Lord; defend us by thy mercy from the dangers of this night." He had a fine voice, but he was not projecting it. I could hear him in the front row by cocking an ear. The people in the back would only see his lips moving. He was not performing an ordinary church service. He was enacting a ritual that happened to have an audience but did not require one.

My eyes were grainy with fatigue. Was it my vision dimming, or the house lights? I looked around and saw the assembly beginning to light their tapers. They thought the dimming effect was part of the ritual, but I knew there was no one in the wings operating the switches. Or no one acting on Henry's instructions. The faces of the crowd looked more relaxed. Dealing with the candles gave them something to do, a channel for their anxieties. The Roque twins were yawning. Mary Fran held her candle in one hand and her rosary in the other. Trudy had already spilled wax on her skirt by tilting her candle and Ella was scolding her for it. None of the traveling salesmen was holding a taper. Dressed so alike, they might have been in uniform. Perhaps they weren't salesmen at all, but members of a religious sect who found the customs of our church idolatrous.

I had counted six or seven travelers when the crowd filed in. Now their numbers had grown. There were ten rows of pews on either side of the center aisle. Except for the two empty rows at the front where I sat alone, one of them was seated at either end of every pew. There were more of them standing at the back, arms at their sides, unnaturally erect, as if they were in drill formation. Their ranks had swelled from half a dozen to over forty. Was there a sales convention going on in the vicinity, or a revival meeting at the Bible camp near Windham? I had a curious notion they were blocking the exits—at the pews, at the rear, at the church door. The door was shrouded in shadows. If they were there, they were invisible.

Henry dropped to his knees inside the circle. His attendants followed his example. His face was set with lines of grief and perplexity. For a moment his voice rose above the murmur of the crowd. "How long, O Lord? Will you forget me forever? How long will you hide your face from me?"

The congregation fell silent. When they resumed their conversations, I thought I heard a note of unrest. They could swallow a certain amount of mumbo-jumbo as long as their leader was strong and confident. "Does he know what he's doing?" whispered Trudy. "I don't like it either," answered Ella. The grumbling died down when Henry got to his feet again, although the words he spoke were not reassuring. "Lord, I believe, help thou mine unbelief." Henry raised the gold crucifix over his head, then pointed it low and in front of him. I looked sideways to see where he was aiming.

The travelers had occupied the two front pews across the aisle. The pews sat twelve people, packed in tightly. Had some of the others come forward? I looked behind me. They were still in their places. Two dozen more had been added to their forces, as if they had multiplied spontaneously. Without thinking, I lifted the long candle beside me and stood it upright between my knees.

The travelers rose as a body. Their movements were laborious, inhibited. The exertion was not mirrored in their faces. Viewed in a mass, their faces were less than ordinary. They were almost rudimentary: mouths drawn in a lipless line, eyes too rounded, flattened noses showing too much nostril, hair so fine and ink-black it might have been painted on their heads. The few I had seen from a distance looked merely similar. At close range, every face was identical, as if they had been cast from a single mold. Reproduction among warm-blooded mammals gives rise to variations in form, not uniformity. I knew what they were. How had I not known them immediately?

Watching them rise, the congregation took a cue from them. Behind me people struggled to their feet, trying to participate in the unfamiliar ceremony. It was an uneven showing. Some were too exhausted to get up, some already asleep, some too burdened by belongings or babies to make the effort. I stood up along with those who could manage it, holding onto the candle as if it were bound to me. Henry raised the cross above his head like the Archangel Michael uplifting his sword of flame. The acolytes circled around him at a quickening tempo, a crude, flat-footed dance of their own inspiration. As they wheeled around him, going clockwise, then counter-clockwise, feet drumming on the chancel paving stones, Henry held forth in a powerful voice, recomposing scripture: "Woe to them by whom offenses come! Whoso offends my children who believe in me, it would be better that a millstone were hanged about his neck and he were drowned in the depths of the sea. Wherefore if your hand or your foot offend you, cut them off; for it is better to go through life maimed than having two hands or feet to be cast into everlasting hellfire."

Among the congregation his words provoked a broken murmur, equal parts of fear and rebellion. I saw people turn to each other, questioning the wisdom of staying in this place, touching the handles of suitcases and baskets, making ready for flight into the open. If the crowd was preparing to retreat, the travelers were pressing forward. Their goal was the sanctuary. Some of them had pushed beyond the pews into the crossing below the chancel steps. For now their advances were checked by Henry's operations. Every pass of the crucifix unbalanced them, bending them backwards like rows of saplings in the wind. If Henry could stand his ground they would topple, uprooted, littering the ground, a heap of inanimate lumber. The skin of Henry's face was shining, lit by a radiance no source within the church could have kindled. Was the light in his face the reflection of God's own countenance? Then surely we were winning.

At that same moment the dance developed a variation, or a hitch in the choreography. Was Emily trying to reverse the direction of the dancers or struggling to break away from them? The look on her face was desperate, ecstatic, a look of martyrdom. Her suffering was in good part physical. On either side of her Ruth and Walter were pulling against her, crushing her hands, wrenching her this way and that way. At length she appeared to give up and get back in step, a piece of cunning designed to make her partners relax their grip on her. In an instant she tore herself free and ran past them, knocking over a votive candle in her headlong flight. She flew up the aisle like a maenad down a wooded mountain. I felt I should follow her in case she should do herself harm. Her nerves were not sound enough for such frenzied exertions.

At the back of the church a figure was standing in the aisle, blocking Emily's passage. Just before impact, Emily stumbled and fell to her knees. Her arms embraced its trousered legs. The figure pulled her to her feet, then pushed her a little away, warding off further demonstrations. Even in the half light I recognized the prodigal daughter. She who was lost had been found. For her sake Emily had broken the magic circle. The fate of many was not so much to her as the recovery of one child. As I watched they disappeared into the blackness of the vestibule, my sister breaking into a run and my mother panting after her.

A gasp rose up from the crowd. Heads twisted to the front, then the back. There was a movement toward the aisles, the pounding of feet, the thud of bodies colliding with the pews, the sound of pew legs, dislodged in the commotion, scraping on the stone. There were people trying to climb over the backs of the pews, people standing on the seats, people dropping lighted tapers, shrieking and stamping on them, people throwing jackets and blankets over their heads, improvising a hiding place. Emily's defection had turned the tables. The travelers were in motion.

From their positions in the rear, on the flanks, and in the vanguard, they pressed into the aisles, advancing at their dragging gait, arms swinging loose, uncoordinated with their footfall. Watching their progress, the dancers slowed to a standstill, frozen in place. Nerveless from fear, their hands fell limp at their sides. Their terror infected Henry, sickening his resolution. The light in his face faded out like a candle flame drowning in wax. He faltered and made a step backwards. The crucifix dropped to the floor, metal ringing on granite.

It was Walter who snatched up the cross, Walter who pushed Ruth and Sally up the steps to the altar. Henry stood alone in the chancel. His friends and his spirit had deserted him. I saw his face as it might look in old age or on his deathbed, sunken, livid, and fleshless, all downward lines of austerity and pain. He was trying to pray, as one prays in utmost privacy, one hand on his chest and the other blindfolding his eyes. Some of his prayer was audible over the crowd noise. "My God, my God, why are you so far from helping me?"

The travelers invaded the transept. They had almost climbed the chancel steps. The nearer they came, the harder it was to see them. Massed in the transept, they were losing substance and definition. Facial features dissolved, body blended into body, until they formed a darkening cloud, a miasma exhaling foulness and frigid air. Insubstantial, they were far more terrible than embodied. In their humanoid guise, they were too like cinema zombies, rickety, slow-moving.

All at once the congregation grew quiet. We had arrived at that point beyond fear where curiosity takes over. Was the priest the travelers' target or the sanctuary? The house lights flickered briefly, off and on, but the sanctuary lamp burned steadily, suspended in its red glass globe above the altar. If they swarmed the altar, would the sanctuary light die out? Would the lights go out all over Christendom? What would they do with us, the sheep penned in the sheepfold, when they captured their objective?

As the blackness surged into the chancel, Henry retreated up the altar steps. Walter's back was to the wall, supporting the women, pressing their faces against his shoulder, sparing them the sight of the malignant cloud. Facing the enemy, Henry braced himself against the altar. The altar was bare. The base of the cross was bolted to the granite block, but the crucifix itself was lying on a seat in the choir stalls, where Walter had tossed it.

The cloud seemed to concentrate its force, regaining the substance it had lost, so dense and impervious to light that it blotted out Henry's legs as far as the knees, mounting upward to obliterate the lower half of his body. Was he there behind the rising darkness or had it consumed him? Without talisman or props, he had one last chip to wager. In a voice like thunder he cried, "Take me, O Lord!" And was answered by a clap of thunder, so horrendous it seemed to issue from inside the chancel. The darkness engulfed him, assuming the shape of his body, as if he had been burned and blackened in a raging fire. He swayed like a collapsing timber, falling headlong down the altar steps. As he lay there the darkness moved from the periphery to the center. It was being absorbed into his body, funneling into the solar plexus.

Peal after peal of thunder rolled over our heads. There was a clatter on the roof, unfamiliar at first, violent enough to damage the shingles. Like members of a desert tribe, we had lived so long without rain we'd forgotten the sound of it. The lights blazed on, mimicked by a flash of lightning outside the windows. Walter was at Henry's side, feeling for a pulse, a heartbeat. I saw Henry lift his head and let it drop again. With an arm under his shoulders, Walter raised him to a sitting position, holding him steady until he could maintain his balance. From that point Henry took it on his own. Like the first man who learned to walk upright, he climbed slowly from his knees to his feet, wavering as he rose, half dazed by the distance he had traveled in that one effort.

As he turned and came toward us, he walked with a noticeable limp, the only evidence of any injury from the fall. On his face was a look of exhaustion and pure relief, a look our volunteer firemen wear after a night of combat, when the spread of fire has been halted and each inhabitant, human and animal, conducted to safety. He limped to the chancel steps and invited us to pray. Every member of the assembly got down on their knees—nonbelievers, Unitarians, and Jews; Catholics and Episcopalians, who kneeled to worship; Congregationalists and Methodists, who were embarrassed by it. Raising his voice to be heard above the torrents pouring down on the rooftop, he uttered the last words he would ever speak as a priest of this parish:

"Almighty God, who are a tower of defense in time of trouble, we give you praise for our deliverance from the peril and dread of this night. By your mercy and none of our doing has the intruder been driven from your temple. Make us worthy of your grace, and ever mindful of the subtlety of our enemies.

"Let the light of your countenance shine upon us and give us peace, both now and hereafter.

Amen."

Afterword

When Dr. Bayer examined Henry's right leg, he found nothing wrong with it. The X-ray pictures of both the leg and the brain (taken by a consulting neurologist) were clean and normal. An orthopedist in Portland concurred. There were no fractures, and no bruising, sprains, tears, or pain in the muscles and ligaments. Warning Henry about compensatory problems on his left side, the orthopedist gave him the name of a physiotherapist associated with the hospital in North Windham, who said, "You're going to have to learn to walk all over again."

After two years of treatments with physical therapists, chiropractors, acupuncturists, and kinesiologists, Henry still walks with a limp. Every one of them eventually suggested he see a psychologist. Henry blamed his disability on inexperience. "I was flying by the seat of my pants," he said. "I took it on. I didn't protect myself." Trained or untrained, all exorcists ran the risk of losing a faculty. "I got off lightly," said Henry. "I could have been blinded. Or struck dumb." For myself, I didn't know which was stranger: the fact that such a fall induced no more injuries than a slight limp or the fact that there was no organic reason for it.

When Bishop Hollins received Henry's letter of resignation, he was as baffled as any of Henry's doctors. It came as a surprise to him, and he disliked surprises. They ruffled his pride. He liked being in the know. In his position, he should have been the repository of diocesan secrets, not a passive respondent to them. If Henry had approached him in confidence beforehand, he might have smoothed the episcopal feathers. Bishop Hollins became suspicious. What was behind this—to his mind—sudden decision? Was there a parish scandal in the offing? Some clerical misconduct, as yet uncovered, that would discredit his own reputation? He sent his canon, Dr. Ethan Prine, to do a spot of investigating.

A pink, tubby man with cold eyes and a ready smile, Dr. Prine wore plain clothes, a sports jacket and a bow tie instead of a turned-around collar, the better to elicit unguarded remarks from his subjects. He made individual appointments with the vestry and a number of longtime parishioners, hoping to catch them out in contradictions. He covered all the bases—moral, financial, liturgical—trying to find out if Henry was leaving under pressure. Were they satisfied with Henry's acquittal of his priestly duties? Was he diligent in the matter of sick calls? Did he allow a "hippie element" to debase the marriage ceremony—handwritten vows, secular music, readings from profane authors? Was he known to endorse the ordination of women? Was he popular with the ladies of the parish? There was a secretary, a young woman in her twenties: he understood she had departed rather suddenly?

Reports came back to us from Michel Roque and Ralph Hiram, the former and present heads of the vestry, that Prine was sniffing around for irregularities in the church account books. Had Henry tried to sidestep the yearly audit mandated by the diocese? Where were the records that itemized disbursements from the rector's discretionary fund? Told that the money for the fund came out of Henry's own pocket, Dr. Prine grew sullen with frustration. The more his inquiries were thwarted, the more he became convinced of a parishwide cover-up.

Prine took to laying traps for his subjects. There were rumors, he averred, that Henry had tampered with the liturgy, celebrating the feast days of saints found in the Roman, not the Anglican, calendar. Confronted with blank stares, he dug the trap even deeper. Spurred on by his own cunning, he dropped hints of confidential sources requesting anonymity, loyal parishioners who had come forward only after painful soul-searching. At that point Dr. Prine sprung the trap. Warning his interviewees that failure to report heretical practices was tantamount to heresy, he demanded confirmation of accounts of "healing sessions" invoking nature gods and the spirits of the dead. Prine never knew how close he came to the mark. Ralph Hiram called the Bishop and complained of gestapo tactics. Dr. Prine was recalled under a cloud and ordered to draft a letter of apology.

The congregation and the town presented a united front. They didn't talk to Dr. Prine; nor did they gossip among themselves. Were they trying to protect Henry? Or to erase unpleasant memories? It took diplomacy and patience to persuade them to talk to me, and I was one of them. They wanted to forget, but I intended to remember. Knowledge forearms us, even knowledge of disastrous possibilities. Everything was relevant to my chronicle: observation, conjecture, hearsay, and the tendency of human beings to belittle or exaggerate events as it suited their self-image. I wanted to record what happened, what seems to have happened, and what didn't happen.

To the third category belongs the abduction of my sister, Hannah, that reverse Persephone, who staged her own disappearance to escape from a too-devoted mother. After knocking around the region, crashing with friends and taking odd jobs, Hannah came back to Dry Falls, as she always did. She and Emily are living together in mutual widowhood. The pattern of their relationship was determined long ago. Each time I visit, the same kind of scene is played out over and over again. Emily made the coffee too weak or too strong and Hannah emptied her cup into a houseplant. Emily patched a hole on the knee of Hannah's jeans. Hannah stormed into the kitchen and ripped the patch out. Emily sneaked into Hannah's studio and did a housecleaning. Hannah brought a bagful of sawdust into the living room and spread it on the rug. After a while I get up to leave. No one stops me. They've forgotten I was in the room. Hannah turns out very little work nowadays and Emily spends less time in her garden. They have limited time for outside activities. They are far too wrapped up in each other.

Released from the corporate hierarchy, Henry seems more youthful than he did when I first met him. The zest he derives from his work releases energy for other aspects of life. He gives lectures all over the Northeast. He has time to serve on the town council and to organize kayak races on the Crooked River. He takes his bicycle out before supper. We have a sexual life on a schedule appropriate to our age, but not, for that reason, uninspiring. We have frequent and earnest disagreements, usually about which cases he should accept and which he should turn down. I've saved him more than once from getting involved with cranks and frauds. The Center receives so many requests for help that we've had to hire an outside reader to sort them into categories.

I lost the most recent argument. Next week Henry takes off for East Readfield, a small town west of Augusta, to look into the strange disappearance of twelve-year-old Mary Belcher. According to eyewitness reports, she was playing Chopin's fifth nocturne in a piano recital at the middle school auditorium. When she finished her piece, she curtsied to the audience, walked off stage right, and has never been seen again, although there were a number of people in the wings at the time—her piano teacher, two other performers and their mothers, and the school custodian. The police launched a statewide investigation, broadcast her picture on the television news, and quickly brought in the FBI. There was a stepfather, a factory worker, who was moonlighting at the local filling station during the concert.

Little Mary made good grades and had a sunny disposition. She was a popular child, whose friends thought of the Belcher house as their headquarters. The case was seven months old and stone cold. It was Mary's mother who wrote to the Center. "She's a runaway," I insisted to Henry. "I don't believe in this perfect family business." "Maybe," he said, and reminded me of the piano teacher's statement. A few seconds after Mary passed her, Mrs. Wilson turned around and saw her opening the door to the emergency exit, some fifteen feet away. "I assumed she wanted to be alone," said Mrs. Wilson. "She had made a few mistakes and I thought she was upset about it." When the police began the search they found a trail of shoe prints (size five and a half, Mary's size, made by the kind of low-heeled pumps she was wearing), leading around the side of the building, stopping abruptly by an outside electrical meter. No other prints of that kind were found anywhere on the grounds. "That's easy," I said. "She took off her shoes and went barefoot." Once again, Henry bested me. "You've forgotten the weather report. It was a wet night in May, a steady drizzle. The temperature was in the forties."

I have finished this chronicle, for whatever use it may be to my townspeople. Henry had expected me to resume full-time work at the Center, writing up case notes and grant applications, running interference with the press, organizing out-of-town investigations. I don't like going out on the road. Generally our cases take us to backwaters where there is no place to stay except those old-fashioned rows of cabins, the precursors of modern motels, and no restaurants for miles except roadhouses where they can heat up a slice of frozen pizza. The locations are uninteresting. The public image of a "haunted house," a granite baronial pile with gables, turrets, and crenellations, derives from gothic novels and is entirely inaccurate. It is amazing how many paranormal manifestations take place in tract houses, commercial lofts, and trailer parks.

Verifying a manifestation is rather like making a movie, as I understand it. More time is spent setting up the equipment—infrared cameras, sensors, motion detectors, tape recorders—than in watching the actors perform. Just when everything is ready, some technical difficulty arises and the day's, or night's, work is wasted. Even if the instruments work flawlessly, we can sit around for days waiting for something to happen. What happens is usually a matter for open debate. Was that blur on the film a ray of light getting through the blackout curtains or the shape of a human figure? Was the sound on the tape an unearthly wail or the wind in the chimney? Everyone has her own definition of boredom. I would rather pluck the leaves from twenty pounds of thyme branches than work on location.

A few weeks ago I made a proposition to Henry and he has accepted it. There is a two-acre plot of land at the end of Nagle's Lane, which runs off Main Street. The land is owned by the Baldwins, whose house abuts it. The Baldwins keep the parcel mowed so it won't revert to forest. When they heard my plans from Lorraine Drago, the Baldwins lowered their price. They were relieved to learn I had no intention of building on it, except, of course, for putting up a storage shed. Someday I hope to add on a glass extension, for starting seeds and wintering over pots of tender herbs. I have money put aside from my earnings and the sale of some Beaulac heirlooms, in particular the attic bed. Henry offered to pay to have the well dug. In the end, my project will prove to be economical. I can grow and preserve all our produce, and eventually market the surplus.

The terms of my proposition are clear and equitable. For six months I will work with Henry in his basement offices; the remaining six months I will tend my allotment garden. In the dark of the year I can manage to work underground. When the winter blows over, I yearn for release into the sunshine. In spite of his robust physique, Henry is a thinking type. I have a limited appetite for theories, abstractions, and shadows. Trapped in Henry's domain, I'd grow haggard and melancholic. I require a more balanced division of mind and matter. I will have some lean seasons in my garden—rainy springs that retard flowering, dry summers that stunt the crops, early frosts that decimate the harvest. I expect them; I even welcome them. They are part of the natural order.

Immersed in the natural world, its cycles and hazards, I will lose any memory or inkling of the worlds beyond it. Working off my pledge all winter in Henry's laboratory, I will be obliged to confront the truth as his research shows it. He believes new lands are intersecting with ours at an increasing rate. In twenty-three years our geographic and psychic boundaries will be all but obliterated. I would like to think his figures are a product of personal bias, a classic case of the experimenter influencing the experiment. Which of us is right? Henry is farseeing, while I am prosaic and shortsighted. This globe, this cloistered earth, is the beginning and the end of my imagining.

Dry Falls, Maine
December 13, 1977

A NOTE ON THE TYPE

This book was set in Janson, a redrawing of type cast from matrices long thought to have been made by the Dutchman Anton Janson, who was a practicing typefounder in Leipzig during the years 1668 to 1687. However, it has been conclusively demonstrated that these types are actually the work of Nicholas Kis (1650–1702), a Hungarian, who most probably learned his trade from the master Dutch typefounder Dirk Voskens. The type is an excellent example of the influential and sturdy Dutch types that prevailed in England up to the time William Caslon developed his own incomparable designs from them.

Composed by Creative Graphics,
Allentown, Pennsylvania

Printed and bound by Quebecor Printing,
Fairfield, Pennsylvania

Typography and binding design by
Dorothy Schmiderer Baker